Sign up for our newsletter to hear
about new and upcoming releases.

www.ylva-publishing.com

Other Books by Jae

Falling
HARD

Jae

Acknowledgments

It's hard to believe, but this is the fifteenth novel I have published. You'd think that would make the writing process a breeze, right? Well, some aspects of it have become easier, but I still occasionally struggle with plot problems.

When that happens, my wonderful team of beta readers is there to offer feedback and encouragement.

A heartfelt thank-you to Melanie, Tricia, Erin, Danielle, Anne-France, Christiane, Alisha, Louisa, Colleen, Helen, Nattalie, and RJ Nolan.

Thanks also to Michelle Aguilar, my editor, and to all the people at Ylva Publishing who work hard every day to make our books the best they can possibly be.

Chapter 1

A WARM ARM STARTLED JORDAN awake when it wrapped around her from behind like a boa constrictor suffocating its prey. Grunting, she opened her eyes.

Bright morning light illuminated a bedroom that wasn't hers and fell onto a string of clothes leading from the door to the bed. The gleaming red numbers of an alarm clock next to her read 8:11 a.m.

Damn. She needed to get going if she wanted to make it home to feed Tuna before heading to the airport to pick up Simone. She pushed back the covers and tried to slip from the bed, but the woman behind her had other ideas and wouldn't let go.

Jordan glanced over her shoulder.

The redhead from last night was snuggled up to her, still asleep, a smile on her face.

Jordan grinned. She loved putting that blissful expression on women's faces. Carefully, she lifted the arm from around her hip and snuck out of bed. Picking up her clothes led her to the door, but leaving without a word wasn't her style. Colleen was still sleeping as she tiptoed past the bed to the bathroom. *Guess I wore her out.*

A shower would have to wait until she made it home. She slipped into yesterday's clothes. Since she didn't want to root through Colleen's bathroom cabinet to see if she had a spare toothbrush, she just squeezed a dollop of toothpaste onto her finger and rubbed it over her teeth.

Just as she was rinsing her mouth, the door opened and Colleen entered, wearing not a stitch of clothing. "Good morning," she said, her voice still raspy from sleep.

"Morning. I hope you don't mind that I helped myself to some of your toothpaste."

"I don't mind at all. I could even offer you my shower…" Colleen stepped closer and wrapped her arms around Jordan, pressing her naked body against her. "And some company."

A shiver went through Jordan. She let out a groan. "I hate saying no to a beautiful woman, but I can't. I have to pick up a friend from the airport, so I really have to go."

Sighing, Colleen withdrew her arms. "Will you call me?"

It would have been easy to just say yes so she could leave without a long discussion, but she never made false promises. She'd already made it perfectly clear last night that she wasn't looking for anything beyond hot, casual sex. But it seemed Colleen needed a reminder of the rules. "Listen, Colleen. I really wouldn't mind a repeat performance, but like I told you last night, I don't do relationships."

Colleen folded her arms across her bare chest as if Jordan hadn't seen every inch of her already. "Never ever? Not even when you meet a woman you really click with?"

Was that what she thought was going on between the two of them? Yeah, they had steamed up the bedroom, but beyond that, Jordan couldn't see herself with Colleen—or with any other woman—for the rest of the month, much less the rest of her life.

"Never ever," she said firmly. With a playful grin, she added, "I'm too gorgeous and too good in bed to tie myself to just one woman and deny the rest of the female population the pleasure of my company."

Colleen shook her head. "God, you're unbelievable."

"That's what you said last night," Jordan quipped.

A light slap hit her in the arm, but then Colleen laughed, and the frown on her face smoothed out.

Jordan smiled. She went back into the bedroom and put on her ankle-high leather shoes before straightening. "It doesn't have anything to do with you, really. You're beautiful and funny and smart." As far as she could tell, at least. They hadn't exactly spent a lot of time discussing politics, science, or literature—or anything else for that matter. She looked deeply into Colleen's eyes, not wanting to leave her with a bad feeling about the entire experience. "Any woman would be lucky to date you."

"But not you," Colleen said.

"Not me. It's just the way I am. A commitment is the one thing I can't promise, but for everything else, you can call me any time." She pressed her card into Colleen's hand.

Colleen read it and wolf-whistled. "You're a surgeon? I should have known."

Jordan grinned and waggled her fingers. "What can I say? We're good with our hands."

They walked to the front door, and Colleen kissed her with a heat that told Jordan that she *would* call. With a spring in her step, she strode toward her Mercedes coupe.

In the dense rush hour traffic on the 101 Freeway, it took her more than an hour to make it from Colleen's posh condo in West Hollywood to her quiet neighborhood in South Pasadena.

Finally, she steered the coupe along the tree-lined cul-de-sac on which she lived.

A large, white moving van was parked at an angle in front of her duplex. It was blocking the driveway, its rear door open and the ramp extended in the direction of the house. Two movers in blue overalls were currently carrying a sofa toward the unit on the right.

After having the house to herself for a couple of weeks, she was apparently getting new neighbors.

She eased the convertible to a stop at the curb, grateful that there was plenty of street parking available, and climbed out.

Her neighbor Barbara was in the front yard, removing dead branches from her azalea bushes. When she saw Jordan, she grabbed her cane and walked over. "Good morning. Looks like your carefree bachelorette days are over." She nodded at the moving van.

"Nah." She'd just have to be a little more careful about entertaining her "lady friends," as Barbara called them, in the fenced-in backyard she shared with the people in the other half of the duplex. Making out in the hammock required too many acrobatics anyway. "Who knows? Maybe the new neighbor is a single woman and a total babe."

Barbara swatted her as if she were a misbehaving child. "Maybe it's an eighty-year-old geezer who'll want you to take a look at his bad hip and keep you up at night because he's snoring loud enough for you to hear through the common wall."

"I'll set him up with you, then." Jordan plucked a leaf from her friend's silver hair.

Something thumped inside the van, and they both turned toward it, waiting for the new neighbor to emerge from the vehicle.

The first thing Jordan saw was a floor lamp, then a worn sneaker. As its owner walked down the moving van's ramp, Jordan's gaze traveled up a gorgeous pair of legs. There was absolutely nothing wrong with the new neighbor's shapely hips, and if she kept Jordan up at night, it wouldn't be because of her snoring.

Her jeans were worn to a soft-looking pale blue and molded to her curvy body. God, she loved a woman in jeans, especially if the woman in question had such a perfect butt.

The stranger entered her part of the house and reappeared a minute later, probably to get another piece of furniture out of the moving van. Now Jordan was able to catch a glimpse of her face too. *Wow.* Her new neighbor looked as fine from the front as from the back.

Her quiet neighborhood had just gotten a whole lot more interesting.

Jordan admired the easy way she moved, graceful but without any pretense. "I think I'll go over and introduce myself."

Barbara shook her head at her. "You're unbelievable."

It wasn't even ten o'clock in the morning, and she'd already heard it twice today. That had to be a record, even for her. "What?" she asked as Barb continued to give her a disapproving look.

"What about Simone?"

"Simone? What about her? We're just friends. Besides, I'm just being neighborly."

"Mmhm. That wasn't what people called it back in my day." Despite her protests, Barbara followed her up the driveway, carrying her cane more than actually using it.

Jordan lightly gripped her elbow and helped her circle around a two-wheeled dolly and a stack of moving boxes that were piled up next to the van, waiting to be transported inside.

When the new neighbor saw them, she paused halfway up the ramp, which brought her chest even with Jordan's eye level. It was hard not to stare at so much God-given perfection, but she managed to keep her gaze on the woman's face. Not a hardship either, really.

She didn't look like one of the models or actresses Jordan often had on her arm and in her bed. The light dusting of freckles across her nose put her into the *cute* instead of the *beautiful* category. By Hollywood standards, she could probably stand to lose a few pounds. She wasn't wearing any makeup, and her blonde hair was pulled back into a slightly messy ponytail, but she was still a very attractive woman—if you went for the girl-next-door look.

Jordan didn't. At least not usually. But something about her new neighbor made it hard to stop staring at her.

Barbara elbowed her in the ribs.

"Good morning," Jordan said belatedly.

"Hi," the blonde answered. "I hope we're not disturbing the entire neighborhood with all the noise we're making."

We, Jordan mentally repeated. Was there a boyfriend or a husband and maybe a gaggle of kids, or was she talking about the two movers helping her? Other than the two men in blue overalls, Jordan couldn't see anyone.

The woman stepped down from the ramp to let the movers unload another piece of furniture.

Compared to Jordan's five-foot-eleven frame, she was petite.

Barbara nudged her again, making her realize she was still staring.

"Oh no, don't worry about it, dear," Barbara said.

Jordan looked back up into the woman's eyes. Now up close, she could make out their color. They were a light green, with copper flecks circling the pupils. With a smile, she offered her hand. "I don't mind noise at all," she said. "I'm Jordan Williams, your better half."

A cute wrinkle formed on the woman's forehead. "Excuse me?"

"I live in the other half of the duplex," Jordan said, pointing at the unit to the left. The duplex had been designed like two individual homes that sat side by side, sharing just one common wall.

"Oh." The new neighbor chuckled, took off the work gloves she wore, and reached for the offered hand. "I'm Emma Larson."

Emma. Jordan had always liked that name. She shook her hand, surprised at the firm grip, and used the moment to check out Emma's fingers. No wedding band or other rings on either hand, and she kept her nails short.

That earned her a tick on Jordan's is-she-or-isn't-she-a-lesbian checklist. "Beautiful name for a beautiful woman," she said with a soft smile.

Emma let go of Jordan's hand and tilted her head in a way that made it appear as if she were looking down at her, even though she was several inches shorter. "Do lines like that actually work for you?"

For a moment, Jordan was taken aback. Few women called her on her flirting within seconds of meeting her. But she always enjoyed a challenge. "That's not a line," she said with an unwavering smile. "It's a fact."

"Ignore her." Barbara nudged her aside and shook Emma's hand. "I'm Barbara Mosley. Welcome to the neighborhood. I'm sure you'll like it here."

"Thank you. I know I will."

"So, what brings you to the area?" Jordan asked. *Relocating for work or to be with a boyfriend...or a girlfriend?* She didn't ask the last part out loud, sensing that she needed to tone it down a little. Apparently, her new neighbor wasn't in the mood for flirting with a woman this early in the morning...or at all.

"What makes you think I'm not from around here?" Emma asked. A grin crept onto her face, making the copper sparks in her eyes dance with mischief. "Did my decidedly un-Californian tan give me away?" She glanced down at her skin that was as white as Barbara's beloved Iceberg roses and looked as soft as the petals.

Jordan laughed. "No, actually, it was the truck." She pointed at the side of the moving van, which advertised the services of a moving company in Portland, Oregon.

"Ah," Emma said.

She didn't answer Jordan's initial question about what had brought her to South Pasadena. Well, maybe she didn't like revealing too much about herself. Jordan could respect that. Besides, the mystique only added to her neighbor's attractiveness.

"Let us know if you need anything." Barbara pointed at her house. "I live right next door."

"Yeah. We'd be happy to help you feel at home here. I know all the best places in town, and I don't mind playing tour guide," Jordan added. Mentally, she reviewed tomorrow's operating schedule. "In fact, if you're an early riser, I could introduce you to the best coffee shop in town tomorrow morning."

"No, thanks," Emma said. "I'll be up to my neck in moving boxes all day tomorrow, so I won't have time for coffee."

The no had come so quickly it was as if she hadn't been tempted for even a second. *I must be losing my edge.* "Maybe another time, then."

Emma gave a noncommittal nod. "Maybe. If you'll excuse me, I have to show them where that goes." She hurried after the movers, who were lugging a chest of drawers toward the house.

Jordan's gaze followed her until Barbara's chuckle interrupted her enjoyment of her neighbor's perfect butt. She turned toward her. "What's so funny?"

"You getting rejected. That's a first."

"Nah," Jordan said. "It's happened before. For some inexplicable reason, there are a few misguided women who are immune to my charm."

Barbara patted her arm. "They don't know what they're missing."

"That's what I tell them."

They grinned at each other.

"I know it's not the same, but do you want to come over and have that cup of coffee with me?" Barbara asked.

Jordan took her hand and squeezed it. Her husband had died nearly three years ago, and her children didn't live in the area, so Barbara sometimes got lonely. Not that she'd ever admit it, but Jordan sensed it, so she made a point of dropping by regularly for a cup of coffee or to help her in the garden. "Normally, I'd love to, but I'm already running late. I'm supposed to pick up Simone from the airport."

"Oh, she's back in town?"

"Yeah, just for a few days. She's got a client in LA who wants to expand, so she's here to take a look at his product line."

"Tell her to come over and say hi. She's such a nice girl. I really don't understand why you don't date her."

Jordan shook her head. "Like I keep telling you, neither of us is in the market for a relationship. We're just friends." Friends with occasional benefits, but she didn't add that, knowing Barb might not understand.

"Friends who I caught making out like a couple of teenagers in that sports car of yours the last time she visited."

Oops. "You saw that?"

"I see everything, young lady." Barbara stomped her cane onto the driveway. "So why aren't you two together?"

"That's... It's just not what we want. We..."

A loud meow interrupted her. Her calico, Tuna, stood at the other end of the driveway, giving her a demanding look.

Saved by the cat. "Sorry, Barb. I have to go. My mistress is calling. Do you need help getting back over to your house?"

Barbara snorted. "I'm seventy-four, not ninety-four. I can walk the few steps to my house just fine." Then her expression softened. "But thanks for asking, dear. Now go and take care of the many females in your life." Again stubbornly carrying the cane instead of using it, she marched back to her house.

Jordan watched her for a moment and then glanced over at the other side of the duplex, hoping for another glimpse of the new neighbor.

Another demanding cry made her tear her gaze away.

"Hold your horses. I'm coming." She hurried up the driveway. "Jeez, if I wanted to get chewed out for not coming home until the morning, I would have gotten a girlfriend!"

Chapter 2

MOVING REALLY WASN'T FOR SISSIES. Emma's back was already aching from lugging around the heavy moving boxes, and she was glad she had arranged a babysitter for Molly ahead of time via Vettedsitters.com.

With Molly out of the house for a few hours, she couldn't get underfoot, and the first thing she associated with the new city would be a fun day at the park, not all this chaos.

Emma counted the neatly labeled boxes stacked against the built-in bookcase in her new living room.

Nine. Which meant there were two more outside. Good thing the rest of her books were stored on her e-reader.

When she went outside to get the two boxes, her neighbor was just leaving the house too.

She had changed, and the white button-down shirt she wore now looked great against her rich dark brown skin and her naturally coiled, black hair, which was cut close to her head and amplified her great cheekbones and her full lips. Her jeans clung to her long, muscular legs and emphasized her slim waist and the slight flare of her hips. Jordan's loose-limbed stride oozed confidence.

Emma touched her thumb to the bare spot at the base of her ring finger, annoyed at herself for even noticing the way her neighbor looked.

When their gazes met across the driveway, Jordan flashed a grin.

Emma couldn't believe the woman had hit on her. Her flirting had been obvious, even for someone who was as rusty as she was. Admittedly, it was a bit flattering and had bolstered her self-esteem, which had taken quite a beating in the past year. Once upon a time, she might have flirted back, but experience had taught her to stay away from a player like Jordan Williams.

She knew Jordan's type. Women like her were easy on the eye but hard on the heart, and she was determined to never again give anyone the chance to hurt her. If she got involved with a woman again at some point down the road, it would be with someone who knew the definition of commitment and faithfulness.

So she just lifted her hand in silent acknowledgment without returning Jordan's smile and climbed into the moving van. Her to-do list was as long as the Great Wall of China, and flirting with the admittedly good-looking new neighbor wasn't on it.

As usual, LAX was a zoo. The automatic doors of the terminal swished open, and Jordan jogged through. Cursing under her breath, she dodged past tired travelers, crying children, and chatting groups of tourists with large suitcases blocking her way.

She craned her neck to follow the signs toward domestic baggage claim. As she rushed past, she glanced at the large digital monitor listing the arrival times of various flights. *Damn.* It showed Simone's plane as having landed an hour ago.

By the time she reached baggage claim, she was starting to sweat. Simone hated waiting, and usually, Jordan hated being late. In her family, being fifteen minutes early had been considered being late, and it had taken her years to become a little more relaxed about tardiness.

Nearly running, she rounded the corner.

There she stood, next to the by-now empty conveyor belt. God, Simone looked good…and annoyed. Her black corkscrew curls bounced up and down with every impatient tap of her foot, and her dark eyes narrowed as she watched Jordan approach.

Jordan cringed. "Sorry," she called across the distance between them. When she reached her, she greeted her with a hug and a kiss that lasted a split second longer than usual between friends. "I got held up."

Simone shook her head at her. "Oh, yeah. I can imagine by what. Or should I say by whom?" Despite the rebuke, there was no bite in her tone, only gentle teasing.

That was the nice thing about being just friends with benefits. No jealousy dramas.

"I wish," Jordan said. "For once, it wasn't a woman that made me late." Well, okay, the sleepover at Colleen's and then trying to flirt with her new neighbor hadn't helped, but if not for Tuna, she could have driven directly from Colleen's condo to the airport. "I had to feed my cat."

A grin spread over Simone's face. She looked left and right to make sure they were alone. "Is that a euphemism for eating pussy?"

Jordan laughed. God, she had missed this crazy woman. "Has anyone ever told you you've got a dirty mind?"

"You did, but you didn't complain back then."

True. They had met right after Simone's high school sweetheart had broken up with her, and Jordan hadn't minded being her rebound woman. She had expected them to go their separate ways after a few hot romps, but instead, they had become friends. "I won't complain tonight either, but the only dirty thing about feeding my cat is the way the kitchen floor looks afterwards."

Simone's laptop bag started to slip from her shoulder, and she caught it before it could crash to the floor. "So you really got a cat? You? The woman who once said getting a pet was the first step toward being tied down with the matrimonial ball and chain?"

"I didn't get a cat." Jordan reached for Simone's suitcase and led the way toward the exit. "The cat got me. One day, it showed up on my doorstep and wouldn't leave, no matter how many times I shooed it away. Finally, I just gave up and took it in."

"I always said that you're just a big old softie," Simone said affectionately. "Before you know it, a woman will sneak into your life the same way."

"Won't happen," Jordan answered with confidence. "Tuna is the only female who's ever gonna live with me."

Simone nearly lost her laptop bag a second time because she was laughing so hard. "Tuna? You seriously named your cat Tuna?"

Jordan shrugged. "She never came when I called her by any other name, but whenever I called 'Tuna' and opened a can, she was right there."

Laughing, Simone followed her to the car. "Thank God you don't want kids, or you'd end up calling them Pizza, Burger, and Cake, after your favorite foods!"

She reached for Simone's laptop bag. "Shut up and give me that thing before you drop it."

"And that's how the little frog found a new home." Emma closed the book and looked down at her daughter to see if she had grasped the meaning of the story.

Molly yawned. She had worn herself out at the park with the sitter and exploring the house, sliding across the gleaming hardwood floor in her socks. "That was a good story, Mommy."

"Yes, it was." She had picked it to help her daughter get settled into her new home and routine.

"At first he was so sad, but then he liked the new house because it was right next to a creek," Molly said as if she had to explain the story to Emma, even though she'd been the one reading it to her.

Emma smiled at how cute she was. "What about you? Do you like our new house too?"

Molly nodded. "I like the tree."

"I bet." Emma laughed. If she had let her, Molly would have climbed the mulberry tree in the backyard.

She waited, but Molly didn't say anything else, and Emma didn't want to force it. She had a feeling that the five-year-old hadn't yet realized that this wasn't just a fun vacation in an exciting new place. Of course she had told her daughter that they would be staying for good, but Molly hadn't fully understood yet that it meant they wouldn't be returning to the only home she'd ever known and to her friends in Portland.

For now, she was content, surrounded by her toys that Emma had unpacked while Molly had been with the sitter.

Molly yawned again and pressed her cheek to Mouse, her favorite stuffed animal.

Emma tucked the covers more securely around her daughter and then bent to kiss her forehead. "Good night. Sleep well."

"Night, Mommy."

She flicked off the bedside lamp and tiptoed to the door, already hearing Molly's breathing fall into the more regular pattern of sleep. At the door, she turned around. The astronaut night-light cast a gentle yellow glow across Molly's face.

For several seconds, she stood in the doorway and watched her before making herself move. She still had several boxes to unpack so Molly would wake up to a house full of familiar objects tomorrow morning.

Several hours later, she folded up the cardboard box that had held her urban fantasy novels and then glanced at her watch. It was already past midnight, and she had slept very little the past two days while they'd been on the road. A wide yawn made her jaw pop.

Enough was enough. The boxes of office supplies would have to wait until tomorrow. So would all the other things going into the tiny third bedroom that she would turn into her office.

Maybe it was a good thing that she'd left behind all of the kitchen utensils, taking only some pieces of furniture, her clothes, her books, and all of Molly's things. Chloe had offered her the ice cream maker, the wineglasses they had bought in Venice, and the knife set their best man had given them as a wedding gift, but Emma hadn't wanted any of it. Those had been *their* things, stuff they had bought together or received as a couple, and she didn't want that reminder every time she caught sight of them.

This was a fresh start, and that meant new kitchen utensils. She'd have to go shopping tomorrow.

She wandered through the still-unfamiliar house, touching a wall here and one of the arched doorways there as if to mark them with her personal scent and make them hers. It was a beautiful house, but—like Molly—she couldn't quite grasp that it was her home now. Maybe it hadn't fully hit her either that there was no going back to the life she'd once had.

Sighing, she stopped in front of Molly's room and peeked in through the door that she'd left ajar so she would hear if Molly woke up.

Even in her sleep, her daughter's small hands held on to Mouse, as if the stuffed animal were a lifeline keeping her afloat.

Had she done the right thing by uprooting their lives and finding a new home for them, or had taking Molly to the town where Emma had grown up been an entirely selfish thing?

Only time would tell.

She tiptoed across the room, tucked the covers closer around her daughter, and watched her for a few seconds longer before sneaking out.

God, she was exhausted. After a quick shower, she slipped into the new bed that had been delivered this afternoon.

The guest room in their home in Portland had been transformed into an office, so Emma had slept on the couch for the last year. Now lying in a real bed felt strange, even though her aching muscles definitely appreciated it. Her thoughts wandered to the last time she'd slept in a bed, back when her life had still been happy and normal. Or maybe it hadn't been, and she just hadn't realized.

Had Chloe held her that last night? Had they made love? Or had it been one of the rare nights that Chloe had been called back to the hospital? Had she returned muttering about wannabe beauty queens who refused to let the ER residents touch their faces and insisted on having a plastic surgeon come in for a few stitches?

Now, of course, Emma could no longer be sure that those emergencies had ever really existed and hadn't been just fabricated excuses so Chloe could spend the night with her lover. Since the infidelity had come to light, everything Chloe had ever said to her had come under suspicion.

Resolutely, she pushed away those fruitless thoughts. She'd lost enough sleep over Chloe during the last year, wondering when it had all started to go wrong and why she hadn't noticed sooner. That had to stop now.

It took a few more minutes before she could shut off her brain and fall asleep.

When she startled awake some time later, it was still dark outside. She reached for her cell phone on the coffee table that served as her bedside table, only to discover that the phone wasn't there. Neither was the coffee table.

Then she remembered. She wasn't in the living room back in their house in Portland. She was in her new bedroom. For several seconds, she couldn't figure out what had woken her. She was still bone-tired, so why the heck wasn't she still asleep?

Banging noises drifted through the wall.

Thump! Thump! Thump!

For a moment, she thought it was Molly, pounding on the wall because she was scared. But before she could jump up and race over to her, she remembered that Molly's room was on the other side of the bathroom, at the front of the house. This wall was the one she shared with Jordan, her new neighbor.

Thump! Thump! Thump!

14

Jesus, what was she doing? Playing indoor basketball in the middle of the night?

Thump! Thump!

Then a loud, ecstatic scream came from the other side of the wall. "Yes! Just like that. God, yes, right there!"

Emma let her head fall back onto the pillow and groaned. Well, at least someone was getting some while she had lived like a nun for the past year.

"Don't stop!"

It wasn't Jordan's voice but that of another woman.

Emma couldn't believe that Jordan had flirted with her and even asked her out for coffee even though she had a girlfriend. Were there no faithful people left on earth?

Or maybe the vocal woman wasn't Jordan's girlfriend but just some stranger she had picked up in a bar.

Why was she even thinking about it? It wasn't any of her business what her neighbor did on her side of that wall—unless it kept her awake.

The banging and moaning lasted for quite some time. Apparently, her neighbor wasn't all talk and no action. Emma had to giggle at the thought and then pressed a hand to her mouth. Since when was she a giggler? She definitely needed some sleep.

But with all the sounds coming from next door, that wouldn't happen anytime soon. The moans, groans, and little screams seemed to go on forever.

Maybe she should have accepted that invitation for coffee after all. Her neighbor had amazing stamina; she had to give her that. Then she grinned wryly and shook her head. Sex with someone like Jordan wasn't worth the inevitable heartache, not even sex that made you scream so loudly that you woke up the neighbor.

After a while, the rhythmic pounding of the headboard against the wall started to speed up. "Yes, yes, yes. God, Jordan!"

Then, finally, there was only silence.

Thank God! Emma hooked one leg over the covers in her favorite sleeping position and prepared to go back to sleep. Just as her thoughts started to drift away and that feeling of heaviness overcame her, the rhythmic banging started again.

Thump! Thump! Thump!

With a grunt of frustration, Emma yanked the covers up over her head. But after a while, she started to sweat. It wasn't because of the hot sex happening on the other side of the wall, she told herself; it was because she was stuck beneath the covers, where the temperature was heating up.

Were they done?

Carefully, she poked her head out from beneath the covers and listened into the darkness.

Thump! Thump! Thump!

"So good."

"No," Emma muttered. "That's not good at all. I have to get up early tomorrow morning, dammit." Why on earth couldn't she at least have straight neighbors? If one of them were a man, their middle-of-the-night romp would have been over already.

"More! Harder! God, yes!"

The framed poster she had leaned against the wall toppled over. She hadn't hung it yet because she hadn't wanted to disturb the new neighbor with her drilling so late in the day. But apparently, Jordan Williams had no such compunctions.

Grumbling, Emma got out of bed, snatched up her pillow and blanket, and marched into the living room. Great. Now she was back on the couch.

At least here she couldn't hear the energizer bunnies next door anymore.

With a grunt, she pulled the blanket up to her chin. What a welcome to the neighborhood!

Chapter 3

JORDAN GLANCED AT THE DASHBOARD clock while she drove. It was already half past six. Usually, she didn't mind the ten-or-eleven-hour days at the hospital, but Simone was only in town for a few more days, so she had promised to take her out to dinner at a nice restaurant.

She had loved having her friend stay with her for the last two days. After not seeing each other for almost a year, their reconnecting in the bedroom had been explosive. But, truth be told, she also looked forward to having her house to herself again, with no one who left their stuff all over and no guilty conscience if she didn't make it home on time because she had ended up having to open a patient's abdomen instead of removing his gallbladder laparoscopically.

When she pulled into the driveway, she once again found something blocking the access to the detached garage she shared with her neighbor. This time, it wasn't a moving van. It was a little girl.

"What the fuck?" Jordan had never had a child play right in front of her house. Sometimes, the neighbors' kids were playing soccer on the street, but unless the ball rolled up her driveway, they usually stayed off her property.

Jordan left the car at the bottom of the driveway and climbed out.

She had lived on this street for almost three years, and she'd never seen this kid before, at least not that she remembered. Maybe it was someone's grandchild here for a visit. She'd never been good at guessing children's ages, but the girl didn't look older than three or four, too young to wander around the neighborhood on her own, especially since it was probably close to her bedtime.

The girl was kneeling in front of the garage, drawing on the pavement with red, blue, and white sidewalk chalk. Half of it dusted her bib overalls and her fair cheeks.

When Jordan rounded the car, she caught a glimpse of what the kid was drawing: some kind of animal with huge triangular ears. Either it was the stuffed lion she clutched in her free hand, or it was supposed to be Tuna, who lay next to the girl, her tail swishing back and forth across the chalk drawing, adding a fourth color to her fur.

"Um, hi there," Jordan said from several steps away, not wanting to scare the kid.

The girl's head shot up, her lopsided blonde pigtails flying. She stared at Jordan with large eyes but didn't return the greeting or say anything else.

Admittedly, her eight-week rotation in pediatrics during med school had hardly made her an expert when it came to kids, but she was fairly certain that children were supposed to be able to speak in full sentences by that age.

"Hi," she said again.

The girl continued to stare.

"Aren't you a little too young to be outside all on your own?"

"I'm not young—I'm five!" the girl declared, scrunching up her nose as if Jordan had offended her.

Jordan had to smile. So the kid was a bit older than she had thought. Maybe she was small for her age, or maybe Jordan needed to brush up on child development. "I was starting to think you couldn't talk."

"Of course I can talk," the girl replied immediately. "But Mommy says I'm not allowed to talk to strangers."

Well, at least the mother had some common sense, even though she let the kid run around alone outside. But then again, maybe that was okay for a five-year-old. Jordan had no idea about the do's and don'ts of raising children.

"That's a good rule," she said because she didn't know what else to say to a child. "My mother taught me the same." She hadn't really. The army posts she had grown up on had been a safe environment for Jordan and her sisters.

The girl colored in the right ear of the animal she had drawn and then peeked up at Jordan. "My name is Molly, and this is Mouse." She held up the stuffed lion.

"Mouse?" Jordan repeated.

Molly nodded as if naming a lion *Mouse* was a logical thing to do. Well, Jordan figured she couldn't complain too much. She had named her cat after a fish.

"What's your name?" the girl asked.

"I'm Jordan, and this is Tuna." She pointed at the cat.

"Jordan?" Molly repeated. "But that's a boy's name! Jordan from my preschool class is a boy."

Figures. The girl thought Tuna was a perfectly fine name for a cat and chose to focus on her name instead. Jordan scratched her head, not sure how to explain.

But luckily, Molly moved on to the next topic before she could think of an answer. "Is Tuna your cat?"

"I guess so. At least I've been chosen as the person who has to pay for all the cat food."

The girl giggled. "Is it a boy cat or a girl cat?"

"She's a girl," Jordan answered.

"Does she sleep on your bed at night?"

Jeez, this kid was asking a lot of questions. Jordan was starting to feel as if she were in a police interrogation. "Sometimes." Not in the last two days, though. Since Simone had arrived, Tuna had looked for a quieter place to sleep. Jordan suppressed a grin.

The girl watched as Tuna rolled over her drawing, getting even more chalk all over her fur. "Bad cat! Stop it!"

"Yeah, stop it, Tuna. No destroying the art."

Tuna stopped rolling, but just as Jordan thought she had finally asserted her authority over her furry roommate, the cat licked her tail.

Jordan blinked. Was that a *kiss my ass*?

"Maybe my mommy will get me a cat too," the kid said.

You can have mine was on the tip of Jordan's tongue, but she had a feeling the girl would take her up on it, and then she might have two very annoyed parents on her hands.

"Where is your mommy?" Jordan asked. "Where do you live?"

Molly proudly rattled off some address in Portland, even though Jordan was pretty sure her mother would have a rule about telling a stranger where she lived too.

Wait a minute... Portland? Did that mean...?

"Actually," a voice to the right said, "that's our old address. We live here now, remember, Molly?"

Jordan looked up.

The door to the neighbor's part of the duplex had opened without her noticing, and Emma stood in the doorway. A hint of sweat gleamed on her forehead, as if she had either worked out or lugged around furniture or moving boxes. Instead of the sexy pair of jeans Jordan had seen her in two days ago, she was wearing gray sweatpants that were baggy at the knees. Even that old, ratty thing couldn't hide her lush curves.

Jordan stared at her. *Damn.* It rarely happened, but apparently, her gaydar had been off. Her cute neighbor was straight. Not that Jordan had ever let that bother her. In her book, most women were straight—until they weren't. But Emma had a kid and very likely a husband, and if there was one rule that Jordan always stuck to, it was to never, ever get involved with someone who was in a relationship.

At least it explained why Emma hadn't been interested in having coffee with her. Maybe she hadn't lost her mojo after all.

"I'm sorry." Emma nodded down at her daughter and the chalk drawings all around her. "It looks like we're blocking your garage again."

"It's okay. We all have to make sacrifices for art, right?" Jordan couldn't stop the wink or the automatic grin she flashed Emma. Flirting with women was ingrained into her DNA, so it was hard to cut it out now that she knew Emma was off the market. Well, establishing a good relationship with her new neighbor was a good thing, even if that relationship would never be extended to the bedroom.

Emma laughed. "Yeah, well, this artist has to go to bed now. Come on, Molly. Let's get you cleaned up and into your jammies." She held out her hand to the girl, apparently not minding the red chalk that clung to the small fingers.

"But Mommy, I haven't finished the cat. Look, it has no tail." Molly pointed at the chalk drawing.

"How about we finish it together tomorrow, after you're back from kindergarten and I'm done with my clients?"

"Yay!" Molly jumped up and skipped across the driveway toward her mother. "Can you draw me a giraffe too? And a Saint Bernard!"

The girl jabbered on and on all the way to the door, and for a moment, Jordan exchanged an amused smile with Emma before both mother and daughter gave a quick wave and the door closed behind them.

Only when her own front door opened did Jordan remember that she had someone waiting for her.

"What are you doing out there?" Simone called.

Jordan looked from Emma's door to the chalk drawing and then to Simone, who was all dressed up, ready to go out. "Um, nothing. Let me take a quick shower and we can go."

As she walked over to her side of the house, Tuna jumped up and ran ahead of her.

"No! Don't let her into the—"

Too late. Tuna slipped past Simone and disappeared into the house, no doubt heading straight for the living room to leave chalk dust all over the couch.

Jordan sighed. She had definitely been right—getting a pet was the first step toward being tied down by the shackles of domesticity. But at least she didn't have to wrangle an energetic five-year-old into bed. The only female she'd take to bed today would go there quite willingly.

Grinning, she sauntered toward Simone to kiss her hello.

The next morning, Molly's first day at school, wasn't off to a good start.

Molly sat at the breakfast table, clutching the spoon without even touching her cereal.

"Hey, little dreamer. Don't forget to eat, or you won't have enough energy to keep up with the other kids in your class."

The spoon clattered to the table. "I don't want to go to stupid school."

Uh-oh. Emma put her coffee mug down. "But, honey, you loved preschool, and I bet you'll love kindergarten just as much."

Molly's bottom lip quivered. "I won't. Kindergarten is stupid. I want to go home."

Emma's heart ached. So far, Molly had seemed to love the new house and getting to stay home with Emma for a couple of days, but now that she was trying to get them settled into their new routine, it stopped being a fun vacation. "This is home now, Molly," she said gently. "Why don't you go today and give it a chance? You might like it."

"No!" Molly kicked the table, toppling over her glass of milk.

"Molly!" Years of motherhood had honed Emma's reflexes. She tried to catch the glass but was a second too late.

The white liquid spilled over the table and splashed onto Emma's lap. She bit back a curse and jumped up. Her wet pants stuck to her thighs, but that would have to wait. Milk dripped onto the floor as she rounded the table, pulled Molly from her chair, and knelt in front of her so that they were nearly at eye level.

"Listen, Molly. I know you miss your old room, and you miss Kenny and Sarah."

Molly stared at the drops of milk on the floor, not looking up into Emma's eyes. "And Mama," she whispered.

Emma swallowed. Her eyes burned, even though she had thought she didn't have any tears left. She wrapped her arms around her daughter and held her tightly, not knowing what to say to that. It wasn't as if Chloe had spent a lot of time with Molly, even when they had lived in the same house, but for a moment, guilt still clawed at her.

To her relief, Molly cuddled against her and hugged her back. After a moment, she pulled back and frowned. "You're all wet, Mommy."

"Yeah, because a certain someone knocked over her glass of milk." She nudged Molly's chin, making her giggle and the tears in her eyes disappear.

It would have been easy to distract her now and change the subject, but Emma knew she would have to address this sooner or later. Still kneeling, she looked into Molly's eyes. "I know you miss her, honey. I'm sure she misses you too." She didn't believe that last statement, but what else was she supposed to say to her five-year-old?

"Then why can't she come live here too?"

"Do you remember when you and Jessica stopped being best friends?" Molly nodded.

"Well, sometimes, that happens to adults too, and then they go their separate ways and no longer live together. That's what happened to Mama and me."

Molly sniffed once and scrunched up her face in that way that meant she was thinking hard about something. "Will you find a new friend, like Kenny and Sarah?"

"I'm sure I will one day, honey." But it wouldn't be the kind of friend who would move into the house and make her daughter cry when she left. "And I bet you'll find plenty of new friends in kindergarten. Want to know why I'm so sure?"

Molly softly swayed back and forth, her hands behind her back. "Because I'm smart?"

Emma chuckled and realized that Molly was repeating what she had often told her in similar conversations. "Well, that and because we're gonna stop at a bakery on the way to school and get cupcakes for everyone."

A broad smile spread over Molly's face. "Cupcakes! Can I pick them?"

"Yes, you may—if you help me clean up the milk. After all, it's your mess, so it's your responsibility."

They worked together to wipe down the table and clean the floor. Of course, Molly was adding to the mess more than really helping.

When they were done, a glance at the clock revealed that they had to leave. No time to change into a dry pair of pants.

Emma grabbed her car keys and Molly's backpack, and they headed out.

Just as they left the house, the door on the other side of the duplex opened and Jordan stepped outside, followed by an attractive black woman of about Emma's age, who carried a laptop bag over her shoulder.

Emma hadn't seen Jordan's girlfriend yet, but she had heard her plenty for the last three nights. She had to admit the two made a nice-looking couple, but she couldn't help wondering if the poor woman knew that her partner had a wandering eye.

"Good morning," Jordan said, and her girlfriend echoed it.

Yes, that was definitely the voice of the vocal woman who had kept her up for several nights in a row. Emma struggled not to blush as she returned the greeting and quickly pulled Molly toward the garage.

Out of the corner of her eye, she saw Jordan walk her girlfriend to a car that was parked at the curb. The logo of a rental company was emblazoned on its side. Apparently, the two of them were in a long-distance relationship or something. Then Jordan pushed her lover against the driver's side door and kissed her.

Christ! This woman really had no shame. Bad enough that she had kept Emma awake with the seemingly endless banging—pun intended—but now she had to suck face with her lover while Molly watched?

Not that Molly *was* watching. She was so used to two women kissing that she didn't even spare them a glance.

Calm down. Yes, her new neighbor was possibly an ass who was flirting with other women even though she was in a relationship, but it was none of her business.

Intent on ignoring them, she strode toward the shared two-car garage, opened the large door, and pressed the button to unlock her Toyota Prius. The key fob didn't beep, and when she reached out for the driver's side door, it didn't open. Frowning, she took a step back and tried again.

Nothing.

She pressed the key fob repeatedly. Normally, a red light flashed, but now it didn't. *Great.* Today, of all times, the battery in the fob needed to be replaced. Had she seen any extra batteries when she had unpacked the moving boxes?

She couldn't remember.

"Mommy?" Molly tried to peer around her to see what was going on. She sounded worried.

"Everything's fine. We'll be on our way in a second." Thank God the car's producers had planned ahead for such emergencies. She pulled the mechanical key from the side of the key fob and inserted it into the driver's side door lock.

But luck wasn't on her side today. When she turned the key, it didn't budge. She carefully pulled it out and tried again—with the same result.

"Is there a problem?" someone asked from the other side of the garage.

Emma looked up and met Jordan's gaze over the roofs of the Prius and Jordan's sports car. "No," she said quickly and tried not to let her frustration show as she jiggled the key in the lock a little.

"We're getting cupcakes," Molly announced.

"Oooh, cupcakes! That's great."

Jordan's very white teeth gleamed against her flawless dark skin. There wasn't a wrinkle in sight, even though Emma guessed her to be slightly older than her own thirty-two years. With the day she was having, Emma found it strangely annoying.

"If I can get the da…dumb door open," she muttered.

Instead of getting into her car and driving off, Jordan came over to their side of the garage. Her gaze wandered down Emma's body, and it took Emma a second to realize she was staring at the way her milk-drenched pants stuck to her thighs.

God, the woman was a pig. Her girlfriend had left less than a minute ago, and here she was, already checking out another woman.

"Something wrong with the car?" Jordan asked.

Emma pulled the key out of the lock and let her hand dangle down. "The door won't open." She demonstrated by pressing the unlock button and halfway expected the door to open and embarrass her, but it didn't happen.

"Hmm." Jordan stepped next to her, and they both bent at the same time to peer into the lock, which brought their faces within inches of each other. When Jordan turned her head to look at her, her warm breath washed over Emma's lips.

Emma's traitorous heart picked up its beat. Quickly, she stepped back to create some space between them.

"I take it you tried the mechanical key?" Jordan asked. Her gaze was no longer on the lock but fixated on Emma's lips.

"I did. It wouldn't open either."

Chloe would have taken the key from her and tried it herself, making Emma feel as if she couldn't even handle as simple a task as inserting a key correctly. But Jordan didn't reach for the key. Instead, she asked, "How long have you had the car?"

"Five years," Emma said. "We bought it when Molly was born." *We.* She squeezed her eyes shut for a second. When she opened them again, she looked right into Jordan's eyes.

Jordan didn't ask questions, at least not about the other part of the *we.* "Have you used the key in the door before?"

"No."

"I'll be right back." Jordan walked back to her side of the garage. When she returned a few seconds later, she pressed something into Emma's hand. "Here. Try this."

Emma stared at the blue-and-white can. "What's this?"

A mischievous grin stole across Jordan's face. "Lube. It can do wonders for orifices that haven't been used in a while."

Was everything the woman said a double entendre? "I can't imagine you having that problem," she muttered under her breath.

Jordan tilted her head. "Sorry, I didn't catch that. What did you say?"

"Nothing."

"Mommy, what's lube?" Molly piped up. "And what's an odi…odifice?"

They looked at each other like two kids who had been caught with their hands in the cookie jar and then burst out laughing. As much as she wanted to, Emma could no longer hold on to her annoyance. "You're getting me in trouble," she whispered to Jordan. To Molly, she said, "She's talking about the door lock, honey. Ms. Williams gave me some lubricant spray to put in the keyhole."

"Jordan, please," Jordan said. "Otherwise, I'll start feeling like a kindergarten teacher, and I think I just proved that it wouldn't be the best job for me."

Emma suppressed a smile, not wanting to reveal that she did find Jordan amusing every once in a while. She nodded her acknowledgment and turned back toward the car door. They really needed to get going. She pulled the cap from the aerosol can and sprayed a bit of the lock lubricant into the keyhole.

"Put a little on the key too," Jordan said. "If you have never used it in the lock before, there could be some dirt in there."

Emma sprayed a little lubricant on the key, inserted it again, and slowly turned it. This time, the lock opened immediately, and she could pull the driver's side door open. "Yes!" Her legs weakened with relief. She had already imagined herself getting the car towed and spending hours at the dealership, and she really didn't have time for that today.

Molly jumped up and down, doing a victory dance.

With a grateful smile, Emma handed back the can. "Thank you. You're a lifesaver."

Jordan returned the smile and tipped an imaginary hat. "Glad I could help."

She might be a player and a cheat, but there was genuine warmth in her brown eyes. Emma felt Jordan's gaze on her as she turned, opened the rear door for Molly, and buckled her into the booster seat in the back before climbing behind the wheel.

When she backed out of the garage, Jordan still stood next to her sports car, the can in one hand while she waved at them with the other.

That evening, when Emma carried the garbage to the curb, Jordan's girlfriend got out of her rental car. With her laptop bag slung over one shoulder, she walked up the driveway. A friendly smile lit up her face as she saw Emma. "Hi."

"Hi." Too embarrassed to stick around for more of a conversation, Emma waved and walked back to her door.

Just as she was about to step inside, a curse made her pause.

"Dammit," Jordan's girlfriend murmured. "If my head wasn't attached to my neck, I swear I'd forget it too."

Emma turned. "Is there a problem?"

"Yeah. Jordan gave me a key, but it seems I forgot to actually take it with me when I left for work this morning." She put down her laptop bag. "Guess I'll just sit here and enjoy the view of this lovely cul-de-sac until she gets back."

Emma hesitated and then gave herself a mental slap. Her embarrassment at having heard the woman have sex was no reason to leave her sitting on the doorstep. "Why don't you come in and have some coffee with me while you wait?"

"Really? That would be great. Thank you."

As she led the stranded woman into the kitchen, Molly came running from her room. "Mommy, can I—?" She slid to a stop when she saw the stranger.

"This is Molly, my daughter."

"Hi, Molly. I saw you this morning, but I didn't have time to stop and chat."

"You kissed Jordan," Molly said.

So she had seen them kiss after all. Emma bit her lip so she wouldn't burst out laughing at the wide-eyed look on the woman's face.

But to her credit, she recovered instantly and smiled. "I did. Jordan tells me you're the famous artist who painted the beautiful drawings on the driveway."

Molly beamed at the praise. "I made them all myself."

"All of them? Wow."

Jordan's girlfriend really was beautiful, especially when she smiled, which she did often. Would she still be so friendly if she knew that her girlfriend had asked Emma out for coffee?

"Molly, this is—" Emma gave the woman a questioning look.

"Simone," she said, "who apparently forgot her manners along with her key."

Emma smiled. In Molly's direction, she added, "She's Jordan's girlfriend and will stay with us until Jordan comes home from work."

"Actually," Simone cleared her throat, "Jordan and I are just friends."

Just friends? Emma stared at her. *Excuse me, but the last time I shouted out a dozen* Oh God*'s at three in the morning, I wasn't with a friend!*

"It's complicated," Simone said with a mild smile. "But we really are just friends."

"Can I have a cupcake, Mommy?" Molly asked, apparently bored with the adults' conversation.

"Now? We just had dinner."

"But I'm hungry."

"Do you want me to warm you up a little of the leftover carrots and peas?" Emma asked, even though she knew the answer already.

Molly scrunched up her nose. "No. I'm hungry for cupcakes."

Emma sighed and decided to make an exception just this once. It had been Molly's first day at school after all. "Okay. But just one."

Seconds later, Molly disappeared back into her room with a pink-frosted cupcake.

"Do you want one too?" If she had counted correctly, there were two left over.

"I really should be a good girl and say 'no, thanks,' but life's too short to deny yourself, so...yes, please," Simone said with an impish grin.

Emma turned on the new espresso machine she had bought the day before and placed the two last cupcakes onto plates. They sat on the couch in the living room. For a minute, silence ruled as they ate their cupcakes.

Simone pulled out a phone. "I'll let Jordan know where I am, if that's okay."

"Sure."

A few quick flicks of her thumbs, and then Simone put the phone back into the pocket of her blazer. "I hear you've only just moved in."

So Jordan had told Simone about her? Had she mentioned that she had asked her out within a minute of meeting her? Probably not.

Emma licked cupcake crumbs off the corner of her mouth and nodded. "On Monday."

"How do you like it so far?"

"I love it. It's quiet, but there are plenty of stores and restaurants just a few blocks away, and the schools are great. I actually grew up here, so I thought it might be nice for Molly to live here. What about you? You don't live here?" She indicated the other side of the duplex.

"God, no." Simone chuckled. "I love staying with Jordan for a few days, but any longer than that and we'd probably end up killing each other. I'm not a slob or anything, but…"

"Life's too short to spend it cleaning and putting things back into their rightful place?"

"Exactly." Simone took another hearty bite of her cupcake. "Finally a woman who understands, unlike Jordan."

Actually, Emma preferred some order too. While she didn't want to feel as if she were living in a museum, with not a single item out of place, a little structure always helped her feel more balanced. She hadn't pegged Jordan for a fellow neat freak.

But apparently, she had misjudged her in other ways too. Jordan might be a player, but she wasn't a cheat. That made Emma feel better about living in such close proximity to her. She didn't want her daughter to grow up around people who thought faithfulness was a thing that had gone out of fashion somewhere in the last century.

"So, where do you live?" Emma asked.

"Chicago. I'm only here for the week to meet with a client."

Emma glanced at the laptop bag leaning against her coffee table. "What do you do?"

"I'm an independent business consultant," Simone said. "Sounds pretty highfalutin, right? It basically means I do research, analyze the data, and come up with fresh solutions."

"That sounds a lot like some of what I d—" Before Emma could finish her sentence, the doorbell rang.

Molly raced to the door.

"No opening the door without me, honey," Emma called. "You know that." She got up. "That's probably Jordan."

Indeed it was.

When she opened the door with Molly at her hip, Jordan stood on the other side of the threshold, a black leather jacket thrown over one shoulder. Her casual confidence seemed to surround her like a magnetic force field.

Emma shuffled backward to resist its pull.

"Hi," Jordan said. "I heard you granted asylum to my forgetful friend."

There it was again: friend. Now that she knew Jordan wasn't in a relationship, she felt guilty for assuming she was a cheat. She couldn't quite look her in the eye. "Um, yes. We're in the living room. Why don't you come in?"

When Jordan stepped inside, the hall somehow seemed smaller, as if she were filling it with her personality.

"We had cupcakes," Molly announced as she followed them to the living room.

Jordan arched her brows as she looked from Molly to Simone. "I thought you wanted to go out for dinner."

"Traitor," Simone mumbled in Molly's direction, but she was smiling. "Yeah, but I was hungry for cupcakes."

She and Emma burst out laughing.

Jordan looked from one to the other. "Want to let me in on the joke?"

"You needed to be there." Simone got up from the couch and kissed Jordan hello.

Even though staring wasn't the polite thing to do, Emma couldn't look away. This wasn't how she would greet one of her friends, but it also wasn't how she would say hello to the love of her life.

Yeah, well, the love of your life is back in Portland with her little medical assistant, so maybe you should stop holding other people to your standards.

She promised herself to give Jordan a chance. Maybe if she looked more closely, she would see the person that Simone saw in her instead of the pathological flirt.

Yeah, just don't look too closely, a sarcastic voice inside her head piped up, sounding annoyingly like her mother, who, at finding out that Emma had filed for a divorce, had helpfully declared that she had never liked Chloe anyway.

"Thanks for the coffee and the cupcake," Simone said when Emma walked them to the door. "It was great to meet you."

"Likewise," Emma answered and found that she meant it. When the door closed behind Jordan and her friend, she resolved to sleep on the couch tonight. Listening to a stranger have sex was one thing, but when you actually had coffee with the woman, that made it even more awkward.

Sleeping in a real bed would have to wait a while longer.

As soon as the door closed, Simone backhanded her across the shoulder. "You dog!"

"Ouch!" Jordan rubbed her shoulder, even though it hardly hurt. "What? What did I do?"

"No wonder you're not planning on moving."

"Uh, what? Why would I move?"

"Because that's what you usually do after three years, and if I'm not mistaken, that's about how long you've lived here."

Jordan shook her head at her friend and took the laptop bag from her to carry it to her side of the duplex. "I have no idea what you're talking about."

"What is the longest you have ever lived in one place?"

"Same city or same house?"

"House," Simone replied.

Jordan thought about it for a moment. "Three years."

"See? The three-year mark is when you usually get itchy feet and start thinking about greener pastures."

Did she, really? Jordan had to admit that she'd recently started to entertain the idea of leaving Griffith Memorial Hospital and doing a fellowship at another hospital. Man, she hated being so predictable. "Then why am I still here, wiseass?"

Simone smirked. "Maybe because you're enjoying the view from your nice little duplex. Not that I could blame you. Your new neighbor is a cutie."

Cutie? Totally hot, that's what she was. And she was nice too. Not that Jordan usually cared about that. "She's got a kid, Simone."

"So? Moms can still be cute, can't they? I sure plan to be once I have kids."

Jordan paused in the middle of unlocking the front door and stared at her. "You want to have kids?"

Simone patted her arm. "Don't worry. Not with you. But yeah, one day, I'd love to have one or two."

Why had she never known that about her friend?

"One day soon, hopefully," Simone added. "Because my biological clock is ticking so loudly that it's starting to keep me up at night. Tick-tock, tick-tock, tick-tock."

Jordan had no idea what to say to that, so she sought refuge in a joke. "Well, I can't help you with that, but if you're not sleeping anyway, I could give your hormones a workout that will keep them in tip-top shape."

Simone's eyes smoldered. She took the key from Jordan, unlocked the door, and pulled her directly to the bedroom without pausing to let her put down the laptop bag first.

Looks like we'll lose our restaurant reservation, was the last clear thought on Jordan's mind before she dropped her leather jacket, set the laptop bag on top, and tackled Simone to the bed.

Chapter 4

"THANK YOU SO MUCH FOR the invitation, Mrs. Mosley," Emma said when her neighbor opened the door on Friday afternoon.

Barbara waved her hand. "None of that Mrs. Mosley thing. I'm Barbara."

"Can I call you Barbara too?" Molly asked, looking around their neighbor's house with big eyes.

"Of course you can. And if that's too much of a mouthful for you, you can call me Barb, like Jordan does." She led them into the living room, where a table was set with a white linen cloth and fine china.

Emma prayed that Molly wouldn't knock over the mug of hot chocolate that Barbara had made for her.

They chatted over cheesecake—Emma's favorite—and coffee, while Emma kept an eye on Molly's mug.

Finally, Barbara reached over and patted her hand. "Relax. I won't be upset if the tablecloth ends up with a stain or two. I have kids of my own, you know?" She pointed at the framed photographs on the mantle.

"Where are they?" Molly asked around a forkful of cheesecake.

"They're both grown now. My oldest son lives in Michigan, and the younger one is in Florida."

Molly's eyes went wide. "At Disney World?"

Barbara laughed. "Not exactly at Disney World, but close enough."

Emma glanced over Barbara's shoulder and studied the photos. One of them showed two men flanking Barbara on either side, towering over her and creating an almost comical effect.

"They're tall, aren't they?" Barbara said. "They get that from their father."

Emma smiled politely, not daring to ask. Was Barbara divorced too, or had her husband...?

"He died about three years ago," Barbara said very quietly. "Heart attack. He had never been sick a day in his life. Maybe that was a blessing, but…" She sighed. "It hit me completely unprepared. Not that you could ever prepare for something like that. I don't know what I would have done if not for Jordan."

"Jordan?" Emma echoed.

A smile ghosted across Barbara's weathered face. "She hadn't been living here for very long when Monty—my husband—died. Before, we exchanged hellos and chatted about the weather when we saw each other in passing, but that was it. But when Monty died, Jordan was the one who really came through for me. She showed up on my doorstep, claiming she had made too much food for herself and would I do her a huge favor and take some of it off her hands. She got me back into gardening and out of the house."

The lump in Emma's throat eased a little. She let go of her fork to gently squeeze Barbara's hand. "I'm glad she was there for you." Who would have thought that Jordan, of all people, would take the time to do something like that for a neighbor she barely knew?

"Oh, yeah, she was. Still is." Barbara chuckled. "She even sat through two bingo evenings with a horde of eighty-year-olds because I refused to go alone."

Emma stared at the mantle. Next to the photo of the bald man who had to be Monty leaned a picture of Jordan kneeling in a flower bed, grinning up into the camera. Apparently, there was more to her neighbor than being a big ol' flirt.

"Jordan is nice. She has a cat named Tuna," Molly said. "I drew a picture of her."

"Really?" Barbara put on a suitably impressed expression.

Molly nodded. "It's on the driveway. Mommy drew a giraffe next to it, but the neck is crooked and we couldn't find the yellow, so we used orange. I can show you!" She was about to slide off her chair and drag Barbara to the door.

"Um, why don't you show her after we finish the cake, honey?" Emma said.

Molly began to eat faster.

Barbara laughed. "I miss having kids around the house. My grandchildren don't visit me nearly enough. If you ever need a babysitter—"

"I'm not a baby," Molly protested.

"Oh, excuse me, whenever you need someone to show Molly how to cheat at Memory, let me know."

Molly giggled.

Emma gave her neighbor a grateful look. All the childhood friends she had made in South Pasadena had long since moved away, and it would be great to entrust Molly to someone she personally knew instead of using the babysitting service. "As long as you don't play for money and win half of my paycheck from Molly."

"I was thinking cookies," Barbara said.

"Yes! Can we have cookies, Mommy?"

Good thing her daughter wasn't shy around strangers. Being able to bake cookies was all the qualification Molly required in a babysitter.

After all she had been through during the past year, Emma had a hard time denying her daughter anything she wanted, but she refused to be one of the mothers who gave in all the time just because it was easier. "No, Molly. Not now. You just had a large piece of cake, and you don't want Barbara to think you didn't like it, do you?"

"No," Molly mumbled. She poked out her bottom lip and hung her head.

"How about we look at your drawings on the driveway now?" Barbara came to her rescue.

The frown instantly disappeared from Molly's face, and she jumped down from her chair.

When Emma felt obligated to get up and follow them to the door, Barbara waved her back down. "You stay and finish your cake. We'll be right back."

Emma sank back onto her chair and watched them go. A slow smile crinkled the corners of her mouth. She was beginning to think that moving here maybe hadn't been such a bad idea after all.

A few hours later, Emma turned on the hot water and squirted some dish soap into the sink. Their plates and pots from dinner piled up to the left, next to more dirty coffee cups than she cared to count. She'd overdone it a little with the caffeine today, but since anything stronger was out of the question when dealing with clients, it had been the next best thing.

She took the first sauce-smeared plate and started to scrub. By the time she rinsed it and put it in the drying rack, part of the stress of the day had melted away.

Chloe had always teased her for wasting time on washing dishes when she had a perfectly good dishwasher, but the mundane task had always helped her think. Whenever she was struggling with a decision or just needed some time to herself, washing dishes was her go-to activity.

It had been at the sink that she had decided to give up her job as executive assistant to the CEO of a large, international company to have Molly.

It had been at the sink that she had decided to move back to South Pasadena.

And now maybe having her hands wrist-deep in sudsy water would help her come to a decision regarding this client. She scrubbed harder at a stubborn bit of sauce on Molly's plate.

D.C. Pane, author of bestselling thrillers and mysteries, was starting to become a *pain* in the ass. She grinned at her own joke for a moment but then sobered.

It really had stopped being funny some time ago. He was quickly becoming her least favorite client. Truth be told, Emma didn't actually know whether the author was a he or a she, since Pane liked to keep a secret identity and refused to talk to her on Skype. When they had talked on the phone, D.C. had sounded pretty androgynous, but she had a feeling she was dealing with a man. At least she wanted to believe that a woman would be more respectful of her time with her family.

Pane, however, expected her to answer his e-mails and direct messages at all hours of the day and night, even on Sundays and national holidays, and he was setting increasingly unrealistic deadlines for the research and marketing projects he wanted her to handle. She had tried talking to him about it, but he didn't seem to get that his expectations were a problem.

She'd given up hope that things would change, so now she had a decision to make. A year ago, there would have been no need to think about it over doing the dishes. She would have told him she couldn't work for him any longer and would have been done with it.

But now things were different. In the beginning, her income as a virtual assistant had been a bonus...a little extra spending money in her pocket or a contribution to family vacations. Now she needed it.

Even though Chloe was paying child support, Emma didn't want to rely on her, at least not a second longer than absolutely necessary. Maybe it was stupid pride, but taking Chloe's money made her skin crawl. For the last year, she had worked hard to expand her client base—which sometimes meant dealing with difficult clients like D.C. Pane.

At least he always paid her on time, and he hadn't even twitched when she had slightly raised her rates two months ago. She needed the money. *Yeah, but I need my sanity too.* She wished she could call one of her friends and get a second opinion, but all of them were friends with Chloe too, so their solution to the problem would probably be to urge her to accept Chloe's money.

Sighing, she rinsed the plate and put it in the drying rack. If she scrubbed it any more than she already had, she would remove the outer coating of the poor plate.

She reached for a glass and ran the dish sponge over it. When she held it up to the light to see if it was clean, her gaze fell out of the window.

The sun was about to set, but Jordan was in the driveway, washing her car with a hand sprayer on the end of her hose because of the drought... if you could call what she was doing *washing the car*. It looked more like an erotic dance performance. She was wearing a pair of cut-off jeans and a T-shirt with a military pattern, its sleeves ripped out to reveal her athletic arms. Emma couldn't tell from this distance, but Jordan either had on headphones or she was dancing to some song in her head. Emma's grandmother had always told her to dance as if nobody was watching, and Jordan was doing exactly that.

She gyrated around the sports coupe, swaying her hips to the unheard rhythm.

Every slide of the sponge over the silver hood of the car looked like a lover caressing a woman's curves. Bits of foam dribbled down her bare arms, and the worn jeans tightened over her sexy butt as she leaned across the hood.

Jesus! Emma exhaled slowly.

Without looking away from the woman in the driveway, she set the glass down before she could drop it.

Wasn't there a commercial like this? But while the muscular hunk washing his car on TV hadn't done a thing for Emma, she had to admit that the sight of Jordan fired up her body temperature in a way that even the hot water in the sink hadn't managed.

Foam and drops of water arced through the air, glittering in the setting sun, as Jordan pretended the sponge in her hand was a microphone and sang into it.

Chloe would have never done something so childish. Emma couldn't help smiling. It was cute...and sexy.

Emma grabbed a knife and scrubbed at it with more force than necessary. Okay, Jordan was not a cheat as she had initially thought, but from her uninhibited flirting Emma guessed her to be a commitment-phobic player. Absolutely not the type of woman she wanted to be attracted to.

The ringing of her phone on the kitchen counter made her flinch as if she had been caught doing something wrong.

She put down the knife she had scrubbed, dried her hands on a dish towel, and reached for the phone. If this was D.C. Pane again, they would have to have another talk about her business hours.

But instead, it was Lori's name flashing across the screen.

Emma relaxed only marginally. "Hi, Lori," she said after accepting the call.

"Hi, stranger," Lori answered. "I've been waiting for you to call and tell me about the new house all week, but it seems now that you are surrounded by attractive Hollywood starlets, you forgot all about your friends in Portland."

"There are no attractive starlets where I live," Emma answered. Not that she needed them. Her gaze went to the driveway, where Jordan was still gyrating around her car.

"Then why didn't you call? Seriously, Emma. Since you and Chloe separated, I rarely hear from you."

Emma clamped her free hand around the damp dish towel. "I know. I'm sorry, but... It's just not fair to draw you and our other friends into our mess."

"Fuck fairness."

The exclamation made Emma laugh. It was so much like Lori. Maybe she was right. She needed friends like Lori in her life.

"I want to be there for my friends," Lori added.

"Chloe's your friend too," Emma said softly.

"Yeah, but it's not like we're that close. You and I have much more in common."

True. They had both worked as executive assistants, so Lori actually understood some of what she did for a living. "I promise to try to call more often, okay?"

"I'll hunt you down if you don't," Lori said, a warning growl in her voice.

"Fair enough."

"So, how do you like your new home?"

Emma directed her gaze out the window and enjoyed the show for a few seconds. "The view from the kitchen is great." She suppressed a giggle. Had she really just said that?

"What's so great about it?" Lori asked.

Emma hesitated, but if she wanted to include Lori into her life a little more, she needed to start somewhere. "My new neighbor. She's out-of-this-world sexy."

"Oooh!" Lori laughed. "No wonder I didn't hear from you! You were busy ogling your yummy neighbor!"

"No, it wasn't like that. I… She…she's a total player. Not my type at all."

"Who said you needed to propose marriage or get serious about her? You could have some harmless fun with her, let her be your rebound girl."

Emma shook her head, even though Lori couldn't see it. "That's not my thing. You know that."

"You're no fun," Lori said. "And here I thought I could live vicariously through you. Try not to turn into a nun, okay? Even though you refuse to tell us what happened, I know whatever Chloe did hurt you. Don't close off your heart…or your legs."

"Lori!"

"What? Just saying. So, tell me, how's Molly?"

They talked for a few minutes longer before Emma hung up. The water in the sink had probably gone cold, but outside, Jordan was still busy with her car.

Emma watched her. Maybe Lori was right. Not about making Jordan her rebound girl, of course, but watching her from the privacy of her kitchen was harmless fun. So what if she found her attractive? So did probably half the population of Southern California. It wasn't as if she was about to march over there, press Jordan against the hood of her car, and declare her undying love. Having a *yummy neighbor* to ogle every now and then was a good thing. At least it proved that her libido hadn't bit the dust along with her marriage. After what she'd been through, she deserved some eye candy. It was safe, especially since she wasn't ready to act on it anyway.

Just as she reached that conclusion, Jordan had apparently decided that her car was clean enough. She stopped dancing and threw her sponge back into its bucket.

A groan of disappointment escaped Emma. The show was over, so now it was time to go back to figuring out her problem with D.C. Pane.

But her gaze followed Jordan as she rolled up the hose and hung it back on its hook next to the garage. When she walked up the driveway, she paused and stared at something on the ground.

What was she looking at? Emma craned her neck.

Jordan's boisterous dancing had sent drops of water across the driveway and had wiped away bits of Molly's chalk drawing. She set down her bucket and took a piece of chalk that Molly had left behind next to a potted plant. Going down on one knee, Jordan gently dabbed at the ground with the towel she had thrown over one shoulder, and when it was dry enough, she redrew the cat's whiskers and ears.

But when the damage to the drawing was fixed, she didn't stop.

What was she doing? Emma bobbed up and down on her tiptoes so she could see.

Finally, the lines Jordan drew formed a second, larger cat next to Molly's.

Emma smiled as Jordan added a mane and a tassel at the end of the big cat's tail. Jordan had drawn a lion—and a pretty good one at that. Her lion certainly looked much better than Emma's sorry attempt at a giraffe.

When the lion was complete, Jordan put the piece of chalk back where she had found it, wiped her hands on her jeans, and looked down at her creation for a moment before nodding and walking out of sight.

Emma stared after her. Her neighbor was an unusual woman. Definitely not one of the cool, aloof players she had met in the past.

Nowhere closer to solving her client problem, Emma pulled the plug from the sink and watched the dirty water swirl down the drain.

Finally, she decided to go back to work for a little while. She might not be able to solve the D.C. Pane problem tonight, but she could at least check in with one of her romance authors so she could get started setting up her Pinterest account tomorrow morning.

The hammock swayed gently from side to side in the rare August breeze that had dried Jordan's damp jeans some time ago. She dangled one leg over the side, sipped her beer, and finished the last piece of the pepperoni pizza that had been her dinner.

Frozen pizza and beer. She chuckled. After several evenings of fancy restaurants and good wine while Simone had been staying with her, she was definitely back to bachelorette life.

She stared into the darkness, barely making out the branches of the tall mulberry tree at the edge of the property and a few stars twinkling in the night sky.

The crickets serenaded her, but other than that and the soft creaking from the hammock, everything was silent. Her new neighbor really didn't make much noise, and the kid had very likely already been in bed by the time Jordan made it home from the hospital. She hadn't heard a peep from either of them while she'd washed her car.

The hammock was set up closer to Emma's side of the backyard, so Jordan could see her neighbor's part of the house from where she was.

There was still a light on in one of the rooms, and she could see Emma sitting behind a desk that was facing the French door leading to the patio. She was wearing a headset, talking to someone.

What the heck did she do for a living? She had mentioned her clients when she had talked to her daughter the other day. Apparently, Emma worked from home. Barbara, who knew exactly when each and every neighbor was coming and going, had mentioned that Emma didn't leave the house at a certain time, other than to drop her daughter off at school and to pick her up again. But obviously, someone in the house made good money; otherwise, they wouldn't have been able to afford renting a duplex in South Pasadena. Jordan had yet to see a husband.

Maybe she works for a sex hotline, her overactive imagination provided.

Movement in the office next door caught her attention.

Emma took off the headset and stretched, her T-shirt molding to her generous breasts.

Jordan's mouth went dry, and she took another swig of beer before forcing her gaze away. *Man, what are you now? A peeping Tom?* Staring at women who didn't know they were being watched normally wasn't her style.

A minute later, the French door opened. Light from the house spilled over Emma from behind, giving her an almost ethereal appearance.

Jordan gulped down more beer.

Emma crossed the patio toward her, carrying something that Jordan couldn't make out. "Hi," she said quietly, as if not wanting to disrupt the peacefulness outside. "I saw you out here, and I thought… I wanted to say thank you for the drawing. Molly will love it once she sees it tomorrow morning."

Jordan hadn't intended for anyone to catch her at that spontaneous action. "How do you know that was me?"

"Um…"

In the dim light that filtered over from the house, Jordan thought she saw her blush. Had Emma watched her draw the lion…and maybe wash her car? Jordan suppressed a smile. Straight or not, apparently her new neighbor hadn't been entirely unaffected by that little scene.

"Well, only you and I share the driveway, so who else could it have been?"

Jordan nodded. "Fair enough."

"I also wanted to say thank you again for your help with the car yesterday."

It was tempting to answer with another joke about the lock lubricant she had provided, but Jordan sensed that Emma was an independent woman who rarely accepted help or had reason to thank anyone, so she just nodded and said, "You're very welcome. I take it the key is still working?"

"Oh, yeah. I replaced the battery, and now all is well." Emma stepped closer and held out a small plate. "This is for you."

Jordan pushed herself up and sat on the edge of the hammock, both feet firmly planted on the ground. She accepted the plate and had to grin when she saw what was on it: a cupcake.

"Molly picked out one for you when we got ours yesterday, but then your friend Simone ate that cupcake, so we got you another one today, as a thank-you for your help with the 'odifice.'"

They both chuckled.

"Sorry," Jordan said. "I had no idea kids were so good at snatching up words from an adult conversation."

"Oh, yes, they are. No matter how focused on something else Molly seems to be, as soon as someone says a word she's not supposed to hear, she's all ears."

"I'll try to keep my potty mouth to a PG level around her," Jordan promised, although flirting with Molly's mother would be hard to resist, even if she was straight and might even be married.

"Thanks."

Before Emma could disappear back inside, Jordan held up her empty beer bottle. "I'm getting myself another. Want one?"

Emma hesitated. Her gaze went to the French door leading to her part of the duplex.

Jordan recognized that gaze. She had seen it on worried parents the few times she had operated on a kid. "Just leave the door open. You'll hear her if she wakes up."

It took another moment until Emma reluctantly peeled her gaze away from the door. "All right."

Jordan pulled over one of the lawn chairs for her and then went to get two beers. When she returned, the slender necks of the bottles held in one hand, Emma had settled into the lawn chair and closed her eyes.

They snapped back open as soon as Jordan stepped outside.

"Long day?" Jordan asked as she handed over one of the beers and settled back into the hammock.

Emma made a sound of agreement.

The chirping of the crickets seemed to grow louder, emphasizing the silence between them.

Jordan looked down at the cupcake she'd set onto a nearby lawn chair. It was a chocolate one, with a decadent dark chocolate frosting, sprinkled with chocolate chips. She tore it in half and held out one part to Emma.

43

"Oh God, no. I ate too many yesterday, and Barbara invited us over for cheesecake earlier today, so now I'd better watch what I eat." Emma patted her curvy hips and her belly.

There was nothing wrong with the way Emma looked, in Jordan's opinion, but it was her body and therefore her choice. Shrugging, Jordan dug in. The taste of dark chocolate exploded on her taste buds. She let out a moan around a mouthful of cupcake.

Emma smiled. "Good, right? They're called Death by Chocolate."

Jordan swallowed and took a sip of beer. "Aptly named. I can already feel my arteries clogging up."

"But what a way to go."

"Yep. Second-best way to die," Jordan said and took another bite of cupcake.

"I'm not even going to ask what you'd consider the best way."

Jordan just chewed and smiled. When the last crumb of cupcake was gone, she licked a bit of chocolate off her fingers. With both feet on the ground, she swayed the hammock back and forth while studying Emma. "Can I ask you a question?"

"Sure," Emma said. Her tone was casual, but Jordan could see her posture stiffen.

Was she expecting Jordan to ask her out again? That wasn't Jordan's style. She might joke around and indulge in a bit of harmless flirting, but a no was always a no in her book.

"When you couldn't get the car to open yesterday, why didn't Molly's father drop her off? I mean, he obviously doesn't live here, but...isn't he in the picture at all?"

Now Emma looked as if she would have preferred to be asked out for coffee rather than have to answer that question. She took several swigs of beer.

"Sorry," Jordan said. "I didn't mean to—"

"No, it's okay." Emma gazed at her beer bottle and circled the rim with her index finger, apparently not realizing how sexy that gesture was. "Molly doesn't actually have a father."

Jordan looked away from Emma's finger and up into her face. "Um, you mean he...he's dead?"

"I hope not."

"You don't know?" Jordan wasn't judging, but Emma didn't seem the type to have a one-night stand with someone and then never contact him again, especially if they had a child together.

"I never met him."

"Um, I might not be an expert on straight sex, but to my knowledge, the birds-and-the-bees thing doesn't work if the bee doesn't actually have some kind of contact with the flower."

"I'm not an expert either, but yes, that's usually how it works." Emma flicked a drop of condensation off her beer bottle and took a long swig. When she lowered the bottle, a slight smile played at the corners of her lips.

Not an expert either... Jordan mentally repeated her words. What was that supposed to—? Her fingers tightened around her beer bottle. "You mean...? But I thought you...?"

Emma cocked her head to the side. "Yes?"

"I thought you were straight."

"Really? I thought someone like you would have better gaydar."

Someone like me? That sounded a little insulting, and Jordan found that, for some reason, she cared what her new neighbor thought of her. "My gaydar did ping when we met, but I thought that was just..."

"Yes?" Emma prompted.

Wishful thinking. "I assumed..." Jordan nodded toward the house. "Well, you have a kid and everything." Man, since when did she stammer like this around women?

Emma's lips curled into another smile. "Lesbians have fully functional uteruses too, you know?"

"I'm aware of that, but you also shot me down pretty quickly, so I thought..."

"You thought the only reason a woman would turn you down is because she's straight? Have you considered that maybe I said no because you're just not my type?"

Of course Jordan hadn't. "Ouch," she mumbled. "Has anyone ever told you that you're really bad for a woman's ego?"

"Somehow, I have a feeling your ego isn't in any danger."

Well, you needed a lot of confidence to cut into people for a living, so Jordan couldn't deny it. "So Molly's father..."

"Is just a number on a sperm donation file," Emma finished the sentence for her and took another sip of beer. "We preferred it that way."

There it was again: the *we* that Emma had mentioned when they had talked about the car. This time, Jordan gave in to her curiosity. "We?"

"My wife and I." Emma dug her teeth into her full bottom lip. "Ex-wife." She emptied her beer in several big gulps, her graceful throat moving as she swallowed.

Before Jordan could say or ask anything else, Emma got up and pressed the empty bottle into her hands. "It's getting late. I'd better go to bed. I have an early day tomorrow. Thanks for the beer."

Jordan watched her go, too surprised by the sudden end of their conversation to even ogle her lush ass.

The French door closed with an audible click, and Emma marched away without making eye contact through the glass.

Jordan knew she should go to bed too. Her hospital ran two ORs for elective surgery even on Saturdays, and she had volunteered to cover one of them. Tomorrow's operating schedule was already a mile long, and there were always emergency surgeries that had to be squeezed in somehow. But instead of heading inside, she sat in the dark, finishing her beer and staring at the light in the other half of the duplex until it finally went out.

So Emma was a lesbian…and divorced.

That thought immediately sparked her interest, but she squashed that spark with a shake of her head. It didn't matter. Emma had a child, so Jordan would be better off steering clear of her. There were plenty of other women who were free to sleep with her with no strings attached.

She emptied her beer, pushed herself up from the hammock, and went inside.

Chapter 5

"THAT WAS FAST," THE NURSE behind the surgical front desk called out to Jordan. "Looks like your horoscope was on target. You're a Leo, right?"

"Right." Jordan paused in front of the counter. "What did it say?"

Evelyn dramatically cleared her throat and read, "Lady Luck smiles on you this week. You're brimming with energy, going through tasks at work like wildfire."

"Sounds accurate so far." It was just seven thirty on a Monday morning, but she had already finished rounds on her post-op patients, making sure that no complications had developed overnight, and had seen the pre-op patients who were being prepped for surgery later today.

"There's more." Evelyn tapped the glossy magazine on her desk. "It also says: An unexpected trip is in your near future. Uranus is in your relationship house, so it might involve a romantic partner. Remember that short trips can be magical for your love life."

Jordan laughed. "I highly doubt it. No vacation on the horizon for me." She hadn't taken any time off in forever, and beyond the bedroom and a few casual dates, she wasn't looking for any magic to happen in her love life.

"Anything else?" Jordan asked. "Maybe I'll win the lottery?"

Evelyn shook her head. "Sorry. Nothing about your finances. But you're supposed to take better care of your health."

One of the surgical residents stopped next to them and peered up at the board that held the OR schedule. When his pager went off, he pulled it from the waistband of his scrub pants and looked at it. "Dammit."

Jordan glanced over, knowing he had taken the pager for a fellow resident who was supposed to have covered the ER but was stuck in traffic. Any emergency could mean that her own cases were getting bumped, and she hated that as much as any surgeon. "What is it?"

"It's the ER," he grumbled. "They need someone to come check out an acute abdomen. I was supposed to scrub in on the Whipple Dr. Soergel is doing in half an hour, but Neuman still hasn't arrived, and if this takes longer..."

Jordan gave him a commiserating pat on the upper arm. She remembered her excitement the first time she had assisted with a Whipple, the most intensive procedure in general surgery. It involved removing the gallbladder, the duodenum, and parts of the stomach, pancreas, jejunum, and bile duct and then attaching it all to the rest of the jejunum. That kind of surgery was rare, so he might not have another chance to witness it again until next year.

She looked up at the large clock on the wall. "You know what? I'll go check it out. I have a little time before my first lap chole of the day."

The resident stared at her.

Jordan made a shooing motion with her hands. "Go before I change my mind."

"Wow...I... Thank you." He trotted off.

Evelyn chuckled. "That was nice of you."

"Don't let it get around. I have a reputation to protect." Jordan sighed and nodded at the magazine. "It seems we've found the unexpected trip I'm taking."

She took the staff elevator downstairs and then stepped through the automatic double doors leading to the ER.

The emergency department wasn't busy yet. On most days, the admissions didn't pick up until nine or ten. Her friend Hope was sitting at one of the computers at the nurses' station, looking at an X-ray.

"Hey, Hope. Shouldn't you be at home with the wife already?" She knew Hope had covered the night shift, which had ended half an hour ago.

Hope turned toward her. "Hi, Jordan. Just finishing up some paperwork. And you know Laleh and I aren't married."

"You moved in together, and last time I saw her, Laleh was talking about getting a kitten. In lesbian terms, that's like being married." Jordan leaned against the counter and gave the nurse behind it a quick glance. She was new and cute. But at the moment, Jordan was here to work, not flirt. "So, where's the acute abdomen you wanted me to take a look at?"

"Mr. Cochran. Treatment room four," Hope said. "He's complaining of nausea and abdominal pain. He's tachycardic and has a temperature of one hundred and one and an elevated WBC count."

"Did you get belly films?" Jordan asked.

"I was just about to take a look at them."

Jordan glanced over Hope's shoulder at the computer screen. "Ooh. There's a pocket of free air in the abdominal cavity. Definitely a surgical case."

Hope shook her head. "Surgeons. You can't resist free air on an X-ray, can you?"

Jordan shrugged. "I'd take a perforated ulcer over a sniffling kid with a sore throat or a guy with a priapism any day. Let's go take a look."

They headed toward the glass-enclosed cubicle. Jordan entered, followed by Hope, and pulled the curtain in front of the glass door to give the patient some privacy. "Good morning, Mr. Cochran." She stepped closer to the treatment table.

Before she could introduce herself, he weakly lifted his head off the treatment table. "Am I finally getting some fucking painkillers? I already told the other nurse I need them."

Jordan quietly looked down at him. He wasn't the first patient who had mistaken her for a nurse, so she had learned to curb her frustration. She knew it happened to all female physicians at least once a week, especially to surgeons like her. Even though things were slowly starting to change, surgery was still a man's field. She had been one of only three female residents in her residency program and the only black woman.

"I'm not a nurse, Mr. Cochran. I'm Dr. Williams from the surgical department. I'll get you some painkillers in a minute, but first I need to examine you."

"The other doctor already examined me," he grumbled. He flicked his gaze toward Hope. Despite his anger, he spoke without moving, remaining so still as if any kind of movement hurt.

"I know, but wouldn't you rather we double-check before cutting you open?"

That shut him up. He grunted and groaned as she snapped on gloves and gently palpated his abdomen, which was completely rigid and slightly distended. A quick check with the stethoscope revealed no bowel sounds.

Jordan straightened. "What's that scrape on your chin?"

"Nothing. It's my damn belly that hurts, not my chin."

How the hell did Hope deal with patients like him all day? Jordan would much rather deal with patients after an anesthesiologist had put them under and she could cut them open. "If you got into an accident, you could have sustained an injury to your abdomen without noticing."

He visibly paled. "A car almost ran me over when I was out riding my bike last night. But it wasn't a bad accident or anything, just a few scrapes."

"Did you by any chance hit your handlebars?"

"Um, yeah. But the pain didn't start until hours later."

That probably meant he had perforated his colon and had now developed secondary peritonitis. "The collision probably perforated your large intestine, and now the tissues that line the inner wall of your belly have become inflamed. You need surgery right away."

He started cursing.

Jordan walked out of the room, followed by Hope. "Did you do an ultrasound of the rest of the abdomen?"

"Of course," Hope said. "No hematomas of the spleen or liver."

"Good. I don't want any surprises when I open him up." She stopped at the nurses' station and addressed the cute nurse. "Call the OR. Tell them they need to bump my cholecystectomy. Mr. Cochran needs to go directly to the OR for a bowel repair."

Apparently, she wasn't the only one taking an unexpected trip today, she thought wryly as she said good-bye to Hope and headed back upstairs to prep for surgery. Maybe Mr. Cochran was a Leo too.

After twelve hours at work, popping another pizza into the oven was tempting, but then Jordan remembered what her horoscope had said about taking better care of her health.

While she didn't believe in astrology, that tabloid magazine was probably right. Some vitamins were in order. She sliced a tomato and a cucumber and improvised a Greek salad with some olives and feta cheese. When she was done, she took it out to the backyard to eat so she could enjoy the evening sun and the fresh air.

As soon as she stepped outside, the fine hairs on the back of her neck stood on end and she had the uncomfortable feeling of being watched.

She hid a grin. Was her neighbor watching her through the office window? Maybe Emma would want to come over for another beer as soon as she had the kid in bed.

She looked over to the other side of the duplex.

Emma wasn't at her desk. The office was empty, as far as Jordan could see.

Probably just her tired brain playing tricks on her. She walked over to the hammock, about to sink into it, when a rustling from the mulberry tree at the edge of the backyard made her freeze and look up.

Something was moving higher up in the tall tree, but she couldn't see what it was.

Jordan put down her salad, walked over, and peeked through the foliage.

She halfway expected to see Tuna perched on a branch. But what she spotted wasn't a cat. A small pair of pink sneakers dangled down from high up in the mulberry tree.

What the fuck?

Jordan pushed some leaves out of the way so she could see more. Emma's daughter was straddling one of the thick branches, holding on with both arms and legs. She peeked down at Jordan through the foliage.

What the hell was she doing up there? She had to be nearly twenty feet up into the tree! If she fell, she would probably break her neck. Adrenaline pumped through Jordan's veins, and she had to force herself to speak softly so she wouldn't startle the girl. "Hi, Molly. It's me—Jordan. What are you doing up there?"

"Eating berries."

Jordan curled her fingers into fists. *Damn.* She should have realized that the mulberries would pique the kid's interest. As a child, she had climbed a lot of trees to stuff herself with cherries, apples, or berries. Back then, she had never stopped to think that it might be dangerous, but now that she was the adult standing beneath the tree, things were different. "I'll get you lots of them, but please come down now."

"I can't." Molly's voice quivered. "I'm scared. I want to get down. I want my mommy."

Oh shit. "Don't cry. Just hold on and don't move, okay?" Jordan's gaze darted around the backyard. There was no ladder, nothing that would help her get the girl down. She tried to remember whether there was one in the garage.

One of the French doors on Emma's side of the house opened. "Molly?" Emma called. "Are you out there?"

"She's here," Jordan answered without turning around or looking away from the tree, as if the power of her gaze could help keep the girl safely on the branch.

A few seconds later, she felt more than heard Emma come up behind her. "Where—? Oh my God! Molly! How did you get up there?"

"I climbed," came Molly's small voice. "But now I can't get down." She started to sob.

"I'm coming!" Without hesitating, Emma gripped the lowest branch and prepared to pull herself up, even though she was wearing a skirt, a top with spaghetti straps, and flip-flops. Her legs beneath the skirt seemed to be bare. She would be getting scratched up good if she climbed into the tree's canopy. Emma didn't seem to even think about it. She was in full warrior-mom mode.

Jordan put a hand on Emma's arm and pulled her back. "Let me do it."

With wild eyes, Emma looked back and forth between the tree and Jordan. "Are you sure? I—"

"Yes. I'm taller and can reach her more easily."

Emma searched her face as if trying to decide if she could put the life of her daughter into Jordan's hands.

"I'll get her down," Jordan said, holding Emma's gaze. "I promise." It was an idiotic thing to say. In her job, she had learned not to make any promises she wasn't sure she could keep, but one glance into Emma's panicked green eyes had made her forget that rule.

Finally, Emma nodded and stepped aside. "Jordan will get you down, honey," she called up into the tree.

Easier said than done. Jordan peered up, searching for a safe grip.

"Should we get a ladder or call the fire department?" Emma asked.

Up in the tree, a branch creaked.

"No time," Jordan said. "I can do this." After taking a deep breath, she gripped one of the lower, almost horizontal branches and hoisted herself up into the tree. She hooked one leg around the branch and then braced her feet on it while she reached for the next one.

I can do this, she repeated to herself. It was just one little tree. She peeked up to where the pink sneakers stuck out of the leaves and then down to the ground, where Emma stood, looking up at her with an anxious expression. *Okay, one rather big tree.* But the knowledge of the scared little girl up there propelled her forward.

Quickly, she realized that her height wouldn't help her—quite the opposite. She wasn't just taller than Emma; she was probably also heavier. Much heavier than Molly in any case. It had been a long time since she'd gone to church, but now she prayed for the branches in the upper part of the tree to hold her.

Halfway up, her climbing slowed because it took more time to find footholds that seemed safe. She had to move closer to the trunk, where the branches were thicker and could carry her weight. Her bare arms were already covered with cuts and scratches, but she ignored them.

"Mommy?" came Molly's trembling voice from above.

"Jordan's coming," her mother called. "She'll get you. Hold on. Not much longer now."

Emma's trust in her felt good. Finally, she was right below the girl. "Hi, Molly. I'm here now."

Leaves rustled, and then Molly's scared little face peered down at her. Tears were running down her cheeks.

Now, how could she get the girl down from the tree without getting her hurt or breaking her own neck in the process? Molly was perched on a branch farther away from the trunk, clinging to it like a koala bear. If Jordan climbed out that far to where the branches grew thinner, she wasn't sure they would hold her weight.

"Can you scoot toward me and give me your hand?"

Clutching her branch more tightly, Molly shook her head.

Damn.

"Jordan?" Emma called from beneath the tree. "Everything okay up there?"

"Yeah," Jordan answered, not wanting to admit that getting Molly down might not be as easy as she had imagined. She was saving people's lives and sometimes working medical miracles for a living; getting a five-year-old down from a tree should be a piece of cake in comparison. "We'll be down in a minute."

She gazed at the branch beneath her. It seemed pretty sturdy and was a little thicker than the one Molly was on. Time to put her money where her mouth was. "Hold on tight, Molly. I'm coming." Not allowing herself to look down, she inched along the rough bark until she was directly beneath her.

Okay, this was the dangerous part. Carefully, she straightened until she was straddling the branch, both legs wrapped around it as if it were a bucking bronco that might toss her off. She let go of the branch with both hands and reached up for the girl.

Molly nearly threw herself at her and grabbed her around the neck, almost dislodging her from her perch.

One arm wrapped around the girl, Jordan grabbed hold of her branch with the other hand to keep them both from falling.

Molly trembled against her, not letting up on the stranglehold she had on Jordan's neck.

Suddenly, climbing a tree seemed the easiest part of her mission. How did you comfort a scared little girl? When she had worked with kids during her residency, she had relied on the nurses to do that, but now, up here, she was on her own.

Gently, she rubbed circles on Molly's back while holding on to the branch with the other hand. "Don't worry. I've got you now, and I won't let you fall. I'll have you down there with your mommy in no time, okay?"

Molly nodded against her, her damp face pressed to Jordan's chest. She sniffled, and something drenched Jordan's polo shirt. She definitely didn't want to know what it was.

Time to get the kid down. But that wasn't as easy as she had expected either. If she used her hands to hold on to the crying girl, she couldn't climb. "Um, Molly, I need you to hold on to me really, really tightly, okay? Because I need to let go of you with one hand."

"Nooo!"

"I need to, or I won't be able to climb. Just pretend you're a koala bear and I'm a tree. Can you do that for me?"

Molly tightened her small arms around Jordan's neck, and her legs wrapped around Jordan's middle until she could barely breathe.

"Great," she croaked. "Just like that."

One hand against Molly's back, keeping her pressed against her body, she used the other to navigate them backward toward the trunk inch by inch.

The branch creaked beneath their combined weight.

"Shit, shit, shit."

Molly lifted her head from Jordan's chest. "Mommy, she said a bad word," she called down.

"Tattletale," Jordan grumbled, still moving them backward. "I think these count as extenuating circumstances."

"What's that?" Molly asked.

"It means she's allowed to say it just this once," Emma called.

Jordan's back hit the trunk. So far, so good. At least the branches were thicker here. But now she'd have to get them to the next branch. "Hold on, Molly."

Slowly, branch by branch, she made her way down the tree. Sweat dribbled down her back and burned in her eyes, but she had no hand free to wipe it away.

It seemed to take forever. Finally, she reached the lower branches.

Her eyes gleaming with tears, Emma stretched up her arms as far as they would go, and Jordan carefully lowered the girl down into her mother's waiting hands.

With Molly safely down, she paused for a moment to wipe her brow before jumping down the rest of the way.

Before Jordan could decide whether she wanted to fall to her knees and kiss the ground, Emma threw her arms around her. She held on to Jordan just as tightly as her daughter had. "Thank you, thank you, thank you," she whispered.

Jordan gently hugged her back, with Molly—still in her mother's arms—buried in between them. Being part of this family hug felt unfamiliar and strange but at the same time unexpectedly nice.

"Can I have ice cream now?" Molly asked after a few seconds. "I'm hungry."

Jordan took a step back and stared at her. A minute ago, the kid had been scared to death, and now she wanted ice cream?

Emma laughed. The relief in her voice was obvious. She kept her gaze on her daughter and avoided looking at Jordan, probably embarrassed at that spontaneous hug. "No ice cream for you," she said to Molly. "You were supposed to play with Mouse, not go outside on your own."

"But Mouse was hungry too. I got him berries." Molly held out her hands, revealing palms that were stained purple from the mulberries.

Great. Half of that had probably made it onto her shirt where the girl had clutched her. But admittedly, it was a small price to pay for getting her down safely. The same elation that she felt every time she saved a patient's life rushed through her.

"I'd better get her cleaned up and to bed." Still holding her daughter with one arm, Emma reached out with the other hand. Inches from touching Jordan's arm, she paused, as if only now realizing what she was about to do, but then squeezed softly. "Thank you again."

Jordan nodded and suddenly felt strangely self-conscious beneath Emma's grateful gaze. She couldn't remember when that had last happened to her. "It was nothing."

"It was everything to me," Emma said, almost in a whisper.

They looked at each other in silent understanding.

"Wait, Mommy! Mouse!" Molly cried.

"What about him, honey?"

"I lost him."

Emma kissed the girl's forehead. "He's probably in your room, waiting for you."

"No. I lost him there." Molly pointed upward.

Jordan tilted her head back to look. A bit of brownish-yellow fur was sticking out from beneath the leaves in the Y where the trunk parted into two thick branches. How the heck had the kid made it up there with the stuffed animal?

"We have to get him, Mommy. He's scared."

Emma reached out with one hand and shook the tree.

Nothing happened.

Jordan stepped next to her and added both of her hands to Emma's attempts to shake down Mouse, but the stuffed lion didn't budge.

Emma muttered something under her breath that sounded like a bad word too. "Okay. I'll get a ladder. You stay here." But when she tried to put Molly down, the girl wouldn't let go, probably still too shaken to let her out of her sight.

"I'll get Mouse down," Jordan heard herself say before she had even realized her mouth had moved.

Emma shook her head. "I can't ask that of you. You already had to climb up once."

56

"You're not asking; I'm offering. It's no problem, really. That tree and I are like this now." She twisted her middle finger around her index finger and winked at Emma. Truth be told, she wasn't eager to get back up on that tree, but she'd never been able to say no to a woman. Apparently, that was true for miniature women too.

"All right. But at least get a ladder," Emma said.

"Nah. It'll be much faster this way." Getting the stuffed animal down would be much easier than rescuing Molly. It wasn't that far up the tree. Apparently, Molly had left it behind halfway up when she had realized she needed both hands to climb. And unlike the kid, she could just toss him down once she reached him.

She pulled herself back up, and this time, she climbed much more quickly because she was already familiar with where the sturdy branches were.

It didn't take long for her to reach Mouse.

Triumphantly, she pulled the stuffed lion out of his perch and held him down for Emma and her daughter to see. "I've got him. Easy as pie. Catch!" She shifted her weight on the branch to toss down Mouse.

A sharp crack sounded beneath her. The branch she was balancing on snapped.

Jordan didn't even have time to scream. She tumbled down, and the ground rushed toward her much too fast. Twigs scratched her arms as she tried to grab hold of them. They slowed her descent but didn't keep her from falling. Wood splintered.

Then she crashed to the ground, catching herself on one outstretched hand at the last moment. Pain shot up her arm.

For a moment, she thought she'd pass out, but then the world swam back into focus, and she saw a pair of bare legs rush toward her.

Gorgeous legs. Dazed, she stared at them.

"Jordan!" Emma put Molly down and knelt next to her. Her hands brushed over Jordan's face, then her body, as if to make sure she was still in one piece. "Oh God, oh God!"

So that was what it took to get Emma to touch her.

"What?" Emma frowned.

Had she said that out loud? Man, that fall must have rattled a few brain cells. Jordan blinked and shook her head to clear it. "I said I'm fine." She put both hands to the ground to push herself up but then flinched as pain knifed through her wrist. Cradling her right arm to her chest with the other hand, she slowly sat up and took stock of the rest of her body.

A few scratches marred her hands and arms. *Shit.* Using the scrub brush and the antiseptic soap before tomorrow's surgeries would hurt like hell. Her ribs and her hips ached; they would probably be covered in bruises by tomorrow. But other than that, everything seemed to be in working order. She hadn't hit her head, and she could move her legs without problems. The only thing that might be seriously hurt was her right arm—and her pride.

Molly stared down at her with large eyes, new tears trickling down her cheeks. "Are you gonna die like Grandma?"

"No, I'm fine." Slowly, holding on to Emma with one hand just in case, she got to her feet. "See?"

Emma held on to her with both hands, as if Jordan would collapse without her help. "Can you walk? I'm taking you to the ER."

No way in hell. She was a surgeon, not a patient. "I told you I'm fine. I don't need an ER."

"I'd rather let someone with a medical degree decide that," Emma said.

"Good, because I do have—"

"A sprained wrist at the very least." Emma pointed. "Look, it's already starting to swell."

Jordan looked down. *Fuck. Fuckity fuck.* She barely held back from saying it out loud, not wanting to be reprimanded by a five-year-old again. Emma was right. Her wrist was already swelling.

"I'm so, so sorry." Emma had gone pale, the freckles on her nose standing out in sharp relief. "I should have gotten a ladder or left Mouse up there."

"Nooo!" Molly shouted.

"It's okay," Jordan said, forcing a smile. "My sisters always told me that a woman would be my downfall one day. I just didn't know she'd be that young."

Emma didn't react to the joke. "Let me get you some ice, and then I'll drive you to the ER."

"I can…"

But Emma was already hurrying into the house, carrying Molly and her stuffed animal with her.

"…drive myself," Jordan mumbled into the now-empty backyard.

Chapter 6

EMMA HATED LEAVING HER DAUGHTER behind, especially after the scare she'd just had, but an emergency room was no place for a five-year-old, and she had no idea how long it would take before anyone could take a look at Jordan's arm. By the time they got back, it would be long past Molly's bedtime and she would be a cranky pain in the ass.

Asking for help wasn't one of her strong suits, but Emma swallowed her pride and went over to Barbara Mosley's house.

The elderly woman opened the door immediately. "Emma! What a nice surprise. Come on in."

"Sorry, I don't have time. I—"

Barbara frowned. "Is the little one all right?" She stared at Molly, who clung to Emma, her face buried against her shoulder.

"She's fine. But Jordan isn't. Nothing too bad, I hope, but she fell out of the mulberry tree and hurt her arm."

"She fell out of a tree?" Barbara looked at her as if she had said a horde of brain-eating zombies had invaded their quiet little street. "How on earth did she manage that?"

"Long story. I don't have time to explain now. If I don't get back in a minute, the stubborn woman will drive herself to the ER. Would you mind coming next door and keeping an eye on Molly until we return? I'll put her to bed before we leave, so I hope she won't give you any trouble."

"Of course," Barbara said immediately. "I'll grab my book and be over in a minute. Tell the stubborn one I'm worried about her and that she should do whatever you tell her."

Fat chance, Emma thought but nodded.

Within fifteen minutes, they were on their way to the ER in Emma's car. Speaking of being stubborn…

"I really could have driven myself, you know?" Jordan said from the passenger seat.

"With that hand?" Emma nodded down to where Jordan pressed a package of frozen peas, wrapped in a dish towel, to her swollen wrist.

"I admit I'm a very hands-on woman." Jordan flashed her a quick grin. "But there are things even I don't use both hands for. Two words: automatic transmission."

This woman was incredible. She was probably in pain, and yet she cracked jokes and spewed sexual innuendo. Did she ever stop?

"This entire mess is my fault," Emma said. "You got hurt because you were trying to help my daughter, and you seriously think I'm going to abandon you and let you drive to the ER by yourself?"

Jordan smiled wryly. "I guess the answer to that question would be a no."

"You can bet your ass on it."

"My, my, Mrs. Larson. You used a bad word," Jordan said, imitating Molly's tone.

Emma glared at her before focusing on traffic again. "It's Ms., actually." She had gone back to using her maiden name before the ink on the divorce papers had even been dry. "And unless you want the doctors to have to take care of both arms, you'd better be quiet."

Chuckling, Jordan did just that.

Emma remembered the hospital in South Pasadena from her childhood, but Jordan directed her all the way to LA. Somewhere beyond Griffith Park, she had her pull into a parking lot.

Above a large red emergency sign, another sign announced that they were about to enter Griffith Memorial Hospital.

"If I have to go to an ER, at least I want to make sure it's the best one around," Jordan said by way of explanation.

"I take it you've been here before?" Emma asked.

Jordan chuckled. "You could definitely say that. I probably spend more time here than at home."

That was obviously an exaggeration. Emma couldn't believe that Jordan would be a klutz who got hurt all the time. Her hands had been sure and steady when she'd climbed the mulberry tree. But maybe she was the type to get overconfident, just the way she had when she had thrown down Mouse.

Emma would never forget those horrible seconds when Jordan had crashed down and had lain without moving for a moment.

"Are you all right?" Jordan asked as they crossed the parking lot.

"I should be asking *you* that."

"I've had worse. As a child, my two big sisters put me on a tire swing and twirled it around and around, telling me I was a cowgirl clinging to a bucking bronco. And then they let go, and the rope the tire swing was on untwisted itself at an insane speed. That bronco tossed me halfway across the playground. Twelve stitches." She pointed at a thin, almost invisible scar on her forehead.

"Ouch. That kind of makes me glad I'm an only child."

Jordan smiled. "Nah. It wasn't that bad." A mischievous twinkle entered her eyes. "At least not once I grew taller than them."

The ER's automatic sliding doors swished open before them.

Emma blinked against the bright fluorescent light as they stepped into the reception area. The smell of hand sanitizer and cleaning products surrounded her.

A security guard in his cubicle waved at them, as did a nurse who passed them.

Wow. The staff seemed really friendly here. Maybe that was why Jordan preferred to come here instead of going to the hospital in South Pasadena.

Jordan walked up to the glass-fronted check-in desk and leaned against the glass in a casual pose, as if she owned the place.

Emma couldn't help admiring her confidence. After the past year, she was still working on regaining her own.

The clerk behind the desk looked up from her computer. Instead of frowning or telling Jordan to take a step back, she gave her a welcoming smile. "Hi, Dr. Williams. I thought Dr. Bender was on call tonight."

Dr. Williams? Emma stared at the clerk, then at Jordan. *She's a doctor?*

"He is," Jordan said. "Unfortunately, I'm not on the fun end of the treatment table tonight." She held up her arm, wrapped in the soggy package of frozen peas.

"Ouch." The clerk gave her a compassionate smile. "Why don't you take a seat in the waiting room? I'll let the ER know you're here. Do you want some coffee while you wait?"

"I'd better not. At least not before I know for sure that this," Jordan held up her arm again, "doesn't require surgery."

Emma's fingers flexed around Jordan's good arm, which she had taken a hold of without noticing. She quickly let go. *Surgery? Oh my God!* She hadn't thought of that. Guilt clawed at her gut. "Do you really think it's that bad?" she asked as she followed Jordan to the waiting room and took a seat on a plastic chair next to her.

"Nah. Merely a precaution. It's probably just a sprain." She stretched out her long legs, entirely comfortable in these surroundings.

"You never told me you're a doctor," Emma said, not quite able to keep from sounding accusing.

"Why would I?" Jordan asked. "You never told me what you do for a living either."

She had to give her that. Their jobs hadn't come up the few times they had talked, so she couldn't hold it against Jordan.

"So far," Jordan added, "my money is on sex hotline operator."

The man across from them, pressing a bloodstained towel to his forehead, gave them a curious look.

Emma nearly fell off the plastic chair. "What?" She burst out laughing, easing her tension a little.

Jordan shrugged. "You work from home, at weird hours, at a job that earns enough to rent a duplex in South Pasadena. I see you on the phone or on that headset of yours all the time. Um, not that I'm watching you or anything."

"No, of course not." Maybe she should have felt that her privacy had been violated, but instead, she couldn't help smiling at how flustered the usually confident woman seemed.

But Jordan quickly recovered and added with a grin, "Plus I can definitely see why people would pay for you to whisper dirty things into their ear."

"I don't work at a," Emma lowered her voice, "sex hotline." Shaking her head, she nudged her with one elbow.

"Ouch." Jordan bent forward and protectively clutched her arm, which Emma had jostled.

"Oh my God! I'm so sorry. I'm an idiot."

Jordan blew out a sharp breath and slowly let go of her arm. "No, it's fine. I'll survive. And that *is* the opinion of someone with a medical degree."

"So, what kind of doctor are you?" Emma asked, partly because she was curious but also because she wanted to distract Jordan from the pain she had caused.

"Not the boring pill-prescribing kind," Jordan said, her brown eyes gleaming with pride. "I'm a surgeon."

Emma automatically slid a little to the side, away from Jordan, on her plastic chair. *I should have known.* Jordan seemed to think she was God's gift to women, just as her ex and most other surgeons she knew did. *Don't be ungrateful.* Jordan had risked her life to save Molly and to get her stuffed animal down, and Emma had seen glimpses of the genuinely caring woman behind the charming-player façade. What she did in her spare time was none of her business.

"What?" Jordan asked, studying her. "You don't like surgeons?"

Before Emma could answer—or even think of a reply that wouldn't make it necessary for her to bare her soul—a tall woman in pale blue scrubs and a white lab coat entered the waiting room.

"Jacqui said you're here. What the hell happened?" Then the doctor seemed to realize Jordan wasn't alone. She ran a hand through her tousled, dark brown hair. "Oh. Hi. I'm Dr. Finlay."

Jordan rolled her eyes. "Emma, this is my friend Hope. Hope, this is Emma."

Hope glanced back and forth between them. "Your...?"

"Neighbor," Emma said firmly, not wanting Hope to think that she was just another notch on Jordan's bedpost.

"Dr. Finlay to room two, stat," the overhead intercom blared. "Dr. Finlay to room two."

"I have to go." Hope strode to the door. "I'll send you a resident. Don't harass him!"

"Me?" Jordan drawled, the picture of innocence.

"Yeah you," Hope called back over her shoulder. Then she was gone.

Emma had expected them to have to fill out some paperwork and wait a while longer, but instead, a nurse came in. "Hi, Dr. Williams. I hear you wanted to check out the quality of the ER tonight."

"Nah," Jordan said. "I already know you guys do great work, especially the nurses on the night shift."

"Flatterer."

God, this woman never stopped flirting, not even when she was sitting in the waiting room of an ER, clutching a damp dish towel and a soggy package of peas to her wrist.

She must have shaken her head, because the nurse's gaze flicked toward her. "Oh. I didn't know she... Um, do you want to come and hold her hand while Dr. Feltner examines her?"

"Oh, yeah, I'd like that." Jordan winked, but there was something else in her eyes. Something that looked like a hint of vulnerability.

Obviously Jordan wasn't entirely comfortable here after all, now that she was the patient.

How could Emma say no, especially to the woman who had rescued her daughter? She nodded and followed the nurse and Jordan into one of the glass-fronted exam rooms.

The nurse pulled the curtain closed in front of the door, placed a rolling stool next to the treatment table, and gestured for Emma to take a seat. Then she carefully lifted the towel-wrapped package of peas off Jordan's wrist and bent forward to examine it. "What happened?"

Jordan flinched a little when the nurse prodded her wrist, but after a second, her lips curled into what Emma was coming to recognize as her signature grin. "I wrestled a lion with my bare hands."

"A lion?"

"Yep. That's my story, and I'm sticking to it. It was a lion. A really wild, dangerous one, right, Emma?"

"Well, kind of," Emma said. "She tried to get my daughter's stuffed lion down from a tree, but then a branch snapped and she fell."

"Spoilsport," Jordan grumbled playfully. "My story sounded a lot better."

The curtain in front of the open door was pulled back, and another nurse stuck her head into the room. "Hi, Dr. Williams. I hear you hurt your wrist. Anything I can do?"

The entire ER staff seemed to know her. Apparently, Jordan was quite popular with the nurses.

"No, thanks, Paula. I'm in good hands."

A third nurse entered to bring Jordan a new ice pack.

"I'll get Dr. Feltner." The nurse who had examined Jordan walked to the door.

"So, do you work in the ER?" Emma asked once they were alone.

Jordan arranged her arm more comfortably on the treatment table. "God, no. The docs down here just keep the patients alive until I can get my hands on them."

Apparently, surgeons in any city exuded that touch of arrogance. Once upon a time, Emma had found it charming, but now she was determined not to let herself be impressed by that type again.

"Seriously," Jordan added, "I couldn't do the kind of work Hope does. I'd rather cut someone open, deal with the problem, and be done with it. Speaking of work... You still haven't told me what you do for a living."

It was probably better to tell her before she again started to speculate about her working for a sex hotline. "I'm a VA."

A wrinkle formed on Jordan's forehead. "You mean you work for the Department of Veterans Affairs?"

Emma chuckled. "No. I'm a virtual assistant."

Jordan squinted over at her. "I've never heard of that."

"It's like a personal assistant, only virtual, via the Internet. Most of my clients are authors, and I help them with things like marketing, proofreading, and research so they'll have more time to write."

"That sounds great," Jordan said. "Too bad I can't have a VA. I sure could use someone to help me with my paperwork so I could have more time to operate."

For a moment, Emma thought she was just faking enthusiasm to be polite. Most other people she told about her job seemed to think she was some kind of secretary who was basically useless because she couldn't even make coffee for her clients since she didn't live in the same city. But Jordan's appreciative smile seemed real. "It *is* great," she said. "I have flexible hours and can work from home, so I get to spend more time with Molly, and I love the variety of work."

Jordan nodded. "That's what I like about general surgery too. The variety of work, I mean. We don't have flexible hours."

Emma couldn't help staring. Jordan made it sound as if they were equals instead of making her feel as if her job wasn't as important. Her ex, Chloe, had taken it for granted that Emma would be the one to give up her job and stay home with Molly so she could pursue her career as a plastic surgeon.

"Evening, Dr. Williams."

Emma jerked at the sudden voice next to them.

A young doctor, probably a resident, had entered without announcing himself. He didn't smile; he just gave Jordan a stiff nod.

Apparently, not everyone in the ER loved Jordan. Or maybe he was nervous about having to treat a fellow doctor.

He sat on a second stool and lifted the ice pack off Jordan's wrist.

Emma peered at Jordan's arm from the other side. Her wrist was swollen. Emma couldn't see it clearly because of Jordan's dark skin, but she guessed that bruises were starting to form. The thought made her stomach churn, and she wished for the dozenth time she hadn't let Jordan climb back up the tree.

"How did this happen?" the doctor asked while he studied the wrist from all sides.

"I fell off a tree and caught myself on my outstretched hand," Jordan answered instead of repeating the lion-wrangling joke.

"What were you doing up in a tree?" The young doctor shook his head at her. "You're a surgeon. You operate on people who hurt themselves doing stupid stuff like that every day. You should know better than to be so reckless."

Emma fought the urge to jump to her defense. The doctor was right. They should have gotten a ladder.

"Yeah, yeah, save the lecture," Jordan grumbled. "I know it wasn't the most clever thing to do, but it was a spur-of-the-moment decision."

The doctor went back to his examination. He eyed the red stains on her shirt. "Other than your arm, do you hurt anywhere else?"

Jordan shook her head, even though from the way she had moved when she had climbed out of the car earlier, Emma guessed that she might have a light headache or at least a few bruises all over her body. "No," she said. "Those are just berry stains."

Emma decided not to say anything, hoping that as a physician, Jordan would speak up if she had any other injury that needed to be treated. Jordan might be stubborn, but she wasn't stupid.

"Can you move your fingers?" the doctor asked.

Jordan slowly wiggled the fingers of her right hand. "Doesn't exactly feel pleasant, but...yeah, I can."

"Does this hurt?" He gently manipulated the joint of her wrist. "How about when I press here? And here?" With each question, he palpated different places on her arm and hand.

Jordan gave clipped replies through gritted teeth.

Each time he pressed down on Jordan's arm or hand, Emma tensed a little more, hoping they would be done soon.

When he pressed on a spot about an inch down from where her thumb met her wrist, Jordan sucked in a breath. "Yeah. Right there. Damn. Hurts like a bitch." She looked at Emma with a crooked smile. "Sorry. Good thing we didn't bring Molly, huh?"

"Yeah, but like you said, these are extenuating circumstances."

They smiled at each other.

The young doctor cleared his throat.

"I'm hoping for a sprain, but it could be a Colles's fracture," Jordan told him. "Make sure you check the ulnar styloid."

He glared at her. "I would have gotten around to it eventually."

"And don't forget the radial—"

Emma squeezed her shoulder. "Why don't you relax and focus on being a patient instead of a doctor?"

"Hallelujah," the young physician muttered loud enough for them both to hear. Finally, after a few more seconds of prodding and palpating, he placed Jordan's arm back on the treatment table and snapped off his gloves. "There's no deformity, but I can't rule out a nondisplaced fracture. I'll order a set of X-rays, and get someone from ortho to take a look since it's your dominant hand."

Emma watched his retreating back as he walked out. All that prodding and torturing Jordan, just for that?

A few minutes later, the nurse who had examined Jordan earlier pushed a wheelchair into the room, and Emma realized that she was still resting her hand on Jordan's shoulder. Quickly, she let go and got out of the way.

"Oh no." Jordan held out her uninjured hand as if to ward off something evil. "I'm not getting into that thing. I hurt my wrist, not my legs, so I can walk just fine."

"It's hospital policy; you know that, Dr. Williams. You don't want me to get in trouble with the charge nurse, do you?" The blonde batted her long lashes at her and invitingly patted the back of the wheelchair.

Grumbling, Jordan slid off the treatment table and into the wheelchair.

This time, Emma had to stay behind and couldn't follow her to the radiology department. Well, Jordan told herself, it wasn't as if she needed someone to hold her hand. Still, she couldn't help looking back over her shoulder as her wheelchair was pushed out of the room. She hated being hurt, and Emma's presence had been surprisingly comforting.

On the way to radiology, nurses and doctors greeted her left and right, and she had to force herself to answer with false cheerfulness. Maybe it hadn't been such a great idea to come here after all. She was used to being the one calling the shots, not the one who was pushed around in a wheelchair like a helpless invalid. It hurt her pride to have her colleagues see her like this.

When she discovered who the X-ray technician on duty was, she wasn't sure if that made it better or worse.

"Hi, Venita." They had slept together a few times when Jordan had first moved to California, but they hadn't seen each other in a while. Jordan wasn't sure why they had drifted apart; she had always liked the warmhearted X-ray tech.

"Hi, Jordan. I heard you were on your way. How are you feeling?"

Great. It was already all over the hospital. "I'll feel better once you've confirmed that it's just a sprain."

Venita gave her a commiserating smile. "Let's get this over with, then." She looked from Jordan to Betty, who was still gripping the handles of the wheelchair. "I'll take it from here."

Air conditioning kept the X-ray room cool, making Jordan shiver as Venita pushed her toward the large X-ray machine hanging from the ceiling. Once she was seated at the end of the radiographic table, Venita gently positioned her wrist and her hand, palm down, on the imaging plate.

"Let's start with the posteroanterior view," she said. "I don't need to ask you if you're pregnant, do I?"

Jordan laughed. "Hardly."

Venita squeezed her shoulder and settled the lead apron over Jordan's chest and lap. "Relax your hand and don't move."

"That wasn't what you said the last time we saw each other," Jordan called after her as Venita walked to the door. She wasn't actually in the mood to joke around, but at least it distracted her from the pain and her growing tension.

"You weren't wearing a lead apron back then," Venita shot back.

"I wasn't wearing anything," Jordan answered, even though she wasn't sure Venita could hear her. "And neither were you."

As the door closed behind Venita, Jordan held her breath, despite knowing it wasn't necessary.

Moments later, Venita stepped back into the room and repositioned Jordan's wrist to take an image from a lateral view.

"How does it look?" Jordan asked as soon as Venita had taken the second X-ray and returned to her side.

Venita freed her of the lead apron. "You know I don't interpret the X-rays; I just take them."

"Not even for me?" Jordan used her most charming smile on her.

Venita chuckled and patted her shoulder. "Nice try. But no, not even for you."

Damn, Jordan thought as Betty pushed her back to her exam room. She really was slipping. First Emma had resisted her charm, now Venita.

It hadn't even been fifteen minutes since Jordan and the nurse had disappeared around the corner, but it felt much longer than that. God, she would be so relieved once they returned and announced that it was just a sprain.

What if it isn't? the pessimistic little voice in Emma's head piped up.

That voice didn't used to be there, but since last year, she tended to view things differently, less optimistically.

A soft knock sounded on the open door to the exam room. Jordan's friend, the tall doctor with the disheveled hair and the incredibly blue eyes, entered. "Hi again. Jordan still not back from radiology?"

Emma threw another glance at the large clock on the wall and shook her head.

"Shouldn't be long now," Hope said. "Mind if I keep you company?"

"No, of course not."

Hope settled on the second rolling stool, looking as if she was glad to be off her feet for a minute. She swept her gaze over Emma from head to toe and back, but there was nothing lecherous about it. "So, you're sharing a house with Jordan?"

"Yes. The house—but not her bed, if that's what you're asking," she said, more candidly than she had planned. God, being here and worrying about Jordan really put her on edge.

Hope stared at her and then smiled. "Um, no, actually, it wasn't. I know how it feels to have people constantly assume we're sleeping together, just because we're both lesbians and Jordan is…well…"

They exchanged knowing glances.

"Popular with the ladies?" Emma suggested, not wanting to bad-mouth the woman who had gotten hurt rescuing her daughter's stuffed animal.

Hope laughed. "Something like that."

So there actually was a woman—an attractive, lesbian woman—that Jordan was just friends with. Who would have thought? Maybe she and Jordan could be friends too. Having a friend in this new city would be great, and beneath all that flirting and bravado, Jordan seemed like a good person.

Footsteps approached, and the wheels of the wheelchair squeaked on the linoleum, announcing Jordan's return before the nurse pushed her through the door.

Almost at the same time, another doctor—probably the orthopedic specialist—entered the room.

"How does it look?" Jordan asked, without bothering to even say hello.

"Hold your horses," the orthopedic specialist said. "I haven't even taken a look."

Emma expected him to stick an actual X-ray image up on a light box and flip a switch so he could examine it, but instead, he moved to a computer with a large monitor along one wall. He typed in something and then clicked a few times before leaning forward to study the black-and-white image on the screen.

Jordan, Hope, and Emma craned their necks.

All Emma could see were two parallel white shadows representing the two bones in Jordan's forearm.

The doctor rubbed his chin. "Hmm."

Emma tensed and rolled her stool closer to Jordan's side. That *hmm* hadn't sounded good.

"Well," the doctor said and turned toward them, "I've got good news and bad news."

"Cut the bullshit, Frank." Jordan waved her left hand at him. "Get out of the way, and let me see that X-ray."

Slowly, the doctor ducked out of the way so that Jordan could see the screen.

Jordan stared at the X-ray for several seconds. "Shit."

"What?" Emma looked back and forth between them. "What is it?"

"I fractured my distal radius," Jordan growled out.

"Which means she broke one of the bones in her forearm, about an inch from the wrist joint," Hope said.

Oh shit. So Jordan's wrist wasn't just sprained after all. Her hand went to Jordan's shoulder again, but she stopped herself before she could actually touch her. "I hope that wasn't the good news you mentioned." Every muscle in Emma's body tensed as she waited for the doctor's answer.

"No, it wasn't. Jordan was actually lucky."

Jordan snorted, but the doctor continued. "The fracture doesn't extend into the joint. It seems stable and well aligned, so she won't need surgery. She'll need a splint or a back slab cast and then a full cast once the swelling has gone down, but in about six weeks, her arm should be as good as new."

Six weeks... Emma groaned along with Jordan. Six weeks in a cast, just because she had let her daughter out of her sight for a few minutes. How could she ever make it up to Jordan?

Chapter 7

SIX WEEKS... AS THEY DROVE back home, Frank's words went through Jordan's mind as if on auto repeat, along with *shit, shit, shit.* She couldn't look away from the back slab cast that covered her arm from her elbow to her MCP joints, leaving only her fingers free.

Six weeks without the use of her dominant hand, which meant six weeks without being able to do surgery. She couldn't even supervise her residents, because if anything went wrong, she needed to be able to take over. No OR for six weeks. She felt like a soccer player who had been sidelined for something that hadn't even been her fault.

"I'm so, so sorry," Emma said for about the hundredth time.

Jordan forced her gaze away from her arm and looked at Emma, who was clutching the steering wheel as if she wanted to strangle it. Her fair skin had gone even paler.

Truth be told, Jordan wanted to be left alone so she could brood on her side of the car, but Emma already felt bad enough, so Jordan put a smile on her face. "Well, at least now I can say I got plastered with you." She held up her arm in the plaster splint, which rested in a triangular sling, and then winced at the pain the movement caused.

The corners of Emma's mouth twitched, but she didn't quite manage a smile.

"It's not the end of the world," Jordan said to both Emma and herself, willing herself to believe it. "I was overdue for a vacation anyway, and my horoscope said I'd take an unexpected trip. I just didn't think it would be a trip to the ER."

Emma sighed. "I'm still sorry."

Jordan didn't know what to say to that, so they were both silent for the rest of the drive.

As soon as Emma parked the car in the garage, Jordan got out and trudged toward her side of the duplex, her usual confident stride absent for the moment.

Emma hurried after her.

In front of the door, Jordan paused and cursed as she tried to pull her keys from the right-side pocket of her jeans with her left hand.

"Let me," Emma said.

Jordan turned toward her. A hint of a smile flashed across her face. "You just want an excuse to get into my pants."

Emma snorted. "Right." But she hadn't considered how intimate it was to reach into someone's pocket when she had offered her help. Well, she wouldn't back down now. Resolutely, she reached out and stuck two fingers into Jordan's front pocket.

The fabric was warm from Jordan's body temperature, and she was overly aware of how close she had to stand to be able to reach into her pocket. Her hand wasn't too steady, so the key ring eluded her.

"Deeper," Jordan said in a breathy tone. "And use more fingers."

Emma paused and stared at her. She wasn't sure what annoyed her more: Jordan's constant sexual innuendo or that the closeness required to fish the keys out of Jordan's pocket didn't leave her unaffected. "You are really enjoying this, aren't you?"

Jordan gave a one-shouldered shrug and a little grin. "Just making the best of a shitty situation."

Another wave of guilt poured over Emma like a bucket of ice-cold water. Sighing, she dug deeper and finally grasped the key ring. She pulled it out, unlocked the door for Jordan, and handed her the keys.

"Thanks," Jordan said, now entirely serious. She took a step into the house and then paused and turned back toward Emma. "Good night. Maybe you could let me know tomorrow if Molly is doing okay."

Emma's annoyance with her instantly vanished. Jordan might be a player, but she could also be incredibly sweet and thoughtful. "I'll check on her in a second, but first let me help you get ready for bed."

Another grin curved Jordan's lips. "You really do want to get into my pants."

Okay. Enough was enough. Emma stepped into the house without asking for permission and closed the door with more force than was appropriate, given the late hour. "Listen, Jordan. Apparently, you surround yourself with women who like the constant flirting and innuendo, but I'm not one of them. I don't go for players like you, and while I admit you're funny every now and then, most of your silly lines get on my nerves. So since we're going to spend more time together in the next six weeks, I suggest you cut it out."

Jordan stared at her and then leaned against the wall with her good side as if needing the support. "You don't hold back, do you?"

Emma glanced at the floor, a little embarrassed at her outburst, and then back up at Jordan. "I did in the past, but it hasn't gotten me anywhere, so now I prefer to make things clear from the get-go."

"I can respect that. I like a woman who knows what she wants." Jordan winced and sent her an apologetic look. "Sorry. Old habits die hard. Or I could just blame it on the painkillers they gave me. So, why are we going to spend more time together in the next six weeks?"

"Because I'm going to help you with everyday things around the house. I had a broken wrist when I was a teenager, and I remember that I constantly had to have my mother help me."

Jordan shook her head. "You're not my mother. It's not your responsibility to—"

"Yes, it is. My daughter and I are the reason you're stuck with a cast for the next six weeks, and I'm a woman who takes responsibility for her actions."

"That's admirable, but you really don't have to help me. I'm used to fending for myself."

Something flickered in Jordan's eyes, and for a moment, Emma imagined that despite the constant stream of women in and out of her bed, Jordan might get lonely sometimes. It made her all the more determined not to let her deal with this on her own. "Please, Jordan. Let me help."

Jordan sighed. "Am I at least allowed to make a joke about not being able to say no to a beautiful woman?"

"Nope." It took all her self-discipline not to smile. She held Jordan's stare, refusing to back down.

"All right. Come on. I'll show you my bedroom—and just for the record, that wasn't a come-on."

When Jordan turned and walked down the hall, Emma finally allowed herself to smile. "I already know where it is," she said before she could stop to think about it. *Damn.* She covered her mouth with her hand, but it was too late to take it back. Maybe Jordan hadn't noticed.

Jordan turned around. "Oh? How's that?"

"Um, I figured you picked the room right next to the bathroom as your bedroom, like I did," Emma said without looking at her. She could feel Jordan's gaze on her.

"Both bedrooms are right next to the bathroom."

Emma shrugged and kept her gaze on the floor. "Yeah, but the other bedroom doesn't have access to the patio."

"True, but... Oh, I get it now! You heard me."

Her cheeks heated. "Not you, really, but...um, your...friend Simone... she's...um, rather enthusiastic."

Jordan grinned, apparently not embarrassed at all. Or maybe she just hid it well. "I had no idea the common wall is that thin. My previous neighbor, Mrs. Fisher, never said anything. But then again, she was hard-of-hearing, so..." She studied Emma. "You could have said something, you know?"

"What kind of introduction would that have been? 'Hi, I'm your new neighbor. Oh, and by the way, could you please abstain from all sexual activity after ten in the evening?'" Emma shook her head. "Besides, it doesn't matter anymore, at least not for a while."

Jordan cocked her head to the side. "Why's that?"

"Because...well..." She gestured at the broken arm.

"There are a lot of other ways to make love to a woman, you know? There's nothing wrong with my—"

"Lalalala, I can't hear you." Emma pressed both hands to her ears and then slowly let them drop away. "And hadn't we agreed that you'd stop the innuendo?"

"Hey, this time, you were the one who started it."

"Touché."

Chuckling, Jordan led her down the hall.

Emma looked around while she followed her. Jordan's side of the duplex was a mirror image of hers: to the left was an open kitchen leading to a small eating area and then to the living room, while two bedrooms flanked the bathroom to the right. The only difference was that Jordan probably used the small office at the end of the hall for something else—and that everything was a lot neater than on Emma's side, without dozens of toys lying around. No matter what she did, by the end of the day, her house looked as if a Toys "R" Us catalog had exploded all over it.

Jordan's bedroom was as tidy as the rest of her house. The bed was made, and a sweatshirt lay neatly folded on top of a dresser. A large photograph of a snow-covered mountain hung on the wall opposite the bed. Instead of a TV, an exercise bike took up one corner.

What did you expect? Handcuffs on the bedposts? A stack of porn on the bedside table? Emma didn't know what she had expected, but not this.

"You know," Jordan said as she kicked off her sneakers, "I really think I can handle it alone. Undressing with just one hand can't be that difficult, can it?"

"Not if you're wearing the right things, but getting out of this," Emma pointed at the short-sleeved polo shirt Jordan wore, "will be a struggle without some help."

"I just put it on before I went outside into the backyard. I can sleep in it and then deal with it tomorrow."

"Not a good idea. There are mulberry stains all over it. Come on." She tugged on the shirt. "We're both adults here."

"Speak for yourself," Jordan mumbled. "I've got the brain of a teenage boy."

Emma smiled. "I noticed." She bridged the space between them and lifted her hands to open the two closed buttons on Jordan's polo shirt. As much as she tried to pretend she was undressing Molly, it wasn't working. Her body was much too aware that she wasn't facing a child. She hadn't undressed another woman in… God, she couldn't even remember how long it had been. Had the sex in her marriage really become that nonexistent, and she hadn't even noticed? Apparently, she had been blind to a lot of things going on in her life.

As she carefully pulled the shirt over Jordan's head and then over the bulky plaster splint, she averted her gaze.

One-handedly, Jordan unbuckled her belt. She struggled with the button and the zipper of her pants for a few seconds but then managed to work them open.

Emma breathed a sigh of relief—until she remembered that putting the pants on tomorrow morning would be much harder to do. She would have to help Jordan with that. "Um…" She cleared her throat. "Want me to open your bra for you?"

For a second, she was sure Jordan would answer with a joke about having lots of practice opening a bra one-handedly, but she just shook her head and reached behind herself with her left hand.

"Thanks," Emma said.

Jordan looked up. "What for?"

"For not saying what I'm sure you wanted to say."

A grin darted across Jordan's face. "That was harder than getting the damn bra open."

The bra dropped to the floor.

Emma tried to look away; she really did, but she couldn't help staring at the expanse of smooth dark skin and Jordan's small, firm breasts. *Now who's got the brain of a teenage boy, hmm?* She snatched her gaze away.

Not that Jordan seemed to mind. She had to be aware that Emma was ogling her, but she just grinned and didn't attempt to cover herself with her arms. She appeared to be completely at ease, standing in only an unzipped pair of jeans in the middle of her bedroom. Without hesitation, she tugged the pants down and stepped out of them before walking over to the bathroom.

Emma stayed behind, pretending it took all of her attention to fold the jeans, the bra, and the stained shirt. Through the door, which Jordan had left ajar, she heard water run into the sink. After a few minutes of splashing and mumbling, probably as Jordan discovered how hard it was to wash herself with just her left hand, everything went quiet.

"Jordan?" she called. "Everything okay?"

"Mmm."

Did that mean yes or no? Emma decided that she'd better go make sure. After a knock on the half-open door, she peeked inside the bathroom.

Jordan stood in front of the sink. Somehow, she had managed to unscrew the toothpaste with one hand, and now she was gripping the toothbrush with her teeth while trying to squeeze out a dollop of toothpaste with her left hand.

Emma took it from her, squeezed out a bit of toothpaste, and handed it back. "Why didn't you call me?"

Jordan turned and leaned against the sink, not bothered by the fact that all she was wearing was a pair of panties and a plaster splint. "You're not seriously planning on following me around to help me out with stuff like this for six weeks, are you?"

Keeping her gaze on Jordan's face, Emma nodded. "If that's what it takes. You'll get better at handling things after the first few days. At least, that's how it was for me. But until then I want to help."

Jordan looked down and examined the toothpaste as if it were the most fascinating thing she'd ever seen. "I'm not used to needing help," she said quietly.

That moment of vulnerability transformed her for a second and took Emma's breath away. "I know. I'm not used to someone climbing trees for me either, but I let you do it anyway. If it makes things easier for you, just imagine me as your very own not-so-virtual assistant. Earlier you said you wanted one, remember?"

"I should have been more careful about what I wished for, hmm?" Jordan said with a wry smile.

Emma nodded. "Lesson learned."

Jordan turned back to the sink and started to brush her teeth. It looked very awkward since she was using her left hand.

For a moment, Emma considered offering her help, but she sensed that Jordan would draw the line there, so she went back to the bedroom. "Where do you keep your pajamas?"

The sounds of Jordan spitting out a mouthful of toothpaste drifted over. "I don't have any."

Emma could hear the smile in her voice. Oh. So Jordan slept naked. She should have guessed that.

"But if it'll make you feel better, I'll put on a pair of scrub pants and a T-shirt or something."

"Not necessary," Emma called back. "I've already seen you naked. Old hat."

Her attempt to play it cool started to crumble the moment Jordan appeared in the doorway. "Oh yeah?" she drawled. "You've seen me *mostly* naked. Big difference. If you don't think it is, you've clearly never seen me in my glorious birthday suit." She teasingly tugged on one side of her panties, pulling them down half an inch.

"Behave," Emma said in her best mom voice and held up the covers for her.

Jordan slipped into bed. The seductive expression was gone as she watched Emma pull the covers over her.

She was more complex than Emma had initially given her credit for. She could go from charming and funny to vulnerable and serious—and back—in an instant.

Gently, Emma placed an extra pillow beneath the broken arm since Hope had mentioned that it was best to keep it elevated to reduce the swelling. "Do you think you'll be able to sleep?"

Jordan nodded.

"Good." Emma resisted the urge to sit on the edge of the bed and straighten the covers. Instead she walked to the door, where she paused and looked back at Jordan. "If you wake up tonight and notice that your fingers are turning blue or cold or go numb…"

"I know. I'm a doctor, remember?"

"Right." Emma couldn't believe she'd forgotten that for a second. *You can never forget that,* she sternly told herself. *She's a surgeon. A player.* She'd have to remind herself of that so she wouldn't confuse the forced intimacy of helping Jordan with something else. The best way to handle this was the way she had suggested to Jordan: pretend she was her VA and Jordan was a client.

Okay. Time to stop hovering and go check on Molly.

"Good night." She switched off the light and closed the bedroom door.

The sound of Jordan's soft "good night" and the sight of her lying in bed with her arm on a pillow accompanied her home.

Chapter 8

JORDAN HAD NEVER BEEN ABLE to sleep on her back, and the dull pain in her wrist had kept her awake for most of the night, even though she'd been exhausted.

At five o'clock, she gave up and climbed out of bed. Normally, she was out of the house within fifteen minutes of waking up, but today everything seemed to take twice as long. As a surgeon, she was usually pretty good with both of her hands—or at least she had thought so.

Now she realized that washing beneath her left armpit without the use of her right hand was a pain in the...armpit. No way would she ask Emma for help with that, though. She didn't mind having a woman undress her, but usually, that happened in a much more pleasant context. Having Emma help her out of her shirt last night...

As she relived the moment, her body insisted that it had been a pleasant experience to have Emma so close, to feel her hands brush her chest as she opened the buttons. At the same time, having to be undressed like a child who couldn't handle buttons made her feel much too vulnerable, and that wasn't a feeling she liked.

She struggled for ten minutes to get her socks and shoes on. Her shopping list was getting longer and longer; an electric toothbrush and slip-on shoes were at the top. Finally, she gave up on trying to tie her shoelaces and just shoved them into the sneakers without tying them.

With the bottle of painkillers and a mug of coffee, she trudged outside to the hammock. Settling into it with the mug in her good hand was a challenge—one she mastered by spilling coffee down her shirt.

"Ouch. Fuck." Maybe one of the lawn chairs would have been a better choice. Since she didn't have a hand free to pull the shirt with the hot liquid away from her chest, she instead blew into the V-neck in an attempt to cool her burned skin.

Of course, that was the moment the French door to Emma's office opened.

Great. Now Emma would never believe that she could handle things without her help.

Jordan quickly stopped blowing and pretended the large coffee stain on her shirt was the latest fashion statement. "Good morning. How's the tree climber?"

At the mention of her daughter, a smile spread over Emma's face. "She's fine. When I looked in on her last night, she woke up for a moment and immediately called dibs on being the first to sign your cast."

Jordan chuckled. "Well, she's got her priorities straight." She looked down at the bandage that held her temporary cast in place, which was open on one side to take the swelling into account. "She'll have to wait until next week when I get my full cast, though."

"How are you?" Emma asked as she came closer. "Did you sleep okay?"

Jordan didn't normally make it a habit to lie to women, but if she told the truth, Emma would feel even more guilty than she already did. "Oh, yeah. Slept like a baby."

Emma squinted down at her. Her gaze seemed to pierce into her, like the X-ray beam that had taken the images of her wrist last night, and see through her just as easily. "Like a colicky baby maybe."

Was she that easy to read? Or did she look that bad? Jordan didn't think that was the case. When she was on call, she often got little to no sleep, so she was used to it. "Okay, it wasn't exactly the best night's sleep I ever had. How did you know?"

"I'm a mother," Emma said with a secretive little smile. "I know these things."

Jordan groaned. "It was bad enough when my own mother said things like that."

Still smiling, Emma knelt down in front of the hammock. She didn't seem to notice or care that the grass was damp.

"What are you doing?" Jordan asked. "Not that I mind a woman kneeling in front of—" *Dammit.* She had done it again. Had little quips and lines like that really become so ingrained? "Sorry."

"Like I said, every now and then, I find it amusing. Just don't overdo it or think that I'll jump into bed with you because of your charming lines."

So Emma did think she was charming. Jordan grinned. That would have to do for now. "Deal. So, what are you doing?"

"Tying your laces." Emma reached for the foot that Jordan had planted on the ground. Before Jordan could protest, she had double-tied her laces.

It wasn't that Jordan didn't appreciate it, but she really detested being treated like a five-year-old. Her pride was taking quite a beating.

Just as Emma was tying the laces of her other shoe, a voice drifted over from the fence that separated the house from Barbara's. "Good morning. How's the arm?"

Jordan turned toward Barbara. "Still broken," she answered in a cheerful voice so her friend wouldn't worry too much. "But at least it's the most beautiful distal radius fracture I have ever seen. I've got the pictures to prove it."

A few drops of dew clung to Emma's knees as she got up.

Speaking of beautiful… Emma's shapely legs were a work of art.

The gate in the fence that separated Barbara's property from the duplex swung open, and Barbara limped through. Her hip always acted up in the morning, so she used the cane for a change instead of just carrying it. She touched Jordan's arm above the edge of the back slab cast, the wrinkles on her face deepening into lines of worry.

Jordan cringed. She loved attention from women—but not this kind. "Hey, it's not like they had to amputate it or anything. I'll be fine." Sighing, she added, "In six weeks."

"What were you doing up in that tree anyway?" Barbara asked in a stern-grandmother tone of voice.

Jordan looked over at Emma, who lowered her gaze to the ground. "Emma didn't tell you when she got back last night?"

"She wanted to check on Molly, so she said she'd tell me the details today. So, what on God's green earth were you thinking, climbing a tree?"

"It's a long story."

"I'm retired," Barbara said, leaning heavily on her cane. "I've got time."

Jordan hesitated.

"She climbed up to get Molly's stuffed lion down," Emma said before Jordan could decide on an answer.

Barbara stared at the mulberry tree, probably wondering how a stuffed animal had made it up there, but she didn't ask. Instead, she bent and kissed the top of Jordan's head. "That was kind of you."

"No big deal."

"I'm making pancakes," Barbara said. "Want to come over and try to beat Jordan's record?" She looked from Jordan to Emma, clearly including her in the invitation.

Emma chuckled. "Normally, I'd love to, but I have to get Molly up and to school, and I have a Skype meeting with a client later."

"I'll come," Jordan said. She'd drive herself to the hospital later to make sure all the t's were crossed and the i's dotted on her paperwork, but other than that, she didn't have anything else to do. At least decimating a stack of pancakes was a challenge she could take on even with one hand.

"I'll drop by after my meeting to see if you need anything," Emma said.

"You don't have to." With a job and a kid and a household to take care of, Emma was no doubt very busy, even without taking care of her on top of everything else. "I can manage on my own."

Emma eyed the coffee stain on Jordan's shirt but didn't comment on it. "I'll be by." She walked toward the house.

Despite her aching wrist, Jordan couldn't resist watching her go. Those curvy hips and nice butt were a better distraction than any painkiller.

The end of Barbara's cane playfully socked her in the left arm, drawing her attention away from Emma.

"Hey, careful, I only have one good arm left." Jordan wanted to make a show of rubbing the limb but couldn't do it with her cast.

"Oh, Jordan?" Emma called from the French door. "What's the record?"

"Eight," Jordan called back with a proud grin.

"Wow."

"I know, I know. I felt like a beached whale afterward, but some things are worth the pain." She hadn't intended to hint at her climbing the mulberry tree to get Molly and then her stuffed lion, but as soon as she had said it, the words took on a different meaning.

Her gaze met Emma's across the backyard. The gratefulness in Emma's eyes made her feel about eight feet tall.

Emma gave her a slow nod, then ducked inside and closed the French door.

"What was that all about?" Barbara asked.

Jordan put her by-now cold coffee down into the grass and pushed herself out of the hammock with her uninjured hand. "Nothing. Come on. I'm hungry and someone promised me pancakes."

Jordan hadn't even made it through her first day not being in the OR, and she was already going stir-crazy. After getting back from the pancake breakfast with Barbara, she had spent two hours at the hospital, doing paperwork and checking on her post-op patients. With her dominant hand out of commission, there wasn't much else she could do, and she could tell that her lingering was getting on her residents' nerves, so she had headed home and tried to read a little.

But holding up the book and turning the pages with just one hand was awkward. She couldn't focus on the plot of the story anyway, too distracted by thoughts of Emma, the next six weeks, and what might have happened if she hadn't discovered Molly up in the mulberry tree.

Finally, she gave up and spent the rest of the day doing little things around the house that she could do with one hand, just to keep herself busy.

Emma had checked on her three times, in between calls with clients and whatever else it was a VA did. She had even brought over lunch, which Jordan had refused because she'd still been full from the pancakes. The fourth time she joined Jordan on the patio, she was barefoot and had changed into a T-shirt that said *mompreneur*.

"Cute," Jordan said, then added, "The T-shirt, not you since I'm not allowed to compliment you."

Emma shook her head at her but said nothing.

Jordan had a feeling she was trying hard not to smile.

Molly ran over, clutching her stuffed lion with one hand. "I'm cute too." She showed off her T-shirt, which was pink and had a roaring tiger on it.

"Very cute. What is it with you and big cats?"

Molly giggled. "I like them. Mommy and I visited them in the zoo a lot. Is there a zoo here?" She looked around as if expecting a giraffe to pop up over the hedges any moment.

"Uh, I have no idea." There had to be a zoo in LA, right? Jordan had never had a reason to know this kind of thing since neither her sisters nor any of her friends had kids.

"Yes, there is," Emma said. "At least there was one when I was a child. But I don't remember if they had big cats. I'll find out tomorrow, okay?"

"Can we put it in your book?" Molly asked.

"Sure." In Jordan's direction, Emma added, "She means my to-do list."

Jordan smiled. "Oh, you're one of those." *A geek, and a sexy one at that.*

"Oh yeah. My ex used to joke that I couldn't find my…um…" She glanced at her daughter. "…butt without my to-do list."

This time, Jordan was proud that she wasn't even tempted to answer with a joke about helping Emma find it. Well, not much, anyway.

"So," Emma rustled the grass with her bare toes and smiled, probably because it tickled, "are you still full from the pancakes?"

"No. I didn't break my record today. Not even close, so that beached-whale feeling has faded away."

"Well, then if you're hungry, why don't you come over and have dinner with us? Cooking with one hand can't be fun."

Jordan hesitated. On the one hand, she would have liked spending more time with Emma, but on the other hand, having dinner at home with Emma and her daughter would probably be a little too domestic for her taste. She was about to say that she would just warm up the lunch Emma had provided when Molly jumped up and down.

"Yay! You can sit next to me. And I don't use my old bib anymore, so you can have it."

"Um, thanks. Well, looks like I'll be joining you for dinner." She couldn't very well disappoint the kid now that she was already so excited.

"Great." Emma received high-fives from her daughter. "Well, come on, then. I'm making burgers. You can tell me your preferences while I cook."

Jordan bit her lip. *Don't say it. Don't say it.* Damn, cutting out the flirty comments was harder than getting dressed with only one hand.

Speaking of her only hand… She was wrenched from her thoughts when Molly gripped her left hand and dragged her toward their side of the duplex.

It was hard to believe, but somehow it had been just a little more than a week since Emma and Molly had moved in. When her friend Hope had moved to LA, it had taken her months to get halfway settled in her new home. Most people were like that, so Jordan had expected to still see some moving boxes or a piece of furniture that hadn't yet been assembled.

The glimpses she'd seen of the living room when she had picked up Simone from Emma's place had made her assume that Emma had quickly relocated any remaining chaos to the other rooms because of their visitor, but now she realized that the entire place looked as if Emma had lived there for years.

A small table with two chairs had been moved into the dining area, and every available inch of wall was covered by hand-drawn pictures that were clearly Molly's. More of them were tacked to the fridge with colorful magnets.

"Looks like you're all settled in already," Jordan said as she looked around.

"Yeah. I didn't want us to feel like we're living in a construction zone, so I tried to get everything unpacked and set up in a hurry."

Jordan's family had moving down to an art form, so she could appreciate someone who managed to pack and unpack just as quickly. "Do we have time for a quick tour before we eat? I'd love to see what you did with your part of the house. I showed you mine, so now you show me yours…your side of the house, of course."

"Of course," Emma repeated with a look that said she knew better. "If you give me a minute, I'll give you a tour. I want to get the patties on the stove first. It's getting close to Molly's bedtime, so I want to have dinner on the table soon."

"I'll show her! Do you wanna see my room?" Not waiting for a reply, Molly grabbed Jordan's hand again. "Come on. I'll show you." She started to drag Jordan toward the front of the house, her pigtails bouncing behind her.

Did the kid ever just walk anywhere? But Jordan had to admit that she'd been the same way as a child. The only pace she'd known was full speed ahead. Her mother had warned her that she would one day be punished with a child just like her. While that hadn't happened, Jordan was now getting a taste of her own medicine.

"Slow down, Molly," Emma called after them. "You have to be careful with Jordan. She can't run, or it'll jostle her broken arm."

Molly slid to a stop. Her eyes went wide, and she stared at Jordan's arm. "Does it hurt?"

"No," Jordan said, even though it wasn't quite true. Because she hadn't eaten much since breakfast, she hadn't taken painkillers yet, and the ache in her arm was beginning to make itself known. "I'm fine. I'm just a little slower than usual, so you'll have to bear with this old lady."

Molly giggled and pointed at a closed door at the end of the hall. "This is where Mommy sleeps."

"I know."

"How do you know?" Molly asked.

Damn. Now she had maneuvered herself into trouble, and she had to talk her way out of it. "My room is right on the other side of that wall, and your mother mentioned that she heard my…um…music."

Molly continued her tour of the house, babbling a mile a minute and introducing each of her stuffed animals by name.

Jordan had decided early on that kids weren't for her, and Molly going on and on about every single toy on the shelves in her bedroom only confirmed that decision. But she had to admit that Molly was pretty cute. Like mother, like daughter.

Finally, after spending ten minutes of oohing and aahing over Molly's bedroom, they moved on to the living room.

Jordan had already seen it when she'd picked up Simone, but she hadn't paid much attention, too tired from a long workday and too surprised at finding Simone with Emma. Now she took in the room more thoroughly. *Wow.*

The built-in bookshelves were crammed full of books; some were even stacked on top of others. Apparently, Emma was a fellow bibliophile. Her taste in reading material was much more diverse than Jordan's. Emma's books were sorted into sections of thrillers and crime novels, romances, paranormal fiction, and business books on productivity, time management, and working from home. If Jordan wasn't mistaken, within each section, the books were neatly arranged in alphabetical order.

Forgetting her resolution not to run with Jordan in tow, Molly dashed toward a shelf that held a vast collection of DVDs. The movies were arranged alphabetically too.

"These are mine!" Molly announced.

Jordan put on a suitably impressed expression. "All of them?"

"Nooo. Just these and these and these." Molly waved her hand at three of the bottom rows.

"And the rest?"

"Those are Mommy's adult movies."

Jordan burst out laughing so hard that she had to bend over and gasp for breath.

Emma walked over from the kitchen at that exact moment. She rushed toward Jordan and gently touched her back. "Everything okay? Are you in pain?"

Slowly, Jordan straightened and wiped tears of laughter from her eyes. She was very aware of Emma's warm hand on her back, making her skin tingle. "I'm fine. I'm just laughing because your daughter showed me your collection of adult movies."

"What?" Emma's jaw went slack, and she pulled her hand away from Jordan's back. "She doesn't... I don't..."

Jordan started laughing again. "I think she meant movies for adults."

"That's what I said." Molly looked from one adult to the other, her small brow wrinkled.

Still chuckling, Jordan reached out to pat her head but then noticed that she couldn't do it with her cast and pulled her hand back. In the process, she bumped it into the edge of the DVD shelf. A painful jolt went through her wrist and then rushed through the rest of her arm. For a moment, she couldn't even breathe.

"Oh God, Jordan. You have to be more careful." Emma took hold of her cast with both hands, as if she could soak up the pain.

"I know," Jordan got out through gritted teeth. She suppressed a curse for Molly's sake.

Emma let go of Jordan's arm as if only now becoming aware that she had taken hold of it. "Where's your sling?"

"At home."

"I know what to do," Molly piped up.

Jordan expected her to suggest getting the sling, but instead, the girl continued, "You need a hug. Mommy says a cuddle makes everything better, right, Mommy?"

"Right."

Molly wrapped her arms around Jordan's thighs and laid her head on her hip.

Jordan froze for a moment. She hadn't expected that trustful gesture. Over Molly's head, she sent Emma a startled gaze.

Emma shrugged and smiled, the corners of her eyes crinkling with amusement.

After a few moments of holding her good arm awkwardly suspended, Jordan lowered her hand to rest on Molly's shoulder and gave it a soft squeeze. "Thank you," she said, surprised to find her voice a little hoarse. "That was a very good hug. I feel better already."

Beaming, Molly stepped back. "Now it's Mommy's turn."

Emma's amused expression instantly vanished.

"You don't have to do that," Jordan said. "One hug is more than enough."

But Molly shook her head. "Two are better."

Jordan couldn't deny that logic—and, truth be told, she didn't really want to. It was only a harmless hug, after all. Just a few seconds of having Emma's body pressed against hers. A shiver went through her at the thought.

"Hug her, Mommy." Molly pushed against Emma's hip as if to shove her in Jordan's direction.

"All right already! I'm hugging. Jeez." Emma bent forward at the waist and laid one arm across Jordan's shoulder, barely touching any other part of Jordan in the process.

"Oh, come on." Jordan shook her head at her. "What are you—a straight woman? This is how two lesbians hug!" She wrapped her good arm around Emma and pulled her into a full-body contact. Her cast came to rest along Emma's back. She had meant to make it a quick embrace, but as soon as she felt Emma's body against hers, all sense of time or propriety seemed to disappear.

She hadn't been able to put on her bra with one hand this morning, so she had gone braless. Emma's warmth drifted through the thin fabric of her shirt, and her perfume enveloped Jordan. She deeply breathed in the light fragrance. It was floral with a note of vanilla that made it innocent yet sensual at the same time. She could feel the roundness of Emma's breasts pressing against her and pulled her even closer. Her eyes fluttered shut, and her nipples instantly hardened. She struggled to hold back a moan.

Man, are you crazy? Her kid is right here! Cut it out. But she couldn't force herself to move away.

After a few seconds, Emma let go and stepped back, not meeting Jordan's gaze. "There. Hug delivered. Now I'd better get back to the burgers."

She turned away so quickly that Jordan wondered whether she'd been just as affected by their closeness.

"I want to put the ketchup on mine," Molly announced, oblivious to what was going on. Then she was off again, rushing after her mother.

Jordan took several deep breaths and stared down at the two hardened nipples poking through her T-shirt. "Behave," she told them before following Emma and Molly back into the kitchen.

She leaned against the kitchen island, keeping a little distance to give her libido some time to cool off, and watched as Emma formed the patties, salted them, and put them in a cast-iron skillet on the stove. While the meat sizzled away, Emma sliced tomatoes, washed lettuce, put a package of French fries into a saucepan of sizzling oil, and answered Molly's curious questions without missing a beat.

Wow. Jordan couldn't help admiring her. A woman who was in full control of her surroundings was unexpectedly sexy.

Emma looked up from the skillet. "Are you all right? Do you need your painkillers? You look a little...dazed."

Jordan blinked to break the spell she'd been under. "I'll take them after we eat. Anything I can do to help?"

"Why don't you and Molly set the table? The burgers will be ready in a minute."

"Sure." Jordan was surprised how well she and Molly worked together. She took each plate from the cabinet, and Molly carried them to the table one by one and then ran back to her so she could receive the next one. Were kids that age always so eager to help, or was Emma's daughter especially well-behaved?

"I can do the knives and the forks on my own!" Molly announced. "Look!" She put them on the table.

The forks were on the wrong side of the plates, but Jordan didn't have the heart to tell her, so she discreetly switched them when Molly ran to get glasses.

Finally, the burgers were ready, and Emma assembled them.

Jordan's mouth watered at the sight of the melting cheddar cheese on the patty. Emma had even put thin slices of fried bacon on each burger. Definitely a woman after her own heart. Yum.

"We don't always eat like this," Emma said. "Normally, I insist on salad or vegetables with every meal, but after the scare we had yesterday evening, I thought we deserve this."

"You won't get any complaints from me. Besides, the tomato and lettuce on the burger should count as salad, right?"

Emma laughed. "Is that your professional opinion as a physician?"

"Absolutely." Jordan gave a decisive nod. "Besides, burgers are good for your mental health."

"Mommy, what's a feesician?" Molly asked.

"It's physician, honey. It means that Jordan is a doctor."

"Ooh!" Molly stared at her with big eyes.

Jordan always got a lot of attention from women for her choice of career, but somehow the kid's adoring gaze felt special, and she found herself standing taller.

"Do you work with Mama?" Molly asked.

"What do you mean?" Jordan looked from the kid to Emma, who pressed her lips together.

"My ex-wife is a doctor too." She turned toward her daughter. "No, honey, she doesn't work with Mama. Jordan works in the hospital where we went to get her cast."

"I want to be a doctor too when I'm big," Molly declared. "Like Mama." She heaved a big sigh and stared off into space, looking so sad that it touched Jordan's heart.

No doubt the kid was missing her other mother.

Emma went over to her, bent, and gave her a hug.

Mother and daughter huddled together like that for several moments. Jordan stood by in silence so she wouldn't disturb them. She had a thousand questions about Emma's ex, but she knew this was not the moment to ask them.

Finally, when Emma returned to the stove, Jordan cleared her throat. "So, do you want to heal kids or work with adults?" she asked to distract the kid from missing her other mother.

Molly's pigtails flew as she shook her head. "I don't want to be a people doctor. That's boring. I will make sick animals all better."

"Boring, hmm?" Jordan mumbled. "No way can my ego inflate around you two."

Chuckling, Emma lifted her daughter onto the kitchen island so she could put ketchup on her burger.

Jordan was glad to see the smile back on her face.

"What do you want on your burger?" Emma asked while keeping an eye on her daughter as she squeezed out ketchup. "Mayo, mustard, ketchup, or BBQ sauce?"

"Actually, do you have any peanut butter?"

Emma stared at her. Even Molly looked up from her burger.

"Peanut butter?" Emma repeated. "You want peanut butter on your burger?" She scrunched up her freckled nose the exact same way that Molly sometimes did. "I think I have to take you back to the ER. You clearly hit your head when you fell out of that tree."

Jordan laughed. "Don't knock it till you've tried it. It's really, really good. Almost as good as—" At the last moment, she remembered Molly. "Um, ketchup."

"Ketchup is the best," Molly declared and squeezed the bottle again, drenching her burger in ketchup.

Emma eased the bottle away from her. "I think that's enough."

They carried their plates to the table, and Emma got a third chair from somewhere.

Instead of taking a seat, Jordan pulled Emma's chair out for her.

Emma paused. "Oh, thanks."

Surely a woman like her couldn't be surprised by such a polite little gesture, could she? Jordan would have bet her next paycheck that she had doors opened and chairs pulled out for her wherever she went—or at least she should. In Jordan's book, women deserved to be treated like queens, especially women like Emma, who single-handedly raised a kid.

Jordan sat and reached for the jar of peanut butter that Emma had placed on the table for her. She tucked it between her thighs so she could unscrew it with her left hand.

"You're not seriously going to spoil that perfectly good burger by putting peanut butter on it, are you?"

"Oh, yes, I am." Grinning, Jordan spread two large gobs of peanut butter onto the top bun before placing it back on her burger. "Want me to peanut-butter your buns for you too?"

Okay, that somehow sounded a little naughty, but Emma didn't seem to have noticed or at least pretended not to.

Jordan was about to grip her burger and take the first bite when she realized that it was much too big to hold with just one hand. Frustrated, she instead shoved a French fry into her mouth and thought about how to attack the burger while she chewed.

"Want me to cut it in half for you?" Emma asked with a knowing gaze. "I did it for Molly too."

Great. There she went again, comparing her to a five-year-old. If they continued like this, her ego would be decimated to the size of a pea by the time she had her cast removed. But certain things in life were more important than pride—and this delicious burger was clearly one of them, so she nodded.

Emma reached over and cut the burger in two neat halves.

"Thanks." Eagerly, Jordan picked up one half and took a bite. The incomparable combination of tender meat, golden-glazed onions, fresh tomatoes, and peanut butter set off fireworks across her taste buds. She let out a moan and chewed with her eyes closed.

When she opened them, Emma had stopped eating and was watching her. Was that a hint of red on her cheeks?

"Can I try?" Molly asked, drawing Jordan's gaze away from Emma.

"Sure."

Emma shook her head. "You're not going to corrupt my daughter, are you?"

"Yep. I sure am." She took the knife and, with some difficulty, cut off a little piece and handed it over to the kid.

"Molly, don't let her lure you over to the dark side," Emma told her daughter.

But Molly just giggled as she put the bite of peanut butter burger into her mouth. She chewed twice, and then her eyes got huge and her chewing sped up. "Ish goo'."

"No talking with your mouth full, honey," Emma said.

Molly gulped down her bite of burger. "It's really good, Mommy. Try." She pointed at Jordan's burger.

"No, thanks," Emma said. "I'll take your word for it."

"I think your mother needs some convincing, Molly." She turned to face Emma. "Come on, where's your adventurous side?"

"I left it back in Portland," Emma muttered just loud enough for Jordan to hear.

At the hint of pain in her voice, Jordan's challenging grin faded away.

Emma sighed. "All right, you two. I'll try it. Happy now?"

"Yes!" Molly high-fived Jordan.

Only when she withdrew her hand did Jordan notice that Molly's finger had been sticky with ketchup, which now clung to her own hand. She wiped it on the paper napkin Emma had provided before putting a piece of her burger onto Emma's plate.

Emma picked up the bite-sized chunk of peanut butter burger between thumb and index finger, as if she wanted to minimize contact.

Jordan couldn't help chuckling.

With a scrunched up face, Emma put the piece of burger into her mouth. Her hand hovered near her water glass as if she was preparing to take a huge gulp to wash it down with. Then the wrinkle between her brows smoothed out. She swallowed, and her tongue darted out to lick a bit of peanut butter off her full bottom lip. A low moan escaped her, sending goose bumps down Jordan's body.

Damn. Jordan had never known how sexy eating a burger could be. She cleared her throat. "So, what's the verdict?"

Emma shrugged and put on an indifferent expression. "It's edible."

"Edible?" Jordan echoed. The urge to reach over and tickle Emma until she confessed to loving it gripped her, but that wasn't a good idea. For one thing, she was at a disadvantage with one hand in a cast, and what was more important, she had no idea how Emma would react to that sort of physical contact. She had to remind herself that she still barely knew Emma, even though it didn't feel that way. "Come on. It's great, and you know it! Just admit it."

"Yeah, Mommy. Admit it."

Emma swiped a French fry through the puddle of ketchup on her plate and chewed it thoroughly before saying, "It's surprisingly…edible."

"I like it." Molly looked at Jordan with big puppy dog eyes. "Can I have your burger?"

"No, honey," Emma said before Jordan could answer. "You have your own, remember?"

"Jordan can eat it."

"I think she'd prefer to eat her own," Emma said.

Jordan glanced at the soggy burger on the kid's plate. Her stomach wept as she took one last glance at the remaining burger on her own plate before handing it over and taking Molly's. "Here."

Emma shook her head at her. "Don't spoil her too much."

"Nah." Jordan took a bite of the ketchup-drenched burger and quickly followed it up with a few French fries while she watched the kid happily dig into the peanut butter burger.

Now that her daughter was busy, Emma started to decimate her own food.

Finally a woman who wasn't afraid to eat a burger and fries! Emma took a huge bite of her burger, not seeming to care that Jordan saw her with bulging cheeks.

Jordan couldn't help comparing her to the women she normally dated. Many of them tried to make a living as actresses or models, so they carefully watched what they ate and stayed away from the junk food Jordan loved. Going out to have a burger and a beer with one of them was out of the question, but she had a feeling Emma would like it.

By the time they were done, all three of them were filled to the gills, and Molly's face was smeared with ketchup and peanut butter.

Jordan stretched out her legs beneath the table and sighed happily. To think that she at first hadn't wanted to accept the invitation to come over for dinner. This was the most relaxed—the most herself—that she had felt around a woman in…well, ever. Not trying to charm her dinner companion was surprisingly relaxing.

Emma patted her belly. "If you can still move, can you go wash your face, honey?"

Molly's pigtails flew as she shook her head. "Don't want to."

Having to wash up must have meant that her bedtime was nearing.

"You have to. You have ketchup all over, and you don't want to ruin your new *Finding Dory* pillowcase, do you?"

Her bottom lip sticking out, Molly shook her head.

"Come on. Off you go. You can take Jordan with you because she doesn't look much better than you do."

Admittedly, eating the kid's burger had been a bit messy because she had used so much ketchup. Jordan got up and followed the girl to the bathroom. Was she supposed to help her, or could five-year-olds wash themselves?

Apparently, this one could…kind of. Molly scrubbed her face with both hands, getting water all over the bathroom floor and her T-shirt. When she dried her face on a towel, traces of red remained behind on the fabric.

"I'll help you," the girl said. Before Jordan could assure her she could wash herself, Molly wet one corner of the towel, gently took Jordan's uninjured hand in hers, and cleaned off the bits of ketchup. Her little face was a study in concentration, and the tip of her tongue poked out of her mouth. Then she tugged Jordan down and ran the towel all over her face.

Jordan held still, touched by how gentle Molly was.

"All done," the girl finally announced.

Jordan glanced in the mirror above the sink. A thin streak of ketchup still marred her cheek. She wiped it off with the back of her hand. "Thank you, kind lady."

Giggling, Molly dropped the towel over the rod and ran back to the kitchen.

Before Jordan had even taken a step, she heard her call, "Mommy, can Jordan read me a bedtime story?"

Jordan stopped and faced her own startled expression in the mirror. *Oh God.* What had she gotten herself into? She could do an appendectomy practically with her eyes closed, but could she read a bedtime story?

It seemed she was about to find out.

Emma leaned against the wall in the dark hallway and listened as Jordan's voice drifted through the door she'd left ajar. It felt strange to be out here and not in the bedroom with Molly. For the past two or three years, she had always been the one who had read Molly her bedtime story.

"There once was a curious little tiger who lived with his mother in the jungle. One day, the little tiger got bored, so he said to his mother, 'I want to—'"

"Not like that," Molly said. "You have to do the voices."

"Um, do the voices?"

Emma pressed her hand to her mouth so she wouldn't laugh. Jordan clearly had no clue about how to read a bedtime story.

"Yes. Mommy always does the voices for each animal."

Just as Emma was about to go in and rescue her, Jordan apparently got it right and continued to read. Her animal noises—the hiss of a tiger and the trumpeting of an elephant—made Molly laugh several times, and Emma smiled into the dark, charmed and grateful that Jordan would go along with what Molly wanted, even if she was clearly out of her comfort zone.

Having Jordan read to Molly also hurt a little, though. It should have been Chloe in there, but she had rarely taken the time to read their daughter a bedtime story, even back when they had still been married.

She just hoped that Molly wouldn't attach herself to Jordan too much. Jordan wouldn't be a permanent presence in Molly's life. Once the six weeks were over and the cast was removed, Jordan would return to her life, which consisted of operating on people and getting women into bed, not of reading bedtime stories and having burgers with her neighbors.

After a while, Jordan reached the end of the story and fell silent.

Quickly, Emma tiptoed back to the living room, not wanting her to know that she had eavesdropped on her interaction with Molly.

Just as she had taken a seat on the couch, Jordan entered and wiped an imaginary trace of sweat off her forehead. "Phew. Mission accomplished. I read her a bedtime story."

"Thank you. I'll go tuck her in, then." She gestured for Jordan to take a seat. "Make yourself comfortable. I'll be right back."

When she returned a few minutes later, Jordan had settled into an easy chair. Emma sat across from her on the couch. "Thanks again for reading to Molly. That was really nice of you."

"No problem. She's a sweet kid."

Emma nodded and allowed herself a moment of maternal pride. At least something in her life was going right. "You're good with kids."

"Me?" Jordan touched her good hand to her chest.

"Yeah, you. You don't think so?"

Jordan let out a chuckle that sounded a little insecure. It was interesting to see this side of her. "I don't know. I never spent much time with kids, not even when I was one."

"Other than the two sisters who tossed you off the tire swing."

They laughed together.

"Yeah, other than that."

Silence fell, interrupted only by the not yet familiar sounds of the house—the ticking of the clock on the mantle, the chirping of crickets drifting in through an open window, the creaking of the easy chair as Jordan shifted positions.

"Do you want—?"

"Thanks for—"

They spoke at the same time and then both fell silent.

Jordan gestured at her to go first. She always did that, Emma had noticed.

"Do you want a glass of wine or a beer?" Emma asked.

A sigh escaped Jordan. "I'd love to have a beer, but..." She held up her cast. "I'm on painkillers, so alcohol isn't the best idea. Unless you want to get me drunk so you can take advantage of me."

Emma wagged a finger at her. "You know what? I'm going to get a piggy bank. Every time you use a line like that on me, you need to give me a buck. I figure by the time the six weeks are over, Molly's college tuition will be taken care of."

Jordan laughed ruefully. "That's a distinct possibility. I'm trying, okay?"

"Good enough. So, do you want something else to drink? I bet your throat is parched after all that storytelling."

"I'm fine. But you can get yourself a beer or a glass of wine, if you want. No need for you to abstain just because I can't drink."

Despite a twinge of guilt, Emma got up and returned with a glass of red wine for her and a bottle of water for Jordan. She opened the bottle for Jordan and handed it over. "You should take your painkillers now too. Where are they?"

"I'm fine."

Why did doctors always have to be such bad patients? Emma sighed. "Where are they?" she asked again.

"Over at my place, on the coffee table."

"Be right back." Emma slipped in and out of Jordan's living room through the open French door and returned with the plastic bottle. She opened it for Jordan and shook out one of the pills. "Here."

Without further protests, Jordan swallowed it.

"So," Emma said once she'd settled back onto the couch, "what was it that you wanted to say earlier?"

"I wanted to thank you for having me over for dinner."

Emma snorted. "It wasn't exactly haute cuisine."

"It was burgers," Jordan said, sounding as if it was the holy grail of dinner foods. "If I have the choice between a tiny portion of some dish with a French name in a fancy restaurant and a burger, I'd rather have the latter."

"Me too." She hadn't admitted that before, even to herself, but she knew it was true. Chloe had been the one who had preferred to dine at expensive restaurants. Of course, Emma had enjoyed going out and having dinner at a good restaurant every now and then, but she would have been just as happy to have burgers at home.

Jordan took a swig of water. "So, how did the meeting with your client go this morning?"

Wow. Emma hadn't expected her to remember, much less ask about it. "Oh. Good. Really good."

"Yeah?" Jordan looked at her as if she expected her to say more.

So it hadn't been a polite question that she didn't really want to have answered in detail. Jordan kept surprising her.

"Yeah. I'm organizing a VBT for her, and she was really happy with what I've done so far."

"VBT?" Jordan asked.

"Oh, sorry. I don't even notice jargon like that anymore. That's a virtual book tour."

Jordan put her elbows on her thighs and leaned forward. "So how exactly does that work? I mean, she can't sign her book online, can she?"

"Well, there are ways to do that, even with e-books, but that's not what a virtual book tour is about. Basically, I'm looking for author blogs where she can guest-post, places where she can do book giveaways, and sites that are willing to review her new book."

"I see. Would I have read any of this client's books?"

Emma sipped her wine. "That depends on what you read. Probably not, though."

"What, you think the only book on my shelf is a copy of *The Joy of Lesbian Sex*?" Jordan asked with a grin.

Heat suffused Emma's cheeks, and she knew it wasn't just from the wine. "No, of course not." Admittedly, she hadn't thought that Jordan would be much of a reader beyond medical journals and maybe some erotica. "I just thought… My client writes paranormal fiction, and I know that's not for everyone."

"I've read *The Dresden Files*, the *Mercy Thompson* series, the *Night Huntress* series, and a few of Karen Chance's books. Oh, and Janet White's *Ghostwalker* series, but she lost me after book two."

"Oh yeah. Me too. I loved her main character in the first two books, but once the romance was introduced, she started behaving like a starstruck teenager with no brain whatsoever."

They talked about books they had both read, and Emma was surprised to find that their tastes in literature were actually pretty similar. Before too long, Emma had gotten up and put together a stack of books for Jordan to read during the next six weeks.

When the clock on the mantle announced that it was midnight, Emma couldn't believe it. When was the last time that had happened to her? When was the last time she'd had any kind of conversation with another adult that didn't revolve around her daughter, for that matter?

Back in Portland, she had met up with friends every now and then. During the last year, those meetings had become rarer, not just because Emma had been busy preparing her move but also because many of her friends had been *their* friends—hers and Chloe's—so their divided loyalties had made things awkward.

Here in California, she hadn't made any friends yet. The only people she talked to on most days were her daughter, Barbara, a couple of clients…and Jordan.

Jordan had stopped her constant flirting—for the most part, at least—but she had pulled out Emma's chair at dinner, and she had complimented her cooking and listened attentively. Emma had to admit that she enjoyed the attention. Being the focus of a woman as confident and charming as Jordan was a heady experience, especially for someone who had basically been ignored by her wife for months, even before the separation.

Of course, Emma didn't intend to take this anywhere, but being treated like an attractive woman for one night felt great. *Yeah, well, you'd better not get used to it.*

"Wow," Jordan said. "I didn't realize it had gotten this late. Do you have to get up early tomorrow, or can you adjust your schedule?"

Emma reached for the disc-bound planner that was her constant companion. The red ink that signaled an important appointment jumped out at her. "I have to drop Molly off at school by seven thirty and then rush home for a Skype chat with a client."

"Sorry I kept you up so late," Jordan said.

"It's okay. Totally worth it," Emma answered and found that she really meant it.

"Yeah, to me too. But then again, I'm the one who can sleep in tomorrow morning, if I want to." Jordan tucked her empty bottle of water beneath her right arm, picked up Emma's empty wineglass, and carried both to the kitchen.

It was a little thing to do, but Emma immediately liked that Jordan was helping to clean up, even though she was a guest.

Emma followed her to the door with the stack of books. "Do you want me to carry those over for you?"

Jordan's eyes twinkled. "You're offering to carry my books for me? Does that mean you want to go steady?"

Emma lightly backhanded her good arm. "You just can't help it, can you?"

"Hey, I've been good tonight…for the most part."

True. Emma had started out inviting Jordan over mostly because she felt guilty but had ended up enjoying her company. "So, do you want my help or not?" She nodded at the books.

"Nah, that's fine." Jordan took the books from her and balanced them against her chest.

"What about getting yourself ready for bed? Do you want me to come with you and give you a hand?" She waved at Jordan's temporary cast.

"I can manage. I'm learning to choose easy-to-put-on clothes, and I didn't put on a bra, so it should be a lot easier than yesterday."

Oh, yeah, Emma had noticed that Jordan wasn't wearing a bra, especially when Molly had urged them to hug. A shiver went through her as she remembered how it had felt to hold Jordan close.

They stood facing each other at the door, with Jordan balancing the stack of books against her chest.

"Well then…" Jordan said. "Thanks again for dinner."

"Thanks for reading to Molly."

"And for introducing you to the peanut butter burger," Jordan quipped.

Emma smiled. "All right. Thanks for that too."

"You're welcome. Good night."

"Good night." Since Jordan had her good hand full of books, Emma reached around her to open the door for her. That move brought their bodies so close to each other that she could feel the heat that emanated from Jordan. A tingle of electricity seemed to engulf her from head to toe. Hyperaware of everything about Jordan, she noticed a dot of dried-up ketchup close to her ear, so she reached out to wipe it away.

Jordan tilted her cheek into the touch. Her lips parted, and she leaned forward, toward Emma.

Oh God. She's going to kiss me. Why was she standing there like a deer caught in the headlights of an approaching car instead of moving away? Her mind screamed at her to step back, but her body wouldn't let her.

It was only the stack of books between them that finally stopped Jordan's forward movement and wrenched Emma from her daze.

Quickly, she stepped back and held out a hand, palm out.

The books thumped to the floor.

They stared at each other, both breathing heavily even though their lips hadn't touched.

"Jesus, Jordan, what are you doing?"

Jordan reached up with her right hand as if to rub her lips, nearly giving herself a black eye with the cast. "I…I thought… You were touching my cheek and I thought…um…"

"I just wanted…" Yeah, what exactly had she wanted? She shook her head to clear it. "I wanted to wipe away the leftover ketchup on your face."

Jordan scrubbed at her face with her good hand and then looked at her fingertips. "Oh. I'm sorry. I really thought… I didn't mean to…"

"It's okay. I know this is what you're used to—having dinner with a woman and then…" She waved her hand. "Well, I guess you don't often say good night at the door."

"Actually, I do. Despite what you might think, I'm not the wham-bam-thank-you-ma'am type. I know how to romance a woman, you know?"

After spending the evening with Jordan, Emma could easily believe that. "I didn't mean to insult you. It's just… We want different things out of life…and from a relationship. If I'm reading you right, you don't want one."

"It was one kiss, Emma—or it would have been one—not a marriage proposal."

"That's just it. For you, a kiss is just a kiss, and sex is just sex."

Jordan shrugged. "What's wrong with that?"

"Nothing—if you're unattached and don't have many responsibilities beyond your job."

"Look, I get that you have responsibilities. But if you think just about yourself for a minute…" Jordan searched her face with an intensity that made Emma feel hot all over. "You are attracted to me, aren't you?"

It really was that easy for Jordan. Emma sometimes wished it were that easy for her too. "That's not the point, Jordan."

"Then what *is* the point?"

"It doesn't work like that for me. I have a daughter. Everything I do affects her in one way or another. I won't subject her to women parading in and out of my bedroom. Can you understand that?"

Jordan didn't look happy, but she nodded grudgingly. "She wouldn't need to know."

"She's five and very clever for her age. How long do you think it would be until she'd start asking about the sleepovers Mommy is having?"

"I could sneak out before she wakes up."

"Sneak out?" Emma shook her head. "No, Jordan. I'm not the sneaking-around type. I deserve better than that." If the past year had taught her anything, it was that.

Jordan ran her good hand through her short, naturally coiled hair. "Yes," she said quietly. "You do. I'm sorry. That was a stupid thing to say. I didn't mean to—"

"It's all right. Let's just forget about it."

They stood facing each other for a few seconds, neither saying anything else. Then both bent at the same time to pick up the books that had fallen to the floor, and their hands touched as they reached for the same novel.

Quickly, Emma pulled back and left the books for Jordan to pick up.

Jordan tucked the paperbacks between the cast and her chest, adding book after book like stones in a wall that separated her from Emma. Once she had picked up the last one, she shouldered the door open. "Good night," she called, already halfway outside.

"Good night." Then the door closed between them.

Outside, Jordan leaned against the door as if her legs wouldn't carry her otherwise. She stared into the darkness and exhaled sharply.

What the fuck was she doing? Since when did she try to talk women into sleeping with her? She never had to beg or resort to her persuasive powers. If a woman wasn't sure a night of passion was what she wanted, Jordan stayed away from her. There were plenty of like-minded women, so why expend so much energy to chase after one who didn't want the same?

Yes, Emma was definitely hot, but so was almost every woman she met. She lived in Southern California after all, the land of Hollywood, where every waitress was an aspiring actress.

No need to pine over the one woman she couldn't have when there were so many more—women who were looking for a fun playmate for the night, not a soul mate or a second parent.

Right?

She gave a decisive nod and pushed off from the door. Emma was her neighbor, she told herself with every step she took toward her side of the house. They could exchange books, but not hot kisses or anything more. Period.

Chapter 9

FOR THE SECOND NIGHT IN a row, Jordan slept very little. With her broken arm up on a pillow, it was hard to find a comfortable position. A few times, she dozed off and fell into a light sleep. Every time she woke, she had the fleeting impression that she had dreamed about peanut butter burgers and kissing Emma, pressed up against her front door.

At half past five, she gave up, climbed out of bed, and went through the awkward routine of dressing herself and brushing her teeth with her left hand.

"Coffee," she mumbled when she padded into the kitchen, like a woman who had gotten lost in the desert and was now stumbling toward an oasis.

While she leaned against the counter and waited for the automatic coffee machine to grind the dark-roast beans and fill her mug, her thoughts drifted to Emma. *Bet she'd kill for a cup of coffee right now, if she hasn't had one yet.* She shook her head at herself. It was barely six. Emma probably wasn't even up yet.

But when she stepped onto the patio and peeked over to Emma's side of the house, there was already light in Emma's office.

Jordan hesitated. *Should I?*

Wouldn't it be better to keep her distance and stay away from Emma after what had happened last night?

But that wasn't even possible. They couldn't escape each other since they lived door to door and Emma had promised to look in on her and help her with whatever she needed while her arm was in a cast. She knew Emma well enough already to realize she wouldn't break that promise, no matter what had happened between them.

Man, nothing happened! It was just an almost kiss. They had to be adults about it.

She made a second cup of coffee and added cream and sugar. While she had no idea how Emma took her coffee, surely a woman who ate a burger with bacon, double cheese, and mayo without a hint of remorse wouldn't prefer black coffee.

Both mugs gripped by their handles in her good hand, she carried them outside to the backyard.

The light in Emma's office was still on. Emma was behind her desk, massaging her temple with one hand while she stared at her computer screen. Jordan wasn't surprised that she was already up and working. By now, she knew that Emma probably tried to get some work done before she had to get Molly ready for school.

She paused on the patio. Should she really disturb her that early?

God. Get a grip. Since when was she so hesitant and full of self-doubt in her interactions with women?

Not allowing herself time to hesitate again, she marched across the patio and toward the open French door leading to Emma's office. Carefully, she used the knuckles on her casted arm to knock on the doorframe.

Emma jumped. Her head jerked around, and then her tense posture relaxed as their gazes made contact.

"Sorry." Somehow, she said that a lot around Emma. "I didn't mean to startle you."

Emma tilted her head in acknowledgment. "That's my I-feel-like-a-zombie startle response."

Had she lain awake for some of the night, thinking about that almost kiss too? Or was it just that she'd gone to bed too late and had not gotten her eight hours of sleep?

You're overthinking again. It doesn't matter. "That's what brought me over."

"Zombies?" Emma asked with a smile.

"Coffee." She held out the two mugs in her hand like a peace offering but didn't enter the office yet. "Or have you already had one?"

"Yeah."

"Oh." Jordan shuffled her feet. "Well, then I'll—"

"But you know what? I'll gladly take a second cup today. This is clearly not a one-coffee morning." Emma rolled back her office chair and waved at her to come in.

Jordan crossed the office toward her and put the two mugs down on the desk. Her gaze fell on several dozen pens, which were sorted by color into three different pen holders. Other office supplies—a ruler, a pair of scissors, and several highlighters—stuck out of a fourth pen holder. Three stacks of Post-It notes, arranged by size, rested next to it. Jordan had to smile at how organized it all was.

"Two?" Emma asked, nodding down at the coffee cups.

"One's mine." She quickly rescued her own mug.

Emma took hers and lowered her mouth toward it like a lover anticipating the joy of a first kiss.

Stop thinking about kisses! Jordan directed her gaze at her own, slightly darker coffee.

After several sips, Emma put her mug down. "Ah. Liquid manna. Thanks."

The ecstatic expression on her face made Jordan smile. "You are very welcome. I thought after last night, I owed you something."

"No need for you to apologize again. It's already forgotten."

Really? Jordan frowned. Normally, she didn't leave women so unaffected.

"It wasn't like you pounced on me like a wild animal in heat. You tried to kiss me, and I said no. No big deal. We're adults and can deal with it."

"True. But actually, I wasn't talking about that." That was a lie, of course, but after that blow to her ego, Jordan felt as if she needed that bit of protection. "I meant I owed you for keeping you up way past your bedtime." She sent her a sheepish grin.

"Oh." Emma took another sip of her cream-laced coffee, probably more to hide her reddened face behind the mug than because she really wanted another hit of caffeine.

"But about the other thing... It's probably not a bad idea to apologize a second time. I didn't mean to cross any lines."

Emma stared down into the depths of her coffee. "It's okay. Maybe we needed to draw a line first. At least now we both know where we stand and can be friends."

"Friends," Jordan repeated, tasting the word. Being friends with a woman like Emma would definitely be a new experience. She had very few female friends—at least not the kind that she didn't sleep with occasionally.

"Yeah." The copper spots in Emma's green eyes seemed to dance. "You know, that strange concept where two people spend time with each other while they aren't in a horizontal position."

"Oh, you'd be surprised what I can do in upright positions," Jordan drawled.

Emma sent her a chiding look over the rim of her mug.

Jordan sighed. "You're no fun," she mumbled into her coffee. "But all right. I could use a boring friend."

A pen sailed across the office and hit her in the chest.

Jordan picked it up and put it back into the correct pen holder.

Emma held out her cup. "To being friends."

They clinked their mugs together and stood in silence for several moments, sipping coffee and grinning at each other.

Emma licked a drop of coffee off her bottom lip. "How did you know how I like my coffee?"

Jordan bit back an *I know what women want, baby* and shrugged. "I figured you for that type of woman."

In the process of taking another sip, Emma paused. Her eyebrows arched up. "What type is that?"

The type with sexy curves instead of a model-thin figure.

Before she could decide whether to voice her thoughts, a timer went off on Emma's computer.

Now it was Jordan's turn for an I-feel-like-a-zombie startle response.

"Sorry," Emma said. "That's my cue to go wake up Molly and get her ready for an exciting day of kindergarten." She finished her coffee with two big gulps and handed back the empty mug. "Thanks again for the extra caffeine. I really needed it."

"You're welcome." Jordan tucked the empty mug beneath her casted arm. In a much better mood, she headed back to her side of the duplex.

Chapter 10

JORDAN STARED AT THE CALENDAR on her kitchen wall. In a neat row were seven crossed-off days—one week since she'd fractured her arm.

One down, five to go.

How was she supposed to make it thirty-five more days without work, without the thrill of surgery, without a chance to head down to the ER for some coffee and a little flirting with the nurses?

Another day lay ahead of her, and she had no idea what to do with it. Normally, she loved to help Barbara in the garden on her days off, but that was out of the question. Now that the swelling in her wrist had gone down, she had to go back to the orthopedic department to get her permanent cast tomorrow, and if the cast got wet before then, Frank and the other ortho guys would have her head.

She had spent an hour on her exercise bike right after getting up, but with only one arm, her workout was otherwise pretty limited. She couldn't even play squash with Hope, as they usually did on Mondays. Of course, she could meet up with Hope later today and have a beer or something, but she knew Hope couldn't wait to get home and spend some time with her girlfriend.

One thing Jordan had always liked about being friends with her was that Hope had never seemed very interested in romantic relationships either. From the time they had met as residents in Boston, Hope had either been single or in relationships that seemed almost as casual as Jordan's one-night stands and short flings.

But now that Hope had met Laleh, that had changed. There was nothing casual about their relationship at all.

Not that Jordan relied on Hope for entertainment. Her address book held the names of dozens of women she could call. But despite what she had almost said to Emma about her tongue not being broken, she didn't feel up to it. It wasn't that she was meeting women just for sex, but usually, that was how the night ended anyway.

It was a bit scary to realize how much she relied on work to fill her days and on women to keep her busy at night.

She flopped down onto the couch.

Immediately, Tuna jumped up and perched on her chest. She sniffed the temporary cast and twitched her whiskers.

"Yeah." Jordan scratched her behind one ear with her good hand. "I want to get rid of that thing too, believe me."

Tuna rolled herself into a ball, kneaded against Jordan's arm for a while, and then promptly fell asleep. She reached across the cat and flicked on the TV.

The familiar sight of two people in scrubs appeared on the flat screen above the glassed-in fireplace.

Jordan knew better, but it was a little like watching a train wreck—you knew it wouldn't end well, but you couldn't look away. She watched as one of the TV show's first-year residents got to scrub in on a coronary artery bypass graft on his very first day of residency.

Yeah, right. Jordan snorted. That wet-behind-the-ears guy wouldn't even know one end of the scalpel from the other. No way would she let him into her OR.

She turned off the TV and threw the remote control back onto the coffee table. It slid across and clattered to the floor.

Tuna lifted her head and then sent Jordan the kind of disapproving glare that only a cat could manage. She uncurled herself, stalked across Jordan's belly, and jumped down.

Jordan got up and prowled the living room. At the French door, Jordan paused and looked outside.

Going over to Emma's was out of the question. They had kept contact to a minimum during the last few days so they could have some time to get over the awkwardness of that almost kiss. Emma had brought her food and helped her wrap her cast in a plastic bag so Jordan could take a bath, but other than that, they hadn't spent much time together.

Just as Jordan was about to turn away from the French door, she caught sight of the mulberry tree. Maybe she could pick the rest of the low-hanging mulberries so Molly wouldn't be tempted to climb up again and get them.

With this new purpose in mind and a large bowl from the kitchen, she went outside.

The late-August heat hit her as soon as she stepped onto the patio.

One of the French doors on Emma's side of the house stood open too, and her voice drifted out of the office.

For a moment, Jordan thought she was on the phone or in a Skype chat with a client and wanted to respectfully duck back into her home, but Emma's voice was too agitated for that.

Was she maybe talking to her ex-wife? Admittedly, Jordan had been curious since Emma had first mentioned her. Who was this idiot who had been stupid enough to let Emma and their kid go? Had they separated on good terms? Was Emma still carrying a torch for her ex?

She knew eavesdropping on her conversation wasn't right, but she still stood rooted to the patio.

Emma got up from behind her desk and started pacing, the phone pressed to her ear. Snippets of the conversation drifted over—things such as "I can't believe it," "meetings," "impossible," and "sitter."

In the two weeks since they had met, Jordan had never seen her so agitated, not even right after she had tried to kiss her.

Finally, Emma hung up and stared off into space, her jaw tightly clenched. As if feeling Jordan's gaze on her, she looked up.

Jordan smiled and gave a weak wave.

Emma didn't return the smile. She moved toward the French door, either to invite Jordan in or to close it.

Jordan didn't wait to find out which one it was. She threw the bowl she still held into the hammock and closed the distance between them with several long strides. "That didn't sound like you're having a good day. Anything I can do to help?"

"No." Emma's expression softened a little. "But thanks anyway."

"Are you sure?"

"Yeah. I have to find a babysitter for Molly within the next hour. There's no school today because it's a teacher in-service day."

"What's that?" Jordan asked.

"It means that teachers go to school for some sort of training but students don't. The problem is that they either gave me the wrong date or I somehow got it wrong. I put it down in my planner for tomorrow." Emma started pacing again. "The sitter service I used before said they have no one available at such short notice, and Barbara has her son visiting this week, and I don't want to take away from their time together." She stopped at the desk and flipped open her planner, which was covered in red ink. "I've got appointments all day. Normally, I would try to postpone them, but one of them is with a new client, and if I come across as unreliable, he might not hire me."

The solution to Emma's problem seemed obvious. "I could babysit." That way, Molly would be out of Emma's hair, and she would have a chance to do something useful. Two birds, one stone.

But Emma didn't break out into a delighted smile, as Jordan had thought she would. "You?" she echoed. "You're volunteering to babysit a five-year-old?"

"Why not? You said I was good with kids."

"Yes, but…"

"But what? You don't think I can do it?" That triggered Jordan's competitiveness. She squared her shoulders. "It's just one little kid. How hard can it be to keep her entertained for a few hours?"

"Famous last words," Emma muttered.

"Oh, come on. Give me some credit. I read her a bedtime story, didn't I?"

"Yes. But that's hardly the same." Emma started pacing again.

Jordan entered the office, blocked Emma's path, and put her good hand on Emma's shoulder to stop her from pacing. She ducked her head a little so she could look directly into her eyes. The copper sparks in the light green irises distracted her for a moment before she remembered what she'd been about to say. "Listen, Emma. You need some help, and I'm here to offer it. You helped me so much during the last week. Let me return the favor."

Emma held her gaze, and Jordan could almost see the gears in her head turning as she struggled to make a decision. "I'm really not sure Molly would even want to go with you."

"Ha!" Jordan said with a slightly exaggerated display of confidence. "That's the one thing you don't have to worry about. You'll be lucky if she wants to go back to you after spending the day with me."

A tired smile crossed Emma's face, but she said nothing.

"We could ask her," Jordan said. "If she doesn't want to go with me, fine. Then she can stay home with you and color while you talk to your clients."

Emma winced, probably as she imagined that scenario.

No way in hell would that kid play quietly for hours while Emma worked.

"I know you mean well, Jordan. But how would you even keep her entertained until my last meeting is over at two?" Emma finally asked. "Remember that you've only got one good arm. Sometimes, I'm struggling to keep up with her, even with two arms."

Jordan feverishly tried to think of something. When she had been a child, she had always played outside—hitting baseballs, climbing trees, building tree forts. But that was out of the question since she couldn't do any of those things with her arm in a cast. Parking the kid in front of the TV was probably out too, but...

"I could take her to the movie theater, for starters. I'm sure there's something playing that would be all right for a five-year-old. The movie will basically do the babysitting for me." She grinned, proud of her genius idea.

"Have you ever been to the movie theater with a five-year-old?" Emma asked.

"Sure." She had been five years old once, and she was sure there had been other five-year-olds watching the same film when her mother had taken her and her sisters to the movie theater on the army post in Germany where they had lived. It had been fun, without any incidents that she could remember. "We'll have a great time. And if Molly gets homesick, I can always bring her back. It's not like I'd be taking her to Australia or something."

Emma hesitated. "Okay. I'll ask her." She left the room.

Jordan watched her go, enjoying the view. Was she supposed to follow her? Without an explicit invitation, she decided to stay back and wait for Emma to return with the verdict.

It didn't even take a minute before Molly burst through the door, jumping up and down like a kangaroo. "The movies, the movies, we're going to the movies!" she sang out.

Jordan couldn't help grinning. "I guess that's a yes."

"Guess it is," Emma said with an indulgent smile.

"Can I have popcorn and nachos? Can we go see *Ice Age*? Can I pick the seats?" Molly was still hopping up and down.

Jordan wasn't even sure what *Ice Age* was or whether it was okay to let the kid have popcorn and nachos. She sent Emma an imploring gaze, hoping she wasn't already disqualifying herself as a babysitter.

"I don't know if *Ice Age* is still playing, honey. But I'm sure you'll find a great movie to watch." Emma took one of the sticky notes from her desk, scribbled something down on it, and then handed it over. "These are my numbers—landline and cell. I'll keep them on all day, so please call if there's anything...*anything*, okay?"

Jordan took in Emma's very serious expression, nodded, and pocketed the note. It occurred to her that she had gotten the phone numbers of probably hundreds of women over the years, but never so she could ask for advice on how to handle a little kid. She stole another sticky note from the desk and only then realized that she'd have to write down her number using her left hand. It wouldn't make her already horrible handwriting any prettier.

Once she was done, she stared down at the crooked numerals for a moment. It would have to do. She stuck the note next to the keyboard.

Emma pulled several bills from her wallet and held them out to her. "Here. For lunch and the movie."

Jordan made no move to take the bills. When she'd been bored a few days ago, she had surfed the Web and stumbled across Emma's website. Okay, maybe *stumbled* wasn't really accurate since she had googled her. Anyway, Emma listed her rates on her VA website, so Jordan could easily do the math. According to her online research, virtual assistants weren't employees; they were entrepreneurs running their own business, so Emma had to pay for her own health care and retirement account, and she didn't get paid sick leave or vacation time. Unless she came from a rich family, Emma wasn't exactly rolling in money.

Frowning, Emma waved the bills.

"Thanks, but I've got it covered," Jordan said.

"That's not how this works. You're doing me a favor, so I can't let you pay on top of it. Take the money."

Jordan sighed and slid one of the bills out from between Emma's fingers. "That's more than enough. We want to go see a movie, not buy the entire damn movie theater...um, I meant..." She glanced down at Molly, hoping she had been too excited to hear it.

"Mommy, she said—"

"I heard," Emma said. She folded her arms over her chest and sent Jordan a glare.

Damn. Um, darn. She really needed to get a grip on her swearing around the kid. If Molly returned from their adventure swearing like a sailor, Emma wouldn't be happy.

"Take the money," Emma said again. "And my car keys. The booster seat is already in the back of the car."

"Thanks, but I've got my own ride. I'll just take the booster seat and put it in my car."

"It's a sports coupe, not a family car, Jordan. No way am I letting you take Molly in that thing."

Jordan sighed and took the money and the car keys. "If you're ever tired of being a VA, you should consider becoming a hostage negotiator. If I were a kidnapper, I would have handcuffed myself by now."

Emma's tense features relaxed a little. "Molly, go get Mouse and your backpack."

Molly rushed from the room like a bloodhound following a scent trail.

"Don't buy her any nachos," Emma said.

"Is she allergic?"

"No. Remember what happened with the ketchup?"

Jordan remembered only too well. A bit of it had ended up on her cheek, prompting Emma to wipe it away and her to nearly kiss her. "Um, yeah."

"Well, cheese sauce won't look any better smeared all over her face, clothes, and the seat in the movie theater."

"Anything else?" Now that she was about to take over responsibility for a little person without any backup, she started to wish there was such a thing as a manual. *Yeah. Maybe* Babysitting for Dummies *or something like that.* She couldn't help smiling at the thought.

"Just…" Shadows darkened Emma's eyes to a murkier green. "Just take good care of her, please."

Jordan frowned. What on earth did Emma think she would do with the kid—go bungee-jumping? "You aren't seriously worried, are you? I might not be the world's most experienced babysitter, but I swear I would never put her in any danger."

A fleeting touch brushed her good arm. "I know. Don't mind me. I guess I'm being overprotective after that whole mulberry-tree incident."

Molly charged back into the room, lugging an orange backpack by one of its straps.

Jordan took it from her. It was much heavier than expected, and the stuffed lion was peeking out at the top. She glanced inside. There were two boxes of colored pencils, a coloring book, a mermaid doll, and a pair of plastic binoculars. Um, how long did the kid plan to stay away from home?

"Honey, I don't think you're gonna need all of that." Emma pulled some of the toys out of the backpack, quickly left the room, and returned with a sweatshirt, which she put in the backpack instead. "In case she gets cold in the movie theater." She knelt down in front of her daughter and took both of her hands in hers.

It was a scene that was touching but at the same time made Jordan uncomfortable to watch, as if she were intruding on a private moment between mother and daughter.

"I'm sorry I can't come with you, but I know you'll have a good time at the movie theater. Be a good girl and do what Jordan says, okay?"

Molly nodded solemnly.

Emma kissed her daughter's cheek, hugged her, and then climbed to her feet.

"Ready?" Jordan slid one strap of the orange backpack, which was much lighter now, over her cast-covered arm.

Molly was next to her in the blink of an eye and slid her hand into Jordan's left one.

The small fingers rested so trustfully in her larger ones that a strange feeling settled over Jordan. She couldn't tell if it was a good or a bad one. Maybe it was a mix of both. With that touch of the kid's hand, the responsibility for her had settled firmly on her shoulders.

But she had survived her own, sometimes chaotic childhood and a stressful residency; spending a few hours with a little girl would be a piece of cake in comparison.

She held on to Molly's hand so she couldn't slip out of her grasp. "Let's go see a movie!"

Molly swung their joined hands back and forth as they walked to the door.

"Wait!" Emma called before they could step outside.

Jordan turned, expecting to get another list of do's and don'ts.

"I, um…" Emma swallowed. "Thank you."

Jordan smiled at her. "No problem. See you sometime after two."

Emma tried to focus on preparing a list of things to talk about during her first Skype meeting, but her attention wasn't on work. When she had realized she had written down Excel sitter instead of Excel spreadsheet, she sighed and put the pen down.

It felt weird to rely on someone other than a teacher, experienced babysitter, or fellow mother when it came to her daughter's well-being. Was she crazy for letting Molly go with Jordan, her womanizing neighbor who had confessed to having no experience with children whatsoever? Had she finally given in just because Jordan had looked at her so earnestly with those deep brown eyes of hers?

Admittedly, she wasn't as unaffected by Jordan's charm as she might like to be, but she hoped that hadn't been a factor in her decision. Despite Jordan's inexperience when it came to babysitting, she had a feeling that Molly was safe with her. After all, Jordan had climbed a tree and risked life and limb to get her and her stuffed animal down. In comparison to that, letting them see a movie together was much less dangerous. What could happen to a supervised child in a movie theater, after all, right?

She picked up the pen, but again her thoughts refused to settle on work. All right. She would allow herself to check on Molly, and then it was down to business.

The sticky note with Jordan's cell phone number was next to her keyboard.

Emma stared at the crooked numerals. They looked like Molly's first shaky attempts to practice her numbers. But then again, Emma had to admit that she wouldn't have fared a lot better if she had to write with her left hand.

She picked up her cell phone and typed in the number. A text message would be better than a call, in case Jordan was driving.

How is it going?

It took a minute for the answer to arrive, and every second ticked away painfully slowly.

> *Emma, it hasn't even been ten minutes! We haven't even made it out of the garage yet. But the good news is that I mastered the fine art of buckling a child into a booster seat.*

Ten minutes? Really? It had felt much longer than that.

> *Sorry. I should have shown you how to do that.*

This time, the answer came immediately.

> *Relax and go back to work. I cut people open for a living; I can figure out a booster seat, even though it's a little tricky with one hand. I've got this.*

Emma sighed. Now she was being one of these annoying overcontrolling mothers that she had never wanted to be.

> *All right. Thanks again and have fun. Drive carefully.*

> *Will do, Mom,* Jordan answered, followed by a smiley face.

Emma put the phone away, adjusted Molly's framed photo on her desk so she could see it better, and went back to her list.

Thank God for mobile Internet. It took Jordan a few minutes, but she finally found a movie theater that still showed the movie Molly wanted to see. With the kid strapped securely into her booster seat, she carefully steered the Prius out of the garage and onto the street.

Barbara and her son were sitting on a bench in front of the house. They stared at her openmouthed as she drove by in Emma's car with Molly in the backseat.

Jordan chuckled. They probably thought she had kidnapped the girl.

Overly aware of her precious cargo, she made sure to stick to the speed limit.

Molly entertained her with a constant stream of chatter about the previous movies she had watched. Obviously, the movie they were about to see was part of a series. The kid didn't stop talking the entire way to the movie theater.

Every once in a while, Jordan glanced in the rearview mirror to make sure Molly was even drawing breath in between sentences. Luckily, she didn't seem to require much of an answer most of the time, which was great, considering Jordan didn't have anything to offer on the topic of a talking sloth and a mammoth that thought it was an opossum.

Molly oohed and aahed over the movie posters that were displayed out front and could hardly contain her excitement when they entered the foyer. She was practically vibrating by the time Jordan had bought the tickets at the glassed-in box office.

As Jordan handed the tickets to the employee in front of the roped-off hallway leading to the individual movie theaters, the kid looked at her as if she were unlocking paradise.

Admittedly, it was a nice feeling to have Molly look at her that way.

As they walked toward their theater, they passed a stack of booster seats similar to the one in Emma's car. Was she supposed to get one for Molly? Jordan shrugged and grabbed one, just to make sure.

Before they reached the concession stand, Molly had her nose in the air, sniffing like a puppy. "Can we get popcorn?"

"Sure." Jordan got into line behind a family with four kids, grateful that she only had to take care of one.

Molly craned her neck to study the machine that made slushed ice drinks.

Finally, it was their turn.

"What can I get you?" The young woman behind the concession stand smiled at Jordan, but it wasn't the kind of smile Jordan was used to. This one definitely wasn't flirty; it was the indulgent smile people gave the caretaker of cute kids.

Jordan frowned. Good thing she didn't have kids. That would definitely cramp her style.

Molly stuck her index finger into her mouth and looked from the popcorn machine to the nachos. "Umm…"

"How about a bucket of popcorn?" Jordan suggested before the girl could decide on getting nachos with cheese sauce.

Molly nodded eagerly. "Can I have a soda too?"

"Sure, why not?"

The bucket of popcorn they received would have been enough to feed a herd of mammoths. Jordan paid and then stared down at the large cup of soda and the popcorn. How the hell was she supposed to get all of that to their seats? She tucked the booster seat beneath her casted arm and reached for the soda, but that still left the popcorn.

"I can carry it!" Molly grabbed it with both hands.

A hail of popcorn landed on the gray carpet as Molly tilted the bucket toward herself.

The kid froze, her eyes wide.

Oh man, she wouldn't start to cry now, would she? "It's okay," Jordan said quickly. "There was too much of it anyway. Just be more careful with the rest." She sent the woman behind the counter an apologetic look and then led the way toward the theater.

With the half-empty bucket of popcorn, Molly ran ahead, pushed open the heavy door with a grunt, and then stopped so abruptly that Jordan nearly bumped into her. "It's dark," she whispered.

"Yeah. Otherwise you can't see the movie on the screen." Hadn't the kid ever been in a movie theater? But she had seemed to know exactly what type of junk food to get. It seemed she had forgotten about some aspects of going to the movies.

Molly latched on to her sleeve as they made their way to their seats.

Since it was only ten o'clock, the movie theater was almost empty, but of course the family of six was sitting right in front of them.

She helped Molly climb up onto the booster seat, and the kid immediately began to attack the soda and the popcorn. If she continued like this, there wouldn't be anything left over by the time the movie started.

Thankfully, it wasn't long before the curtains parted and the ads began to play on the big screen.

Molly gave them her full attention, seemingly completely fascinated. When the movie started, she began to comment on anything and everything, even things that had nothing to do with the movie at all, and she didn't lower her voice to do so. Apparently, she hadn't yet grasped the difference between watching a movie in your own living room and watching it in a movie theater.

The father of the family in front of them turned around, and Jordan ducked down in her seat. "Um, Molly, you need to be a little quieter, or the people won't be able to hear the movie."

Her gentle rebuke seemed to work—for all of a minute.

Kids, Jordan discovered, had a really mean brand of humor. A belly laugh burst from Molly when Sid the sloth got his lips stuck on a block of ice.

Clearly, they didn't share the same type of humor or taste in movies. This animated movie made no sense at all. Why the hell was the prehistoric saber-toothed squirrel flying around in a spaceship? And even more confusing, why would it keep trying to bury the damn acorn and store it for winter? It was the Ice Age, for fuck's sake, where winter lasted for several eons!

Molly didn't seem to mind. Of course, the scientific concepts in the movie, such as volcanoes, magnetism, and asteroids, went right over her head. After a while, she began to fidget in her seat. Her feet bumped the back of the seat before her, making the father sitting in front of them turn around and glare again.

"Careful, Molly." Jordan gently took hold of her shoes and guided them away from the back of the seat.

"How long before the movie is over?" Molly asked.

Jordan stared at her, then at her wristwatch. It hadn't even been ten minutes since the movie had started. "Um, a little while. Don't you want to see it anymore?"

Molly nodded. "I want to see it." Gaze on the screen, she continued to fidget, sliding down in the booster seat, then pulling herself back up, just to start the routine all over again.

Should she say something? Ask her to stop? "Um…Molly…"

"I need to go," Molly said.

"Go?"

"Go pee."

Oh. No wonder, after all the soda she had gulped down. "Um, okay." Jordan got up.

Molly slid out of her booster seat and grabbed hold of Jordan's good hand. Her fingers were sticky from the popcorn or some soda she might have spilled.

Walking slowly, Jordan led her down the stairs through the dark movie theater and then to the nearest restroom. At the door, she hesitated. Could five-year-olds take care of business on their own? Damn, she really needed that *Babysitting for Dummies* book.

Molly looked up at her as if expecting her to follow, so Jordan pushed open the door to the ladies' room.

The automatic lights flared on, and Molly marched to one of the stalls and closed the door before Jordan could ask if she could manage on her own.

Oh. Good. "Um, I'll wait here." She wiped her damp forehead and then realized that her hand was now sticky too. *Great.* She grimaced.

Maybe, just maybe, Emma had been right. Going to the movies with a five-year-old was not for sissies!

By the time the movie was over and they left the darkened theater, Jordan felt a little like the animated animals who had saved their icy planet from being destroyed by an asteroid.

"It was so funny when the rock hit Scrat," Molly said as she skipped along the hall toward the exit.

Jordan raised her eyebrows. For much of the movie, Molly hadn't seemed to pay much attention to it, but as they went back to the car, she went on and on about every little nonsensical detail. She shook her head. Kids were a mystery.

"So, is the rat your favorite character?"

Molly laughed as if Jordan had made the funniest joke ever. "He's a squirrel, not a rat."

"Oh, yeah. Of course. My mistake. So, is he your favorite?"

"Nooo." Molly shook her head.

"Then who is it?" As they reached the Prius, Jordan unlocked it and opened the door for the girl.

Molly climbed onto the booster seat in the back of the car and seemed to think about it for a moment. "Shira."

Jordan had to smile. She should have known. Of course Molly would love the saber-toothed tiger that had been voiced by Jennifer Lopez. "You've got good taste, kid."

As Jordan got behind the wheel and started the car, she glanced in the rearview mirror. "How about some lunch?"

Molly shook her head. "I'm not hungry."

Well, after that bucket of popcorn, that wasn't surprising. But what else was she supposed to do with the kid? She still had at least two more hours to kill before it was time to take her home.

Her genius idea about the movie theater had turned out not to be so genius after all. How else could she keep Molly occupied?

Think, think, think! What had she liked to do as a child? She immediately dismissed the first two ideas that came to mind, climbing trees and beating up the boys who thought they could order her around.

She fondly remembered the summer they had lived in Italy. She and her sisters had spent so much time at the beach that her mother had joked about them growing webbings. Little had she known that fifteen-year-old Jordan had mostly gone so she could admire the girls at the beach. Well, that and eat ice cream.

Ice cream! That's it! The child who couldn't be entertained by ice cream had yet to be born. "I know you said you're not hungry, but…could I interest you in a trip to the ice cream parlor?" she asked, watching Molly's reaction in the rearview mirror.

Molly let out a squeal. "We're going to get ice cream? Really?"

Jordan couldn't help smiling at her enthusiasm. So she had guessed right. "Really." She changed course and drove toward the nearest ice cream parlor.

The kid immediately started to chatter about what ice cream flavor she would be getting, listing her many favorites.

By the time they had finally found a parking space, she still hadn't made a decision. Jordan chuckled to herself. Just choosing an ice cream flavor—much less eating it—would probably keep her busy until two.

The scent of warm chocolate, freshly pressed waffles, and roasted nuts wafted toward them when Jordan opened the door of The Scoop.

"Yum," Molly said, her nose up in the air. Then her gaze went to the long glass case with dozens of metal tubs of ice cream and several containers of toppings. Her eyes went wide.

Jordan laughed. She might have to call Emma and tell her they were going to be late.

A middle-aged woman stood behind the counter. Her lips were pressed together as she watched them approach, without even a hint of a smile.

What the hell was her problem? It wasn't because she—a black woman—had entered the store with a little white girl, was it? *Oh please. Not today.* Jordan didn't want anything to spoil Molly's fun.

"What can I get you?" the woman asked, still not smiling.

"How about a scoop of strawberry in a cup, with a little cut-up fruit sprinkled over it?" Jordan suggested, remembering that Emma had said she normally tried to feed the kid vegetables, fruit, and salad every day.

Molly scrunched up her nose. "I hate strawberry."

"Pineapple?" Jordan said hopefully.

The girl shook her head, making her pigtails fly left and right. Her nose nearly pressed to the glass, she stood on tiptoe and studied the metal containers of ice cream as if world peace depended on her making the right choice.

A blender whirred somewhere in the back, then went silent, and a second vendor stepped out of another room.

Jordan immediately recognized her. They had met at the gym last year and had slept together once or twice, but after switching to the gym at her squash court, Jordan hadn't seen her again. "Hi, Kimberly. I didn't know you worked here."

Kimberly stopped, a tall glass of milkshake clutched in her hands. "Oh. Hi." She looked startled. Was she just surprised to see Jordan here, or hadn't she expected her to remember her name?

For some reason, she got that reaction every now and then, and it always annoyed her. Just because she wasn't in the market for a long-term relationship didn't mean she was an asshole who treated the women she slept with like interchangeable objects and didn't even care about them enough to remember their names.

Kimberly's gaze went from Jordan to Molly and back. "Wow, I... I had no idea you have a child."

Her colleague nudged her with an elbow. "It's not hers, stupid," she said, not even trying to lower her voice. "Are you blind? She's the nanny."

The nanny? Jordan couldn't believe her ears. The woman seriously thought she was Molly's nanny? *Do I look like a nanny?*

To the ice cream vendor, she probably did. In her book, black women who bought ice cream for little white girls had to be the nanny. Never mind that she had a medical degree from Johns Hopkins University and made five times as much as Molly's mom. The color of her skin was enough for the woman to assume she had to be the nanny.

Jordan gritted her teeth. *Don't react. If you do, she'll take it as a confirmation that you're just an angry, loud black woman.*

"Nooo." Molly laughed as if the vendor's idea of Jordan as her nanny was absurd. "She's not my nanny. That's Jordan. She's my friend."

A lump formed in Jordan's throat. For a second, she was ready to buy the kid every last flavor in this damn ice cream parlor.

The older vendor huffed, took the milkshake from Kimberly, and stalked away.

"Sorry," Kimberly said into the awkward silence. "Um, what happened to your arm?"

"She got hurt when she climbed the tree to get Mouse down for me," Molly said and gently touched Jordan's cast.

"Well, I'd say she deserves some ice cream, then, don't you think?" Kimberly said.

Molly nodded.

"So, what do you like?" Kimberly looked at Jordan with a flirty smile. "And don't tell me you prefer vanilla."

"Nope. I'm definitely not a vanilla type of girl." Jordan was tempted to flirt a little more, but not in front of the kid. She checked the flavor labels attached to the glass case. "A scoop of peanut butter crunch in a cup, please."

Kimberly scooped a generous portion of peanut butter ice cream into a plastic cup and slid it over the counter toward Jordan.

"Thanks."

"And you? Have you decided what you want?" Kimberly smiled down at Molly, the metal scoop at the ready.

Molly chewed on her index finger for a moment. "Peanut butter…or chocolate…or cherry." She stared at the metal tubs for a moment longer before looking up and declaring, "Chocolate."

"Good choice," Kimberly said. "Do you want a cone or a cup?"

Again, Molly gave it serious consideration for a minute. "A cone, please." She watched as Kimberly scooped the chocolate ice cream into the cone. Eagerly, she held out her hands to receive it.

Jordan paid and tipped Kimberly for her patience with Molly, hoping she wouldn't have to share the tip with her ignorant colleague. "Let's sit over there at one of the tables." After what had happened at the movie theater, she didn't fully trust Molly's ability to walk and eat ice cream at the same time.

"I'll pick one!" Molly ran ahead.

"Jordan!" Kimberly stopped her before she could follow.

She turned.

"Here." Kimberly rounded the counter and stuffed something into her pocket since Jordan was holding her cup of ice cream in her good hand.

Probably her phone number, Jordan thought. But when she sat at the little table and pulled it out, it was a thin stack of paper napkins.

"Trust me," Kimberly called from behind the counter. "You're gonna need them."

Jordan ate her peanut butter ice cream, enjoying the crunchy bits in it, while she watched Molly lick her ice cream. Bits of chocolate already stained the girl's chin, so Kimberly had been right. She would need those napkins. "Good?" she asked with a grin.

Molly nodded, too busy eating to give a verbal reply. She held out her cone for Jordan to try.

"Um…" Soggy cone and thoroughly licked ice cream. Yum. She resisted the urge to make a face and bent forward to lick away a bit of melting ice cream that was about to dribble down. "Yummy."

"Very yummy." Molly looked at her expectantly.

It took Jordan a second to figure out why. "Oh. Want to try some of mine?" When Molly nodded, she put a bit of peanut butter ice cream on her bright yellow plastic spoon.

Instead of taking the spoon from Jordan, Molly opened her mouth like a little bird expecting to be fed.

Carefully, Jordan spooned the ice cream into her mouth and prayed that history wouldn't repeat itself and she would end up having to eat the chocolate ice cream while Molly took over her peanut butter crunch.

"Yum, yum, yum," Molly said and then went back to licking her own cone.

Phew. Jordan grinned at her own relief at not having to eat the soggy cone.

When they had finished their ice cream and were about to get up and leave, a small metal tray was slid onto their table.

Jordan looked up. She hadn't ordered anything else.

Kimberly pointed to the two tall glasses of milkshake on the tray. "It's on the house. I'm really sorry for what she," Kimberly jerked her head in the direction of the other employee, "said."

Jordan had known that she liked her for a reason. "Thank you. I hope they're not taking it out of your wages."

Kimberly just smiled. "Enjoy."

"That was a nice lady," Molly said when Kimberly had walked away. "Is she your friend?"

"Um, yeah, I guess so. Want to try the milkshakes to see which one you want?" she asked, hoping it would distract Molly from asking about how she'd met Kimberly.

Molly nodded and pulled the tray toward herself.

"Careful. And let's clean you up first." Molly's face was covered in chocolate from one ear to the other.

Molly raised her chin and held still, obviously expecting Jordan to clean her up instead of doing it herself.

Grateful for the napkins that Kimberly had given her, Jordan used them to wipe off the kid's face. But the paper napkins were too thin and quickly became soggy. She threw them into her empty plastic cup and went to the counter to get more napkins from the dispenser.

Kimberly watched her with a grin. "This is your first time, right? Babysitting, I mean."

"I never thought a woman would say that to me again." Jordan smirked. "But yeah, it is. That obvious?"

"A little."

127

A thought occurred to Jordan. "You don't have kids, do you?" Maybe she should have asked that question a little sooner, before she had slept with her.

"No." Kimberly laughed. "Just a gaggle of nieces and nephews. I learned to always bring plenty of baby wipes for situations like this." She pointed over at Molly, who was swinging her feet back and forth while she eyed the milkshakes.

Jordan grabbed a handful of napkins. "I'll make sure to do that next time." That thought gave her pause. Did she really want there to be a next time? She didn't even like kids all that much, did she?

Molly might be the exception, she admitted to herself as she walked back toward the table. Babysitting her was exhausting as hell, but at least she was no longer bored.

It took three more napkins to clean every trace of chocolate off Molly's face. With each one, the girl became more impatient to finally try the milkshakes. When Jordan finally declared her face clean enough, she grabbed for the nearest glass—and promptly knocked it over.

A flood of milkshake spread over the table and splashed onto Jordan's jeans.

Her hand shot out and caught the glass before it could fall to the floor and shatter, but it was too late to save the milkshake. Most of it was all over the table and her lap. Even the bandage holding her back slab cast in place was spattered with what looked like cherry milkshake.

"Oops." Molly went very still and ducked her head. "I'm sorry."

Jordan sighed. "It's all right. I guess we decided that this milkshake will be yours." She pointed at the leftover glass. "Just be more careful with this one, okay?"

Molly nodded and held on to the glass with both hands.

Another trip to the napkin dispenser was in order. Maybe she should invest in baby wipe companies. They probably made a fortune if all kids were like this.

When she pulled several napkins from the dispenser and started to clean herself up, Kimberly leaned across the counter. "You know, I admit I have been thinking about getting another chance to make you wet, but this isn't exactly the way I imagined it."

Jordan sighed dramatically. "This kid is definitely cramping my style."

Kimberly sobered. "Are you…um…dating her mother or something?"

"No. You know my idea of dating includes," she lowered her voice, "hot, sweaty all-night sex, not family visits to the zoo."

"Yet here you are." Kimberly gestured toward Molly, who was slurping her milkshake, still holding it as if her life depended on keeping it safe.

Jordan froze in the middle of rubbing splashes of cherry milkshake off her cast. "Um, yeah, but that's different. I'm just…"

Kimberly held up a hand. "No need to explain anything. I just wanted to make sure I'm not intruding on another woman's territory."

Flicking a piece of cherry off her knee, Jordan shook her head. "I'm no one's territory, you know that."

"Good." Kimberly reached across the counter and pressed something into Jordan's hand, and this time, it wasn't a napkin—it was her phone number.

Maybe the kid wasn't cramping her style all that much.

Her day of babysitting wasn't even over, but Jordan had already learned three essential rules that should have made it into *Babysitting for Dummies*, if such a book even existed: One, make the kid go to the restroom before seeing a movie. Two, always take plenty of napkins or baby wipes. Three, never, ever give an already energetic child so much sugar.

Molly was practically bouncing in the backseat, jabbering away a mile a minute and jumping from one subject to another that was so completely unrelated that Jordan could barely keep up. Her head was reeling.

She couldn't return the kid to Emma like this; otherwise, Emma would think she'd fed the girl some Ecstasy instead of ice cream. It was time to burn off some of that sugar. Jordan leaned against the car, googled playgrounds in the area, and dismissed a few that didn't look very nice.

Oooh. This one. It had a tube slide. Jordan remembered loving them as a child, and Molly seemed like the kind of girl who wouldn't be scared to try them out.

As they walked toward the playground twenty minutes later, her guess was confirmed. Molly let out a squeal when she saw the shiny stainless-steel tube slide. She started walking faster, nearly running on her short legs and pulling Jordan along by the hand she held.

Jordan refused to let go since there were cars whizzing by on the street. Only when they entered the playground did she release Molly's hand.

Molly pressed her stuffed animal into Jordan's hand and took off toward the slide, kicking up bits of sand with every step.

A wooden fortress formed the center of the playground. A net of ropes in a climbing frame on one side and two ladders led up to a platform. Two twisting metal tubes gleamed in the sun, making Jordan wish she had gotten her sunglasses from her car before starting on this adventure.

Molly reached the ladder. Gripping the lowest rung with both hands, she looked up at the platform, about twelve feet high, and hesitated.

Apparently, she needed a little help. Jordan was just about to head over and lift her partway up or climb up with her when someone said next to her, "Give her a minute."

Jordan turned.

A cute brunette several years younger than Jordan sat on one of the benches, eating animal-shaped butter cookies. "She'll climb up once she sees my son making it to the top." She pointed toward the slide. "See?"

Jordan glanced back toward the wooden fortress.

A little boy climbed up the ladder, past Molly. After pulling himself up onto the platform, he leaned over the railing and shouted something down to Molly.

With a determined expression on her little face, Molly started to climb up too.

Jordan tensed. Her gaze followed every movement Molly made, every grip of her hands, every careful slide of her feet. One wrong step and the girl would fall and, despite the soft sand beneath, possibly hurt herself. When Molly reached the top, Jordan started breathing again and turned back toward the brunette. "She made it," she said and then had to chuckle at herself. She sounded so proud as if she had given birth to the girl herself.

The brunette smiled and nodded. "Why don't you sit? I have a feeling you're gonna be here a while. Now that she made it to the top once, she won't want to stop."

Jordan's gaze flicked back and forth between the woman and Molly. "Won't I have to catch her once she pops out of the other end?"

"She's what…five?" the brunette asked.

"Yeah."

"She'll let you know if she wants your help. They're big on independence at that age."

At least one of them seemed to know what she was doing. Jordan sat next to her on the bench.

"Cookie?" The brunette held out the package to her.

"Aren't they for him?" Jordan pointed at the little boy, who now exploded out of the other end of the slide.

"I won't tell if you won't." The brunette grinned.

Jordan's gaydar started to ping. She returned the woman's smile and added a wink. "It'll be our little secret." Who would have thought? Now she could add playground to the list of places where she had flirted with a woman.

"Jordan, watch!" Molly's distorted voice drifted down the tube.

The wrap-around metal of the tube blocked Jordan's view, but she obediently fixed her gaze on the end of the tunnel.

Squeals—half-scared, half-excited—echoed through the tube, and then Molly popped out from the end. Her momentum carried her past the end of the slide, and she landed in the sand on her bottom with a thump.

Jordan jumped up.

But Molly was already back on her feet. "Did you see?" she shouted.

"I saw." Jordan sat back down. "You were great."

Molly raced around to the other side of the fortress and climbed up again.

Jordan took the second cookie the brunette nudged her way. *Rule number four,* she mentally added. *Always bring cookies to soothe your nerves.*

Her phone vibrated. When she pulled it out of her back pocket and checked it, she found a text message from Emma. It was the third one.

> *How are things going? Has that energetic daughter of mine run you ragged yet?*

To her own astonishment, Jordan had enjoyed her day with the kid. But, truth be told, she would be just as glad once she could hand over Molly to her mother. Keeping up with a five-year-old was exhausting.

But if she admitted that, Emma would start to worry.

Not in the least. She's been an angel.

Now I know something's wrong, came Emma's immediate reply. *What happened?*

Molly slid down the tube again, and when she made it out of the other end, she waved.

Jordan waved back with her casted arm while typing an answer with the other hand.

Nothing happened. Everything is fine. I promise. Now go back to work and let us have fun.

Aye-aye.

Smiling, Jordan closed the text-messaging app.

The brunette nodded toward the cell phone in Jordan's hand. "Your... um...partner?"

So the woman had a gaydar in full working order too. "Nah. I don't have one of those. That was my neighbor. Molly is hers. I'm just the last-minute babysitter."

"Hurray for babysitters." The brunette offered her another cookie.

Jordan stretched out her legs, ate her cookie, and watched Molly plunge down the tube.

The two kids raced each other again and again to see who could make it down the slide faster. Before a winner could be declared, the package of cookies was empty, and the brunette stood with a glance at her wristwatch.

"It was great to meet you. Maybe we'll see each other again around here."

Jordan shrugged. "I don't live here, but... Well, I don't know your personal situation. But if you are interested, we could go out for dinner sometime. Something more adult than animal-shaped cookies," she added.

The brunette laughed. "Why not? I'm divorced, and an adult dinner sounds wonderful."

"Great." Jordan patted her pockets until she found her card and held it out. She didn't let go as the brunette wanted to take it from her, so they both held on to it, their fingers lightly touching. "In the interest of full disclosure... I'd really love to take you out, but I'm not looking for anything serious."

"Me neither. I'm still not over his father," the brunette pointed at her son, "so an adult dinner...and maybe an adult something else...is all I want too."

So she was bi? Jordan didn't care either way. "Perfect." Jordan let go of the card. She watched as the brunette took her son's hand and walked away.

Molly and the little boy waved at each other.

"Hey," Jordan called after the woman. "I never got your name."

The brunette looked back over her shoulder. "It's Emma."

Emma. Wow. What were the chances? Apparently, she had a thing for attractive single moms named Emma at the moment.

Molly rushed past her on the way to the ladder. Her cheeks were red, and one of her pigtails had gotten loose.

"One more time, okay?" Jordan called.

"Okay," Molly called back, already reaching for the bottom rung.

When Molly popped out the end of the slide again, Jordan got up from the bench and handed the stuffed animal back to Molly. "All right. Let's go."

"Can I go on the swing?" Molly looked up at her with big, imploring eyes. "Pleeeease."

How could she resist? "Sure."

"Yay!" Molly ran to the swing set on the other end of the playground.

God, hadn't she burned off all that sugar by now? Apparently not.

Molly sat on the swing and started pumping her legs. Her right hand gripped not just the chain but also Mouse's tail. The stuffed animal's mane and the girl's hair blew back and forth in the wind. "I can fly! Look, Jordan!"

Jordan laughed. "Yeah, you—"

On the next forward swing, Molly let go of the chains with both hands and jumped off the seat.

"Molly!" Jordan dashed forward to catch her but was a second too late. The girl landed in the sand with a loud thud.

All Jordan could do was catch the heavy rubber seat before it could swing forward and hit Molly in the head. She landed in the sand on her knees next to the girl. "Molly! Jesus! Are you okay?"

Molly sat up and immediately burst into tears. Her entire front and her stuffed animal were covered in sand.

In the face of ruptured major arteries and other emergencies during an operation Jordan had stayed calm, but now panic gripped her. *Triage,* she told herself, seeking refuge in the familiar medical term. *First make sure she isn't seriously hurt, then get her cleaned up.*

"What's wrong, Molly? Where does it hurt?" She desperately tried to see if there was any blood beneath the sand but couldn't make out anything.

Molly was crying so hard that Jordan barely understood her.

"What? Your mouth? Your mouth hurts?" *Oh God.* She hoped the kid hadn't bitten through her tongue or knocked out a tooth. Why oh why had she allowed her to get on that damn swing? "Can you open your mouth and show me your teeth?"

Still sobbing, Molly opened her mouth wide.

No blood and all teeth seemed intact. She blew out a breath. "Are you sure it's your mouth that hurts?"

"Mouse," Molly sobbed again and held out the stuffed animal.

"Oh." Jordan held back a relieved laugh. It wasn't Molly's mouth that was hurt; it was Mouse!

The stuffed lion's right front paw was dangling only by a thread, and cotton wool peeked out from the near-amputated limb. Apparently, Molly had landed on it. Mouse might have even cushioned her fall and saved her from hurting herself.

Jordan's heart was racing and only slowly settled into a more normal beat. God, that kid had given her the scare of her life!

"It's not so bad, Molly." She gently rubbed her back. "I can fix him for you once we're home."

Molly's tears slowed. "You can? Promise?"

"Promise," Jordan said. "I'm a doctor, remember?"

"Like Mama." Molly sniffled noisily.

Jordan didn't like being compared to the woman who had been stupid enough to let Emma and their daughter go, but she nodded. "Yeah. Just like her. I promise Mouse will be as good as new in no time. Want to go home and fix him?"

Molly gave her a watery smile and nodded. Snot trickled from her nose.

Ugh. Jordan patted her pockets and then triumphantly pulled out a napkin that had been left over from the ice cream parlor. It wasn't baby wipes, but it was better than nothing.

Gently, she cleaned Molly's face, had her blow her nose, and then stood and brushed the sand off her clothes. She even tried to redo the pigtail that had gotten loose, but with only one good hand, it was an impossible task. Finger-combing Molly's hair would have to do. "There. Now you're pretty again."

Molly threw herself forward and wrapped both arms around her.

Surprised, Jordan stumbled back half a step before catching herself. Her good hand came to rest on Molly's shoulder. "Um, is everything okay?"

Molly nodded against her hip. "Can you carry me?" she asked, her voice muffled against Jordan's jeans.

"Of course. You carry Mouse, and I'll carry you." She bent and picked up the girl with her left arm.

Molly snuggled against her, both arms around Jordan's neck. She was silent as Jordan carried her to the car. The complete silence from the normally talkative girl was starting to worry Jordan.

"Are you sure you're okay?"

Again, Molly nodded.

When they reached the car, she seemed reluctant to be put down, but with only one good arm, Jordan didn't have a choice. She helped her climb into her booster seat and then settled Mouse into her lap.

Jordan walked around the Prius and got in too. When she started the car and steered them toward home, Molly hadn't yet said anything. She was still silent when they drove north on the Pasadena Freeway.

It wasn't until they passed the Dodger Stadium exit that Molly said, "Jordan?"

"Yes?" Jordan glanced at her in the rearview mirror.

Molly was stroking the stuffed animal's mangled paw. "Can Mouse get a cast just like yours?"

"Sure." Jordan was so glad the kid was talking again that she would have said yes to anything, even though she had no idea how to get a cast for the stuffed animal.

"I want to sign it!" Molly started to go on and on about the cast they would make for Mouse and what she wanted to draw on it.

Who would have thought Jordan would ever be so glad to listen to that nonstop chatter? With a big grin on her face, she drove them toward South Pasadena. Now she only needed to smuggle Molly into her side of the duplex so she could clean her up a little more and fix the stuffed animal without Emma noticing.

Chapter 11

DONE! EMMA CLOSED HER LEATHER-BOUND planner with a thump and got up from her desk chair. Her back muscles had stiffened up, making her groan. She'd been so immersed in her work that she had forgotten to get up and stretch every now and then.

It had been a productive day. Despite thinking of Molly and her emergency babysitter every few minutes and fighting the urge to send another text message, she had managed to check off every single task on her to-do list.

Sometime during her last Skype call, she had thought she heard the garage door opening and closing, but she must have been mistaken. If they were back, surely Molly would have burst into the room by now.

When she stepped onto the patio for some air, she discovered that the French door leading to Jordan's living room stood open. It hadn't been open earlier today, had it? So were they back after all?

It was a quarter past two, so maybe Jordan had let Molly stay with her for a while longer so Emma could wrap up work.

She couldn't remember when someone had last done her such a huge favor, especially someone she still didn't know very well. Emma resolved to find some way to make it up to Jordan.

She crossed the patio to Jordan's side of the house.

Voices drifted through the open French door—her daughter's excited chatter, interspersed with Jordan's deeper voice.

As she came closer, she could understand what was being said.

"There's a lot of sand in the wound," Jordan said. "We'll have to clean it out before I can stitch it."

Instantly, Emma's heart started to hammer against her rib cage in a rapid staccato. *Oh God.* So something had happened after all! Molly was hurt!

She rushed inside.

Jordan and Molly were both kneeling in front of the low coffee table that served as some kind of operating table. Emma couldn't see what exactly was being stitched up because Jordan's athletic back blocked her view.

She crossed the room in two more hurried steps. "Molly!"

They both turned around.

"Mommy!" Molly jumped up, rushed toward her, and threw herself into Emma's arms.

Emma's eyes fluttered shut as she held her daughter, who still seemed to be in one piece. Gently, she put her down and held her at arm's length to see where she was hurt.

Only then did she realize that Molly wasn't wearing the T-shirt she had put on this morning. She was dressed in a pale green scrub top that covered her entire body like a dress. Other than her unusual clothes, she seemed just fine. No bleeding wounds. Emma couldn't even detect any bruises.

"Mommy, come look! We're per..." She looked at Jordan, who nodded in encouragement. "...performing surgery."

So Molly wasn't the patient after all. Now more curious than worried, Emma let herself be dragged to the coffee table, which was covered in pristine white tissues. On top of it lay their motionless patient.

Mouse had nearly lost one paw during whatever adventures they'd had today. Emma didn't dare ask just yet.

Jordan was wearing scrubs too, and while they weren't exactly formfitting, there was something about the way she wore them—as if they were a second skin—that made Emma take another look.

Molly knelt next to Jordan again, drawing Emma's attention away from Jordan's scrubs.

"Needle," Jordan said and held out her left hand.

For a moment, Emma could easily imagine how she was in an operating room, confidently guiding her team and using her skilled hands to save a patient's life.

Very carefully, Molly picked up a sewing needle from the table and placed it on Jordan's palm.

Emma bit back a grin at how serious she looked while doing it, every inch the dutiful surgical assistant.

Jordan gazed down at the needle and seemed to realize that she couldn't get it threaded with just one hand.

"Need a hand—pun intended?" Emma asked before Jordan could do something stupid in front of Molly such as putting the needle in her mouth while she tried to thread it.

"Have you ever assisted with a surgery like this?" Jordan asked.

They both looked at her with equally skeptical gazes.

Emma drew herself upright. "I even made a teddy bear when I was in sixth grade."

"I'd say she's qualified. What do you think, Molly? Should we let her help?"

"But she doesn't have the special clothing." Molly pointed at the scrubs she and Jordan were wearing.

"Doesn't matter, as long as she's not touching our patient."

Molly tilted her head and seemed to think about it for a few seconds. "Okay. Mommy, you can help." She slid a little to the side so Emma could kneel next to them.

"Thanks a lot, Doctor." She gave Jordan a sidelong glance. "She's got the bossiness down to an art form already. Maybe she really will become a doctor one day."

Jordan grinned. "Don't look at me like that. I didn't teach her that. She must get it from her mother—and I'm not talking about your ex."

Their fingers brushed as Jordan handed her the needle. Jordan's skin was warm and felt good sliding over hers. Emma gritted her teeth, annoyed with herself for thinking such a thing. One womanizing surgeon in her life was more than enough, so this was as close as she would ever get to Jordan's skin.

Her fingers weren't too steady. She needed three tries until she could finally hand back the threaded needle. This time she was more careful not to touch Jordan's fingers with her own.

"All right. Molly, this is the part where I need your help with the surgery. Do you think you can hold the patient's arm like this," Jordan demonstrated, "while I stitch him up?"

Molly nodded eagerly. Her little chest puffed out with pride at being handed such an important task.

Emma craned her neck so she could see past Jordan and make sure she wasn't coming anywhere near Molly's hands with that needle. But she needn't have worried.

With Molly holding the loose paw in place, Jordan put in a neat row of stitches. For using her left, non-dominant hand, she was remarkably nimble. Finally, she studied the paw from all angles and moved it left, right, up, and down. "Looks like the patient is all healed. What do you think, Molly?"

"Can I listen to his heart?" Molly pointed at the stethoscope that hung around Jordan's neck as part of her surgery outfit.

"Of course." Jordan bent her head so Molly could slip the stethoscope from around her neck.

Molly took it without hesitation. Her daughter had never been shy, even around strangers, but it still surprised Emma how casually Molly touched Jordan's shoulders as she took the stethoscope. Apparently, they had bonded today. Molly fumbled with the earpieces for a moment before managing to slip them into her ears.

Jordan watched her with a smile. "The other way around." She helped her put the earpieces in the right way. "And then you put the bell of the stethoscope in your hand to warm it up a little so it's not so cold when you put it on Mouse's chest."

Molly took the metal disc into both of her hands. "One, two, three," she said, showing off her ability to count. She pressed the bell of the stethoscope to the lion's chest, listened with an intent expression, and finally pulled the earpieces out of her ears. "All healed," she declared.

They high-fived each other.

"So the patient doesn't need a cast after all, Dr. Larson?" Jordan asked.

Molly put a finger in her mouth, which she sometimes did when she was debating the pros and cons of a decision. "Maybe he is a little not healed."

Jordan grinned, wrapped a bandage around the lion's paw, and then handed him over to Molly for inspection.

"Hmm." Molly turned the wrapped paw this way and that. She knocked on the bandaged limb and then, more gently, on the slab of plaster beneath Jordan's bandage. "But it's not hard like yours. It's not a real cast."

"Um…" Jordan scratched her head and sent Emma an imploring gaze. "Help," she whispered to her.

"Yes, it is, honey. It's a special lion cast while Jordan has a cast for humans."

Molly looked skeptical for a moment before nodding. "Can we still sign the special lion cast?"

"Of course." With the fabric markers she had gotten Molly last Christmas, that shouldn't be a problem. "Want to go over and do it?" She pointed to their side of the house.

"Yes!" Molly ran to the door, but Emma quickly blocked it.

"Aren't you forgetting something? Have you said thank you to Jordan for taking you to see *Ice Age*?"

Mouse still clutched in one hand, Molly ran back to Jordan and hugged her. "Thank you."

Was it just her imagination, or did Jordan look a little less awkward than before at being hugged by a little child?

Molly let go and skipped out the door.

Emma and Jordan both watched her go and then turned toward each other.

"I can't thank you enough for watching her," Emma said. "You really were a lifesaver."

"That's what we surgeons do," Jordan said with a grin. "Save lives, right?"

The mention of surgeons in general made Emma stiffen, but she tried to brush it off and remind herself that Jordan wasn't Chloe. "I guess."

"How did it go with your new client?"

A smile chased away Emma's tension. "Great. He hired me. Just on a trial basis for now, but it's promising."

Jordan gave her an encouraging nod. "You'll blow his socks off with your mad VA'ing skills."

That kind of trust in her felt good. "Thanks." She looked over her shoulder. "I'd better go before Molly finds the fabric markers by herself and tests them out on the couch. Thanks again. I owe you."

Jordan waved her away. "It really was my pleasure."

They nodded at each other, then Emma hurried after Molly to get the fabric markers and to find out what her daughter and their neighbor had been up to today.

Finally! It had taken ages for Molly to settle down and fall asleep. She had gone on and on about her day with Jordan until the moment her eyes had fallen shut.

Emma got up from the edge of the bed and tiptoed out of the room. At the door, she glanced back.

Her daughter was sound asleep, using Mouse and his newly signed special cast as her pillow.

When she entered the living room, dusk was already falling. She walked up to the French door and peered outside. In the fading light, she could make out Jordan lounging in the hammock, one of her long legs hanging out so she could keep swaying a little.

Emma laughed to herself. Jordan was probably just as worn out as her daughter. She deserved some peace and quiet, but Emma also wanted to thank her again after everything Molly had told her about her day with Jordan.

She got two beers from the fridge and stepped outside, leaving the French door open so she would hear if Molly got up and was looking for her.

Jordan stopped swaying and looked up at her as she walked over.

"I thought you could use this." Emma held out one of the beers. "Or are you still taking painkillers?"

"Not today. I was on duty."

Emma understood. Jordan hadn't wanted to take anything while she was responsible for Molly. A new wave of gratefulness gripped her, mixed with a bit of guilt. She admitted to herself that she had misjudged Jordan. Just because she wasn't the commitment type didn't mean she was selfish and irresponsible.

She pressed the beer into Jordan's hand. "Um, do you mind some company, or would you rather be alone and enjoy the quiet?"

"No, that's fine. Stay, please. I'd love to have a beer with you."

Emma settled down cross-legged in the grass next to the hammock.

They took a sip of beer and listened to the crickets.

"So," they both said at the same time.

Jordan gestured at her to go first.

"How did things really go today?" Emma asked. "And don't try that she-was-a-total-angel spiel again. I know my daughter. When she gets overexcited, she can be quite a handful."

"It was fine, really."

Emma gave her *the* look—the one that usually made Molly stop whatever she was doing. "Mouse nearly lost his paw; Molly had more sand in her hair than the Sahara, and if I'm not mistaken, your cast acquired a few interesting-looking stains today."

Jordan rubbed her cast on the scrub pants she was still wearing as if that could remove the stains. "So you want the truth, hmm?"

"Of course. I can take it. I've lived with that bundle of energy all her life, and I admit I've had moments where the thought 'just thirteen more years' might have crossed my mind."

The sound of Jordan's soft laughter made Emma smile in return.

"It really was fine," Jordan said. "But oh my God, she's got more energy than a nuclear plant! Of course," she added with a sheepish grin, "that could have to do with me feeding her popcorn, soda, ice cream, and a milkshake."

"Jeez, no wonder she was on such a sugar high." Emma shook her head. "Typical rookie mistake. You're a doctor; shouldn't you know better?"

"Guess I wasn't thinking with my doctor brain. But at least she didn't puke, and she had fun. Well, I think she did. It kind of ended on a down note when she decided she could fly and jumped off the swing. That's when Mouse lost his paw."

Emma sighed. "She really has no sense of danger sometimes. Once, she tried to jump down from on top of a slide, just to show me that she could do it. It wasn't a very high one, but still she could have gotten hurt if I hadn't stopped her. And let's not even mention her climbing up the mulberry tree." She shuddered at the thought and then pushed it away. "But she did have fun today. I think you rank up there with a day at Disneyland now, and that's the highest praise in her book."

Jordan's very white teeth flashed against the darkening sky. "I rank higher than Disney?"

"Jeez, I shouldn't have mentioned that. As if you aren't already arrogant enough." Emma hoped her tone made it clear that she was only teasing.

"Confident," Jordan said.

"Well, Miss Confident, I said you rank up there with Disney, not that you top the list."

"Details, details. That will teach you to never, ever doubt my babysitting skills again. They are top-notch, baby." Jordan polished her nails on her scrub top.

"Umm… Do I need to mention popcorn and soda and ice cream and milkshake, which, by the looks of it, ended up mostly all over your cast?"

"Hey, I didn't buy her that milkshake."

"No?"

Jordan sighed and took a long pull of beer. "We got it on the house as an apology for the vendor mistaking me for Molly's nanny."

"Her nanny? Why would he or she think that?"

"Apparently, I look like a nanny." Jordan's full lips formed a bitter line.

Emma let her gaze wander over Jordan's body: the casual yet confident pose, the secure grip her strong hand had on the beer bottle, her dark flashing eyes, and her short hair. "Um, no, you don't. Most of the babysitters I had so far were teenagers or students who were short on cash. I'm pretty sure the jeans you had on this morning cost more than all of my jeans together."

"Well, the woman didn't look at the brand of my jeans. She just looked at the color of my skin."

Emma couldn't help staring. "You mean she assumed you must be the nanny because you're black?"

"Yup." Jordan gulped down more beer. "I get that a lot. Well, not the nanny thing, but people making stupid assumptions. When I was a resident at Mass General, some of my fellow residents implied that I only got into the residency program because of affirmative action. Guess it was easier for them to think that instead of admitting that I got in because I worked my ass off during the entire four years of med school."

"Wow." Emma shook her head. "I'm sorry. People really can be ignorant assholes. What did you say? To the woman in the ice cream parlor, I mean. Did you correct her?"

Jordan chuckled, and her tense posture relaxed. "I didn't have to. Your daughter did it for me. She declared me her friend, and that was that."

A warm feeling of pride spread through Emma's chest. Molly could be quite a handful, but she didn't have a mean bone in her body. "I really hope I'm raising her to become an adult who doesn't make such stupid assumptions based on other people's skin color, gender, or sexual orientation."

"For what it's worth, I think you're doing a great job. And after today, I know it can't be easy being a single mom. I don't know how you do it."

Warmth suffused Emma's cheeks. Secretly, she had to admit how good it felt that someone—Jordan—had noticed instead of taking it for granted. "Well," she said, trying not to show how much Jordan's praise pleased her, "it's not like I have a choice."

"Sure you did. Not about the single part, maybe, but about being the mom part. It's not like you can get pregnant by accident if you're in a relationship with another woman after all."

"Thanks for the lesson in Human Biology 101, Doctor."

Jordan gave her a regal nod. "You're welcome."

They sat sipping their beers for a few minutes. Emma leaned back on her free hand and stared up into the night sky. This was the nice thing about being back in California: you could sit outside and enjoy a warm summer night without worrying that it might rain.

"There's one thing I've been wondering for a while," Jordan finally said.

Emma's relaxation evaporated. She had a pretty good idea what Jordan was about to ask. Since they had touched on her being a single mom, it was only natural for Jordan to wonder what had happened to her marriage. *Yeah, I'm still wondering that too.*

"What's that?" she finally asked, trying to sound neutral. She kept her gaze on the label of her beer bottle.

"Why aren't there any fireflies in California?"

Emma looked up at her. "Seriously? That's your question?"

Jordan nodded gravely. "Yes. Haven't you ever noticed? I mean, I've seen plenty of fireflies when I lived in Massachusetts. We also had them in Maryland, North Carolina, Georgia, and Wisconsin, but I haven't seen a single one since I moved here."

After putting her beer bottle down, Emma leaned back in the grass on her elbows and gave it some serious consideration. "It's probably too dry for them here in SoCal. Which is too bad. I would have loved to see one."

"You've never seen fireflies?"

Emma shook her head. "Just in one of Molly's Disney movies."

"Wow. You missed out on a great experience. Whenever we lived in a state that had them, my sisters and I collected them and put them into glass jars—with holes in the lid for air, of course. We called them twinkle bugs."

Emma couldn't help smiling as she imagined Jordan as a little girl. "Aww. That's cute."

"It was kind of magical, like a meadow dusted in fairy light."

Hiding another grin behind her beer bottle, Emma studied her. Who would have thought that Jordan would have such a soft, poetic side? The more time she spent with her neighbor, the more unexpected traits she discovered—and she had to admit that she liked these hidden layers.

"So," Jordan stopped staring into space and turned her head to look at her, "where was that firefly-lacking place where you grew up?"

"Here, actually."

"Here? Like *here* here?" Jordan pointed at the spot of grass where Emma was sitting.

"Well, not in this house, but in South Pasadena, just two blocks from the public library. I grew up climbing all over the aerial roots of that majestic Moreton Bay fig tree next to the library."

"Guess the tree-climbing is genetic," Jordan said, the amusement clear in her voice.

"Maybe. But I never had to be rescued from a tree like a stray kitten."

"Good for you because there might not have been such a charming knight in shining armor around."

Emma gave the hammock a soft nudge, making it sway. "Knight in scrubs, you mean. One who ended up having to be rescued herself."

"Well," Jordan said with a wink and a shrug, "sometimes, fairy tales in real life don't always have a happy ending."

"No, sometimes they don't." Emma suppressed a sigh.

"So it's the homesickness that brought you back here?" Jordan asked after a few moments of silence. She emptied her beer and put the bottle down into the grass next to Emma. When she withdrew her hand, it lightly brushed Emma's knee.

Emma absentmindedly rubbed the spot as she considered her answer. "Not really. Yes, it's beautiful here, but I also loved Portland. I've lived there since high school, so it was home."

"Why move away, then?" Jordan studied her, and Emma felt her gaze like another brush of her hand. "You don't have to answer that if you—"

"It's fine," Emma said. She didn't want to give her past that much power over her that she would avoid it. When she had decided to leave

Portland, she had promised herself to analyze her failed marriage, learn from it, and then move on. Unfortunately, she hadn't quite made it to the move-on stage of the process yet. But Jordan deserved an answer. "As much as I liked Portland, staying there kept me in a never-ending loop of reliving memories. Don't get me wrong; not all of them were bad, but after the way my marriage ended, even the good memories felt tainted somehow."

"I understand," Jordan said gently.

Did she, really? Emma couldn't imagine any woman cheating on Jordan. If anything, it would be the other way around.

"How long were you married?"

"Too long," Emma muttered. Then, realizing how bitter that sounded, she added, "Eight years. Of course, the state didn't call it a marriage back then. Chloe and I got together ten years ago, long before Oregon even had domestic partnerships for same-sex couples."

Jordan gave an impressed whistle as if she couldn't imagine being with one woman for so long. "Eight years. Wow. What happened?"

Emma sighed. "I keep asking myself that. Let's just say that apparently, those eight years and our marriage vows didn't mean as much to her as I thought and leave it at that. What about you?" She realized she had been rubbing the bare spot where her wedding ring used to be with her thumb and quickly pressed her hand flat into the grass.

"Never been married, never intend to marry."

"No, I meant, where are you from?"

"Everywhere," Jordan said.

What kind of an answer was that? Emma gave her a searching look.

"My father was in the army, so we moved around a lot."

"You're an army brat?" Somehow, that fit Jordan. She seemed different from most people Emma had met before.

Jordan nodded, her face in the almost darkness unreadable.

Emma found herself curious to learn more about Jordan's life. Well, if Jordan was to be the first new friend that she made in South Pasadena, getting to know each other was the natural thing to do, right? "Was that a good or a bad way to grow up?"

"It had its challenges, but personally, I wouldn't trade my childhood for anything. The only thing I found tough was transitioning to the civilian world. I really struggled to fit in when I went to college."

"Really?" That was the last thing Emma had expected. Jordan seemed so easygoing and approachable; she would have bet money on her having been one of the popular girls who got along with everyone.

"I wasn't an outcast or anything. God knows, if growing up in a military family teaches you one thing, it's how to adapt to new surroundings, so I made a ton of new friends wherever we went. But after two or three years, my dad always got new PCS orders and we had to move again, so my sisters and I learned quickly that friendship is a temporary thing."

"Wow. I can't imagine growing up that way. I still remember how heartbroken I was when my parents decided to move to Portland when I was fourteen."

Jordan shrugged. "It was normal for us. The concept of having the same friends since kindergarten totally baffles me."

"Do you have any close friends now?" Emma asked.

"My sisters are pretty much my best friends."

Emma smiled. "Despite throwing you off the tire swing?"

"Despite that, yeah." Jordan laughed. "And then there's Hope, of course. When we met, we could instantly relate to each other for some reason, even though she's not a general surgeon and we were in different years of our residency. I recently found out that she grew up in foster care and moved around a lot too, so maybe that's why."

The dark-haired ER doctor with the incredibly blue eyes had still seemed very different from Jordan—crackling with energy and a little disheveled where Jordan was laid-back and clearly paid more attention to her appearance, wearing nice shirts, expensive jeans, and a perfume that always made Emma sniff like Molly did when she smelled popcorn.

"How about you?" Jordan asked. "Do you have any friends or family still in the area?"

"No. Most of my friends moved away, and I'm an only child. It's always been just my parents and me, and they moved to Florida after my father retired."

Jordan tilted her head. "And moving there after your divorce wasn't an option?"

Emma barked out a laugh. "Living within a fifty-mile radius of my parents? No, thanks." She softened her tone when she realized how bitter she sounded. "They have never been very supportive of me, especially not after I came out to them. But South Pasadena was a nice place to grow up, and I wanted Molly to have that too. To give her…"

"Roots," Jordan finished the sentence.

Emma nodded. It was nice to have someone who understood. "Plus I didn't want to move all the way across the country. I wanted some distance, but I like knowing my ex can get on a plane and be here to visit Molly within less than three hours." Not that Chloe had made use of that option so far. She suppressed a sigh.

They were both silent for a while.

"So, where did you live as a child?" Emma finally asked.

"Where didn't we live? Let's see…" Jordan counted it off on her fingers, starting with the fingers of her good hand. "There was Maryland, Georgia, Texas—twice, North Carolina, and some other states that I barely remember because I was too young. We also lived in Italy and in Germany for a while."

Emma was getting whiplash trying to imagine moving around so much. "No wonder I couldn't place your accent."

"I have an accent?" Jordan asked.

"No, that's just it—you don't have one. Somewhere from the Midwest was my best guess, but I also thought I heard a bit of a southern accent every once in a while."

"I didn't know you paid so much attention to my lovely voice," Jordan drawled.

Emma nudged the hammock again. Admittedly, Jordan's voice was pretty nice to listen to, but she didn't need to tell her that. "It's something I do with everyone I meet. Whenever I have a new client, for example, I guess where he or she is from, and I haven't been wrong yet. I just couldn't place you."

"I pick up accents pretty fast. I was drawling like a champ two weeks after moving to Texas."

"Do you speak any German or Italian?"

"Just enough to charm the ladies and to order ice cream, beer, and Swabian Spätzle."

Emma couldn't help laughing. "You've got your priorities straight."

Jordan folded her good arm behind her head. "Yep."

"What about your sisters?" Emma asked.

"They like ice cream, beer, and Spätzle too, but they're not much into charming the ladies. Well, Nia had this bi-curious phase a few years ago…"

"No, I meant, was it as hard for them to adjust to civilian life as it was for you?"

"Probably even harder. I always knew I wanted to be a surgeon, so that grounded me. But Shawna was bouncing around from job to job, never finding one that suited her, until she finally joined the army too. And Nia is on her third marriage."

Emma blew out her breath through her teeth. One divorce had been bad enough, but going through it twice and then finding the courage to marry again… Emma couldn't imagine doing that. "Wow."

"Yep. Compared to them, I'm the steady, settled-down one."

"Have you ever considered it?" Emma asked, unable to keep herself from giving in to her curiosity. "Settling down?"

"Never. The thought of living in the same place, waking up to the same woman every day for the rest of my life sends shivers down my spine—and not the pleasant kind." Jordan shook herself and rubbed her right upper arm with her left hand as if she really had goose bumps. "That would be like having the same thing for dessert every day."

"Yeah, but what if it's the world's best dessert, something like chocolate fudge cupcakes with salted caramel frosting, sprinkled with toasted pecans?"

Jordan licked her lips. "Sounds yummy. But what if I'd want to sample other cupcakes too? I really enjoy the freedom of picking whatever dessert I want, whenever I want. I'd rather have that freedom than be stuck like my mother."

"Oh. So your parents… They weren't happy together?"

"God, yes, they were. Deliriously so. Still are."

"But?" Emma prompted.

Jordan toed the ground and set the hammock swaying softly. "I don't know. I just always felt that my mother gave up too much when she married my father. She was a very talented musician. She plays six instruments, most of them self-taught. Could have done it professionally if she'd wanted, but I rarely heard her play when I was growing up."

"Why not?"

"She was practically like you."

"Intelligent, pretty, and extremely nice?" Emma quipped, surprising herself with how relaxed she felt around Jordan.

Jordan laughed. "That too. But I meant she was almost a single mom. She was the one who kept the family together whenever my father was deployed to a war zone."

"She must be an incredible woman."

"She is." The pride in Jordan's voice was unmistakable, and Emma hoped that her own daughter would someday talk like that about her. "She practically raised me and my sisters singlehandedly. I know she has no regrets, but she gave up a lot. Maybe I'm too egoistical, but I'm not ready to do that."

"A surgeon being egoistical? No. That's just not possible."

Jordan reached down and pinched her.

Emma jumped. It had barely hurt, but Jordan's hand on her thigh had sent shivers down her body—and they *had* been the pleasant kind. "Okay, okay, have all the cupcakes you want. I don't know why I'm defending monogamy anyway. It's not like I had a lot of success with it."

"But it's still what you want," Jordan said, and it didn't sound like a question.

"Yes. With the right cupcake, I do."

They were both silent for a few minutes, the soft melody of the crickets surrounding them.

"Great," Jordan said after a while. "Now I'm in the mood for cupcakes."

Emma laughed. "We'll get you some on the way back from the hospital tomorrow."

"Um, you don't need to come with me. I can drive myself just fine."

"I didn't say you couldn't, but I'm still driving you." Jordan barely needed her help for everyday things anymore, so driving her to her doctor's appointments was the least she could do. "At what time do you want to leave? The appointment is at nine, isn't it?"

"Isn't it in your big leather-bound planner?"

"Of course it is."

"Did I rate the red ink?" Jordan flashed her a teasing grin.

So what if she took her color-coding seriously? It really helped with her job, and Emma refused to be embarrassed about it. "Red is only for top-priority stuff like meetings with potential clients that I want to impress."

Jordan stuck out her bottom lip the way Molly sometimes did. "So you don't want to impress me?"

"Do I need to?" Emma paused. Christ, what was she doing? Was she flirting with her, just when Jordan was starting to behave?

But to her surprise, Jordan didn't answer with some flirty innuendo. "No," she said very seriously. "I already am impressed." She languidly stretched her tall body, making the ropes of the hammock creak, and yawned. "I don't know how you keep up with that daughter of yours every day. I admit she tired me out."

Emma got up from the grass, took hold of the hammock with one hand to keep it steady, and held the other hand out to Jordan. "Come on, then. To bed with you."

"To bed with me?" Jordan purred. "Finally!"

There she was: the old Jordan. This time, Emma was almost relieved about it. Their conversations had touched on some pretty raw emotions for her and probably for Jordan too. She had to admit that Jordan continued to surprise her. She hadn't thought she would turn out to be the kind of person with whom she could have that type of conversation.

Jordan gripped her hand in a secure grasp and let herself be pulled out of the hammock.

Her momentum brought them within inches of each other, their hands still clasped. Jordan's heady scent surrounded Emma, inspiring stupid thoughts about what it would feel like to lift up on her tiptoes and kiss her good night.

Are you out of your mind? She's not a one-cupcake woman, remember? Quickly, she pulled her hand from Jordan's and took a step back. "How about eight?"

"Um, eight what?" Jordan blinked down at her.

"Eight o'clock. Tomorrow." Emma shook herself out of her daze. "That should give us enough time to make it to the hospital, even if traffic is bad."

"Oh. Yeah. Eight. Sounds great. I'll bring coffee."

"Deal. Good night." Emma went inside and closed the French door without allowing herself to look back.

Chapter 12

WHAT ON EARTH WAS TAKING so long? Getting X-rays of Jordan's arm had gone much faster last week, hadn't it? Emma peeked out of the waiting room, but there was still no sign of Jordan. God, she hoped her wrist was healing properly. Surely someone would have come and told her if there was something wrong and Jordan had to have surgery after all...

A scrub-clad woman walked down the corridor.

Emma tensed, but then she recognized her as Jordan's friend Hope, who paused when she saw her. "Um, hi. Emma, right?"

Emma nodded, impressed that Hope had remembered. That was quite a feat, considering how many women she probably saw Jordan with.

"Are you here with Jordan?" Hope asked.

"Yes. She's getting her full cast today."

"I know," Hope said. "That's why I came up."

Jordan rounded the corner and strode toward them. Either hospital policy didn't require her to use a wheelchair outside of the ER, or she had talked a nurse into letting her walk.

Emma went to meet her. "Finally! Is everything okay?"

"Everything's fine," Jordan said. "It just took some time to get dressed after I seduced the X-ray tech."

Emma stared at her. "You...?"

"Don't believe a word she says," Hope said from behind her. "This isn't Seattle Grace or whatever they call it now. Real on-call rooms don't get as much action in a year as the ones in *Grey's Anatomy* do in a single episode."

"Unfortunately, she's right." Jordan let out an exaggerated sigh. "The boring truth is that radiology was backed up."

"So everything is all right with your wrist?" Emma asked.

"I'll know as soon as my favorite doctor takes a look at it—or lets me have a peek at the X-ray." Jordan looked at her friend expectantly.

Hope shook her head, making her disheveled hair fly. "I'm not your doctor; I'm your friend. Besides, I don't work in ortho."

"Yeah, but everyone here knows you, so can you do me a favor?" Jordan asked. "I need a cast."

"I know. That's why you're here. But like I just said, I can't treat you."

"Oh, come on." Jordan winked. "I let you experiment on me when you were a resident."

Emma looked back and forth between them. Experiment? Had Hope practiced drawing blood on Jordan, or was Jordan implying that there had ever been more than friendship between them?

"Hush." Hope glowered at her. "That was different. Besides, doctors don't put on casts. We have cast techs for that; you know that."

"The cast I want you to do isn't for me." Jordan looked around as if making sure no one was listening in on their conversation. "It's for a lion."

A lion? Emma stared at her. She couldn't mean…?

"Um, you're aware that I'm not a vet, right?"

"Not a real lion. It's…" Jordan reached for the backpack she had handed Emma earlier, when the nurse had come to accompany her to radiology. When she opened it, a familiar stuffed animal peeked out.

"You brought Mouse?"

Hope looked back and forth between them as if they were speaking a foreign language.

"Yeah well…" Jordan shrugged, studied the linoleum floor, and rubbed her neck. With her dark skin, it was hard to tell, but Emma had the impression that she was blushing. "I saw him sitting on the kitchen island when I brought you coffee earlier, so I thought why not take him too? I bet Molly would love it if he got a real cast, not just a special lion cast."

Sudden tears burned in Emma's eyes, and she quickly blinked them away. Probably just PMS. But admittedly, that was a very touching gesture. She couldn't believe how sweet Jordan could be.

A broad grin spread over Hope's face. "I thought you didn't like kids?"

"I never said that. I said I didn't want them. But for the record, I'm a stellar babysitter, right, Emma?"

"The best," Emma said. "Well, if we ignore the fact that you fed my daughter enough sugar to keep all the Hershey factories in North America in business for a month."

Hope laughed. "I did the same to Laleh's niece the first time Laleh left me alone with her." Her eyes shone as she said the name.

So did that mean that Jordan's friend was in a relationship?

"So?" Jordan dangled the backpack in front of Hope. "Will you take care of Mouse?"

"Mouse?" Hope echoed.

"The lion," Emma and Jordan said at the same time.

"Sure, I can do that." Hope reached into the backpack to pull out the stuffed animal.

Jordan groaned. "Just take the entire backpack. I want to keep this between you and me. I've got a reputation to protect, you know?"

Hope chuckled. "Yeah, right. So, what color do you want for his cast?"

Jordan looked at Emma. "What do you think?"

"I bet Molly would love it if Mouse's cast matched yours."

A thin line of worry creased Jordan's brow. "What's her favorite color?"

"Pink."

Jordan winced and stared down at her arm as if already imagining a pink cast covering it.

"Preferably with glitter," Emma added. God, it was fun to tease her.

Now Jordan started to look a little nauseated.

Emma allowed her grin to show. "Just kidding. Her favorite color is actually green."

"Phew." Jordan wiped her brow. "I can live with that. Your patient would like to have a green cast—no glitter," she said to Hope. "And make sure you use enough Webril so the fiberglass won't cut into his paw or make it damp."

Her friend shook her head at Jordan, her eyes twinkling. "Oh, so suddenly you're an expert on how to treat stuffed animals?"

Jordan raised her chin. "I was the surgeon who reattached his severed limb, so yeah, I guess that makes me an expert."

Emma could only imagine the turf wars that might sometimes be fought between the ER and the surgery department.

"Be right back." Jordan's backpack slung over one shoulder, Hope walked away.

For a moment, they were alone in the corridor in front of the waiting room.

Emma stepped closer and lightly put a hand on Jordan's left arm, but before she could thank her for her thoughtfulness, a nurse waved at them. "Hi, Dr. Williams. I've got treatment room four all ready for you."

Apparently, all of the staff in the orthopedic department seemed to know Jordan too.

Emma took her hand away and followed them to the glass-enclosed room.

As soon as the nurse was gone, Jordan pulled the curtain closed behind them and moved to one of the computers.

"Um, what are you doing?"

"Taking a look at my X-rays," Jordan answered while she logged in to the computer.

"Are you allowed to do that? I mean, you don't work in this department, and you're here as a patient."

"She's right," someone said behind them.

A salt-and-pepper-haired doctor had entered the room. It was the same orthopedic specialist who had taken a look at Jordan's arm the evening she had broken it. He glared at Jordan with his arms crossed over his chest.

Jordan didn't appear intimidated in the least. "Oh, come on, Frank. Don't tell me you wouldn't want to take a look at the X-rays if you were in my shoes."

He shouldered past Jordan, sat on a rolling stool in front of the computer, and clicked back and forth between two black-and-white images.

A ball of tension formed in Emma's stomach. She stepped next to Jordan, who was trying to peek at the screen. Before Emma could stop to think about what she was doing, she had reached out and taken hold of Jordan's uninjured hand.

Jordan turned her head and looked at her, surprise written all over her face, but then her features relaxed and she smiled.

Emma wondered whether she should withdraw her hand, but Jordan held it firmly and she didn't want to start a tug-of-war, so she left it where it was.

"The X-rays look good," Jordan said, peering around the other doctor. "The bone hasn't shifted, so everything is still well aligned."

They looked at each other and beamed as if they had just won the lottery.

The orthopedic specialist clearing his throat interrupted their eye contact. Emma quickly let go of Jordan's hand.

"I was just about to say the same," the doctor said. "A cast and a little bit of patience should do the trick." He patted Jordan's shoulder, gave Emma a nod, and left.

A few minutes later, a young Asian American woman entered the treatment room, probably the cast tech Hope had mentioned. "Hi, Dr. Williams."

"It's Jordan, remember?" Her tone was friendly, but to Emma's relief, she didn't seem to be flirting.

"Um, I wasn't sure..." The cast tech flicked her gaze toward Emma.

"It's fine, May. She saw me fall out of the tree, so she already knows I'm not an authority figure who everyone is so in awe of that no one dares to call me by my first name."

"Don't listen to her," May said, addressing Emma. "Of course everyone here is in awe of her. She's one of the best general surgeons in the city."

Jordan squinted skeptically. "I bet you say that to all the surgeons."

"Only to the ones who end up on my treatment table." The cast tech finally seemed relaxed enough to joke back. She closed the door behind her and pulled the curtain in front of it. "So, shall we get started?"

"Yes. Let's get it over with. Someone promised to get me cupcakes on the way back." Jordan took a seat on the treatment table and put her arm up on a padded board.

Emma sat on a rolling stool on the other side of the treatment table, where she could watch without getting in the way.

May took a piece of gauze that looked like a sock that was open on both ends and rolled it up over Jordan's injured arm. When everything was wrinkle-free, she took a roll of some white padding—probably the Webril Jordan had mentioned—and wrapped it around the arm from the knuckles to almost her elbow. Each layer overlapped with the one below, creating a thick padding that would protect the skin.

Jordan observed the young cast tech like a hawk watching its chicks during their first attempts to fly. "Make sure you—"

Emma touched her back. "She's got this," she whispered.

"Right." Jordan heaved a sigh.

May sent Emma a grateful glance before donning a plastic apron and gloves. Her back to them, she turned toward a basin. Water splashed. "I met Dr. Finlay outside. She said you want pink, right?"

"What? No! I said green."

When May turned around, she wore a broad grin and held a roll of dark green fiberglass.

"Hahaha. Didn't Hope tell you not to mock your patients?" Jordan grumbled.

The curtain in front of the open sliding door was pulled back, and Hope entered. "Did I just hear my name?" She looked from Jordan to the cast tech. "Everything going well in here?"

"Oh yeah," Jordan said. "Everything's fine. How's your other...um, project?"

"The procedure was a full success." Hope let the strap slide down her shoulder and handed the backpack to Emma.

Had she really managed to put a cast on a stuffed animal? Emma peeked inside. There he was. Mouse was sporting the same green cast that May was applying to Jordan. Molly would be over the moon. Emma could already imagine her excited squeals. She got up from the rolling stool and gratefully squeezed Hope's arm. "Thank you so much. That was really kind of you."

"Hey, what about me?" Jordan protested immediately. "It was my idea."

Hope waved her hand. "Ideas are a dime a dozen. It's the execution that counts."

God, these two could be like two competitive alpha females. "A big thank-you to you too." Not wanting Jordan to think that she'd said it just because it was expected of her, she leaned forward and kissed her on the cheek.

Jordan's skin was warm and soft. *God, so soft.* And that perfume or deodorant of hers... Whatever it was, it made Emma want to bury her nose against Jordan's neck so she could inhale it. She had to force herself not to linger.

Jordan's eyes went wide. Her good hand went up, and she touched her cheek with her fingertips. For several moments, she looked like an inexperienced teenager who had never been kissed before.

It was such an unexpected expression on her that Emma couldn't help smiling.

"Hold still," May said as she wrapped another layer of the damp roll of fiberglass around Jordan's arm.

"It's hot." Jordan frowned down at her wrist.

Yeah, Emma felt overly warm too.

"That's normal and will fade away as the cast dries," May said.

"Um, right."

May finished the casting and folded back a bit of the padding and the gauze beneath over the edge of the fiberglass.

"Looks good." Hope gave the cast tech a nod and then patted Jordan's shoulder. "Call me if you need anything."

"Sure," Jordan said, but Emma knew her well enough by now to know that she wouldn't.

May inspected Jordan's cast one last time and then, apparently satisfied with her work, nodded. "Make sure to keep the cast clean and—"

"Dry. Yeah. I know the drill. I'm a doctor, remember?" Jordan slid from the treatment table. "Come on." She gripped Emma's elbow with her good hand as if she couldn't wait to get out of there. "Let's get the patient home."

May gave them a look as if she was wondering why on earth Jordan was referring to herself in the third person.

Chuckling, they headed for the elevator.

Jordan leaned back in the passenger seat and tried to ignore how much she disliked not being the one behind the wheel. Emma was a good driver, so she couldn't complain. As she stretched out her legs, she accidentally jostled her backpack, which she had put down at her feet.

Thinking about what was inside made her smile. Was it stupid that she was looking forward to seeing Molly's face when she laid eyes on Mouse's new cast?

"Hot date?" Emma asked from the driver's seat.

"Huh?"

"You've got such a broad grin on your face that I was wondering if you've got a hot date planned for tonight."

Not wanting to admit what she had really been thinking about, Jordan shrugged. "Nah, not really. I'm just glad the arm is healing well."

Emma instantly sobered, any hint of teasing gone. "Me too. I don't know what I would have done if it looked like you might have some permanent damage..."

A rash of goose bumps went down Jordan's back. "Let's not think about it." She forced a smile. "The arm is fine, and I even escaped a pink cast."

They both laughed a little too loudly.

Rush hour was over, so they made good time on the freeway, and Emma didn't have to focus on traffic too much.

"Your friend seemed really nice," she said after a while.

"You mean Hope?" Jordan waited for Emma's nod of confirmation before continuing. "Yeah, she's great."

Emma rubbed her index finger over the steering wheel as if she had discovered a speck of dirt. "Were you ever...you know...a couple?"

"I don't do relationships, remember?"

"Right. What I meant was...um..."

Aww, how cute. Emma was actually blushing! Mercifully, Jordan decided not to tease her about it. "Have we ever played doctor with each other?"

"Um, something like that, yes. I mean, it's obvious that you've known each other for a long time, and I know you don't... Well, how do I say this? You don't seem to be just friends with a lot of women, at least as far as I can tell."

"I'm just friends with Barbara," Jordan pointed out.

"Please! She could be your grandmother!"

"I'm also just friends with Laleh, Hope's girlfriend." Jordan hesitated and then admitted, "Although I did ask her out for coffee the first time we met."

"Wow. I bet that went over well with Hope."

"They weren't together back then. I would never hit on my best friend's girl. Even I have my limits." It surprised Jordan how much she wanted Emma to know that about her.

Emma nodded. "Any other women on your very short list of female friends?"

Jordan smiled. "You," she said. "I'm friends with you."

Emma tilted her head in acknowledgment and was silent for a few seconds. "All right. What about Hope? Are you saying you're just friends with her too?"

"Yep. Not that I didn't try for more." Jordan chuckled as she remembered that day, more than six years ago. "I think I hit on her within five minutes of meeting her—and she shot me down just as fast."

"Must be a record," Emma muttered.

"No, actually, I think you hold the all-time record. I'm not even sure you said 'hi' before calling me on my lines."

"I did say 'hi.' I even introduced myself—and then I shot you down. You deserved it."

Hard to believe that it had been little more than two weeks ago. "Maybe I could have been a little more...subtle."

"A little?" Emma snorted. "Try a lot. If you approached Hope like that, no wonder she shot you down."

"You know what? I'm actually glad she did." As she said it, she realized it was true. "If she hadn't, we would have slept together, and that would have been the end of it. But because she rejected me, I saw her as a challenge and wanted to spend more time with her."

As their exit approached, Emma signaled and changed lanes. She waited until she had pulled onto the off-ramp before asking quietly, "Is that why you're spending time with me? Because I'm a challenge? A tough nut you want to crack?"

Was that what she was doing? Biding her time in the hope of getting Emma into bed one day if only she was patient? She tried to be very honest—with Emma and with herself. Emma deserved as much from her. "Well," she said slowly, giving herself time to think, "no one who's got even one functioning brain cell would kick a woman like you out of bed for eating crackers." She peered at Emma to see how she was reacting to those open words.

Was that a hint of a smile on her face?

Encouraged, Jordan continued. "And it's no secret that I can be a little... hormone-driven at times. But I listened, you know? I heard what you were telling me. You've already got one female in your life—Molly—and she comes first. That's how it should be. So a fun fling with your hot neighbor isn't in the cards for you. I accepted that—even though I still think you're missing out on the greatest experience of your life."

Emma chuckled. "I don't know how I'll survive, but I probably will."

"So, to answer your question, I keep hanging out with you because I enjoy your company—even if it's not in the bedroom."

"Ditto," Emma said. She stopped the car at a red light, and they smiled at each other.

Maybe one day, Jordan would have this exact same conversation with another woman, and she would tell her that she was actually glad Emma had shot her down because it had been the beginning of a beautiful friendship.

One day.

"Done!" Molly declared. "Can we go over to Jordan's now?"

Emma looked at her daughter's plate and had to suppress a smile. Molly had shoved the remainder of her potatoes beneath an uneaten lettuce leaf. "That's not empty, Molly. I know you can do better than that."

With an aggrieved sigh, Molly picked up her fork and shoveled down the rest of her food.

"Slow down! Jordan and her cast will still be there in a few minutes."

Cheeks bulging, Molly reached for her glass with both hands and gulped down her water. "And my surprise?"

"That too."

Molly opened her mouth and stuck out her tongue to show that her mouth was empty. "All done. Can we go now?"

Emma was tempted to tell her they could go as soon as they had done the dishes, but, truth be told, she couldn't wait either to watch Molly get her surprise. "All right. Let's go."

Molly didn't have to be told twice. She jumped up and took Emma's hand. Emma barely had time to grab a pack of Sharpies before she was dragged out the door.

"What's my surprise?" Molly asked as she marched across the patio, Emma in tow.

"It wouldn't be called a surprise if I just told you, would it?"

"Is it a bicycle?"

"Um, no. No expensive gifts unless it's your birthday or Christmas, you know that."

"A pony?"

And that's not expensive how? Emma laughed. "Why don't you just wait until Jordan shows you? And don't forget to say thank you, okay? What she did was very nice of her."

Molly nodded five or six times in a row. "She's nice."

That adjective hadn't been one she would have used to describe Jordan the first time she'd met her, but if you looked beyond the surface, Jordan was surprisingly sweet and considerate.

"Yes, she is."

Jordan wasn't in her hammock or anywhere on the patio, where she normally spent her evenings.

Molly ran ahead and pressed her nose to the glass of the French door to peek into Jordan's living room. "I don't see her." Her voice quivered with disappointment.

"I bet she's home." After their trip to the hospital, Jordan had looked pretty beat, so Emma couldn't imagine her having gone out again, and she had said that she didn't have a hot date planned for tonight. "Maybe she's in the kitchen. Let's knock."

Eagerly, Molly hammered her fist against the glass.

"Molly! I said *knock*, not kick in the door."

Her daughter gentled her knocking.

Nothing moved on the other side of the glass. The living room remained empty. Just when Emma was beginning to worry, the French door to their left opened, and Jordan stood in the doorway of her bedroom.

Her hair was mussed, her eyes not fully open, and one of her cheeks had a crease from the pillowcase. "Hi." Her voice was a little husky from sleep.

Oh shit, was Emma's first thought. Then, not too far behind, was the second: *Aww, how adorable.* With her sleepy smile, Jordan looked much younger than the thirty-four years that Barbara had revealed her to be. She wore only a white tank top and a pair of panties.

As Emma's gaze traveled down her bare legs, her thoughts went from *adorable* straight to *hot.* She reached up and touched her mouth as if to make sure she wasn't drooling. "Um, I…I'm sorry. Did we wake you?"

The muscles in Jordan's long legs shifted beneath her skin as she stretched, making the edge of the tank top slide up.

Je-sus! Emma tore her gaze away before they had to drive back to the ER—this time for a heatstroke.

"Wake me?" Jordan gave her an amused smile. "You probably woke half of South Pasadena."

"Sorry. I guess…uh…Molly got a little carried away." Her brain refused to form more words. God, what was wrong with her? Was she suddenly channeling Jordan? It was just a pair of legs. Naked legs. Gorgeous legs. But still… She saw more bare skin on the covers of her romance-writing clients' books every day, and she had already seen Jordan in her underwear when she had helped her undress. Seeing her in her sleep attire shouldn't be a big deal. "We…um… We'll come back later."

"Nah. It's all right. It was just a little nap. I'm actually glad you woke me, or I wouldn't have gotten any sleep tonight." Jordan stepped back, clearing the doorway. She looked wide-awake now, as if she hadn't been asleep a minute ago. "Come on in. I bet you're here for the surprise."

"Yes!" Molly pushed past Emma and stepped into Jordan's bedroom as if this were the most normal thing in the world. "And your cast. Can I put my name on it?"

"Sure." Jordan reached for a pair of sweatpants on the dresser and pulled them up her long legs.

Emma didn't know whether to be relieved or disappointed. Slowly, she followed Molly inside.

"Here it is." Jordan sat on the edge of the unmade bed. As she held up her cast, the wide armhole of her tank top, necessary to fit over her cast, revealed a glimpse of her braless breast.

Wow. They had come over so Molly could get her surprise, and now Emma was the one who had gotten one first. She tried not to ogle Jordan and valiantly kept her gaze on the shiny hardwood floor.

"Mommy! Moooommy!" Molly waved her hand as if she had called Emma several times already. "Can I have the pen?"

"Oh. Sure." Emma held out the markers.

Molly picked the red one and carefully signed her name in big letters across the top of the cast before switching to the black marker. With the tip of her tongue poking out from between her lips, she added a little drawing.

When she was done, Jordan studied her cast. She pointed at what looked like a stick figure. "Is that me?"

"Nooo. That's a tree."

"Oh. Sure. I can see it now."

"Wait, I'll draw the berries." Using the red marker, Molly added little dots all over the tree.

It did look like a stick figure with chickenpox, but Emma bit her lip and didn't say anything.

Jordan grinned at her over the top of Molly's head, apparently thinking the same.

"There." Molly had added a big red heart on the other side of her name.

A heart... Oh, Molly. It was cute, and Emma loved how easily her daughter showed her affection, but at the same time, she couldn't help worrying. *Please, please don't get too attached.*

If Jordan's track record remained true, she would move away eventually, or she would fade from their lives once her arm healed and she went back to work. After Molly had already had to say good-bye to her other mother, Emma didn't want anyone else to hurt her.

She raised her gaze to Jordan's face to see how she would react to that sign of Molly's affection.

Jordan stared down at the red heart. She swallowed and smacked her lips as if her mouth had gone dry. The smooth-talking womanizer was speechless.

If circumstances had been different, Emma would have found it amusing.

Jordan cleared her throat. "Thank you, Molly. My cast was a little bare. It looks much nicer now."

"Mommy can put something on it too. Then it will look even better. Here, Mommy." Molly extended the black marker toward her.

Emma took it. With Jordan sitting on the bed and her standing, she wouldn't be able to reach the cast very well, so she went down on one knee. As she slid closer, her other knee brushed the outside of Jordan's thigh. Emma pressed her lips together and tried to ignore the leg resting against hers.

Jordan put her arm on her lap so she could hold it still.

Very aware of Jordan's closeness, Emma gripped the marker and signed her name on the green fiberglass. "There."

She wanted to stand and get some distance, but Molly shook her head. "You have to draw something too."

Emma added two dots and a curved line, turning the A of her name into a smiley face.

But Molly frowned down at her contribution. "No, Mommy. Draw a real picture."

Marker poised above the cast, Emma thought about it. "What should I draw?" She looked from Molly to Jordan. Her drawing skills weren't any better than her ability to ignore the warmth of Jordan's thigh against her knee.

"Do a giraffe," Jordan said. "I liked the one you did on the driveway."

"You liked that one? Are you sure you hurt your arm, not your head?"

Jordan laughed. "Okay, I admit that giraffe was pretty...um, special, but I still liked it."

So Emma set out to draw a giraffe. Under the observant gazes of her captive audience, she made it stretch its head to nibble at the berries on Molly's tree.

"It's eating the berries, look, Jordan!" Molly clapped.

The giraffe's knees looked a little wobbly, and the neck ended up being too long, but it was recognizable.

When she was done, she capped the marker and stood. "Don't say I didn't warn you."

Jordan brushed her fingertips over the flank of the giraffe. "Thank you. She's beautiful."

"She?"

"You made her wear lipstick, so I assumed..."

"That's not lipstick. Her lips are red from the mulberries." Emma heaved a sigh. "No one understands my art."

"Don't be sad, Mommy." Molly took hold of Emma's leg and patted it comfortingly. "She didn't know what mine was either."

"Hey, I don't have much practice with cast drawings," Jordan said. "But that might change in a minute. Want to go over to the living room and get your surprise, Molly?"

"Yes!"

They trooped over to the living room, with Emma bringing up the rear. *Speaking of rear...* She couldn't help noticing how good Jordan's butt looked, even in the baggy pair of sweatpants.

She quickly looked away and focused on the brightly wrapped package on the coffee table. "You wrapped it?" Emma whispered.

"Badly." Jordan laughed. "I needed four tries until the tape finally stuck on the paper instead of my cast or," she lowered her voice, "Mouse's mane. But I thought it might make for a nicer surprise."

God, why couldn't Jordan have a twin sister who didn't run the other way at the mere mention of the word *commitment*? Once she was ready to start dating again, Emma hoped she would meet someone who was half as sweet as Jordan.

Molly reached for the wrapped package but then hesitated. "It's not my birthday yet."

"That's fine," Emma said. "Go ahead and open it."

She and Jordan settled down on the couch, close but not touching, and watched Molly tear off the paper in one-point-five seconds flat.

Unbidden, a memory of Molly's last birthday rose in Emma's mind. It had been just a few days before she had caught Chloe cheating. She and Chloe had sat on the couch in their house in Portland, watching Molly open her presents. As Molly had cheered and exclaimed over every gift, they had kissed each other, the taste of chocolate cake lingering on Chloe's lips.

She'd had her whole life mapped out—birthdays, Christmases, Valentine's Days, graduations. Every single event had one constant: Chloe. Not for a second had Emma imagined that she'd end up here, a single mom, sitting on her neighbor's couch while Molly opened her present.

"You okay?" Jordan whispered.

Emma sat up straighter. "Yes. I just—"

Molly's squeal interrupted her. "It's a cast! A real one! It's green, like Jordan's! Mommy, look!" She hopped around the coffee table, nearly falling in her haste to get to Emma and show off Mouse's cast.

Emma caught her before they had to return to the ER for a cast for Molly.

They both oohed and aahed over the tiny green cast around Mouse's paw as if they hadn't seen it before.

Molly threw her arms around them, forcing them into a group hug.

Great. Just when Emma had forgotten how nice and warm Jordan's body felt and how wonderful she smelled.

"Mommy, can I have a giraffe on it too?" Molly asked when she finally let go of them.

It would have to be the world's tiniest giraffe, but Emma nodded. Just as she finished her drawing, her cell phone rang. It was the ringtone she used for her clients, and she didn't even need to look at the display to know which client it was. Unless it was an emergency, no one but D.C. Pane would call after six.

"I need to get that. It's a client of mine."

"But Mommy, I want to go over and show Barbara Mouse's cast!"

Emma looked back and forth between her ringing phone and her daughter. Before she was forced to make a decision, Jordan said, "Why don't I take her over to Barb's? That way, we can both show off our casts."

Emma hesitated. Should she really allow her daughter to spend more time with Jordan and grow closer to her? Yesterday, when she had accepted Jordan's offer to babysit, she hadn't imagined it would become an issue. She had thought Jordan would realize that interacting with a little girl required too much of her attention or that Molly would lose interest in this fascinating new person once she spent a few hours with her. Neither had happened.

When Emma didn't answer, Jordan playfully puffed out her chest. "Hey, I'm supersitter, just with a cast instead of a cape. We'll be fine, and I'll have her back with you in a few minutes."

You're overreacting. It's a short visit with Barbara, not letting her move in with Jordan. "Okay." Emma kissed the top of her daughter's head, slid her finger across the phone's screen, and strode toward the door. "D.C.? I think we need to talk."

Chapter 13

JORDAN SIGHED HAPPILY. *I THINK* I'm in love. She flipped to the next page and chuckled at the characters' verbal sparring. Normally, she wasn't much of a romance reader and had bought this book only because she had loved book one of the sci-fi series.

But now she found herself reading just as much for the love story as for the political intrigue, the clever plot, and the fascinating alien culture the author had created.

Yep, she definitely had a book crush. Who could resist a woman like Salomen, even if she was fictional? She wondered whether Emma had read the book. Actually, Salomen reminded her a little of Emma. They might not belong to the same species, but they were both proud, headstrong, and family-oriented.

The French door to Emma's unit swung open.

Speaking...or thinking of the devil...

"Jordan!" Steps trampled over the patio.

Not for the first time, Jordan wondered how one tiny kid could manage to sound like an entire herd of elephants.

Seconds later, Molly crashed into the hammock, nearly tumbling Jordan to the ground.

She caught herself with her good arm and scrambled upright to plant her feet firmly on the ground. "Careful, kiddo! One arm in a cast is more than enough for me. Where's the fire?"

"Come quick!" Molly tugged on Jordan's good arm.

Worry lanced through her, setting her heart pounding. Had something happened to Emma?

"We're baking cookies! Come help us."

Jordan, already half out of the hammock, sank back. This kid would give her a heart attack one of these days. Baking cookies didn't constitute an emergency in Jordan's book. Speaking of books... Hers had fallen to the ground. She picked it up and brushed a few stalks of grass off the cover.

"Molly," Emma called from the French door, "leave Jordan alone. Maybe she doesn't want to bake cookies or has something better to do."

Jordan glanced at the novel. She really wanted to know what would happen next. But on the other hand... "What kind of cookies are you making?"

"Peanut butter," Emma and Molly answered in unison.

Okay, that decided it. *Sorry, Salomen.* Peanut butter cookies and getting to sneak glances at Emma while she made the dough beat reading about stubborn alien women. She put the book down.

"I'd love to help. That is..." Jordan studied Emma more closely. She looked cute in her I-wear-my-cape-backward apron, but not even a hint of a welcoming smile curved her lips. For a relaxed Saturday afternoon with her daughter, she seemed remarkably tense. "...if you really want me to."

"Why wouldn't we? More people to help with the cleanup later on." Emma smiled, but it looked a little forced.

"Are you sure?" Jordan asked. "I really don't have to join you. I would understand if you want this time just for you and the kid."

Emma sighed. "I'm sure. Really. It's not you, I swear. I just have a lot on my mind." Now her crooked half smile reached her eyes. "Not a line that you hear a lot, do you?"

"Nope. Usually, all women have on their mind around me is—"

"Jordan!" Emma waved toward Molly, who hung on their every word.

"What?" She gave Emma her most innocent look. "I was about to say peanut butter cookies. So let's go bake."

"Oh my God," Emma mumbled around her mouthful of yumminess. "Is there anything better than homemade cookies that are still warm from the oven?"

"I could think of a thing or two." Jordan winked and reached for another cookie.

"Of course you could." Emma shook her head at her. "Have you ever realized how often you talk about," she glanced toward the bathroom to make sure Molly was still busy brushing her teeth, "sex?"

"What's wrong with that?" Jordan broke a cookie in half, licked her fingers, and stretched out her legs beneath the kitchen table. Maybe it was because they were talking about sex, but suddenly each little move was filled with a sensual eroticism that made the air in the kitchen seem to crackle. "This is the twenty-first century. Women are allowed to talk about sex—and to enjoy it."

The low rumble of her voice made Emma hot all over. No amount of denial could put it off to the heat from the oven. "I know. It's just…" She couldn't explain why it annoyed her so much. Maybe because she wasn't having any. After the week she'd had, she could have used the stress relief. "It seems to be on your mind a lot. Have you ever not wanted sex?"

"Sure. During my residency, I worked such grueling hours that I often couldn't muster the energy to go out with a woman, much less sleep with one. I was all talk, no action back then. Maybe I'm still making up for that, sowing my wild oats. And just for the record, I haven't had sex since this," Jordan lifted her arm that was stuck in the cast, "happened."

Emma let out a low snort. "That's been how long? Barely two weeks. You won't get any sympathy from me."

Interest sparked in Jordan's brown eyes. "So it's been a while for you? Hasn't there been anyone since you and your ex separated?"

Emma shook her head. "For the last year, the only thing I took to bed was my favorite battery-operated device."

Jordan nearly inhaled half of a cookie. Coughing and wheezing, she bent forward and gasped for breath.

A sly grin darted across Emma's face. Finally she had been the one to leave Jordan breathless with a quip. "What? I was talking about my e-reader."

"You're evil, woman. Really evil." Jordan patted her own chest as if to dislodge cookie crumbs that had gone down the wrong pipe.

"Can I help it if you've got a dirty mind?"

Jordan's coughing finally stopped. "So," she gazed across the table at Emma, "you don't really have stock in double A batteries?"

Emma flicked a piece of cookie at her. "I'm not discussing my love life—or lack thereof—with you, Jordan Williams."

"You were the one who started it with your little e-reader joke."

Hmm. True. Normally, Emma wasn't one to talk about sex with her friends, not even as a joke. She wasn't a prude by any means, but somehow, she had never gotten into the habit of talking about her love life, partly because she knew Chloe wouldn't have liked it. But Jordan's relaxed attitude made it easy to talk to her. "I just don't—"

"My teeth are brushed, Mommy," Molly called from the bathroom.

"Saved by the kid," Jordan muttered.

Emma got to her feet. "I'll tuck her in, read her a bedtime story, and be right back. Don't eat all the cookies."

"No promises." With a grin, Jordan reached for another cookie. "You'd better read fast."

It was nice to know she would be returning to an adult—a friend—to talk to and a kitchen that smelled heavenly. Emma realized that she was a lot more relaxed now than she had been before Jordan had joined them. Maybe it was the baking, but she had a feeling that it also had to do with Jordan's company.

It took two stories until Molly finally settled down enough to sleep.

"Phew," Emma said when she reentered the kitchen. "Seems like I forgot the most important babysitting rule today too."

"Easy on the sugar?"

"That's the one," Emma said with a nod. When she looked around her kitchen, she realized that Jordan had begun the cleanup. She had put the batch of cookies that had been cooling on the wire rack into a Tupperware container and had piled up all the dirty mixing bowls, cookie sheets, and measuring cups to the left of the sink. "You don't need to do that. I can do it later."

"I don't mind. It's the least I can do after eating half your cookies." Jordan added a used whisk to the pile of dirty dishes.

"No, really." Emma tried to guide her away from the sink, but Jordan was dragging her heels like a stubborn mule. "Jordan, let me..." Okay, time for an embarrassing confession. "I'm not just being polite. I like doing the dishes."

Jordan gave her a skeptical look.

"It gives me some thinking time. Chloe talked me into using the dishwasher a few times, but I realized I get grouchy if I don't get that bit of time to myself. I know it sounds stupid, but doing the dishes is almost like meditation to me." Her cheeks went hot, and she directed her gaze at the kitchen floor, which, as she discovered, was dusted with flour.

Gently, Jordan touched three of her fingers to Emma's chin and guided her head back up.

The intimacy of the touch made Emma shiver. She gazed up into Jordan's dark eyes. Instead of a you've-clearly-lost-your-marbles look, she encountered understanding and a bit of heat in Jordan's eyes.

From only a few inches away, Emma discovered that Jordan had traces of flour in her hair and on her cheek from when Molly had enthusiastically dumped the flour into the mixing bowl, sending up a cloud of flour dust.

Emma's fingers itched to reach up and wipe away the flour. *Are you crazy? Remember what almost happened the last time you removed a bit of food from her face? Hands off!*

As if she had come to the same conclusion, Jordan dropped her hand away and took a step back. "Doesn't sound stupid at all," she murmured. "I've never told any of my colleagues, but I actually enjoy scrubbing before a surgery. It's like a ritual. While I stand at the scrub sink, I go over the procedure and try to anticipate anything that could go wrong. By the time I step into the OR, I'm one hundred percent focused."

Emma hadn't expected that. Jordan's understanding settled over her like a warm coat on a cold winter day.

"So," Jordan nodded toward the dishes, "do you want me to leave you to your cleaning and thinking?"

"No," Emma said without having to consider it. "Please stay. That is, if I'm not keeping you from something."

Jordan's gaze went to her side of the house. "Well, now that you mention it, there's this really attractive woman waiting for me..."

Emma stared at her. Jordan had a woman waiting yet she had spent the entire afternoon baking cookies?

"Don't look at me like that." Jordan laughed. "She's fictional, so she really doesn't mind waiting."

"Oh. Oooh. You mean...?"

"Yeah. Salomen is just a character from a book."

"Salomen? Don't tell me you're reading *Without a Front*!"

A delighted grin spread over Jordan's face. "You read it?"

"Devoured is more like it."

"I knew you'd like it. Salomen is great, isn't she? I can't resist a headstrong woman like her."

Emma shrugged. "Personally, I liked Andira better. There's something about these strong, honorable warrior types… It might sound old-fashioned, but I like people with that kind of integrity."

"Then maybe you should be on the lookout for a woman like that. They don't just exist in books, you know?"

Emma led her into the living room and waited until they had both settled on the couch before she said, "I don't know if I'm ready for that. I almost drowned, so now I'm a little reluctant to dip my toes back into the dating pool."

"Understandable. But you know what they say. The best way to get over someone is to hook up with someone else—and that's not an attempt to talk you into sleeping with me. I… I'm your friend, and I want you to be happy."

"Thanks." Emma put her hand on Jordan's arm just over the edge of the cast and let it rest there for a moment before pulling back. "I'm not unhappy, you know? I'm learning not to rely on others for my happiness. How am I supposed to make someone else happy if I can't be happy on my own?"

"I agree." Jordan's serious expression was replaced by a mischievous grin. "And if you would take a battery-operated device other than your e-reader to bed, you'd get plenty of practice at making yourself happy."

Emma's cheeks felt as if they were flaming. "Jordan!" She pushed her with one shoulder.

"Ouch, hey, careful. Injured lady here!"

"If you'd actually act like a lady, I wouldn't need to push you."

"I admit the ladylike thing has never been my forte. It's way overrated, if you ask me."

Emma nudged the bowl she had brought from the kitchen toward Jordan. "Cookie?" If Jordan was busy eating, she would stop giving her pointers on masturbation.

"Oh God, no. I'm gonna be sick if I have any more. I didn't think I'd ever say so, but apparently, there is such a thing as too much of a good thing."

After taking one last cookie for herself, Emma pushed the bowl to the corner of the coffee table farthest from her so she wouldn't be tempted anymore.

"So," Jordan said after a while, "earlier, when Molly invited me to join the baking adventure, you said you had a lot on your mind. If there's anything I can help you with…"

"I don't think so."

"Are you sure?" Jordan asked. "I'm a good listener. All of my patients say so."

"Um, excuse me, but aren't they all under anesthesia when you operate on them?"

"Okay, I admit there's not much talking and listening going on in the OR. But seriously, if you want to talk…"

Emma exhaled a breath. So far, she had avoided talking about it with anyone, mostly because she hadn't wanted to be unprofessional by bad-mouthing a client. But D.C. didn't keep to professional boundaries either, so maybe it was time to talk about it.

"Do you remember the call I got on Monday, when we were over at your place to sign the cast?"

Jordan nodded.

"That was a client of mine. His name is—" She stopped herself. Jordan read a lot, so there was a chance she'd heard of D.C. Pane or might even be a fan. She didn't want to spoil her enjoyment of his books or hurt his book sales. "Let's call him…" Her gaze went to her DVD shelf for some inspiration. "…Darth Vader."

A chuckle escaped Jordan. "Let me guess. He's not your favorite client."

"Not by a long shot. But it seems I'm his favorite VA, and that's the problem," Emma muttered.

Jordan stiffened next to her. Any hint of amusement vanished off her face. "You mean he's behaving inappropriately toward you? Want me to pay him a little visit? I'm a surgeon. I know all the ways to hurt a person."

"Don't tempt me. No, he wasn't being inappropriate. At least not the way you think. He apparently thinks VAs are robots who are awake and willing to do his bidding twenty-four/seven. He doesn't seem to get that I'm in my office all the time only because I work from home. He bombards me with e-mails, and if I don't answer within fifteen minutes, he follows it up with direct messages on Twitter, Facebook, and all my other social media channels. If that doesn't work, he starts calling me."

"Jesus. That's like being on call all the time. I assume you talked to him about it?"

"Three different times." Emma sighed. "He apologizes, but after a day or two, he's back to his old ways. He's a workaholic. His entire life revolves around his publishing career, so he doesn't understand that most people actually like spending some time doing something else."

Jordan nodded slowly. "I've got colleagues who are like that."

"How do you deal with them?"

"For the most part, I don't have to. It's the residents who need to work with them, and there's not much they can do about it. But you can. You're a freelancer, right? You could just drop him as a client."

"Is that what you think I should do?" Emma asked.

"Yes," Jordan said without the slightest hesitation. "You deserve better than that."

She paused as if remembering the same thing that was going through Emma's mind: It was the exact phrase Emma had used after their almost kiss, when Jordan had suggested she sneak out of Emma's bed before her daughter woke up in the morning.

Jordan cleared her throat. "I mean, you don't need him as a client, do you? You've got others. Why keep him if you don't need him to make a living?"

Emma had started to ask herself the same question. "I feel like I owe him. He was one of my first clients, and he brought me a lot of business by mentioning on social media what a good job I was doing as his VA."

"So send him a bunch of flowers and then drop him."

The dry response made Emma laugh, easing her tension. Chloe had been the same. For her, most things were a black-or-white matter. Emma had to admit that it simplified life if you didn't take every *if*, *when*, and *but* into consideration. Still, she couldn't help herself. "But what if he'll take other clients with him? If he talks to his writer buddies and starts spreading ugly rumors about me..."

A low growl rose from Jordan's chest. "He wouldn't dare!"

"Trust me, he would."

"So you're stuck with him unless you're willing to risk your career?" A deep line dug itself between Jordan's eyebrows. "That's not fair!"

Emma sighed. "No, it's not. But that's what it comes down to."

"Are you sure you don't want me to pay him a visit? A broken kneecap might discourage him from trashing you on social media." She looked so fierce as if she actually meant it.

It was completely unreasonable, but her passionate defense felt good. "No, thanks." She lightly touched Jordan's cast. "One broken bone is enough for now."

Jordan slid down a little, leaned her head back against the couch, and stared off into space. "What if you made him think you no longer work as a VA? Tell him you fell madly in love with your hot neighbor and now spend every waking moment having steamy sex with her."

Emma snorted. "That would probably make it into his next book. It wouldn't work anyway. His writer friends who are clients of mine would tell him that I'm still VA'ing for them."

"Damn," Jordan muttered. "That broken-kneecap idea starts looking better and better. Is there anyone who could help?"

"Breaking his kneecap?" Emma offered a weak smile.

"No, I mean, could you ask your other clients for help somehow?"

Emma shook her head. "I don't want to get them involved if this turns into a mudslinging match."

"You're too good for this world. I hate that you're in this situation."

"It's okay. I'll make it through this. I hope." Emma glanced at the clock. "I'd better get started on the dishes."

Jordan got up from the couch, and Emma walked her to the French door, where Jordan turned and regarded her with a serious expression. "Listen, if there's ever anything you need... If you get into a tough spot financially, or—"

"I'll be fine." No way would she take money from Jordan, even though she appreciated the offer.

"Man, you're stubborn."

A tiny smile ghosted across Emma's face. "I thought you liked stubborn women?"

"Maybe I should reconsider," Jordan grumbled. "It's more fun in fiction than in real life."

Emma bit back a protest. What the heck was she trying to accomplish—to convince Jordan to pursue her, just when she had come to enjoy their friendship?

Jordan stepped onto the patio and then turned. "Thanks for the cookies."

"Thanks for listening."

They faced each other across the threshold. Jordan looked as if she wanted to say something else, but instead, she took a step forward, back into the house and right into Emma's personal space.

Emma's heartbeat picked up. *Oh God. What...?* Would Jordan do something crazy and try to kiss her? Her brain screamed at her to back away, but she stood rooted to the spot, drawn in by Jordan's body heat as she stepped even closer.

Then Jordan's arms were around her. Not for a kiss, as Emma's mutinous body realized with some disappointment, but for a hug—the lesbian kind, as Jordan had once called it, with their bodies touching from ankle to shoulder.

Jordan's arms engulfed her in a cocoon of warmth and that indescribable scent.

Emma had no time to resist. Okay, truth be told, she had no *desire* to resist. She wrapped her arms around Jordan's trim waist and sank against her as if her bones had liquefied. Her cheek came to rest on Jordan's shoulder as if it was the most natural thing in the world. It sure felt like it.

Her eyes fluttered shut, and all thoughts of work and D.C. Pane faded to the background. God, she hadn't realized how much she needed to be held until this very moment. Her body hummed contentedly, caught in a strange state between relaxation and arousal that she had never experienced before.

Did this feel the same to Jordan? Jordan's body was warm and soft and welcoming, but the muscles in the arms that held her felt taut.

Finally, it was Jordan who pulled back first.

Emma stared at her. "Um, what was that?"

Jordan shrugged and shuffled her feet. "I just thought... You looked like you needed a hug. And that's what friends do, right? Give a hug when needed."

"Yeah." Emma exhaled slowly. She could still feel the ghost imprint of Jordan's body against hers. "Thank you."

Jordan smiled—not that big, charming grin that she sometimes flashed but a quieter, softer one. "My pleasure. Good night." She lifted her hand in a short wave and disappeared into the darkness.

Emma stood staring after her and then kicked herself into gear. Time to do the dishes—and some thinking. *About D. C. Pane,* she told herself firmly. Not about how good Jordan's body had felt against hers. It had been just a hug between friends after all.

Chapter 14

ON MONDAY MORNING, AS SOON as she had returned from dropping Molly off at school, Emma plopped down into her office chair and powered up her computer with a lump in her throat.

Yesterday, she had penned a very polite "I quit" e-mail, and since then, she had deliberately stayed away from her in-box, not wanting to spoil the weekend by checking to see if—and what—D.C. Pane had replied.

She sat there for a few seconds, fiddling with a pen, before she worked up the courage to open Outlook. Her fingers tightened around the mouse as she waited for her e-mails to download.

With a ping, several new e-mails materialized in her in-box.

Emma bit the end of her pen. She wanted to close the program and go back to bed. *Oh, come on. Be a woman.* She forced herself to take a closer look.

Three of the e-mails were from other clients, giving instructions on projects they wanted her to do. She dragged those into her to-do folder.

The next one was from Chloe. Great. Now they were down to exchanging e-mails. She opened it.

It was an apology for missing her every-other-day phone call to Molly yesterday. Well, it wasn't her that Chloe needed to apologize to, and she told her ex-wife that in no uncertain terms. She wasn't in the mood to mince words.

The next e-mail was from her friend Lori, carrying the subject line *How's it going with your hot neighbor?*

Emma groaned. Lori had sent her messages like that since she had first told her about her new neighbor. She ignored it for now.

The e-mail below Lori's was marked high priority—and the sender was D.C. Pane.

The mouse arrow hovered over the e-mail for several seconds before she found the courage to click on it.

Bracing herself, she started to read.

> Emma,
>
> To say that I'm beyond disappointed in your unprofessional behavior is an understatement.
>
> If you can't keep up with the projects I'm giving you, you could have just said so instead of sending me this passive-aggressive e-mail.

Passive-aggressive? Excuse me? She had labored for two hours on Sunday morning, carefully penning the e-mail as politely and professionally as she could.

Because she had wanted to end it in a civilized way, she had avoided going into detail and listing reasons that could be interpreted as blaming him for the failure of their working relationship. Apparently, that had just encouraged him to speculate about her reasons for resigning, and of course, it couldn't have anything to do with him.

Jordan's broken-kneecap suggestion started to sound better and better. Gritting her teeth, she continued to read.

> But fine, I accept your resignation. Given your constantly late responses, it might be better anyway. If I want to stay on the best-seller lists, I can't afford to work with people like you, and neither can my friends.

Emma gave the keyboard tray a forceful shove that made it snap back with a crash.

She jumped up and started to pace. Her greatest fear seemed to have come true. That last sentence was clearly a threat. D.C. knew a lot of people in the writing community, who in turn knew a lot of people.

As she paced, a ding from her computer announced more incoming e-mails. No doubt they were from D.C.'s writer friends, telling her she was fired as their virtual assistant.

Close to tears, Emma bunched her hands into fists. Her little company, which she had carefully built up over the last two years, was crumbling before her eyes, all because of this asshole.

A knock on the open French door nearly made her jump out of her skin.

"Good morning," Jordan called. "Is this a good time for your second coffee?" She held out the mug.

"Does it have any rum in it?"

"Rum?" Jordan paused in the doorway to stare at her. "Um, no."

"Cognac?"

"No."

"Then I don't want it." Emma dropped back into her office chair.

Risking life and limb, Jordan entered despite Emma's not exactly welcoming glare. "Is everything okay?"

"Nothing is okay!" Emma wanted to grab her pen holder and throw it across the room, followed by every other item on her desk.

Jordan set down the mug. "You got a reply from Darth Vader. How bad is it?"

"Bad." And she hadn't even looked at her other e-mails. God, if all of the clients who were friends with D.C. no longer wanted to work with her, she was a goner. She wouldn't be able to keep up with her rent or—

"Do you have any appointments this morning?" Jordan's voice broke into her panicked thoughts.

"What? No. I'll be updating client websites today. If I have any clients left."

Jordan rounded the desk, nudged Emma's hand out of the way, and powered down her computer with a few clicks.

"What the heck do you think you're doing?"

"You can't work like this." She took Emma's hand and tried to pull her up from the chair.

"Says who?" Emma stiffened her body, making herself heavier, and attempted to free her hand.

But Jordan was stronger and practically lifted her to her feet. "Says anyone with eyes in their head. Jeez, stop being so—"

"So what? Passive-aggressive?"

"So damn stubborn."

"Then stop being so controlling!" Emma's shoes screeched across the floor as Jordan pulled her toward the door. "I got enough of that with my ex."

Jordan instantly let go of her hand and regarded her somberly. "I'm not trying to control you. I'm trying to make you feel better. I know exactly what you need right now: a good, long—"

"Oh, stop it, Jordan!" Emma snapped. "I'm not in the mood for your silly innuendos!"

"Drive along the ocean," Jordan finished her sentence. "Tsk, and people say I've got a dirty mind!" Her crooked grin faded away immediately, and she looked into Emma's eyes. "Do you really think you'll get anything productive done the way you feel right now? You'll drive yourself crazy, sitting around, waiting for the other shoe to drop. Come on. You know I'm right. Come with me."

This time, Jordan didn't try to pull her to the door.

Emma hesitated. "Molly—"

"Is at school, isn't she?"

"Yeah, but—"

"I'll have you back in time to pick her up. I promise." Jordan held out her left hand, palm up.

Sighing, Emma slid her hand into it. Jordan's fingers curled around hers. Her grip was warm and steady, and their hands fit together so well, as if they had been molded around each other.

Okay, now you're losing it. Maybe she needed a time-out more than she had realized.

When Jordan led her through the hall, Emma reached for her sunglasses and the car keys on the chest of drawers next to the door.

"You won't need those. The keys, I mean. We're taking my car."

"But—"

"Trust me," Jordan said, giving her fingers a soft squeeze.

After Chloe's betrayal, trust no longer came easily to Emma. "I'll need my keys to get back into the house."

"Then take them, but we'll still take my car. Okay?" Jordan looked into her eyes.

Emma held eye contact for a few seconds before blowing out a breath. "Okay."

As soon as they were clear of the dense city traffic, Jordan stepped on the accelerator. The convertible's engine purred as they flew along Pacific Coast Highway with the top down.

She eased up on the gas and kept her gaze on the road ahead for the most part, not wanting to take any risks with Emma onboard, but every now and then, she couldn't resist peeking over at her.

Emma's cheeks were flushed from the wind that whipped her long, blonde hair across her face. She made no attempt to brush back the tangled strands, letting the ocean breeze do whatever it wanted. The sun streamed over her face as she tilted her head back. Her eyes were hidden by a pair of sunglasses, but Jordan had the feeling that they were closed, giving her the opportunity to study Emma without being caught.

God, she was beautiful. Jordan gripped the steering wheel more tightly with her left hand and forced her gaze back to the road. What Emma needed at the moment was a friend, not a woman lusting after her, and Jordan vowed to be that friend, even if it killed her.

But seeing Emma so unguarded, so vulnerable didn't make it an easy task.

The tight line of her mouth had relaxed, and a slight smile graced her lips. Her bottom lip was stained blue, probably from a pen she'd been nibbling on in frustration earlier, and it drew Jordan's attention like a beauty spot.

She imagined herself rubbing away the stain—and then kissing those soft lips. *Girl, you really need to get laid. Two weeks has clearly been too long for you.* She shook herself as if that would get rid of the amorous thought. No such luck.

"Something wrong?" Emma asked.

It was the first time she had spoken since they had gotten into the car.

"Um, no. You just have a little ink or something right there." She gestured at her own mouth.

Emma flipped down the sun visor on the passenger side and craned her neck to see herself in the tiny mirror. "Jeez. I look like a clown."

You look gorgeous. Jordan bit her lip before she could voice her thought. She didn't want her to think she was dropping her a line.

Emma rubbed at her bottom lip with the back of her hand. When she was satisfied that the stain was gone, she put the visor back up. "Thanks."

She fell silent again.

Jordan didn't try to make conversation, leaving it up to Emma whether she wanted to talk. Apparently, she didn't, and that was just fine with Jordan. She reveled in the feeling of the sun on her skin, the wind ruffling her short hair, and the vibrations of the engine humming through her. This was freedom, and to her surprise, having Emma with her only added to this feeling instead of taking away from it.

They cruised along the highway hugging the coastline for nearly an hour before Jordan started to head back.

She sensed more than saw Emma tense in the passenger seat.

Clearly, she wasn't ready to return home and face whatever had happened with Darth Vader.

So instead of following PCH to where it turned into the Santa Monica Freeway, she took the Ocean Avenue exit and then turned left onto Colorado Avenue.

Emma didn't react to the change of direction at first, as if she had completely handed over control to Jordan and not even paid attention to where they were going.

That kind of trust felt good, especially after Emma had been so reluctant to go with her.

When Jordan steered toward the parking lot at the Santa Monica pier, Emma turned her head. "What are you doing?"

"Since you're not interested in trying out my proven methods of relaxation, I thought I'd give a PG option a shot." She found a free parking spot and turned off the engine. After pressing the button that raised the convertible top, she got out of the Mercedes.

Emma sat in the car for a moment longer, as if reluctant to leave that safe heaven, before following her.

The scent of hot dogs, suntan lotion, popcorn, and sea-salted air engulfed them. Seagulls squawked overhead; waves broke along the sandy beach in a soothing rhythm, and the boom of rap music drifted over from the boardwalk.

Jordan offered her arm, and Emma slid her hand into the crook of her elbow. Despite Emma being several inches shorter, they immediately found a comfortable rhythm. They strolled along the boardwalk lined with snack stands, seafood restaurants, and souvenir shops, circling around break-dancers and artists selling their work to the tourists.

At the edge of the pier, they stopped, leaned against the railing, and watched the anglers for a while. The breeze from the ocean ruffled Emma's hair and colored her cheeks, making it easy for Jordan to imagine how she might look after a night of—

Oh, stop it. Jordan cleared her throat. "Are you hungry?"

Emma shrugged. "A little." She stared ahead, to a sailboat gliding over the waves farther out. "I didn't have breakfast earlier. Too nervous."

"Come on." Jordan offered her arm again. "Let's feed you." She steered her over to a small shack and got into the short line that was already forming, even though they had just opened.

"Um, Jordan…" Emma tugged on her arm and pointed at the sign on the shack. "They are selling hot dogs on a stick."

"Oh, yeah." Jordan nodded happily. "Isn't it great?"

"It's ten in the morning."

"Is there a law that restricts eating corn dogs to a certain time of day?"

Emma shook her head at her. "You were clearly skipping classes on the day they covered a healthy diet in med school."

Jordan laughed and pulled her forward as it was their turn to order. She studied their offers for a moment. Sugar-free cherry lemonade and turkey corn dogs, as if that would make much of a difference. *Only in LA.*

"What can I get you ladies?" the young woman behind the counter asked.

Jordan kept her gaze on the food despite the fairly skimpy shorts and the tight uniform top the woman wore. Today, Emma deserved her full attention.

"A beef dog on a stick and…" She turned toward Emma.

"What the heck. Make that two."

They grinned at each other like two criminals who had just conspired to rob a bank.

The woman dipped two sausages on a stick into the batter and then deep-fried them.

"Do you mind sharing a lemonade?" Jordan held up her casted arm. "I can't hold my corn dog and a cup."

"Sharing is fine."

Jordan smiled. Being with Emma was so uncomplicated, compared to some of the women she had hung out with in the past.

Once Jordan had paid, they sat on nearby steps, where they could see the ocean.

Jordan took a big bite of her crispy corn dog and hummed. "Yum. Heaven."

"You're easy to please."

You've got no idea. Jordan said nothing and just continued eating.

Emma took a careful nibble, followed by a larger bite. Her long, sensual moan made Jordan squirm.

"See?" she said, her voice a bit husky. "Some things are great at any time of the day."

Emma looked at her expectantly.

"What?" Jordan put her corn dog on the paper plate on her lap and wiped her mouth to see if she had mustard smeared all over her face.

"I'm waiting for the inevitable sex reference."

Jordan shrugged. "I thought I'd behave for a change."

Emma's smile made Jordan feel as if she had just finished a successful surgery.

They ate their corn dogs and drank the fresh lemonade, their fingers sometimes brushing as they passed the cup back and forth.

If circumstances had been different, Jordan would have considered this a perfect date. A bit of lemonade dribbled down her chin at the thought. *Are you crazy? You don't date women with kids!*

Maybe having a corn dog at ten in the morning hadn't been such a bright idea after all. The cholesterol was already clogging up her arteries, compromising the flow of blood to her brain.

Finally, Emma wadded up her napkin and leaned back on her step. "What now? Home?"

The look in her eyes reminded Jordan of Molly when they had left the movie theater, ready for more adventures. "No. There's one more thing."

"If you're getting me a funnel cake stick, I might puke."

Jordan chuckled. "Don't worry. I learned my lesson with Molly." She led them past an arcade and two girls practicing up on a trapeze, over to the Ferris wheel that was perched over the ocean.

"Oh. Wow. Are we going up?" When Jordan nodded, the copper sparks in Emma's green eyes seemed to light up. "I haven't done that in ages. My parents sometimes took me as a child. Do you come here often?"

"Is that your best line, Ms. Larson?"

"What? No, I... That wasn't—"

"Relax. I'm teasing. Actually, this is my first time going up on a Ferris wheel."

Emma stared at her. "Okay, there has to be some law against *that*. You've never been on a Ferris wheel? Never, ever?"

"Not that I remember. My dad was deployed most of the time when I was little, and when I was a teenager, I thought the Ferris wheel was much too tame for me. I preferred the wilder rides that made the girls cling to me." She flashed Emma a grin.

Emma bumped her with a hip. "Won't work with me. And I'm paying, so put that wallet away. It's the least I can do…since you're gonna lose your Ferris wheel virginity to me." She got into the line in front of the ticket booth, leaving behind a speechless Jordan.

She stared at Emma's back for several seconds; then a slow smile spread over her face, and she hurried after her.

It was crazy, Emma told herself. Here she was, on a Monday morning, when she should be at home, working and worrying about her career—about to step onto a Ferris wheel.

But when the red gondola stopped in front of them and the operator waved at them to get on, she followed Jordan without hesitation.

Maybe this time away from it all, high up above Santa Monica, was exactly what she needed.

They settled onto the red leather seats on opposite sides of the swaying basket.

Soon, the wheel began to turn, and their car rose into the air, carrying them higher and higher.

Emma peered past the Ferris wheel's metal struts. The sun glittered on the endless panes of the Pacific, and the yellow tracks of a roller coaster curved below them. She glanced over at Jordan, who had her legs stretched out to Emma's side of the gondola and seemed completely unconcerned about the light rocking of their car as it climbed higher.

Of course. Jordan didn't appear to be scared of much—except for commitment. If she'd been in Emma's shoes, she would have put D.C. Pane in his place, the consequences be damned.

Sometimes, Emma envied her a little, but she knew she couldn't live her life like that.

When their car reached its highest point, the wheel stopped as the operator waited for passengers to get on or off.

"He sent me an e-mail," Emma heard herself say before she had consciously decided to speak.

Jordan didn't ask whom she meant.

"Calling me passive-aggressive and unprofessional."

"That little worm!" Jordan jumped up, making the car sway wildly. She quickly sat back down. "Sorry. I just…" She gave Emma a smile that looked more like a wild animal showing its canines. "Are you sure you don't want me to break his kneecaps?"

"Believe me, I had some pretty violent fantasies myself. I might take you up on your offer once I read all of the other e-mails."

Jordan's grip on the metal railing tightened until her knuckles went white. "Um, other e-mails?"

"Yeah. I didn't dare look at them, but I'm sure they're from his writer buddies, letting me know I'm fired."

"Shit."

"Yeah. Exactly my thought."

"No, I mean…" Jordan unclamped her hand from around the railing and ran her fingers through her hair. "Do you have your phone with you?"

"Um, yeah. I always have it with me just in case Molly's school calls. What—?"

"Check your e-mails, please."

"Now?"

Jordan nodded, her full lips compressed to a tense line.

What the heck was this all about? Emma pulled the phone from her back pocket, slid her finger across the screen in a zigzag pattern, and then touched the app icon for her e-mail program.

It took a moment for her e-mails to download.

Up here, the wind from the ocean was chilly, and Emma shivered a little while she waited but couldn't tell if it was actually from the breeze or from nervousness.

"Are you cold?" Jordan asked.

Emma nodded. "A little."

Jordan got up, this time more slowly.

"What are you—?"

Just as Jordan crossed the space between them, the wheel started to move, and their car lunged forward, tossing Jordan against her.

A shot of adrenaline spiked through her, and she made a wild grab for Jordan so she wouldn't topple over the edge.

When the gondola stopped swaying, she realized she'd dropped her phone. Instead, she was holding on to Jordan with both arms, her hands dangerously close to her tight ass while her face was pressed against her breasts. Jordan's knee had somehow come to rest on the seat between Emma's thighs, pressing between them.

Her eyes fluttered shut, and her heart started to race. This time, it had nothing to do with adrenaline. Her body strained against Jordan.

Everything spun, and it took her a moment to realize that it was the Ferris wheel.

Desperate, she shoved against Jordan's hips, creating a few inches of space between them so she could think more clearly. "Jesus, Jordan! What are you doing?"

Jordan slid onto the leather seat next to Emma as if her knees had turned into a wobbly mass. "I just… I wanted to warm you up."

Mission accomplished. Thanks a lot. She was anything but cold now. "How?" she got out. "You're not even wearing a jacket."

"Um, just…" Jordan lifted her good arm and mimed wrapping it around Emma's shoulder.

It was tempting to cuddle up and get lost in Jordan's warmth, but whatever Jordan offered, it was only temporary, she reminded herself. "Thanks. I'm fine."

The Ferris wheel carried them toward the ground. From Emma's position, it looked as if they would be dipped straight into the ocean. *Which wouldn't be too bad. I could use some cooling off.*

Jordan's leg, which rested against hers in the tight space in the gondola, wasn't helping.

Her phone dinged from somewhere beneath the seat, reminding her of what she'd set out to do before Jordan's body had collided with hers, making her forget everything else. She picked it up but then hesitated. Did she really want to spoil what was turning out to be a nice day by reading a bunch of *you're fired* messages?

"You want to see this," Jordan said as if sensing her thoughts. "Trust me."

As the Ferris wheel carried them back up to the top, Emma flicked her thumb across the screen. *God.* It was worse than she had expected. She had ten unread e-mails in her in-box. Her finger shook as she tapped on the first one, opening it.

Jordan pressed closer on the seat, either to provide warmth or to read the e-mail along with her.

The touch of their bodies from knee to shoulder was now comforting rather than arousing. With Jordan's presence next to her, Emma found the courage to lower her gaze and read.

The e-mail wasn't from one of her clients. In fact, it wasn't from anyone she knew.

> *Dear Ms. Larson,*
>
> *My name is Marion Whisman. I'm a virologist who publishes regularly in medical journals and academic textbooks. I'd love to spend more time on my research and less on proofreading and all the other tedious details, so I would be interested in hiring you as a virtual assistant.*
>
> *If you have a few minutes, could we set up a call to talk about it?*
>
> *Best regards,*
>
> *Marion Whisman*

Emma blew out a breath. So at least one of the messages hadn't been a client dismissing her. Quite the opposite.

"Read another," Jordan said.

"We're missing the view." Emma pointed to the ocean glittering beneath them. "I wouldn't want your first time to be a disappointment."

Jordan chuckled. "You don't have to worry about that. And we can always do it again. So, please, read."

With the wind whipping around her, Emma opened the next message in her in-box. Then the next one. And the one after that until she had made it through all of the e-mails.

None of them were from clients wanting to fire her. They were all similar to the one from Ms. Whisman. What the heck was going on? Why were all these academics trying to hire her as their virtual assistant? Where had they even found her, all at the same time?

The only thing they had in common was that they were all working in the medical field, but normally, scientists, associate professors of surgery, and physicians didn't require her services. Most of them had assistants, lab techs, and nurses to help them, or they muddled through on their own.

Emma froze and then jerked around to face Jordan, making the gondola sway. "You! You made this happen, didn't you?"

A pleased half smile on her lips, Jordan nodded. "Darth Vader you do not have to fight alone. On your Jedi friends you must rely, young Padawan."

"Jesus, Jordan! You scared me half to death! I thought all these e-mails were from clients about to fire me!"

The grin on Jordan's face withered away. "I'm sorry. That wasn't my intention. I just... I couldn't sleep after you told me about Darth Vader and how he could destroy your career. I was thinking about what I said in the hospital, that I would love to have a VA to do my paperwork so I could spend more time doing surgery, and I thought a lot of my friends and colleagues are probably the same. So when I got up on Sunday, I started making a few calls, and Hope made a few calls...and it kind of snowballed from there."

"Jordan, you can't just..." Emma forced herself to take several deep breaths. "I know you mean well, but these people," she waved at her phone, "they don't really need a VA, at least not one like me. I specialize in working with novelists. They are all academics who publish in medical journals. That's not my area of expertise at all. I would be about as useful to them as Molly would be as an OR nurse."

"Well," Jordan said with a hint of a smile, "she did a good job assisting me when I operated on Mouse."

The corners of Emma's mouth wanted to curl up into an answering smile, but she forced them down. This was serious. Chloe had had a tendency to take over and try to run her life for her too, and she had vowed to never let it happen again. "I appreciate what you were trying to do for me. Really. But this is something I have to handle on my own."

Jordan stared down at her hands, which were lying on her lap. "I just hate sitting around, doing nothing while this asshole might ruin your career. I'm a surgeon. If I see a problem, I take a scalpel and cut it out." Her gaze veered up to meet Emma's, and the helplessness she read in her eyes touched Emma.

She reached over and put her hand on Jordan's. "I get that. And you *are* doing something."

Jordan gave her a doubtful look.

"Just because you can't go after Darth Vader with your lightsaber doesn't mean you aren't helping. This is helping." Emma nodded at the gondola, which was about to reach the top of the wheel for the third time.

"Yeah?"

"Yeah." Emma gave her hand a squeeze. "But that final battle is one I have to fight alone. Can you understand that?"

Jordan nodded.

"Thank you." She slid her phone back into her pocket but left her other hand where it was, resting on top of Jordan's.

They rode that way in silence until it was time for them to disembark.

Emma climbed out of the gondola and kept a hold on Jordan's hand so she could help her onto the platform too. "Come on, Yoda. I think I want a funnel cake after all."

Jordan pulled into the garage next to their duplex and turned off the engine. It was probably childish, but she didn't want to let Emma go. She wanted to back out of the garage and take her somewhere else, anywhere else, as long as their day together wasn't ending.

Emma didn't seem in a hurry to get out of the car either.

They sat in the sun-warmed leather seats for a few moments, neither of them saying anything.

Emma's fair cheeks were tinged red from the wind and the sun. The freckles on her nose had multiplied, making Jordan smile.

"What?" Emma rubbed at her face. "Do I have powdered sugar from the funnel cake on my face?"

"Um, no." What was it with them and the traces of food they wanted to remove from each other's faces? "It's just... You got some sun. It looks good on you."

Emma's cheeks reddened a bit more. "Thanks. It was good to get out for a bit."

Neither of them made a move to get out of the car.

For a few seconds, only the soft ticking as the engine cooled off interrupted the silence.

"I'm sorry," they said at the same time.

"For scaring you with the e-mails," Jordan added.

Emma waved her hand. "You were trying to help. Of course, you did it in true let's-use-the-scalpel-first-and-ask-questions-later surgeon style, but it's the thought that counts." She reached across the console between them and lightly touched Jordan's thigh. "I'm the one who needs to apologize. I wasn't very nice to you when you came over with the coffee. I took my frustration about Darth Vader out on you, and yet you kidnapped me and spent part of the day with me. Thank you."

The fingers on Jordan's leg squeezed softly, sending a shot of excitement straight to her core.

"You're welcome," Jordan said, trying to sound completely unaffected. "Did it help? The kidnapping, I mean."

"Yes. It's been years since I've done such a spur-of-the-moment thing, but it was just what the doctor ordered."

"Literally."

They grinned at each other.

Did Emma realize her hand was still on Jordan's thigh? Jordan cleared her throat. "So now that we both apologized, is this the part where we kiss and make up?"

She'd meant it as a joke to lighten the mood and distract herself from the feel of Emma's fingers on her, but Emma's gaze immediately went to her lips.

Jordan groaned. Emma's heated gaze drew her in like a magnet. God, those eyes... The copper flecks in Emma's irises seemed to smolder, setting something deep inside of Jordan on fire. She leaned across the middle console and slid her good hand into Emma's windblown hair. Emma's scent—fresh air, funnel cake, and a hint of vanilla—engulfed Jordan and made the rest of the world fall away.

At the caress of Jordan's fingertips along her scalp, Emma shivered and let out a low moan.

Instantly, Jordan wanted to hear her make that noise again. Leather creaked as she shifted in her seat and guided Emma toward her.

They were both breathing fast, Emma's hot breath fanning over her face.

"Jordan," Emma husked out, and Jordan loved the way her voice dipped as she said her name. "This is not—"

"I know."

But neither of them was backing away. Their faces moved toward each other inch by inch.

Emma's eyes fluttered closed a heartbeat before their lips met.

So soft. So full and warm. Jordan struggled to keep her eyes open, then surrendered and closed them as she tilted her head and caressed Emma's mouth with her own. Her tongue traced the outline of her lips, exploring their shape, then dipped just inside.

Emma breathed out a soft sigh and opened her mouth. Her warm tongue met Jordan's, stroking fiery trails along it.

Emma's fingers on her leg flexed. Her other hand came up and clasped Jordan's nape, her short nails digging into the skin, sending sparks of need through Jordan.

Her taste made Jordan's head spin. Waves of heat rolled through her body. She wanted to lick every single inch of her, to consume her. Now. She reached for Emma, needing her closer.

In the cramped space, her cast collided with the back of the seat.

All her senses buzzing, Jordan felt no pain and ignored it.

"Stop!" Emma pulled away until her back was pressed against the passenger side door. "What the heck are we doing?"

"Kissing," Jordan said as she tried to get her breathing under control. Okay, not the most intelligent reply, but it was all she could think of: kissing Emma again.

Chest heaving, Emma lifted her hand to her kiss-swollen lips and stared at her. Slowly, she shook her head. "Not a good idea."

"Why not?"

"You..." Emma pressed her fingers to her mouth once more before dropping her hand to her lap. Instead, her tongue flicked out as if she could still taste Jordan. "You're becoming a very good friend to me. A little sex is not worth destroying that."

A little sex... That stung. But then again, it was all she ever offered women, so maybe Emma was right, even if Jordan's body screamed otherwise. She sank against the driver's side door and rubbed her thigh as if that could erase the imprint of Emma's touch on her leg. "You're right. I'm sorry. I...I guess I got carried away."

"It's not just your fault. I kissed you back."

God, yes, she had.

Emma didn't look at her, intent on studying something on the cast. "Let's just forget about it, okay?"

Jordan nodded and then, when she realized Emma couldn't see it, said, "All right. If that's what you want."

"I'd better get inside. I have a lot of e-mails to answer before I pick up Molly." Emma opened the passenger side door and scrambled out of the car. With her hand already poised to close the door between them, she paused. "Thanks again. For everything today."

Before Jordan could answer, she shut the door and was gone.

Chapter 15

WHEN EMMA'S TIMER BEEPED, REMINDING her to get up from her desk and move around, she realized she had been staring into space for the last fifteen minutes.

In the two days since her impromptu trip to the pier with Jordan, she hadn't gotten as much work done as usual. Her mind had been too busy replaying every second of that trip a hundred times, especially the last few minutes in the garage.

It had been one of the worst mornings of her life, followed by one of the best days...and one of the best kisses.

Okay, who am I kidding? Probably the best kiss. Not that she would ever admit that out loud, especially not to Jordan. She was a fool to have let it happen and to keep thinking about it, as if she didn't have other things to worry about.

Nothing could ever come of it. She knew that. Jordan wasn't the relationship type, and as much as Emma was tempted to say "to hell with it," she wasn't the one-night-stand type. She had never managed to sleep with someone without becoming attached, and that would only lead to heartbreak with Jordan.

No matter how much her libido urged her in Jordan's direction, she'd have to wait until someone more dependable came along—even if that someone wouldn't look half as good in shorts and a tank top.

She realized she had walked over to the French door and was peeking into the backyard, where Jordan was busy rearranging the patio table and the lawn chairs. The muscles in her good arm bunched as she dragged a giant sun umbrella from next to the hammock.

Without conscious thought, Emma took a step toward her but then stopped herself. If Jordan wanted some help, she would ask. Admittedly, they hadn't talked much in the last two days. Any time she saw Jordan in the backyard, she was itching to join her. Without her realizing it, they had developed a routine in the three and a half weeks since she had moved in. Jordan would bring her a second cup of coffee in the morning, and they would meet on the patio for a beer and some conversation in the evening, after Molly was in bed.

She missed that.

Oh, come on. That's ridiculous. You were with Chloe for ten years, and you don't miss her that much.

Granted, Chloe had broken her heart—and Jordan hadn't.

But she will if you continue like this!

Fed up with herself, she whirled around, away from the French door with its perfect view of the patio table and Jordan, and marched back to her desk.

She opened her e-mail program and scanned the messages. Her heart no longer beat faster every time she checked her e-mails. That was the one good thing about obsessing over Jordan and their kiss. It had distracted her from worrying about other clients firing her.

Fortunately, this had only happened with one client. Either D.C. didn't have as much influence in the writing community as she had thought, or he was too busy with his writing to take the time to ruin her career.

With that immediate crisis averted, she had plenty of time to think about Jordan.

Instead of checking her e-mail, she caught herself staring out the open French door and noticed that Jordan was no longer alone in the backyard. An attractive stranger had joined her and was now pressing her slim body against Jordan's in an embrace that looked a little too intimate for Emma's taste. Long, black hair flowed down the stranger's back, and her melodious laugh drifted across the patio.

Emma white-knuckled her favorite coffee mug. She had known that Jordan would sooner or later bring other women to the house, but she hadn't counted on it happening so fast.

Two days ago, Jordan had kissed her with such passion, and now she was hugging another woman as if there were no tomorrow.

What did you expect? Jordan was a female version of Casanova, she reminded herself. Seducing women—many women—was her favorite pastime.

But whenever Emma was with her, it didn't feel that way. Jordan's focus was on her so completely it was as if no other woman existed.

That's probably what makes her so successful with the ladies.

It certainly seemed to work on the attractive stranger in the backyard. The Middle-Eastern-looking woman ran her hands over Jordan's cast.

Ugh. Emma had seen enough. She jumped up, hitting her knee on the keyboard tray in the process, and limped to the kitchen for a much-needed change of scenery.

"Mommy," Molly called from the living room, where she was playing with her Legos, "you used a bad word. Are these extending circustances?"

It took Emma a second to shake off her annoyance and grasp that her daughter meant *extenuating circumstances.* She'd learned that term from Jordan. "Yes," she called back through gritted teeth. "They certainly are."

"Nice horse," Laleh said, pointing at the cast.

Jordan covered the drawing with her hand. "It's a giraffe. Can't you tell?"

"Oh. Um, no. Well, it's not too bad for a little kid."

"Molly was the one who drew the heart and the tree. The giraffe is her mother's."

"Oops." Laleh laughed. "I'm sure she has other talents."

Jordan glared at her. "Yeah. She does."

A line dug itself between Laleh's dark, perfectly arched brows. "You know I'm just teasing, right? What's going on with you?"

"Nothing. I'm just…" *What? PMSing? Overly protective of Emma? Moody as hell because I've barely seen her for the last two days?* She ignored the inner voice. "Sick and tired of this cast."

Laleh lightly rubbed her shoulder. "Hang in there. Just three more weeks."

On the one hand, Jordan couldn't wait to get rid of the damn cast. But on the other hand, she didn't want to think about what would happen when she was fully healed and Emma no longer had a reason to check on her. Their friendship felt shaky right now, so would it survive her going back to work?

Jordan decided not to think about it for now. "So, what is taking Hope so long in the kitchen?"

At the mention of her partner's name, Laleh's face brightened into a beaming smile. "She's warming up the rest of the food."

"The rest of the food?" Jordan gestured at the bowls and plates arranged on the table. "There's already enough to feed the entire neighborhood!"

Hope stepped onto the patio through the French door, carrying two steaming bowls. "There's no such thing as too much Persian food," she and Laleh said in unison. Their gazes met and held, and they smiled at each other as if nothing else in the world existed.

Jordan looked back and forth between them. Sometimes, her friends seemed so much in tune it was as if they were reading each other's minds. She had never thought she would see her friend Hope so much in love. They were disgustingly cute together.

"Maybe you should invite your neighbor," Hope said, pointing to Emma's side of the duplex. "She's watching us like a starving hyena."

Emma? Jordan whirled around.

But no, it wasn't Emma who lay on her belly in the living room, her chin propped up on one hand, Legos abandoned next to her.

"Hi, Molly," Jordan called over.

"Hi, Jordan." Molly jumped up and took a few steps forward. At the open French door, she stopped and eyed Jordan's friends.

"It's okay. This is the doctor who did Mouse's cast." Jordan pointed at Hope.

"Really?" Molly ran over and stared up at Hope. "It's a good cast."

"Um, thank you." Hope looked just as uncomfortable as Jordan had felt around Molly at first.

Now, after almost a month of near-daily interaction, she had gotten used to talking to a minihuman.

"Next time, I want a white one," Molly declared. "It's better to draw on."

"Next time?" Jordan echoed. "I'm not getting another one, and neither is Mouse."

Molly stared at her with sad eyes. "Not even a pretend one?"

Jordan wavered. God, how did Emma manage to ever say no to this kid? *Same way she said no to you when you kissed her.* "We'll see."

Molly squeezed past her to peer at the table. She started counting the bowls and plates but gave up halfway through. "Are you having a birthday party? I have one soon."

"See?" Jordan gave Laleh a gentle nudge before turning back to Molly. "No. This isn't a birthday party. My friends apparently thought I'm really hungry."

"I'm really hungry too."

"Haven't you had dinner yet?"

"Yes, but..."

A smile crept onto Jordan's face. She had witnessed a similar exchange several times over the past couple of weeks. "Let me guess... You're hungry for this food."

Molly nodded eagerly.

"Why don't you go and ask your mother if she and you can join us?" Laleh said before Jordan could stop her. "There's enough food for everyone, and I'd love to meet your mother."

"Okay!" Molly ran back into the house as fast as her short legs would carry her.

"Great," Jordan muttered. *This might become awkward.*

"What's wrong?" Hope asked. "Your neighbor... She and you seemed pretty friendly. She even drove you to your appointment at the hospital."

"Yeah, well..." How was she supposed to explain? She wasn't even sure she knew what exactly was going on between them.

Hope stole a piece of the lavash bread and popped it into her mouth. "Yum. This is great, *delbar-am*." Chewing, she gave Laleh an appreciative glance before returning her attention to Jordan. "Oh, let me guess. You slept with her, and now you're ready to move on, but she wants to play house."

"What? No!" For the second time within minutes, Jordan found herself glaring.

"No? What is it, then? Come on, Jordan. Don't act like in ninety-nine out of a hundred cases, I wouldn't be right."

Okay, she might have a point, but Emma was the one-in-a-hundred woman, and it bothered her that Hope assumed she was one of her usual hookups. "I didn't sleep with her."

"But you want to," Laleh said softly. She studied Jordan with her intense dark eyes. "Right?"

In the past, Jordan had never hesitated to talk about the women she had pursued, but now she found herself wanting to protect Emma's privacy. "I..." She flicked her gaze toward the other side of the duplex, making sure that Molly wasn't yet returning with Emma in tow. "I… She… We… We kissed."

"So?" Hope said. "What's the big deal? You've kissed half of the women in the greater LA area."

Jordan snorted. "You're exaggerating."

"Slightly."

Laleh put her hand on Hope's arm, stopping her from saying more.

"Besides," Jordan said, "it wasn't like that with Emma."

"No?"

"No. This is… Emma is… I don't know." Things were different with Emma, but she couldn't say why or how. Frustrated with her inability to explain what was going on, she ripped off a piece of bread and stuffed it into her mouth.

When Emma stepped onto the patio, dragged by a very determined Molly, Jordan nearly choked on her mouthful of lavash.

It wasn't that Emma was wearing anything special. She hadn't even put on makeup. But her black shorts clung to her full hips, and the aquamarine top brought out the green in her eyes. The spaghetti straps revealed a charming smattering of freckles on her shoulders, and Jordan instantly wanted to follow their path with her lips.

She forced her gaze up to Emma's eyes. The copper sparks in her irises seemed to glow. Was Emma still angry about that kiss? Jordan refused to avert her eyes and back down. Emma had kissed her back after all, so there was no reason for her to feel guilty.

"Hi," she said softly.

"Hi," Emma answered.

Great. After all the conversations they'd had in this very backyard, now they were down to a single word. Jordan hated the awkwardness.

"Mommy, look!" Molly dragged her mother past Jordan, to the table.

Jordan breathed a sigh of relief but then noticed that Laleh and Hope were giving her curious looks. She tried to muster some of her old cool. All she managed was a weak smile.

Growling, she grabbed one of the plates. "Hey, Molly. Have you ever had fesenjan?"

Someone handed Emma a plate, but she was too distracted by watching Jordan put a selection of different dishes onto Molly's plate to pick anything for herself.

When Hope stepped next to her, she quickly looked away and started spooning some of the eggplant dish onto her plate. "Thanks so much for including me and my daughter. The food looks delicious, and it's been ages since I had Persian food."

As much as she didn't want to like the attractive stranger who had apparently made all these dishes, she had to admit that she seemed to be a great cook—and a nice person.

Hope wrapped her arm around the woman and pulled her against her side. "Laleh makes the best Persian food on this continent."

The woman bumped her with her hip, but she was clearly glowing under Hope's praise. "Nonsense. My aunt's cooking is much better. And you're getting quite good at making fesenjan too."

They shared a gentle kiss.

Did she just say...Laleh? Emma stared at them. "Oh, so you're Laleh, Hope's partner?"

Laleh nodded. "Yes, I am. Pleased to meet you."

"Emma Larson."

They shook hands. Laleh's grip was warm and friendly.

Gosh. She should have known the moment she'd seen her with Hope, but her brain hadn't been working at one hundred percent lately. *Clearly not, or you wouldn't have kissed Jordan.*

Emma watched Jordan's friends interact with each other while she put two stuffed vine leaves, a little fesenjan, and some melon salad on her plate.

They radiated happiness. The bitter part of her insisted that they couldn't have been together for very long. Had she and Chloe ever looked that good together, as if there was nothing that could tear them apart? If they had, it had been an illusion.

When they all sat at the table, Hope chose the chair next to Laleh, and Molly had already climbed onto the chair at the head of the table, leaving Emma to sit next to Jordan.

With all the bowls and plates on the table, the space was a bit cramped, so their arms brushed while they ate. It shouldn't have been a big deal, but Emma was overly aware of every little touch.

Jordan struggled to get the meat off the skewer on her plate. Finally, she tried to hold the skewer with the fingers of her casted arm while using her fork with the other.

Without saying anything, Emma took the plate away from her, removed the skewer, cut the meat into pieces, and then handed back the plate.

"Uh, thanks." Jordan looked a bit dazed, as if no one had ever cut her meat for her.

The expression on her face made Emma smile. "Sorry. It's the mom reflex." Her feelings for Jordan were anything but maternal, though.

"So, how's your work situation?" Hope asked. "Jordan didn't want to go into detail, but she was pretty determined, calling me at six in the morning on a Sunday, insisting that I call or e-mail everyone I know right away. Did any of them end up hiring you?"

Emma stared at Jordan, who bent her head over her plate. Heat shot up her chest, part embarrassment at having Jordan's friends involved in her job crisis, part gratefulness at how determined Jordan had been to help her. "They wanted to," she finally answered. "But I specialize in assisting fiction authors, not people writing for academic presses."

"So that didn't work out, then? Sorry to hear that," Hope said.

"Well, something good came of it. I realized that if Jordan is willing to get her friends involved, it would be pretty stupid of me not to use all of my own resources too. It doesn't mean I'm unprofessional or a helpless damsel in distress."

Jordan looked up from her plate. "You asked your clients for help?"

"Just the ones I have a more personal relationship with. And I also contacted some of my VA colleagues, just in case they had more clients than they could handle."

"And?" Jordan's fork hovered over her food.

A smile curled Emma's lips. "And now I have three new clients to replace Darth Vader and the other one I've lost."

"Darth Vader?" Hope and Laleh echoed.

Emma and Jordan grinned at each other as they shared the inside joke. God, it felt good to have that carefree connection back, even if it might be only for a moment.

"The guy who was stupid enough to not just fire her but to threaten her too," Jordan said, a snarl in her voice.

"What exactly is it you do for a living?" Laleh asked.

"My mommy helps write books," Molly said before Emma could answer. "When I'm big, I'm gonna be a writer too."

"I thought you wanted to be a doctor or a veterinarian?" Emma asked.

Molly scrunched up her face as she thought about it. "Can't I be both?"

"You can be whatever you want to be," Emma told her. With a humorous undertone, she added, "As long as you don't become a surgeon."

"Hey!" Jordan elbowed her lightly. "I'll have you know that surgery is a very honorable profession!"

"Yeah," Hope added. "If you can't be a real doctor, being a surgeon is a good second choice."

Jordan put her fork down and mock-glared at them. "Ah, so that's how it's going to be. The minute I introduce you to each other, you're ganging up on me."

"Yes," Emma, Hope, and Laleh shouted in a chorus.

Molly slid off her chair and ran to Jordan's side of the table. "I can be on your side, Jordan."

Everyone laughed.

Jordan carried the last empty bowl in from the patio and added it to the pile of dirty dishes in the kitchen. She looked around. Emma stood at the sink; Hope and Laleh had just left because Hope was covering an early shift tomorrow, and Molly was nowhere to be seen.

"Where's Molly?"

"I sent her over to Barbara's with the leftover adas polo," Emma said. Her hips swayed as she energetically scrubbed one of the bowls.

Jordan tried not to watch, but her gaze was drawn to Emma time and again. "Are you sure you don't want me to just toss everything into the dishwasher and be done with it?"

"I'm sure."

"Thinking time, right?"

Emma sent a quick smile back over her shoulder. "Exactly."

What was she thinking about? Did she sometimes think of the kiss they had shared? "Emma..."

"Jordan, listen..."

They spoke at the same time.

Emma turned away from the sink so she could look at Jordan. Foam ran down her fingers and dripped onto the tiles.

Without looking away from Emma's eyes, Jordan handed her a dish towel and gestured for her to go first.

Emma dried her hands and then bunched the towel into a ball, kneading it between her fingers. "I hate this," she burst out. Her eyes widened as if she had surprised herself with her words.

Jordan swallowed. "Hate…what? Living here? Having dinner with me and my friends?"

"No. God, no. I love living here, and your friends are very nice." Emma directed her gaze at the floor for a moment and then peeked up through lowered lashes. "And so are you."

Nice… Jordan mentally repeated the word. It should have sounded positive, but somehow, the compliment fell flat. She wanted to be much more to Emma than just *nice*.

"I hate that we can barely look each other in the eyes," Emma added. "I hate that we're tiptoeing around each other, careful not to go into the backyard at the same time."

Jordan exhaled. "Yeah. I hate that too."

"If we both hate it, why are we behaving like this? It's silly. It was just a kiss, right? Not worth all this drama."

Jordan forced a smile. "I beg to differ. It wasn't just a kiss. It was an *awesome* kiss, rating at least a hundred on a scale from one to ten."

Emma chuckled. "All right, I admit it. It was…okayish."

"Okayish?" Jordan drew out the word.

"Yes. I didn't suffer too much."

"You!" Jordan dug the fingers of her good hand into Emma's ribs and started tickling her.

Squirming and laughing hysterically, Emma dropped the dish towel and tried to back away, but the sink stopped her retreat. "Jordan!" she got out between squeaks and laughter. "Stop it."

"Or what?" Laughing along with her, Jordan trapped her between the counter and her own body.

"Or I will… I will…"

They stared at each other.

Jordan's fingers paused, and she became aware of how intimate their position was—their bodies pressed close, her hand just beneath Emma's breast. The copper sparks in Emma's eyes seemed to draw her in.

"Or I'll..." Emma made a desperate grab for the kitchen hose and swung it in Jordan's direction.

"You wouldn't da—"

Cold water drenched her before she even got the word out.

Emma laughed as Jordan scrambled to escape the spray. "You looked like you could use some cooling off." Then she paled and dropped the hose into the sink. "Oh shit. Your cast! I'm so, so sorry. I'm an idiot."

Jordan had forgotten about it too. Now she quickly checked to see if it had gotten wet. "It's fine. My face and shoulders took the brunt of it."

Emma took the abandoned dish towel and ran it over Jordan's shoulder and upper arm, stopping the water from dripping down onto the cast.

They again stood so close that Jordan could sense Emma's body heat. As the thin towel brushed along her neck, she shivered. Her nipples hardened.

"Emma," she gasped out, not sure what she was doing—warning her away or beckoning her closer.

Emma seemed to take it for the latter and leaned closer.

The ringing of Jordan's phone startled them apart.

As soon as Emma was no longer touching her, Jordan's brain started to work again. God, they had almost done it again, and this time, Jordan wasn't sure they would have stopped with a kiss.

Her normally steady fingers shook as she fumbled her phone from the pocket of her shorts.

"Hi, Jordan," a woman's voice said. "This is Emma."

"Emma," Jordan repeated, staring at Emma, who had backed away and was now mopping up the water on the floor.

At the sound of her name, she looked up, and their gazes met.

"Yes?" Emma—the Emma who was in the kitchen with her—sent her a questioning look.

Quickly, Jordan shook her head. "Um, nothing," she whispered, covering the phone with one hand for a moment.

"Yeah," the woman on the phone said. "Emma from the playground, remember?"

"Of course I remember." Jordan's body still felt alive with Emma's closeness, and she had to make a conscious effort to sound halfway normal. "Good to hear from you. I wasn't sure you would call."

"Jackson was sick, so I couldn't leave him with a babysitter, but now he's back to his old self, so I thought I would call and see if you're still up for that adult dinner…and maybe the adult something else," she added, dropping her voice to an intimate whisper.

Very aware that Emma—her Emma—could hear every word she said, Jordan turned her back. Why the hell did she feel as if she were cheating on her? *Ridiculous. And wait a minute…* Had she just thought of her as *her* Emma? They weren't in a relationship. All these confusing feelings had to stop. Right now. She needed to clear her head, and Emma—the Emma from the playground—was the perfect person for that. "I'd love to," she said, trying to sound more enthusiastic than she felt.

"Great," Emma number two answered. "How about next Saturday?"

Jordan hesitated. *Are you stupid? What's there to hesitate about? A beautiful woman wants to go out with you. Say yes, idiot.* "Sounds good to me," she said. "What time do you want me to pick you up?"

"How does seven sound?"

"Sounds fantastic," Jordan answered.

"I'll text you my address. Or do you want *me* to pick *you* up?"

"No," Jordan said quickly. Even though she chided herself for being stupid, she didn't want the two Emmas to meet. "No, that's fine. You don't need to drive all the way to South Pasadena. I'll pick you up at seven."

"Great. I'm really looking forward to it."

"Um, yeah, me too." She wasn't. At least not the way she usually did when she was going out with a woman she'd just met. But this was a familiar, soothing routine. She knew exactly what she wanted from *this* Emma, without a hint of the confusion that colored her interaction with the other Emma.

When she finished the call and put her phone away, Emma stood at the sink, scrubbing for all she was worth.

Did she even care that Jordan had made a date with another woman?

"Emma?" she asked.

"Hmm?" Emma didn't look up, all her attention on a bowl she was scrubbing.

"Are we okay?"

Now Emma did look up. She half turned and gave Jordan a smile. "Of course we're okay. We both know that we're better off as friends, right?"

"Right. Friends."

Emma reached out a hand and then seemed to realize that it was sudsy. She wiped it on her shorts before giving Jordan's shoulder a quick squeeze.

The simple touch set Jordan's body on fire. She wished it had been a hug instead. She wanted to press against Emma and hold on, but she knew it was a dangerous thing to wish for.

Emma wanted the white-picket-fence scenario that had always been a nightmare rather than a dream to Jordan. She couldn't give her that, so she had no right to hold her.

Her body screamed out its protest as she stepped out of touching range.

Emma turned toward the sink and dropped the next bowl into the soapy water.

Chapter 16

THE NEXT MORNING, EMMA FINISHED scheduling tweets and Facebook posts for her new clients and then glanced at the clock. Almost nine. Around this time, Jordan usually came over to bring Emma her second cup of coffee.

She looked out through the open French door, but there was no sign of Jordan yet.

Maybe she had overslept. Maybe she'd had her date with that woman last night.

It bothered Emma—and the fact that it bothered her bothered her even more. She was Jordan's friend, period. As a friend, she had to accept her exactly the way she was, and that included accepting her womanizer tendencies. Wishing that Jordan were different—that things between them could be different—was a waste of time.

The ringing of her phone wrenched her from her thoughts. A glance at the display revealed that the call had nothing to do with work. It was Chloe. Emma's money was on her calling because she had no clue what to get Molly for her birthday. In the past, Emma had always been the one to take care of buying presents for friends and family members.

She lifted the phone to her ear. "Good morning, Chloe," she said and then paused, a little surprised to find how easy it was to be civil to her ex-wife. Maybe she had finally reached that moving-on stage.

"Morning. Um, I'm not interrupting your work, am I?"

Emma moved the phone away from her ear and stared at it for a moment before moving it back. "Who are you, and what have you done with Chloe?"

"Hardy-har-har."

"I'm just surprised. You've never bothered to ask before." In the past, Emma hadn't noticed, but now Jordan had set new standards for her by constantly respecting her work.

Chloe sighed. "Listen. I'm calling about Saturday. Something has come up. Something important."

Emma's entire body stiffened. "No. No, Chloe. Don't do this."

"Like I said, it's something important."

"And our daughter's birthday isn't important?"

"I didn't say that. It's not like I have a choice, okay?"

"You promised her you'd come." Emma snorted into the phone. "But then again, promises never meant much to you, did they?"

"Emma, please. Don't make this about us."

Emma ran her free hand through her hair and slowly counted to ten. "Is there any way you could take a later flight? I can have Molly take a nap in the afternoon and then let her stay up a little longer if—"

"No," Chloe said. "That won't work. I'll be in New York this weekend."

Emma wondered what was in New York that could be more important than their daughter's birthday. She didn't ask.

"I'm really sorry, Emma. I promise I'll make it up to her."

What could she say to that? She'd stopped trusting Chloe's promises.

"I have to go," Chloe said. "Give Molly a hug and a kiss from me, okay? I'll try to call her on Saturday. Talk to you then."

Try? A ball of anger lodged in her throat, threatening to choke her. Before she could force out the words past that lump, Chloe was gone. Not that Emma knew what she would have said. She sat there with the phone in her hand. God, how was she supposed to tell Molly that her other mother wouldn't come to her party after all? That she had something more important to do?

Molly wouldn't understand. How could she? Emma wasn't sure she understood it either.

Chloe had missed events in Molly's life because of work before, back when they had still lived in Portland, but never something as important as her birthday party.

Tears of frustration burned in her eyes.

A light knock sounded on the open French door. "Hey, ready for another coffee?"

Emma quickly put the phone down and wiped at her eyes with her free hand. "God, yes," she said, trying to sound normal. "Beyond ready."

Jordan crossed the space between them, the mug with the large red smiley face that she always reserved for Emma in her hand. Her gaze never left Emma, and her frown deepened with every step. "Are you...are you crying?"

"No."

"What happened?" Jordan put the mug down and knelt in front of Emma, one hand on her knee in a gesture of comfort. "Did Darth Vader do anything to—?"

"No. This has nothing to do with him." Emma would gladly deal with a dozen Darth Vaders if it meant she could spare her daughter the pain of finding out her other mother wouldn't be there for her birthday. She stared at her phone and then down into Jordan's brown eyes. They were full of worry and compassion. "Chloe called. She was supposed to come to Molly's birthday party, but she won't be able to make it after all. Seems something more important came up."

"Oh, Emma. Poor Molly. I'm so sorry." Ignoring her cast, Jordan took Emma's hands into both of hers and gave a soft squeeze.

They stayed like this for a minute, holding hands. Jordan's steady grip grounded Emma in a way she hadn't thought possible.

Finally, she heaved a sigh. "Nothing we can do about it now. I can just try to break it to Molly gently."

Jordan rubbed both thumbs along Emma's fingers, sending tingles up and down her body. "Want me to put Chloe on the list of people whose kneecaps need to be broken?" she asked with a crooked smile.

Emma laughed and suddenly had to fight back renewed tears. Jordan's support felt good. "Ask me again once I've told Molly. She hasn't seen Chloe since we moved here. I'm sure there'll be tears."

Jordan's grip on her hand tightened. "I'm sorry. Anything I can do?"

"Thank you, but I don't think so." Emma paused. "That is... Would you come to the party? I know it's short notice. I wanted to ask you before but with...um, you know, the kiss and everything and Chloe coming here, I wasn't sure it was a good idea."

"And now you do? Want me there, I mean?" Jordan asked.

Looking down at their entwined fingers, Emma nodded. "I know Molly would like it if you came—and me too," she hastened to add. "Nothing big. Just me and half a dozen overexcited kindergarten kids."

"Sounds…um…lovely." The corners of Jordan's mouth curled up into a half smile. "I'll be there. When's the party?"

"Saturday."

"Uh…this Saturday?"

"Yes." Emma watched as Jordan's brow furrowed. "You've got other plans, haven't you? Just forget about it. You don't need to—"

"I'll be there," Jordan said again. "What time do you want me to come over?"

"The party starts at three."

"Want me to come over at two to help with the preparations?" Jordan asked.

Emma stared at her. God, this woman was too good to be true.

"What?" Jordan asked as she kept staring. "Two doesn't work for you? Would one be better?"

"Uh, no. I was just thinking what a great friend you're turning out to be." She would be crazy if she did anything to jeopardize that.

Instead of answering with a joke or a flirty line, Jordan glanced at her shoes and then up into Emma's eyes. "Thanks. You're pretty okayish as a friend too."

They smiled at each other until an alarm on Emma's computer interrupted their eye contact.

Jordan, who had still been kneeling in front of her, got up from her crouched position. "Duty calls?"

"Yes. I've got a Skype call with a client in five minutes."

"Then I'll let you get back to work." Jordan walked to the French door.

"Jordan," Emma called before she could step outside.

Jordan turned.

"Thank you," Emma said. "For the coffee—and for being such a good friend."

"You said *great* friend," Jordan corrected.

"Oops. Of course. My mistake." Jordan's competitiveness made her shake her head in amusement. "See you later." She gave one last wave before putting on her headphones. Her gaze remained on Jordan until she disappeared from sight.

Instead of plopping down in her hammock, Jordan went back to her living room and closed the French door, not wanting Emma to overhear the phone call she had to make.

She sat with the phone in her hand for a minute, not sure what she should say. Finally, she shrugged. No big deal, right? That was the joy of not being in a relationship—she didn't have to justify her actions to anyone, only to herself.

Emma number two—she really had to ask her what her last name was—answered the phone on the second ring.

"Hi, Emma. This is Jordan Williams."

"Hi." Emma sounded pleased to hear from her. "What a nice surprise! Couldn't wait until Saturday to talk to me?"

Jordan chuckled but then sobered when she remembered why she was calling. "Um, actually, I'm calling about Saturday. I…I can't make it."

For several seconds, only the sound of Emma's soft exhalation drifted through the phone.

"Can we…um, postpone? Something came up. Something important." She imagined that Chloe might have said something similar when she had called Emma. Great, now she felt like an asshole. "I'm really sorry. I know you had a babysitter booked already, and I swear I normally wouldn't do this. But… You remember Molly, don't you? The kid I was babysitting when we met."

"Of course," Emma said. "Jackson…my son…couldn't stop talking about her for the entire week."

Jordan smiled. Emma might have a heartbreaker on her hands one day. "Yeah. So, it's her birthday this Saturday, and her mother invited me to her party, and I really didn't want to disappoint Molly by saying no."

"Molly?" Emma asked. "Or her mother?"

"Emma…"

"Forget it. That was a stupid thing to say. I know you said no commitments. I was just thinking that for someone who doesn't want a commitment, you sure are committed to this friend."

Jordan rubbed her neck. Before she could think of something to say, Emma spoke again.

"About postponing our date… I'll have to check with my babysitter or my sister first to see when they are free. Can I call you back?"

"Sure."

They talked for a few minutes more before ending the call.

Jordan slid the phone onto the coffee table and flopped down on the couch. Who would have thought that she would ever cancel a hot date to attend the birthday party of a little girl?

The birthday party was a success, at least judging from the shrieks and squeals the kids let out as they raced each other through the backyard, balancing eggs on large spoons.

Resisting the urge to cover her ears with her hands, Jordan sank onto one of the large coolers and surveyed the fruits of their labor.

Earlier today, she and Emma had worked together to set up benches and a large table, which now looked as if a horde of pigs had descended on and then abandoned it. Balloons, streamers, and a *happy birthday* banner hung from the mulberry tree and the bushes surrounding the backyard.

The birthday presents, which Molly had opened an hour ago, had been moved to the side to make room for the party games. Now Shira, the stuffed saber-toothed tiger Jordan had gotten her, sat in the little basket of the bicycle that had been a gift from Emma. The envelope tied around the tiger's neck held tickets to the Los Angeles Zoo.

Molly had squealed for a full minute. The memory of it made Jordan smile.

"What a nice party," Barbara said from where she sat in one of the lawn chairs, a plate with a half-eaten piece of birthday cake on her lap. "When I was little, no one went to all this trouble for a child's birthday party."

"I think Emma went all out because she wanted to make sure Molly has a nice birthday," Jordan said, "despite her other mother not being able to make it."

Barbara shook her head. "Poor little one. I would have killed my Monty if he had ever missed one of our sons' birthdays."

"Trust me. It crossed my mind," Emma said as she stepped out of the house with a jug of orange juice for the kids.

Jordan wanted to jump up and help, but Emma waved her back down. "You helped enough already. Sit and rest. I've got this."

She sank back onto the cooler and watched Emma hand out glasses of juice to the kids.

Molly wandered over and perched on the cooler next to Jordan, dangling her legs.

"Hey, birthday girl," Jordan said. "Don't you want any juice?"

Molly shook her head.

Uh-oh. Barbara and Jordan exchanged concerned gazes.

"Aren't you enjoying your party?" Jordan asked.

Molly nodded but still didn't give a verbal reply.

With a sinking feeling, Jordan looked around for Emma, but she was still handing out juice. *Time for Supersitter Jordan to step up to the plate.* "Want to tell me what's wrong?"

Molly kicked her heels against the cooler, then stopped the racket and stared at her knees. "My mama couldn't come to my party. She has to work."

So that was what Emma had told her. Jordan swallowed. What was she supposed to say now? She glanced at Barbara, who had leaned back in the lawn chair and looked entirely content to let her handle the situation. *Thanks a lot, Barb.* "That sucks." She winced as soon as she'd said it.

Molly stared at her and then started to giggle.

Well, at least her bad word had brought the girl out of her funk. But with a glance toward Emma, Jordan decided that maybe she should add something of value. She slid a little closer and wrapped one arm around Molly's small frame. "You know, when I was little, my father was a soldier. He was gone a lot."

"Even on your birthdays?" Molly asked with big eyes.

Jordan nodded. "Sometimes even on my birthdays."

"What did you do?" Molly asked, hanging on her every word.

"Not much I could do. I just tried to make sure I doubly appreciated the people who *had* made it to my party."

"Like your mommy?" Molly asked.

"Exactly."

"Hmm." Molly dragged her heels along the cooler and looked out over the backyard, her little brow furrowed as if deeply in thought. Finally, she jumped up and ran across the patio.

At first, Jordan thought that she had become thirsty and wanted to get a glass of juice, but then Molly threw her arms around her mother in an exuberant hug.

Barbara chuckled. "My, my. You're good at this!"

Heat rose to Jordan's face, and she was grateful for her dark skin that hid her blush. "I wish. Most of the time, I'm totally winging it and hoping no one will notice."

Barbara's gaze was still on her. "So you and Emma...?"

"No," Jordan said quickly. "You know I'm not the settling-down kind."

"Oh yes. Settling down would be awful, right? You'd have to spend all your time with just one woman." Barbara gave an exaggerated shudder, making her silver locks fly. "And—heavens beware—you might even have to attend a child's birthday party and sit in a backyard full of screaming six-year-olds who had too much cake." She made a show of looking around. "Oh, wait! You *are* at a birthday party in a backyard full of screaming children, and if I'm not mistaken, you haven't had a woman other than Emma over in at least a month!"

Jordan grimaced. "Seventy-four is a little late to start a career as a comedian, don't you think?"

"It's never too late to give your life a new direction, my dear," Barbara said.

Jordan groaned and got up. "I think I need some juice—or something stronger."

When Barbara entered the kitchen with a stack of plates, Emma rushed over and tried to take them from her, but Barbara sidestepped her despite her bad hip.

"You're a guest," Emma said. "You're not allowed to help."

"I'm a *friend*," Barbara said. "Besides, Jordan is helping too, so why can't I?"

"Because she won't take no for an answer."

Barbara chuckled. "I imagine she's not used to hearing no from women."

Emma sighed at the reminder that Jordan didn't normally spend her days at the birthday party of a now six-year-old. Jordan seemed to have had so much fun refereeing the sack races that it was easy to forget that her idea of family and commitment was usually sleeping with the same woman twice.

"I've known Jordan for almost three years, but I had no idea she's so good with kids. Whenever my grandchildren visited, she made herself scarce. But look at her with Molly." Barbara pointed in the direction of the backyard, where Jordan and Molly were making a race of picking up trash. Their competitive shouts and cheers drifted in through the open French door in the living room. "Aren't they cute together?"

Emma couldn't help smiling. "Lethally cute."

Barbara put the stack of dishes down next to the sink. "Well, you know… You two are pretty cute together too—you and Jordan."

The comment caught Emma off guard. Her own parents were anything but relaxed about her sexual orientation, so they had never commented on her and another woman, at least not in a positive way.

Barbara laughed at the probably not very intelligent expression on her face. "I might be old, but I'm not blind."

"Have you…? Did Jordan…?"

"No." Barbara patted her arm. "She didn't say a thing. She's too much of a gentlewoman for that. But like I said, I'm not blind."

Emma turned her back to run water into the sink. "Nothing to see."

"No?"

She didn't need to see Barbara to know there was a knowing smile on her face. "Okay. There was one kiss." She squeezed the plastic bottle a bit too strongly, making an explosion of dish soap squirt into the water. "Almost two," she added under her breath, "or three."

"I knew it!" Barbara tapped her cane onto the tiles. "So what are you going to do about it?"

"Do?" Emma dropped a plate into the water. Soap bubbles scattered in all directions and settled down on her face. She wiped them away with an abrupt flick of her hand.

"Well, in my day and age, a kiss was usually followed by another date… and another kiss…and then…"

Emma wanted to clamp her hands over her ears. It was freaking her out a little to discuss this with someone who was older than her mother. She turned around and shook her head. "Not this time."

A frown deepened the lines on Barbara's face. "You're not going to give her a chance?"

"That's just it, Barbara. She doesn't *want* a chance. At least not a chance at anything more than... Well, you know."

"How do you know? Have you asked her?"

Emma opened and closed her mouth a few times, like a carp that had been tossed out of its pond. "Um, no, but—"

"Maybe you should."

Emma stared at her. *What the...?* Could it really be possible...? She shook her head at herself. *Nonsense.* Barbara was a family woman and a romantic. She wanted to see her two favorite neighbors together, but that didn't mean it was likely to happen. It was better not to let herself indulge in daydreams, or she would be in for another rude awakening.

"I don't need to ask to know it's not what Jordan wants. I heard her set up a date with another woman not too long ago." The thought made her ache the same way she had when she had caught Chloe cheating. *Christ. You're being silly.* It was hardly the same.

"Then maybe you need to give her some incentive not to go."

"What? No. I don't want... I can't..."

Before Emma could stammer out a full sentence, Barbara smiled, gave her a pat on the arm, and shuffled from the kitchen.

Chapter 17

On Wednesday evening, Jordan paused and stared at Emma, her beer bottle halfway to her mouth. "You've never tried it? Seriously?"

Emma leaned back in the grass on one elbow and shook her head. "Never had an opportunity."

"Well, you've got one now." Jordan motioned to the hammock without getting out of it. "It's big enough for two. Come on. You can lose your hammock virginity with me."

"Um, wouldn't it be safer if I tried alone?"

"Safer…maybe. But not as much fun." When Emma flicked the cap of her beer at her, she ducked and then climbed out of the hammock. "Okay, okay. Try alone. Mi hammock es su hammock."

Emma put her beer down into the grass and scratched her head as she squinted at the hammock. "Um, how do I do this? Feet first or…?"

"No. Backside first. Like this." She demonstrated and then got out again so Emma could try it. It was fun to watch her as she lowered herself and then fought to keep her balance.

Finally, Emma lay back and swayed back and forth. "Wow. This is nice."

"Yep. Looks like you've got the hang of it now." Jordan chuckled. "Literally." She handed Emma her beer and then sat in the grass next to her and looked out into the darkness. God, she loved evenings like this. All that was missing were some fireflies.

"Um, Jordan?" Emma said after a while. "There's something I've been meaning to ask you."

Why the hell did her pulse start to hammer? Just because Emma was in her hammock now didn't mean she would ask to get into her bed next. But Jordan couldn't help sounding a little breathless as she asked, "What is it?"

"Well, my friends have been on my case about me starting to go out again and having more of a social life, so I was wondering..."

When Emma paused and directed an expectant gaze at her, Jordan froze. Emma wanted to go out...with her? A strange mix of terror and elation filled her chest. Before she could consider her reply, Emma continued.

"I was wondering if you would mind babysitting Molly next Saturday." Jordan stared. "You want me to...?"

"I know it's a lot to ask. You helped me with the party last Saturday already, so if you've got other plans, of course I understand."

"That's not it." She didn't have any plans. Emma number two hadn't called her back yet, and to her surprise, Jordan wasn't itching to go out with any other woman. "I just..." She took a swig of beer. *You just what? You seriously didn't hope she wanted to go out with you, did you?*

It would never work. For Jordan, going out was usually just the first course of a meal that ended with a night of hot sex as the dessert. For Emma, going out was the main dish...the first in a row of main dishes that would lead to having dinner together every day for the rest of their lives.

"I would love to watch Molly for you," she finally said, hoping she sounded more enthusiastic than she felt. "We'll make peanut butter burgers and then Molly will introduce me to the first of the *Ice Age* movies."

Emma stuck her arm out of the hammock and squeezed her shoulder. "Thank you."

Even another gulp of beer couldn't wash away the tingle the touch set off. "No problem, really. So, where are you going?"

"A colleague of mine...another VA who lives in Glendale...asked me if I want to meet her for dinner, and I'd hate to say no. Wendy was the one who referred one of the new clients to me."

Just a colleague. A work-related thank-you dinner, not a date. Jordan smiled. "Tell her yes. I'll watch Molly."

Within ten minutes of entering Emma's side of the duplex on Saturday evening, Jordan learned another valuable lesson of babysitting: never handle knives while you're watching the kid's mother getting ready to go out.

She was in the middle of slicing the tomatoes for their burgers. When Emma entered the kitchen in search of her purse, Jordan nearly cut off the index finger of her already-injured hand.

Oblivious to the near mishap, Emma put in her second earring as she crossed the room. She wore a navy-blue jersey dress that would have looked simple on any other woman. The way it hugged Emma's curves and draped over her butt stole Jordan's breath. She had even put on light makeup, which Jordan had never seen her do before. The result made her wish Emma had gone to all this trouble for her, not that virtual assistant.

Jordan put the knife down and pretended not to stare.

"What?" In a self-conscious gesture, Emma ran her hand through her blonde hair that fell down her back in soft waves.

"Uh, nothing. You look great." That was an understatement of epic proportions. Like a bee drawn to honey, Jordan left the tomatoes behind and followed her into the hall, where Emma put on a pair of sexy sandals. Jordan suppressed a groan. All of this would be totally wasted on a thank-you dinner for some straight colleague.

But then again, Emma hadn't mentioned her colleague's sexuality.

The thought made Jordan stiffen. "This colleague of yours... Is she a lesbian?"

"I have no idea." Emma slipped on the second sandal and then straightened. "I know she works for a lot of LGBT authors so it's possible, but I didn't ask."

"Oh." A new feeling, one she'd never experienced before, clawed at Jordan's chest. Whatever it was, she didn't like it one bit.

"Does it matter, even if she is?" Emma asked.

"Of course it matters!" Jordan realized that she had raised her voice and made a conscious effort to speak more softly. "I mean, if she's a lesbian, she could mistake your thank-you dinner for a date."

Emma lifted her chin. "So what? You were the one who said the best way to get over someone is to hook up with someone else, right?"

Had she really said that? Jordan wanted to slap herself. "Um, yeah. I mean, it works for people like me, but you are different. You..."

Emma slipped into a fitted blazer that gave her outfit a businesslike flair and made Jordan feel a tiny tad better. "Don't worry, Mom." She patted Jordan's shoulder. "I'm just meeting her for the first time. I won't do anything you wouldn't do."

"That doesn't rule out much," Jordan muttered and followed her to the door.

Emma said good-bye to Molly, who ran over, clutching two DVDs she wanted to watch with Jordan. Her hand already on the door, Emma hesitated. "If anything happens or you or Molly need anything, you've got my number, right?"

"I do." Jordan held up her phone. "Don't worry. Nothing will happen. Relax and have some fun." *Just not too much.*

Emma kissed Molly's forehead one last time. For a moment, she looked as if she was about to kiss Jordan too, but then she opened the door, stepped outside, and walked in the direction of the garage.

Jordan's gaze followed her until she vanished out of sight.

This movie didn't make any more sense than the one she and Molly had watched in the movie theater. The saber-toothed squirrel was still trying to bury his acorn. But at least the interactions between the grumpy tiger and the human baby were funny.

Jordan hoped she was doing a better job as a babysitter. But, truth be told, she wasn't paying all that much attention to the movie. She was too busy wondering how Emma's thank-you dinner/date was going.

Had Emma's colleague greeted her with a kiss? Did she like the dress as much as Jordan had, and did Emma like whatever the other VA was wearing? What were they talking about over dinner? Were they already planning a second date?

Her overactive imagination jumped ahead to the woman spending the night at Emma's. She clutched the armrest with her good hand at the thought of Emma taking the damn VA outside to the backyard—their backyard—to count stars or to neck like two teenagers. God, she really wasn't sure she could watch that.

You're being stupid, she told herself. Even if the colleague was a lesbian, they wouldn't move in together after the second date. Emma was more careful than that. She was the kind of woman who wanted to know more about the person she dated than just her bra size.

But the tension wouldn't leave Jordan's body.

At least Molly seemed totally relaxed, cuddled up to Jordan on the couch. Was she even still awake? She hadn't laughed at the funny scene when the talking sloth's tongue had gotten stuck on a block of ice.

Jordan peered around Molly to see her face.

"Jordan?" Molly said, making her jerk back in surprise.

"Yes?"

"My tummy hurts."

Oh shit. At that moment, nine years of medical training went down the drain, and panic rose. *Calm down, idiot.* A stomachache was a common complaint among kids and usually nothing to worry about. But knowing that didn't help her now. She slid out from her position as Molly's pillow so she could take a look at her. "Where exactly does it hurt? Here?" She gently pressed on Molly's right lower abdomen.

Molly shook her head. "It hurts everywhere."

Okay, that wasn't very helpful, but at least it didn't look like appendicitis. The pain would be more localized if that were the case. "Do you need to go to the bathroom?"

Molly nodded.

"All right. Then let's get you to—"

Puke splashed onto her T-shirt.

Oh shit. Jordan stared down at herself.

Then Molly started to cry.

Helplessness gripped Jordan. "Don't cry. You'll feel better soon."

Still crying, Molly started to heave again.

No time to hesitate. Jordan stripped off her soiled shirt, picked up the girl, and carried her to the bathroom, where she promptly lost the rest of her burger.

Ugh. Jordan suspected that neither of them would feel the desire for a peanut butter burger anytime soon. She held Molly and stroked her hair until the heaving stopped. Gently, she helped her strip off her pajama top and washed her face.

Molly didn't stop crying the entire time.

Jordan cradled her against her body. "Sssh. You're making your poor stomach even sicker. Come on. Let's get you to bed." She picked her up again, ignoring any damage it might do to her healing arm. A half-forgotten memory rose as she carried her toward Molly's bedroom. Whenever she or her sisters had been sick, they had been allowed to sleep in their parents' bed, which had been a no-no at any other time. It had made her feel special and cared for.

Hoping it would be okay with Emma, she pushed open the bedroom door, settled the girl in her mother's bed, and tucked the duvet around her. The pillow smelled of Emma, making Jordan smile and Molly stop crying.

She sat on the edge of the bed and brushed a damp strand of hair from Molly's forehead. "I'll be right back, okay?"

"No! Don't go!" Molly clung to her.

"I'll just get a bucket and something to drink for you and be right back. I promise."

Reluctantly, Molly let go. She looked up at Jordan and started sniffling. "I want my mommy."

Oh man. Jordan's respect for pediatricians grew. How did they manage to deal with sick children all the time? Seeing Molly suffering felt as if someone was squeezing her heart. "We'll call her in a second, okay? But first, you need something to drink."

"O-okay."

Jordan rushed to the kitchen and rooted through the cabinets in search of some Pedialyte or some other electrolyte drink. She couldn't find any, so some water would have to do for now. With a bucket, a small glass of water, and a clean pajama top, she returned to Molly's bedside.

She sat on the edge of the bed again and helped her put on the new pajama top. Her casted arm wrapped around the girl, she guided her to take tiny sips of water so she wouldn't upset her stomach even more. Then she put the glass on the bedside table and felt Molly's forehead. If she had a fever, it was a low-grade one.

"Can we call Mommy now?" Molly asked.

She looked drowsy, as if she would fall asleep any second. Should she really call Emma? It would probably scare the poor woman to death. But she had promised Molly, and Emma hadn't taken too kindly to Jordan trying to make decisions for her. She tried to put herself in Emma's shoes. If she were Molly's mother, she'd want to know if she was sick. So Jordan nodded and pulled out her phone.

If this was what she had to look forward to once she started dating again, Emma decided that staying single might be an attractive option.

Wendy was perfectly nice, and she could certainly be considered good-looking. Emma's gaydar had also pinged as soon as they had met in front of the restaurant. They should have been a perfect match, especially since their jobs gave them something in common and Wendy had declared her love of kids before they had even ordered their dinner.

But there wasn't any kind of spark for Emma. It didn't matter, she told herself. Neither of them had called this a date, and making a new friend who lived in the area would be great.

Jordan had told her to relax and have some fun, and that was exactly what she would do. The problem was just that she didn't feel very relaxed. For some reason, she couldn't be herself with Wendy. She felt like an actress who struggled to get into her role. God, she wished she'd stayed home to watch *Ice Age* for the thousandth time and to tease Jordan about her peanut butter burger.

"Is something wrong?" Wendy asked.

Emma was startled out of her thoughts. "Um, wrong? No." She forced a cheery smile. "Everything's great."

"Then why do you keep glancing at your watch?"

Oh no. Had she really done that? Emma felt like an ass. She had wanted to thank Wendy for her help, yet here she was, spoiling her evening. "I'm sorry." She peered across the table at her. "It's just that... My daughter didn't feel so great this morning. She seemed to be doing better, but I always hate leaving her when she might not be one hundred percent."

It was true, even though it wasn't the real reason for her distraction. She couldn't pinpoint what the heck was going on with her.

"Why didn't you call me? We could have postponed our date."

Date... So Wendy did consider it a date? Or had it just been a figure of speech? "No, that's all right. She seemed to be perfectly fine when I left, trying to decide which movie to introduce Jordan to first."

"Jordan?" Wendy asked.

"My..." *Neighbor? Babysitter? Woman whose kiss still makes me weak in the knees every time I walk into the damn garage and see her sports car?* Finally, she settled on "friend."

"So you have found a reliable babysitter for your daughter?"

"Oh, yeah. Jordan is great. She even got Mouse—my daughter's favorite stuffed animal—a cast of his own, and she kidnapped me for a drive along the beach and—" She snapped her mouth shut when she realized Wendy was giving her a blank stare, probably not very interested in hearing her sing the praises of her babysitter.

"Good," Wendy said. "I'm very glad you got your childcare situation sorted out. Because I'd love to meet up with you more often."

Meet up? Did that mean date or hang out as friends? God, why did things between two lesbians have to be so complicated? "I'd really like that, but... Okay, this is going to sound incredibly arrogant, but I'm not sure I'm ready to—"

The ringing of her phone interrupted.

"I'm sorry," she said as she dug it out of her purse. "I have to take this. It could be Jordan. I mean, my babysitter."

Wendy sighed. "Go ahead."

The name flashing across the display was indeed Jordan's. Cold sweat broke out all along Emma's back. Jordan wouldn't call unless something was wrong. Her index finger shook as she swiped it across the tiny screen. "What happened?"

"Molly's fine," was the first thing Jordan said.

Relief flooded through her for a moment, but then her brain bombarded her with other things that could be wrong. "And you? You didn't re-injure your arm, did you?"

"No. I'm fine too. Molly just had a bit of an upset stomach and wanted to talk to you."

"Oh no. Poor Molly. Hold on a second." Emma put down the phone and gave Wendy an apologetic look. "I'm really sorry to do this, but my daughter is sick. I have to go, but please stay and allow me to treat you to dinner."

When Wendy nodded, she put several bills on the table and hurried to the door. "Okay, Jordan. I'm on my way. Put her on."

Emma had probably broken the land speed record—and a few traffic laws—on the way home. Hurriedly, she unlocked her front door and then rushed down the hall without even taking the time to take off her blazer or put down her purse.

The door to her bedroom opened, and Jordan stepped out. "She's sleeping," she whispered.

Emma stood and stared, her poor brain busy processing the different things going on—among them Jordan stepping out of her bedroom, dressed in only a pair of low-slung jeans and a beige bra that was three shades lighter than her skin tone.

Jordan. Half-naked. Her bedroom.

This might have been an erotic dream, if not for her daughter being sick.

Jordan followed her gaze, not the least bit self-conscious about her state of undress. Not that she had reason to be. She was gorgeous. "Molly got sick all over my shirt."

"Oh God. I'm so sorry." Emma tiptoed past her, very aware of the fact that Jordan's torso was nearly naked as their shoulders brushed. She peeked into her bedroom.

Jordan must have brought the night-light over from Molly's room. It illuminated the bedroom just enough for her to make out Molly's sleeping form, bundled up under the duvet, Mouse by her side.

Quietly, Emma pulled the door closed and tiptoed back.

Jordan followed her to the living room.

"What happened?" Emma took off her blazer, threw it over the back of the couch, and plopped down on the sofa.

"We hadn't even made it halfway through the movie when she told me she had a tummy ache and then threw up before we could make it to the bathroom—or I could get out of the way." She gestured at her chest, drawing Emma's attention back to her bra-encased breasts.

It took some effort to tear her gaze away.

"I swear it wasn't my peanut butter burger," Jordan added.

A ghost of a smile formed on Emma's lips. "I know. She seemed a little off this morning, but earlier, when you came over, she was back to her old self. Otherwise, I would have never left."

"Hey, you don't need to feel guilty." Jordan sat on the couch next to her. "Even moms deserve a night off every now and then, and there was no way you could know that she'd get sick."

"Do you think she'll be fine? Or should I take her to a doctor?"

"I am a doctor, remember?"

"You're a surgeon, not a real doctor." The teasing made her feel better, and she realized she was more relaxed now—even with a half-dressed Jordan and a sick daughter—than she had been in the restaurant with Wendy. Life was really weird sometimes.

Jordan let out a growl but then admitted, "I called Hope as soon as you hung up, just to make sure I did everything right. She said that we need to keep Molly hydrated and she should be fine. It's probably a bout of gastroenteritis that will run its course."

"Thank you, Jordan." She knew what it meant for Jordan to swallow her professional pride and call her friend for help. A wave of gratefulness gripped her. She wanted to sink into Jordan's arms for a hug, but with Jordan being nearly topless, that wasn't a good idea. All that naked skin just inches away seemed to make the air crackle between them. "Thank you for taking such good care of her."

"If I'd known she would be asleep by the time you got back, I wouldn't have called you," Jordan said.

"I wanted to be called. Besides, I was being the worst date in the history of mankind anyway."

"You being a bad date? I don't think so." Then Jordan seemed to really think about what they had just said and lifted her eyebrows. "Wait a minute... So this *was* a date after all?"

"Wendy seemed to think so."

"And you?" Jordan asked quietly.

"I..." *Wanted to come back here to be with you and Molly.* God, this was so stupid. She was setting herself up for another broken heart.

"Mommy?" Molly's voice drifted over from the bedroom.

Emma jumped up. "I'm coming, Molly."

Jordan got up too. "Um, can I borrow a top?" She chuckled. "I don't want to damage your reputation by being seen leaving your house in my underwear."

Her cheeks warming, Emma reached for the blazer that hung over the back of the couch. "Will this do?"

"Yes. Thanks."

Their hands brushed as she gave Jordan the blazer.

It was too short for Jordan and too wide at the bust, but she settled it around herself like a cape of honor and pulled up the collar as if wanting to breathe in Emma's scent.

"Jordan, I..." She bit her lip before she could say—or do—something stupid. "I really can't thank you enough."

"No thanks necessary." The expression in Jordan's eyes as she looked down at Emma was warm, almost tender.

"Mommy!"

Emma tore her gaze away from Jordan's. "I have to..." She pointed in the direction of the bedroom.

"Go. I'll be back in half an hour with some Pedialyte for Molly."

"You don't have to—"

"I know."

"Thank you," Emma said again. Their gazes met again and held. The look in Jordan's eyes was steady and reassuring, promising to be there for Molly—and for her—but there was something else, something deeper there. No time to linger on it.

Emma turned and hastened toward the bedroom. She felt Jordan's gaze follow her as she hurried to her daughter's bedside.

Chapter 18

JORDAN HAD JUST TAKEN A big bite of her chicken wing when her phone vibrated, dancing on the table next to her. With one arm in a cast and the fingers of her other hand full of grease and red sauce, she couldn't take the call. With a grunt, she glanced at the screen.

Emma.

For a moment, her heartbeat picked up like a Pavlovian response before she realized it wasn't *that* Emma calling. It was the woman from the playground. The woman she had stood up for a child's birthday party.

"Want me to get that for you?" Hope asked.

"Uh, no, that's—"

The rest of the words died away as Hope, in full take-charge physician mode, had already reached for the phone.

"Jordan Williams's phone," she said in her best secretary voice.

Jordan wiped her hand on a paper napkin and snatched the phone away from her. "Hi, Emma."

"Um, am I interrupting something?" Emma number two asked.

"No. Please excuse my immature friend." She gave Hope a glare. "How are you doing?"

"Good, thanks. I'm calling to see if you're free tomorrow. My sister is in town, so she could watch my son."

"Wow. That's…um, great."

"So?" Emma drew out the word. "Saturday?"

Jordan hesitated. Now that Molly was doing better, she and Emma had planned to take her to the zoo on Sunday morning.

Then she slapped her own forehead. *You're seriously thinking about turning down a hot date with a woman because you want to be well rested for a family outing to the zoo? What the hell is wrong with you?*

"Saturday sounds great," she said.

A fun date and a night of steamy sex with a beautiful woman was exactly what she needed, right? It was what she had always wanted, and that wouldn't change now. Maybe a sexy romp in the sheets with Emma number two would get her confused brain back on track.

They agreed that Jordan would pick her up at seven and then ended the call.

"Wow." Hope reached for another chicken wing from the plate in the middle of the table, but instead of eating it, she waved it at Jordan. "You're dating Emma? That's great! I really like her. Why didn't you tell me?"

"What? No, not *that* Emma. This was just a woman I met. Her name happens to be Emma too."

"Just a woman?" Hope repeated. "I've seen patients who were in the process of passing a kidney stone look happier than you do now. Correct me if I'm wrong, but that was a booty call, wasn't it?"

Jordan sighed, took a chicken wing, and swirled it through the spicy red sauce. "Kind of."

"You don't look very excited. Isn't the woman your type?"

Jordan tried to picture Emma—her tall body, cute smile, and dark hair, but instead, the image of the blonde Emma superimposed itself over it. She tried to shake it off and flashed a grin. "Hey, you're talking to me. Every good-looking woman between twenty-one and forty is my type."

"What's the problem, then?"

"There is no problem." Jordan took a bite of the wing to end the conversation, but Hope continued to look at her.

Jordan sighed. *Dammit.* She and Hope didn't have sensitive chats. They were best buddies who talked sports, women, and medicine. But now, since getting together with Laleh, Hope had become more in touch with her emotions. Sometimes, it was a pain in the ass. "I'm just not really in the mood, okay?"

"You? Not in the mood? Damn. Hell just froze over."

Jordan shrugged. "It happens."

"Then why not tell her that?"

"Nah. I can't do that. I already had to cancel our first date because of Molly's birthday party."

"Um, why didn't you make an appearance at the birthday party and go out with this woman afterward?"

"Um, because…" *Damn.* Why hadn't she even thought of that option? "Guess I didn't think of that."

"Maybe because you aren't that into her in the first place."

Jordan groaned. God, she was so messed up it wasn't even funny. "Enough about me. Let's change the topic."

"Sure. How's your patient?"

"My… Oh, you mean Molly. She's doing great. Bounced right back the next day."

Hope grinned. "Good. And how's her very attractive mother?"

Jordan picked up a chicken bone and threw it at her. So much for changing the topic.

"How about some dessert?" Emma number two purred as they left the restaurant and paused next to Jordan's car. The gleam in her eyes made it very clear that she wasn't talking about food.

This was familiar territory—except for the fact that it was normally Jordan who asked that question and backed her date against her sports car so she could kiss her senseless.

"You don't have to go home to your son?"

Emma grinned. "My sister is taking care of him tonight." Lowering her voice even more, she added, "The whole night."

"Hurray for babysitters," Jordan murmured and reached around Emma to open the passenger side door for her. "Your place, then?" she asked as they both got in.

Emma shook her head. "My sister is there with Jackson. How about your place?"

"Um, sure." So what if Emma—Emma number one—might see them? No big deal, right? Her neighbors had seen her with many different women over the years. She was a free spirit, not accountable to anyone.

Jordan started the engine.

Emma's hand began to roam over Jordan's thigh as soon as she pulled out onto the street.

"Emma," she groaned.

The hand moved even higher up her thigh and cupped her through her pants.

"Jesus!" Jordan jerked the steering wheel a little before grasping it more tightly. "I'm driving!"

"Are you complaining?" Emma asked, a smile in her voice.

Was she? Her body definitely wasn't. She couldn't even remember when she had last gone without sex for more than four weeks in a row, so she was beyond ready to end her dry spell. "No." She hissed as Emma rubbed her softly through the fabric of her pants. "Wait! You'll make us crash."

Emma moved her hand to a safer spot just above Jordan's knee.

Jordan blew out a breath. God, she was wet. She squeezed her legs together and sped toward South Pasadena.

Emma rinsed the last plate, put it into the drying rack, and looked down at the pile of dishes she had done. Her fingertips were starting to prune from the water, but she wasn't anywhere close to getting the tornado twirling through her mind to settle down.

Even if she pulled out every last plate and glass from the cabinets and washed them, she doubted she would find a solution to what was bugging her.

There *was* no solution. Jordan had never made a secret of the fact that she wasn't the settling-down kind, and Emma wasn't conceited enough to believe that she would be the woman who could change Jordan's mind. Any attempt to do so would be stupid. A player like Jordan didn't change her spots, and Emma couldn't afford to gamble on her possibly being an exception.

As much as her body—and maybe, just maybe her heart too—might pull her in Jordan's direction, she knew Jordan wasn't the Princess Charming who would sweep her off her feet to live happily ever after with her.

If she couldn't even make Chloe be faithful, how was she supposed to keep the biggest flirt on this side of the Mississippi committed to her?

It was impossible. She and Jordan weren't destined to be more than friends. The sooner she accepted that, the better for them both.

As if on cue, headlights cut through the darkness on the other side of the kitchen window, and Jordan's sports car turned into the driveway and then disappeared into the garage.

Jordan was home.

Emma hadn't seen her all day, and now a buzz of anticipation spiked through her. Maybe they could sit outside in the backyard for a while and talk about their days.

But when Jordan stepped out of the garage, she wasn't alone. A woman clung to her like a leech, her arms around Jordan and her mouth attached to her neck.

Emma wanted to wrench the window open and hurl one of the plates at the bitch, but she knew she had no right to be upset. She whirled around, away from the spectacle in the driveway, and stomped into her bedroom.

There she paused abruptly and stared at the common wall. *Oh God.* She would hear them…would hear every little moan and groan and breathless gasp Jordan would coax from the woman's throat. Maybe she would even hear the sexy noises Jordan made as she climaxed in this stranger's arms.

The thought made her clench her teeth. She wanted to walk out and hide in the living room, as she had done her very first night in the new house, but for some reason, she couldn't make herself move—at least not in that direction.

Instead, she pressed her ear to the wall.

Had that been a groan or just the creaking of a floorboard?

She stopped herself. God, she was making a fool out of herself, and she had sworn to never, ever do that again over a woman. Sudden anger, mostly at herself, built in the pit of her stomach.

Don't you ever learn, you idiot?

She wrenched her ear away from the wall. The anger evaporated as quickly as it had come. Deflated, she crawled into bed, where she curled up into a ball and drew the covers over her head.

Tears burned behind tightly closed eyes. She hadn't felt so miserable since the night she had caught Chloe with that damn medical assistant.

Jordan nearly dropped the key as Emma ran her tongue along the sensitive shell of her ear. "Jesus. Give me a minute. I can't get the door open like this."

As she fumbled with the lock, her mind flashed back to Emma number one fishing in her pants pocket for the keys. The memory made her smile.

"See?" Emma number two trailed her fingers over Jordan's lips. "Now you're getting into the mood."

Jordan's smile faded. She suppressed a sigh and finally got the door open. One glance back to the other side of the house, which lay in darkness, and then she closed the door behind them.

Emma was on her in a heartbeat, almost tackling her against the wall. Her lips wandered down Jordan's neck.

Jordan gasped as she started to suck.

Emma was touching her in all the right ways, in all the right places. Her body didn't have any complaints. How the heck could it still feel so wrong?

"Bedroom," Emma got out between nips at Jordan's neck.

Jordan hesitated.

"What's wrong?" Emma lifted her mouth from Jordan's skin.

"Nothing." She grasped Emma's hand and pulled her toward the bedroom.

The light flared on as she flicked the switch, revealing Emma stripping off her top.

Jordan couldn't help staring. Emma was beautiful, but she didn't have curves that she could get lost in for days on end or freckles that she wanted to trace with her tongue.

"Emma," she whispered.

Emma number two looked up from where she was trying to pull down Jordan's zipper. Her eyes were smoldering, but they were the wrong color. "Yeah?"

Not you, Jordan wanted to say but, of course, didn't. God, what was wrong with her? She had never, ever thought of someone else while sleeping with a woman. She had always been fully present in the moment, focused on the person she was with. Now her thoughts weren't with the woman right in front of her; they were with the woman on the other side of this wall.

The woman who would be able to hear everything if Jordan had sex with her namesake. In the past, Jordan might not have cared; she might have even found that little bit of exhibitionism hot. But now...

When Emma slid her hand into Jordan's open pants, Jordan grasped her wrist. "No," she got out. "I...I can't."

Emma pulled her hand back and glared at her. "What the fuck?"

"I'm sorry. I guess, I'm not in the mood."

"Not in the mood?" Emma huffed. "You're soaking wet."

Jordan bit her lip to stop herself from saying *not because of you*. Sure, her body was reacting to Emma's touches, but her mind kept picturing the other woman with that name. "Sorry," she said again.

Emma rubbed her forehead as if she couldn't process what was happening. "Are you kidding me?" She put her hands on her hips. "You were the one who invited me to an adult dinner, and you didn't leave any doubt what tonight would be all about."

When Jordan lowered her gaze and mumbled, "I know. I'm sorry," Emma pulled her top back on with jerky movements and then paused as if giving Jordan one last chance to change her mind.

Jordan stood frozen to the spot, her pants open and her head spinning.

Muttering curses all the way, Emma stalked to the door. "I can't fucking believe this."

"Emma, wait!" Jordan pulled up her zipper and hurried after her. "Let me drive you home."

"Don't bother. I'll call a cab."

The door banged shut behind her.

Jordan sank against the wall. *Fuck.* Her reputation was ruined. And so was her sanity.

She wasn't sure how long she had leaned against the wall, but after a while, she pulled out her phone. She needed to talk—to someone who could help her make sense of this jumbled mess that was her mind.

Her first thought—*call Emma*—was crazy. She was the reason for this mini-meltdown.

Hope, Laleh, Simone, or even Barbara would have been better choices. But Jordan's mind latched on to one name in her contact list: Nia. Her oldest sister had always been her go-to person whenever she needed to talk.

She tapped the contact and lifted the phone to her ear.

It rang. And rang. And rang.

Just when Jordan wanted to hang up, Nia answered.

"Hi, big sis. It's me—Jordan."

"Hey, what's up?"

Jordan hesitated. But she knew she needed to get it out. "I went out with a woman tonight, and I...um, I took her home with me."

For a moment, only silence filtered through the line. "And you're calling me at midnight to tell me that...why?"

Midnight? Jordan flinched. *God.* She really was losing it. "I'm sorry, Sis. I didn't realize it had gotten so late."

"It's okay," Nia said. "Talk to me. You're not calling to tell me you've gotten laid, are you?"

"No. It wasn't like that this time. I...I couldn't go through with it."

"What do you mean? Is it because of your arm?" Her tone colored by amusement, she added, "Don't worry. You won't have that cast for much longer. I'm sure you'll survive going without sex for a few more weeks."

Jordan stared at her cast. Her gaze lovingly traced the contours of the giraffe with the overly long neck. "No. This isn't about the cast. You know me. I don't need two hands to make a woman—"

"Lalalala," Nia chanted. "TMI, TMI. There are things I don't need to know about my baby sister."

"There's nothing to talk about anyway," Jordan grumbled. "I couldn't touch her...or let her touch me."

Her sister gasped. "Jordan... Are you okay? Did something happen to you?"

Nervous laughter burst from Jordan. "I'm fine. Don't worry. It's nothing like that. I just... I met someone."

Silence filled the line.

"Nia? You still there?"

"Um, yeah, sorry. I just... Wow. I didn't see that coming."

Jordan sighed. "Neither did I."

"Tell me about this someone."

"She's a woman."

Nia chuckled. "I gathered that." More silence filtered through the line, as if Nia needed a few seconds to wrap her mind around Jordan's revelation. "Is she the one you took home with you tonight?"

"I wish," Jordan murmured. More loudly, she said, "No. It's not like that between us. She...she's got a daughter, Nia."

Her sister whistled through her teeth. "Wow. My sister, the wild child, finally falls in love, and it's with a mom."

"Oh, no, no, no." Jordan shook her head, even though Nia couldn't see it. "Who said anything about being in love? You know I'm not the falling-in-love type."

"If it's not love, what has you so out of sorts?"

Another sigh escaped Jordan. "I don't have a clue. That's why I'm calling you." She paced up and down in front of her bed. "You've been married three times. You should know these things."

Nia laughed. "If I knew these things, I wouldn't have needed to marry three times to get it right." In a more serious tone, she added, "Tell me about her. How did the two of you meet?"

"She moved in with me about six weeks ago."

This time, the silence was so deafening as if Nia had even stopped breathing.

"She...what? Jeez, Jordan! I know lesbians like to U-Haul, but isn't this a little fast, especially for you? And why the hell am I only hearing about this now?"

A smile ghosted across Jordan's face. "Calm down. I didn't mean it like that. Remember how I told you Mrs. Fisher moved out? Emma and her daughter moved into the other side of the duplex."

"Ooh! So she's the one who made you climb that tree."

"She didn't make me, but yeah. That's what started this whole thing, whatever this is. Because I couldn't work and was home all the time, we started spending time together, and I realized I really like spending time with her, and now...now..."

"And now you and your hot mom...?" Nia prompted.

Jordan groaned. "Don't call her that."

Very quietly, Nia asked, "You really care about her, don't you?"

Jordan plopped down onto her bed and bounced on the mattress a few times. It didn't help to settle her spinning head and neither did Nia's question. "No. Yes. Maybe, but... Dammit. I'm so fucked up, Sis. I don't know what to do."

"What do you *want* to do?"

"March over, knock on her door, and then kiss her senseless as soon as she opens it."

"So what? You never had a problem doing that before. Remember when I caught you with Vonda when you were sixteen?"

Not that old story. Not now. "It's different with her…with Emma. Sure, I could kiss her senseless. Been there, done that. But what would come after that? I can't sleep with her once or twice and then walk away. She deserves…more." That's what it always came down to; it was just that she had no idea what *more* might mean—and whether she could give it.

"What would you do, then? Marry her and raise her daughter?"

Jordan sucked in a sharp breath. "I…I don't know. I haven't thought that far ahead." She kicked off her shoes and sank onto the bed more fully. "Or maybe I have, just for a second, and that's what's scaring the shit out of me," she finally confessed in a whisper. "What if it turns out I really can't do the forever thing? What if I regret it and start feeling stuck at some point? What if I'm back to looking at other women next week or next month or next year?" She sat up again. "I can't do that to her. I have a feeling that's exactly what her ex did, and it broke Emma's heart."

"Jordan, Jordan," her sister said, a smile in her voice. "Want to know what I think?"

"What?" Jordan leaned forward, eager for some wisdom to guide her.

"I think it's pretty obvious that you're already thinking more of her than of yourself. Maybe you're not as bad at relationships as you think. I know you have a big heart. You could love her if only you'd let yourself."

Jordan swallowed. Love? She had never been in love. Sure, she'd had a few crushes here and there, and she was certainly no stranger to lust, but love? Big, all-consuming, let's-buy-a-house-and-live-happily-ever-after love was a whole other ball game. She had never felt that—or wanted to feel it.

It had to be something else, right?

Slowly, she turned her head and stared at the common wall separating her half of the duplex from Emma's. Whatever she felt for her was something she had never experienced before. "I… That's… I don't know, Nia. I really don't know."

"Have you talked to her about it?" Nia asked.

"No. I don't think I'm ready for that. I need to figure this out for myself first. Otherwise, I'd only end up hurting her."

"You," Nia said, and a crackling in the line sounded as if she had tapped the microphone, "are so in love."

"Would you stop saying that? I'm not!"

"Are too."

"Am not."

"Are too."

Jordan sighed. "This must be why I called you instead of Shawna—your penchant for mature conversation."

"Listen, little sis," Nia said, now completely serious. "I understand where you're coming from. I really do. When I met Rob, I was scared shitless too. I mean, you know how my marriage to Ethan ended, and don't even remind me of the disaster with Brandon. After that, I wasn't too eager to get involved, much less married again."

"How did you get over that fear?"

Nia let out a laugh. "Who says I did? I just figured Rob and I might as well be scared together."

Jordan settled against the headboard, the back of her head coming to rest against the common wall. "Nia?"

"Yeah?"

"Don't give up your day job to become a motivational speaker."

This time, they laughed together, and some of Jordan's tension receded.

"Just take your time," Nia said. "If this is right for you, you'll figure it out."

For the first time in years or maybe ever, Jordan lacked the confidence in herself to believe that.

"Hang in there," Nia said. "And keep me posted. I want to know what happens with that hot mom of yours."

Jordan let out a growl. "Nia."

Her sister chuckled.

Jordan thanked her, said good-bye, and ended the call. Wearily, she closed her eyes and again rested her head against the wall, very aware that only a few feet might separate her from the woman who would keep her up tonight.

And tomorrow morning, she would visit the apes and the bears with her.

Too bad that wasn't a euphemism. She and Emma would take Molly to the LA Zoo. With a wry smile, she rolled off the bed and trudged toward the bathroom for a shower—a cold one.

Chapter 19

IF NOT FOR MOLLY'S CONSTANT chatter, it would have been a very quiet drive to the zoo.

After having slept for only an hour or two the previous night, Emma felt as if her eyelids weighed a ton, and Jordan didn't look much more awake as she dropped into the passenger seat of the Prius.

Yeah, but the reason she didn't get any sleep is because she probably had sex all night long.

Not that Emma had heard anything. Every once in a while, she had stuck her head out from under the covers. No gasps or moans had drifted through the common wall.

But that didn't mean a thing. Jordan and her latest conquest probably hadn't even made it to the bedroom before ravaging each other. Emma couldn't think about anything else, so she was grateful for Molly's endless questions about the zoo animals that distracted her from the images in her mind.

As soon as they got out of the car and entered the zoo, Molly dragged them to the giraffe house, grasping Jordan's good hand and Emma's right one.

"Look, Mommy! A baby giraffe! Awww!"

"I see it." The baby giraffe looked tiny next to the four adult animals, even though the sign next to the enclosure said that it was already taller than the average human. Emma smiled as she watched it prance around. "Cute."

"Very cute," Jordan said. "Almost as cute as the one on my cast." With her fingertips, she touched the crooked giraffe Emma had drawn.

What the heck? She had just slept with another woman, and now she was practically caressing Emma's giraffe! Emma wished she could see her eyes so she could guess what was going through her mind, but Jordan was wearing a pair of dark sunglasses. Admittedly, she looked sexy as hell wearing them.

"Did you see that, Jordan?" Molly tugged on both their hands. "It's got a black tongue!"

Jordan craned her neck. "Which one?"

"All of them!"

Emma stared too, but not at the giraffes and their tongues. Was that…a hickey on Jordan's neck? It was hard to tell with Jordan's dark skin, but it sure looked like one.

Jordan turned her head, about to say something to her, and caught Emma staring. Her good hand went up to cover the spot on her neck.

I knew it! It was a hickey.

So what? It wasn't as if Jordan was her girlfriend. She could get a hickey whenever she wanted.

But Emma couldn't help the feelings of betrayal, hurt, and anger churning through her. Knowing that Jordan had slept with another woman was one thing; seeing proof of it was another. She whirled around, away from Jordan and the sight of her hickey. "I'll get us some ice cream. Molly, please stay with Jordan." Not knowing—and not caring—where she might find an ice cream stand, she stormed off.

"Emma, wait!" Jordan jogged after her.

Emma whirled back around. "What?"

Jordan rubbed her neck and then dropped her hand to dangle next to her thigh. "I… It's not what it looks like."

Of all the million things she could have said, this one was the worst. A ball of anger gathered deep inside of Emma and then exploded outward. Her vision went red. "If I hear that one more time, I'm gonna… I'm gonna…" She clenched her hands into fists and struggled to keep her voice down so Molly wouldn't hear her.

Thankfully, her daughter was still clinging to the wall around the giraffe enclosure, watching the calf.

"One more time?" Jordan asked. She slid her sunglasses onto her head and stared at her as if trying to read a book written in hieroglyphs. She looked tired, but Emma was too angry to care right now.

"It's what Chloe said when I caught her…"

Jordan's jaw muscles bunched as she gritted her teeth. "I'm not Chloe."

Emma took a deep breath and tried to smooth the jagged spikes of her anger. Jordan was right. This was a different situation, and it wasn't fair to transfer her feelings about Chloe's betrayal to Jordan. "No. You're not. And we're not in a relationship." Maybe saying it out loud would finally get her brain to grasp that simple concept. "Who you sleep with is none of my business."

"But...I'd like it to be your business."

They stared at each other. Jordan looked just as stunned as Emma felt. She lifted her good hand and pressed her fingers to her mouth as if she couldn't believe the words that had come out of it.

Emma's heart slammed against her ribs as if it were being pulled toward Jordan. "W-what's that supposed to mean?"

"I...I don't know." Jordan tried to run the fingers of her right hand through her hair and nearly knocked herself in the head with her cast. Her sunglasses tumbled into the grass next to the path, but she made no move to pick them up. "I want you to know that nothing happened last night."

New anger sparked alive in Emma. She pointed at the hickey. "That's not nothing." Their different concepts of what did or didn't constitute *something* was reason enough to end this conversation. Now. Nothing good could come of it. She and Jordan were too different to make anything longer than a one-night stand work.

"I didn't kiss her, much less..." Jordan's gaze flicked to Molly. "Anything more. I swear."

Emma wanted to believe it, but she wasn't sure she could. "It doesn't matter." She slid the strap of her purse higher on her shoulder like a soldier adjusting a weapon. "I'll go get that ice cream now."

"Emma..."

"Please. Let it go. This isn't the time or the place."

Jordan sighed and then nodded. She finally bent to pick up her sunglasses.

Emma turned. God, she hoped the ice cream stand was all the way across the zoo. She needed some time away to get her head on straight.

"Emma?" Jordan's voice reached her before she had taken three steps.

A mix of anticipation, hope, and fear made every muscle in her body tense. Slowly, she turned back around. "Yes?"

"Peanut butter," Jordan said. The slightest smile curled one corner of her mouth.

Emma stared at her.

"The ice cream. I want peanut butter if they have it."

Peanut butter. Of course. A wave of affection swept over Emma. And that was just fine. She could like Jordan and be friends with her. But if that was all it was, why did the mere mention of someone's favorite ice cream flavor nearly make her tear up? She quickly turned around before Jordan could see it. "Got it," she called over her shoulder and marched away.

The ten minutes it had taken to get ice cream cones hadn't been nearly enough time to settle her emotions or find answers to the many questions ricocheting around her mind.

While she carried the cones back to the giraffe house, Jordan's words still echoed in her head on auto repeat: *I'd like it to be your business.*

What the heck did that mean? Was that a hint that Jordan wanted more than just friendship? But what exactly did *more* mean where Jordan was concerned? Sleeping together whenever they felt like it?

What exactly did Jordan want from her? And, for that matter, what did she, herself, want? If Jordan's comment suggested a friends-with-benefits arrangement like the one she had with Simone, could she live with that?

She kicked out at a piece of bark mulch on the path in front of her. No. At least this one thing she knew for sure. She had always been a one-woman woman. Her reaction to seeing Jordan with the stranger last night told her that she could never share her that way.

But a part of her couldn't help hoping and wondering: what if *more* meant something else—a real relationship? Was there a chance for them to be happy together?

That's crazy. You'd be handing over your heart for her to stomp on it, just like Chloe did.

She had promised herself a year ago to never, ever take that risk again. But now she was no longer sure if that promise was even realistic. Wasn't love always a risk—a leap of faith that you just had to take?

Love? Oh, come on. That's not what this is...is it?

She and Jordan had known each other for less than two months, even if she felt as if she already knew her better than she had known Chloe after half a year of dating.

She was more confused than ever, and Jordan didn't seem to know what to do about this whole mess any more than she did.

Maybe time would tell. If she waited a little bit, the situation might resolve itself without her having to make a decision one way or the other.

In about a week, Jordan would have her cast removed, and if her arm had healed well, she'd go back to work—and maybe right back to her old lifestyle. Maybe last night had already been the beginning of Jordan's return to her adventurous sex life. She and Jordan would stop spending so much time together. No more baking cookies or hanging out in the backyard, wishing for fireflies.

The thought made her chest ache.

Well, she would have to tough it out and pretend she was fine for Molly's sake, the way she always had.

She rounded the last corner to the giraffe house. Her gaze immediately zeroed in on Jordan, who was kneeling next to Molly, pointing at something in the giraffe enclosure that made Molly laugh.

The ache in Emma's chest returned. Jordan was so good with Molly. She was a big part of what had made Molly feel at home in South Pasadena so fast.

She and Jordan would have to get over whatever was going on between them. Another messy breakup wasn't an option, or Molly's little heart might shatter—along with her own.

Jordan looked up as if feeling Emma's gaze on her. A tentative smile formed on her lips, so unlike the confident grin she normally flashed.

Not knowing what to say, Emma stepped up to them and held out the ice cream cones. "One scoop of peanut butter crunch. And chocolate for you, Molly."

Molly and Jordan eagerly reached for their cones.

Jordan bent her head and licked off a bit of ice cream that was starting to melt and dribble down the side.

Emma tried hard not to stare at the way her tongue flicked over the sweet treat, but Jordan's moan made her shiver deep inside.

"Yum. This is good," Jordan said. "Thank you. What do I owe you?"

"Nothing. You don't owe me anything, Jordan."

They stared at each other and then looked away at the same time.

God, why did every glance, every word they exchanged suddenly have a deeper meaning?

"Um, I mean, you already paid for our zoo tickets, so this is my treat."

"What did you get, Mommy?" Molly asked while she happily ate her chocolate ice cream.

"Banana peanut butter ripple," Emma answered.

Lips already lowered to her ice cream, Jordan paused and looked back up. "Ooh! Have I finally seduced you over to the dark side?"

"No. No seduction going on here." She forced herself to hold Jordan's gaze to make sure she got the message. "A little hint of peanut butter in my banana doesn't mean anything. When it comes to...ice cream, we're too different. I think we can agree that it's safer if both of us stick to our own preferences. Otherwise, it could get messy."

Ice cream dribbled down Jordan's long fingers as she looked at Emma, but she didn't seem to notice or care. "I don't know. Maybe you're right, but—"

"But messy is fun," Molly declared, her face already smeared with chocolate ice cream.

"Not for me," Emma said, still looking at Jordan.

Finally, Jordan sighed and lowered her gaze to her cone. She looked as if she had lost her appetite. "Man," she muttered. "Why the he...heck is ice cream so damn complicated?"

The corners of Emma's mouth twitched into a half smile. "I don't know. Sometimes it just is."

Molly looked back and forth between them as if doubting the adults' sanity. Then she shrugged and went back to devouring her ice cream. "Can we go see the tigers now?" she asked once they had all finished their ice cream.

"Tigers it is," Emma said, forcing a cheerful tone into her voice.

Molly took their hands again. Connected this way, they made their way to the tiger enclosure.

Chapter 20

AT HALF PAST SIX ON Monday evening, Emma slid the headphones off her ears, paused the audio of the author interview she was transcribing, and listened into the silence of her house. Had that been the doorbell?

Nothing.

Just as she was about to put her headphones back on, the doorbell rang again.

She jumped up and hurried to the door. Was there something wrong with Molly?

No. If she had gotten sick again, Jessie's mother would have called her, not just dropped her off at home.

The first thing she saw when she opened the door was a giant wicker basket with a yellow bow.

"Emma Larson?" the man behind the basket asked.

"Yes."

"I've got a delivery for you, ma'am." The deliveryman held out the gift basket.

Automatically, Emma reached for it. *Wow.* That was heavy. What on earth had she done to deserve it?

For a second, she thought it might be an apology gesture from Jordan. Chloe had sent her flowers too the morning after she had caught her cheating. Ever since then, deliveries like this one left a bad taste in her mouth.

No, sending a gift basket instead of apologizing face-to-face wasn't Jordan's style. Besides, she had nothing to apologize for, even though it kind of felt that way to the emotional part of Emma's brain.

"Who's it from?" she asked.

He glanced at his clipboard. "Someone named Francine Barcowsky."

The name didn't ring a bell. She signed the form the deliveryman held out to her, closed the door, and carried the gift basket inside.

A white envelope stuck out from between a pineapple and a bottle of red wine. She plucked the envelope from the basket, pulled out the card, and read it.

Dear Emma,

Thanks so much for the great job you did with the book launch for The Sky Above. I know you are a huge part of the reason why it's selling so well, so this is a small token of my appreciation.

Enjoy!

Fran Barrows

a.k.a. Francine Barcowsky

Smiling, Emma slid the card back into its envelope. What a class act! A client like Fran made up for a hundred D.C. Panes.

She took a quick inventory of the goodies in the basket, then picked a box of Godiva chocolate truffles and carried it back to her desk, where her transcription was waiting.

Since Molly was having a sleepover with a new friend she had made at school, she had planned to work late. At least if she kept herself busy, she wouldn't think of Jordan all the time.

She popped a dark chocolate truffle into her mouth, sent off a quick thank-you e-mail to Fran, and then went back to work.

An hour later, the box was half-empty and the transcribed interview had been sent off to the client.

She powered down her computer, got up, and stretched, groaning.

I wonder what Jordan is doing. The thought came uninvited, but it refused to go away. She peeked out through the French door.

The sun had just set, and darkness was falling, but she could still see well enough to recognize that the backyard was empty. Maybe Jordan wasn't home.

Maybe she's with hickey woman. Jealousy churned in her gut. She didn't like the feeling, and she liked herself even less when she was like this. It was childish, really. She and Jordan weren't involved. They had agreed to each stick to her own "ice cream" preferences so they wouldn't create a mess.

Thinking of ice cream made her stomach grumble, and she realized that, except for the half dozen truffles, she hadn't eaten anything since lunch. She wasn't in the mood to cook just for herself, so she grabbed her gift basket, a wineglass, and a corkscrew and carried them outside. Once she was on the patio, she opened the bottle of red wine and arranged her impromptu picnic on the patio table.

As she took a seat and then poured herself a glass of the Château Faizeau, she peeked over at Jordan's side of the duplex.

There was no light in any of the three rooms facing the patio. Where was Jordan?

Stop thinking of her. When had she lost the ability to enjoy her evening off without wishing she could spend it with Jordan?

Emma took a big sip of wine. Her cheeks instantly warmed. *Phew.* That stuff was potent—much more potent than the bottle of light beer that she usually had with Jordan. She'd better be careful, especially since she had never tolerated wine well. Chloe had always teased her about that.

Well, she's not here to judge.

Emma took another sip while thoughts of Chloe and Jordan jumbled through her mind. Before she knew it, the glass was empty, and she had yet to eat anything.

Movement from the right drew her attention.

The hammock swayed in the light evening breeze.

Should she...? It would be a lot more comfortable than this plastic chair. She grabbed the bottle, her empty glass, and a package of red velvet cookies and headed over to the hammock.

After setting her goodies down into the grass, she lowered herself into the hammock and lay back. Jordan's scent seemed to cling to the fabric, surrounding her like an embrace. When her eyes fluttered shut, she forced them back open.

None of that! Separate ice cream cups, remember?

She bit her lip, reached down for the bottle, and refilled her glass. Softly swaying back and forth, she drank the deep ruby wine and stared into the falling darkness.

Jordan was right. Evenings like this one really would have been more perfect with fireflies. *And with Jordan.*

She took another sip of red wine on her nearly empty stomach.

Before she could scold herself for thinking about Jordan again, Jordan's voice drifted, as if conjured up by thinking her name. "Hi."

Jordan stood at the now-open French door, backlit by the light from her living room.

"Hi. I didn't know you were home." Emma attempted to climb out of Jordan's hammock, but the swaying didn't make it easy. She felt like a turtle lying on its back.

Jordan waved her back down. "Stay. As I said: mi hammock es su hammock. And no, I wasn't home. Just got back."

From a visit to hickey woman's place? Emma bit her lip. *Note to self: red wine doesn't help to counteract jealousy.*

"I picked up Barb from her bingo group and then just drove around," Jordan added, as if hearing the unvoiced question. "Driving does for me what washing the dishes does for you."

What had she been thinking about on the drive? Couldn't she get their conversation at the zoo out of her mind either?

Grass rustled as Jordan walked closer. Her gaze went from Emma to the gift basket on the patio table. "Are you having a picnic?"

"Um, yeah." Although she had forgotten all about the cookies and the rest of the basket's contents once she'd started on the red wine. "It was a gift from a client for a job well done."

"I'm glad you're getting some recognition for the great work you're doing."

"You never worked with me, so how can you know I do great work?"

"I know you...at least a little," Jordan said softly. "You don't do anything halfheartedly."

"No. It's all or nothing with me."

They stared at each other.

Great, now they were back to hidden messages. They really needed to work up the courage to talk more openly. But she needed more alcohol for that.

Emma tore her gaze away and took another gulp of wine. Her head was starting to spin, but she had no idea if it was from the wine or from Jordan's presence. *I'd better eat some of those cookies to soak up the alcohol.* She reached for the red velvet cookies and ripped open the package with so much force that several cookies spilled out.

Jordan caught one. "Um, here." She reached out to hand it back.

"Keep it." Emma nodded down at the bottle of wine resting in the grass. "Want to join me? It's a Château Something."

Jordan quirked a smile. "Are you by any chance a little drunk?"

"No. This is my first glass." Or was it? "Okay, maybe the second." It was empty, and she poured herself another.

Jordan sat cross-legged in the grass next to the hammock and munched her cookie but shook her head as Emma again offered her wine. "Where's Molly?" she asked after a while. "In bed?"

"I hope so. She and Mouse are having a sleepover with a new friend from school."

"On a school night?" Jordan raised her eyebrows.

Part of Emma felt criticized for her parenting decision; the other part was amused at Jordan's sudden maternal instincts. "Normally, I don't allow weekday sleepovers, but her friend wanted so much to go to the zoo with us yesterday, but she's highly allergic to pretty much all types of animals. I thought making an exception just this once would be okay."

"Ah. That was nice of you."

Their hands touched as they both reached for another cookie at the same time.

That little brush of Jordan's fingers against hers made Emma's entire body feel alive in a way she had never experienced before, and she knew it had nothing to do with the effect of the wine.

"Emma?"

God, she loved the way Jordan said her name, even though she wasn't looking forward to what she knew would be coming. She forced herself to look at Jordan, knowing she couldn't avoid a real conversation—one not involving ice cream metaphors—forever. The almost darkness made it a bit easier. "Hmm?"

"You have hinted at it a few times, but you never told me what exactly happened with Chloe."

Chloe? She had been sure Jordan would ask about them—not that there was such a thing as a *them*. But maybe whatever they had couldn't be seen independently of what had happened between her and Chloe. The failing of her marriage would forever influence how she approached relationships.

Emma let her head drop back into the hammock and stared up into the night sky. "We were together for ten years. Ten years, two months, and four days, to be exact. Most of my adult life, really." She sighed and circled the rim of her wineglass with her index finger.

Jordan's eyes tracked the movement in the near darkness, but she didn't interrupt.

"I thought she and I would grow old together. We had a pretty good life." The circling motion started to make Emma a bit dizzy, so she stopped it and took a sip of wine instead. "At least I thought so. Chloe apparently didn't share that opinion."

"What happened?" Jordan asked, her voice lowered to almost a whisper.

"Chloe…she was a plastic surgeon in a private practice."

Jordan waved her hand dismissively. "A plastic surgeon? And you've been comparing me to her all this time? That's not a real surgeon."

Emma sent her a look that made Jordan mime pulling a zipper closed across her lips. Telling this story was hard enough without any interruptions. She had never talked about the details with anyone before, but Jordan needed to hear them. Or maybe she herself needed to hear them, to remind herself why there was no chance for happiness with someone like Jordan.

"Anyway, Chloe had been talking about her medical assistant every now and then, mentioning how efficient she was. I thought she was talking about drawing blood and filing patient records, not about…" She paused to take a sip of wine, but it didn't help against the bitter taste in her mouth. "Not about how great she was at going down on her."

Jordan leaned forward and placed her good hand on the edge of the hammock but didn't try to touch Emma. The compassion coming off her in waves warmed Emma as much as the wine.

"We're a walking cliché, aren't we?" She laughed, a sound bare of any humor. "I caught her cheating with her assistant—in our own bed. And when I walked in on them, she gave me the classic line."

"It's not how it looks," Jordan murmured.

Emma nodded. Her throat burned too much to talk.

"That's why you got so angry when I said that yesterday," Jordan said.

Emma nodded and gulped more wine without tasting it, ignoring the light-headedness that was starting to set in. "I won't go through that ever again. I won't."

"You shouldn't have to. I would never, ever cheat on you." Jordan raised herself onto one knee and leaned forward so she could look her in the eyes. Her entire body vibrated with the need to make Emma believe that.

Emma stared at her and blinked several times. She lifted the glass to her lips once again and then frowned as she seemed to realize it was empty. With an unsteady hand, she reached for the bottle.

Jordan snatched it away. The bottle was three-quarters empty. "Maybe you should slow down, or you'll be drunk in no time."

"I'm not drunk." Emma glared, and then her expression softened. "Okay, I might be a teeny-weeny bit tipsy." She held her thumb and forefinger a fraction of an inch apart, looking as if she had to focus hard to measure the correct distance.

God, she was cute. And definitely on the drunk side of tipsy. "Have you had dinner yet?"

"Yeah. I had…" Emma's brow furrowed as if she was thinking hard about it. "Cookies. And truffles."

"That's not dinner. Come on. I'll make you something to eat."

"No peanut butter burgers," Emma said.

A smile made its way onto Jordan's face. Seeing Emma drunk was amusing, but it also made her sad because she had a feeling Emma had only drunk so much because their conversation at the zoo had brought up a lot of painful memories. "No peanut butter burgers. I promise."

Emma dropped her empty glass onto the grass and swung her legs down onto the ground. When she sat upright, she grabbed hold of the hammock with both hands. "Hold on to the hammock, please."

"It's not swaying—you are. Come on. I'll help you." She offered Emma her good hand.

Emma took it, but instead of pulling herself up, she sat and ran her thumb over the back of Jordan's hand as if marveling at the feel of it. Then she stopped and giggled. "You might be right." She wasn't slurring her words, but she spoke slowly as if picking every word with great care. "Maybe I am a little drunk."

"Yep." Jordan smiled down at her. "Ready?"

Emma blinked. "I don't know." She blinked again. "Oh. You mean... to get up. Yeah."

Jordan pulled her up.

As soon as she was on her feet and took a step, Emma stumbled and fell against her.

Jordan caught her, the cast coming to rest against the small of Emma's back.

Emma leaned against her and put her head down on Jordan's shoulder. She smelled of chocolate, red wine, and some other enticing scent that Jordan couldn't identify. The warmth of Emma's body filtered through her clothes. Their bodies fit together like a worn, comfortable glove to a hand. No other woman had ever felt so good in her arms.

They stood like this for a moment, Emma leaning heavily against her. Warm breath bathed the base of Jordan's neck, and Emma's lashes fluttered against her cheek. Her hands slid up Jordan's back.

Oh God. She had a feeling if they stood like this for a few seconds longer, Emma would try to kiss her—and she wasn't sure she was strong enough to resist.

Her body screamed in protest, but Jordan forced herself to create some space between them, while her good arm remained wrapped around Emma so she wouldn't stumble and fall.

Slowly, she led her through the open French door into Emma's side of the duplex and then steered her toward the bedroom.

Emma dragged her heels. "What about my peanut butter burger?"

"I thought you didn't want a peanut butter burger?"

"Oh." An adorable wrinkle formed on Emma's forehead. "Didn't I? I don't know what I want."

"Yeah." Jordan sighed. "Me neither. And that's the problem. Or maybe I do know, and that comes with its own set of problems."

"W-what?"

"Nothing." They would have to talk about it, but not while Emma was drunk and might not remember a word in the morning. "I think you need sleep more than you need food."

She pushed open the bedroom door with her shoulder and flicked on the light. Emma seemed to have forgotten about the burgers as Jordan led her to the bed. Obediently, she sank down on it and then looked up at Jordan, her cheeks flushed. In the low light of the bedroom, she looked like an angel—a very tipsy angel.

"Can you take off your shoes?" Jordan asked.

"Shoes?" Emma blinked.

Was she staring at her mouth? Jordan rubbed her tingling lips.

Snatching her gaze away from Jordan's face, Emma directed it downward, at her shoes. "Of course I can." She looked at her like an insulted three-year-old and then set out to prove herself. But the laces of her sneakers wouldn't cooperate. Just as Jordan was about to push aside her hands and help, she finally got them untied and kicked off her shoes. "There."

Jordan waved at her to continue, but Emma stared at her without comprehension. "Um, you'll sleep more comfortably if you take off your pants."

A mischievous grin tugged on Emma's lips. "Want to do it?" she asked, her voice a seductive purr.

Under different circumstances, Jordan would have been on her before she had been able to finish that question, but not like this. Not when Emma might regret it in the morning. "Um, I..." She cleared her throat. "I think it's safer if you do it."

"Spoilsport," Emma grumbled. She flopped onto her back from a sitting position. Her hand went to her zipper and slid it down so slowly that Jordan could hear each individual click-click-click. The button popped through its hole. Then Emma arched up her hips and tried to tug her jeans down. Her underwear slid partway down with it.

Jordan caught a glimpse of trimmed blonde curls before she guiltily forced her gaze away. *Oh man.* She couldn't decide if this was heaven or hell—or maybe a delicious mix of both. She knew Emma wasn't teasing her on purpose…or was she?

She peeked at Emma, who was still struggling with her pants. No. She was just pretty uncoordinated now that the effects of the wine had set in. How could Emma think she would seduce her in this state?

Well, there probably isn't much thinking going on in that brain of hers right now.

Emma grunted and writhed in her attempts to strip off her jeans.

Sweat broke out along Jordan's back—and, admittedly, a few other places on her body might have become a little damp too. Finally, when she couldn't take the torture anymore, she decided to intervene. "Let me help."

Immediately, Emma lay still and peered up at her. Her expression was a mix of burning desire, childlike innocence, and complete trust.

Jordan's breath caught, and she wasn't sure which element affected her the most. Her fingers shook as she reached down and pulled Emma's panties back up.

"I thought you wanted me to undress?" Emma said. The timbre of her voice sent goose bumps down Jordan's spine.

"Just…" She had to stop and clear her throat. "Just your pants." Careful not to use her casted hand too much—or, worse, tug down the panties too—she pulled down Emma's jeans.

Emma's skin was like warm silk beneath her fingers.

Resisting the urge to touch her was incredibly hard, but there was no way she would take advantage of Emma's trust.

With the pants halfway down her legs, they both paused and stared at each other.

Emma's pupils were wide and a little unfocused, but it was the longing in her eyes that made Jordan's breath catch.

One of Emma's hands came up. She touched Jordan's cheek with her fingertips, a gesture so tender that Jordan started to ache all over. She covered Emma's warm fingers with her good hand, cradling them against her cheek.

"You're so beautiful," Emma whispered.

Jordan couldn't remember the last time someone had told her that. Sexy, hot, attractive—sure. But not *beautiful.* "So are you," she whispered back and swiped a loose strand of hair back behind Emma's ear. God, she wanted to kiss her so much…to lose herself in Emma, but it wasn't right.

"Kiss me." Emma's words echoed her desire. She threaded her fingers through Jordan's hair and tugged her down. "Please."

The touch of her fingers against her scalp might have been the most erotic thing Jordan had ever felt. Her knees weakened.

With a moan of approval, Emma pulled her down farther.

"Emma," Jordan groaned, not sure if it was a protest or an encouragement. Her eyes fell shut a moment before their lips were about to meet.

Emma's warm breath teased her lips.

Oh God, yes. Yes! But another voice in her head shouted, *No. Not like this.*

At the last moment, Jordan powered herself back up on her shaking left arm. "No." Gasping for breath as if she'd just completed a marathon, she stared down at Emma. The glittering copper sparks in Emma's irises were almost her undoing.

Emma covered her face with both hands. "I'm sorry," she mumbled from behind that cover. "I just… I can't think straight when I'm around you."

Despite the thick sexual tension between them, Jordan felt the corners of her mouth twitch into a half smile. "Thinking straight is overrated anyway." She sat on the bed next to her and gently pulled down Emma's hands. "You don't have to apologize. I want you. Please don't doubt that."

A low moan escaped Emma.

"But not like this," Jordan added. "Not when you're drunk."

"Tipsy," Emma corrected.

"Very, very tipsy. I've never slept with a woman who was dr—very tipsy, and I'm sure as hell not gonna start with you. You…" *You mean a lot to me.* But that, too, would have to wait until Emma was sober. "You deserve better."

Emma's eyes were glassy, and for a moment, she looked as if she was close to tears, but then she smiled.

Gently, Jordan tugged Emma's jeans down the rest of the way, folded them, and set them on the dresser. Then she turned back toward Emma and settled the covers over her.

Emma snuggled beneath them and stared up at her. "Thank you," she said after several seconds, and Jordan had a feeling she was talking about more than just tucking her in.

"You're welcome." Jordan went to get her a glass of water, grateful to have a moment to cool off and get herself under control. When she returned, she expected to find Emma asleep.

Emma's eyelids had sunk down a little, but she opened them more fully when Jordan put the glass down on her bedside table. "Wet," she said.

Jordan blinked and swallowed against a suddenly dry mouth. "Um, excuse me?"

"Water." Emma's flushed cheeks took on an even deeper shade of red. "I meant water. Thank you for the water."

"Oh. You're welcome. Good night, Emma." Taking a slight risk, Jordan bent and kissed her forehead. Emma's skin was warm and soft, and Jordan barely resisted the urge to explore more of it.

One of Emma's hands came out from beneath the covers, and she touched Jordan's cheek again, this time just cradling her and gazing into her eyes without trying to pull her down.

It occurred to Jordan that it was much more intimate than any kiss could have been.

They remained like that for a few moments; then Emma yawned.

"Sleep well." Jordan forced herself to straighten and walk to the door.

"Jordan?" Emma's voice stopped her before she could leave the room.

She turned. "Yeah?"

"Have you...?" Emma licked her lips. "Did you really not sleep with her?"

So it was still on Emma's mind, even in this state. "I swear I didn't. I didn't even kiss her."

They looked at each other for several moments before Emma nodded. "Okay." Apparently satisfied with that answer, she closed her eyes. Before Jordan could turn away a second time, she opened them again. "Why didn't you?"

Jordan shook her head. If she bared her soul, she didn't want to do it to a woman who might not remember it in the morning. "Let's talk about it tomorrow. I promise to explain it then."

It seemed to take Emma a couple of seconds to process that answer or maybe to decide that Jordan's promise was enough for now; then she nodded. "Okay."

At least Emma was a relatively docile drunk. Jordan turned to leave.

"Jordan?" Again, Emma's voice reached her before she could step across the threshold.

Jordan couldn't help smiling. Somehow, this reminded her of putting Molly to bed—minus the sexy striptease and the almost kiss, of course. She turned. "Yes?"

"Will you stay?"

Oh God. She couldn't share the bed with Emma, could she? Before she thought of an answer, Emma's eyes fluttered closed, and her deep, rhythmic breaths revealed that she had fallen asleep.

Saved by the sandman. Jordan didn't know whether to be relieved or disappointed. She stood watching Emma sleep for a while, then flipped off the light and tiptoed out of the bedroom.

Remembering that the gift basket was still in the backyard, she went out to get it and then closed the still-open French door. She walked into the kitchen, got a glass out of the cabinet, and put it onto the counter, along with a bottle of the Pedialyte left over from when Molly had been sick. Emma would probably need it tomorrow morning.

It was a little strange to be in Emma's kitchen when she wasn't there, but at the same time, it surprised her how at home she felt—and it probably wasn't just because Emma's side of the house was a mirror image to her own.

When she was done with her hangover preparations, she glanced toward the front door and hesitated.

Emma had wanted her to stay, so stay she would.

She kicked off her shoes and jeans, settled down on the couch, and pulled the comforter over herself. "Good night, Emma," she whispered again. "I'm here."

The first thing Emma became aware of when she woke the next morning was her splitting headache. Her temples pounded like a drum in a marching band.

Carefully, she opened one eye and squinted against the piercing sunlight streaming in through the window.

Oh God. How much had she drunk last night?

She was pretty sure she hadn't emptied that bottle of wine. How on earth could you get drunk on two...okay, three...glasses of red wine? Somehow, she seemed to have managed.

Her mouth felt and tasted like a fuzzy sock. *Ugh.* She shuddered and tried not to gag.

When she opened her second eye, she peeked at her alarm clock. A little after seven. She thanked the patron saints of hungover single moms that she had no work appointments this morning and wouldn't have to pick up Molly until this afternoon. But then again, if Molly hadn't been at a sleepover, she would have never allowed herself to drink so much.

A glass of water sat next to her alarm clock on the bedside table. *Jordan.* Jordan had put it there.

Oh no. Emma clutched her throbbing temples as she remembered what she had done last night. Couldn't she at least suffer from a merciful blackout that wiped out the memories of her drunken advances? But no, every moment was etched into her brain with laserlike precision.

She covered her face with her hands, the way she had last night. Had she really tried to get Jordan to kiss and undress her? How embarrassing. Thank God Jordan had put a stop to it.

Emma sighed. To be rejected by Jordan Williams... She had to be the only woman on earth that had ever happened to. Or the second one, if what Jordan had said was true and she really hadn't slept with that woman the other night.

Emma believed her. She hadn't believed Chloe when she swore it had been the first time she had ever cheated on her, but things were different with Jordan. The way Jordan had looked at her when she had put her to bed... There had been no room for lies.

I want you, Jordan had said. That hadn't been a lie either, and neither had the tenderness in her eyes. But what did it all mean?

They needed to talk.

Where was Jordan now? Dimly, Emma remembered asking her to stay just before falling asleep, but Jordan had been too honorable to get into bed with a drunk woman.

Emma sat up. A wave of nausea hit her, and the room started to spin. She clutched her churning stomach with one hand and her head with the other.

When the merry-go-round finally stopped, she reached for the glass of water with both hands and sipped it as if it were the elixir of life.

Feeling slightly less like a zombie, she braved getting out of bed. Every step toward the bathroom made her head pound. *Oh God.* Why hadn't Fran just sent her a signed paperback as a thank-you?

She relieved herself and then brushed her teeth and gurgled with mouthwash to get rid of the awful taste. The rattle of the toothbrush as it plopped back into the glass made her wince. She headed through the hall toward the kitchen, coffee the only thing on her mind. But something made her stop and peek into the living room.

The sight she encountered made her forget about her pounding head for a moment.

Jordan had stayed. She was on the couch, half covered by the comforter, the arm with the cast dangling over the edge.

Aww. Emma leaned against the wall and watched her. For the first time, she became aware of how familiar Jordan's features already were to her: the elegant arc of her eyebrows, her broad nose and high cheekbones, and her full, kissable lips. She knew each feature so well it was as if she had caressed them a thousand times. Her fingers curled against her palms as she remembered cradling Jordan's face in her hand last night.

Jordan's limbs started jerking the way Emma's childhood beagle's paws had when he had dreamed, and she mumbled something unintelligible.

Emma smiled. "Sweet dreams," she whispered into the space between them.

Before she could tiptoe to the kitchen, Jordan opened her eyes and looked directly at her.

Caught, Emma froze.

"Good morning." Jordan sat up.

God, how could she be so wide-awake so fast? It must have been a surgeon thing, because Chloe had been the same way.

"Morning," Emma mumbled.

"Damn. I overslept," Jordan said. "I wanted to bring you breakfast in bed."

"Oh God." Emma pressed one hand to her mouth. The thought of food made her queasy.

"That's what women usually say to my *dessert* in bed," Jordan quipped. Then she grimaced and rubbed her face. "Sorry. I shouldn't have said that. Old habits die hard."

All of them? Emma wanted to ask, but she wasn't ready for that discussion. At least not before she'd had coffee, a shower, and some painkillers, not necessarily in that order.

Jordan pulled back the comforter and got up from the couch. She had slept in her panties and the shirt from last night. Her jeans were neatly folded on the coffee table, and Emma couldn't help watching as she pulled them up her long, athletic legs.

The hangover might have killed her appetite, but apparently not her libido.

It was only when Jordan gave her a slow perusal that she realized that she was wearing the same outfit Jordan wore—a wrinkled T-shirt and a pair of panties, minus the jeans.

"Headache?" Jordan asked when Emma continued to stare without saying anything.

"Oh yeah. I feel like a pile of bricks hit me on the head."

Jordan's grin managed to be amused and compassionate at the same time. "Nope. No bricks involved. Just most of a bottle of red wine."

"I never did well with red wine," Emma mumbled, her cheeks heating. "I don't know why I drank it."

"No?" Jordan's gaze seemed to drill into her.

Emma sighed. "Okay, maybe I do know. But I need painkillers and coffee before we delve into that topic. My head's too foggy to think clearly."

"Come on, then."

Jordan led her into the kitchen as if it were her own, and Emma surprised herself by letting her play hostess. She sank onto the chair Jordan pulled out for her and put her head on her folded arms on the small table. From there, she watched Jordan prepare a tray.

"Voila," Jordan said when she finally set it down on the table, "breakfast of champions. Well, wine-drinking champions."

Emma frowned down at a plate of dry toast and a purple liquid in a glass. "What's that? Where's my coffee?"

"No coffee until later. We need to rehydrate you first. Drink up—doctor's orders."

Groaning, Emma reached for the glass and drank a few sips. Whatever it was tasted very sweet and grape-flavored.

"Do you have any Ibuprofen in the house?" Jordan asked.

Emma nodded. "Bathroom," she said between sips of the sweet liquid.

Within less than a minute, Jordan was back with a bottle of painkillers.

Eagerly, Emma opened it and shook out two of the pills. "No other miracle cures that they taught you in med school?" she asked after swallowing them.

"Not drinking usually works, but other than that—nope. Sorry. You'll just have to be patient and wait it out."

Wait it out... That's what Emma had done during the last few weeks— waiting for her mind to reign over her heart and her body, for her longing to be held in Jordan's arms to fade, or for someone else to come along and make her forget Jordan.

She had a feeling it wouldn't happen, no matter how long she waited. Coming to a decision, she emptied her glass and pushed the plate with the toast away.

"Finished?" Jordan asked. When Emma nodded, she took the tray away.

"Can you give me a minute to take a shower?" Emma asked. "Then I'd like to sit on the couch and talk."

"Uh, yeah, of course." Jordan sounded tenser than Emma had ever heard her, including the minutes while they had waited to find out whether she needed to have surgery for her arm.

Emma stumbled to the shower and tried not to think about the conversation they were about to have. When she stepped out of the bathroom, she was starting to feel better—at least physically. Emotionally, she was a wreck. Her heart started to pound more urgently than her head as she walked toward the living room.

This was it. They would talk about it now—about last night. About them.

Oh God. Was she really ready for it? But ready or not, she knew she couldn't avoid it any longer—didn't want to avoid it any longer. If she did, she would drive herself crazy.

Nausea threatened as she entered the living room.

Jordan was already seated at one end of the couch.

For a moment, Emma eyed the easy chairs, but then settled down next to her. No avoiding this. The faux leather of the couch still seemed to hold some of Jordan's body heat, and Emma cuddled against it, trying to soak up as much as possible.

Their arms rested against each other, but neither of them pulled away.

"How's the head?" Jordan asked before Emma could decide how to start this conversation. "Did the shower help, or would you rather do this another time?"

Was she chickening out? "Do you want to—?"

"No," Jordan said quickly. "I just wanted to make sure...with your hangover and everything...that you feel up to it."

Emma stared down at her knees. She had put on a pair of sweatpants, but she felt as exposed as she had earlier, in just a pair of panties. Voicing her feelings was harder than she had imagined, but she didn't want to hide or play games. "My brain feels very muddled, but that has nothing to do with my hangover."

Jordan tugged loose a few threads from the edge of her cast. "I know what you mean," she murmured without looking away from the cast.

Good. At least they were on the same page when it came to that. A tiny seed of hope took root in Emma. Maybe they would be on the same page about what they wanted too.

For a moment, she wished she had a cast to tug on too, since she didn't know what to do with all that nervous energy swirling through her. "You know," Emma said when she couldn't stand the silence any longer, "when I first woke up and remembered what I had done last night..."

"No need to be embarrassed," Jordan said.

"That's nice of you to say, but I find it pretty embarrassing. And that's part of the reason why I wanted to tell you to forget about it."

Jordan turned her head and studied her. "But?"

The tension in Emma's body increased until she thought one of her tendons or muscles would snap. She took a deep breath. Jordan had been the brave one in the zoo, but Emma had practically told her to shut up, and now it was her turn to put herself out there, at least a little bit. "But we keep saying that, don't we? And it doesn't seem to be working."

"No," Jordan said slowly, "it doesn't seem to work at all."

They sat in silence for a moment until Emma said, "Can I...? Can I ask you something?"

Jordan licked her lips. "Um, sure."

The tension was so thick, it almost seemed to materialize into a cloud between them.

"What you said in the zoo…that you'd like it to be my business who you sleep with…what exactly did you mean by that?" Emma stared at Jordan, not wanting to miss her reaction.

"I…" More loose threads came free. If their conversation continued like this, Jordan wouldn't need to have the cast removed—she would take it off thread by thread right here. "I'm not sure. I just said it without thinking."

"Oh." Emma looked away, not wanting Jordan to see how much of a disappointment that was. "So you didn't mean it?"

"No. I mean, yes. Jesus, Emma, I'm so turned around right now, I don't know what direction is up and what is down. The only thing I know for sure is that there's something between us…something more than horniness or sexual attraction…and I'm pretty sure I'm not the only one who feels that way." Jordan peeked at her. For the first time since Emma had met her, she looked almost shy. "Am I?"

Emma's throat was dry, so it took her a few seconds to make her vocal cords work. Or maybe she needed these moments to take this leap and put her heart on the line despite her fears. "No," she got out. "No, you're not. But here's the thing… You told me more than once that you can't imagine eating the same dessert every day for the rest of your life. And I could accept that as long as we were just friends, but now…" She heaved a sigh. "I can't help it. Maybe it's old-fashioned, but…I'm a one-cupcake woman. Once I find the one dessert I like, I don't want to keep sampling others… and I don't want my favorite cupcake to be nibbled on by other people."

Jordan gulped audibly. She turned a little on the couch so she could fully face Emma. "And…and you think that I could be your favorite cupcake?"

"When I moved here, I wasn't looking for a…cupcake. After Chloe, I thought I would stay away from desserts for the foreseeable future. Even if I had been looking, you at first certainly didn't seem like the type of dessert that would be to my taste."

"But?" Jordan prompted.

The hopeful gleam in her eyes gave Emma the courage to continue. "But you keep surprising me."

"In good ways?"

"In very good ways." Emma's throat closed with emotion, so she paused for a moment. "You're smart, confident, and a lot more sensitive and reliable than most people give you credit for, and you make me laugh and feel safe like no one else."

"Don't forget damn hot," Jordan quipped, probably to break the tension.

Emma smiled. "All right, I admit it. You look pretty...okayish too."

They both chuckled, but it sounded nervous.

"During the last couple of weeks, I realized that in many regards you're exactly the type of cupcake I'm looking for," Emma said. It was hard to admit to, especially to herself. Coming so close to perfection, yet never reaching it... It hurt. She sighed and forced herself to go on. "We seem so compatible in a lot of ways. We both like order, and we have the same taste in books, and I love how supportive you are of me and my job...and you're fantastic with Molly and..." She stopped herself when she realized she was babbling. "But in this one very important thing, we're not compatible at all. I want to enjoy the same cupcake for the rest of my life—and you want a sampler plate."

Now that it was out, her tension deflated a little, and she sank against the back of the couch. Hesitantly, she peeked over at Jordan to see her reaction.

Jordan's features were in constant motion, the muscles beneath the smooth skin shifting too fast to settle into one specific expression that Emma could identify. She opened her mouth, closed it again, cleared her throat, and then finally spoke. "That sums it up pretty well."

Tears burned in Emma's eyes. She let her pounding head fall back against the couch. "Yeah." Unfortunately, it did.

"At least it would have been a very accurate description of what I wanted in life six weeks ago—a sampler plate. Having fun with a lot of different women, maybe have a second bite if I really enjoy being with one..."

Emma's stomach churned. Did she really need to hear all these details?

"Relationships mean compromise and sacrifice—at least that's the way I always saw it. Like what my mom gave up when she married my dad. Like what you gave up when you had Molly."

"It's okay," Emma said. As much as it hurt, she knew she had to accept Jordan's choices. "You don't need to say anything else. I understand that you can't or don't want to—"

Jordan touched Emma's arm before pulling her hand away. "Let me finish. I need to get this out before my brain freezes in terror," she said with a wry smile.

So she was scared too. Emma wanted so much to take her into her arms and comfort her, but she knew they needed to talk this out before one of them gave in to the fear and ran.

"That's how I saw it: freedom and fun versus compromise and sacrifice. A no-brainer, really. I thought I'd made my choice for life. But this," she tapped her cast, "slowed me down and forced me to look at my choices for the first time in years. I'm starting to get what my mother always tried to tell me. Relationships aren't all about compromise and sacrifice. They are also about support and intimacy. About bringing out the best in each other and growing with each other."

"Not all of them," Emma couldn't help saying as her mind flashed back to that moment when she had stepped into their bedroom and caught Chloe with her medical assistant. "But ideally...yeah."

"So, I'm starting to wonder..." Jordan paused and ran the fingers of her good hand through her short-cropped hair. "Are these short flings really what I want at this point of my life? Or am I just clinging to them because that's what I'm used to?"

Emma barely dared to breathe while she waited for Jordan to continue. If that wasn't what Jordan wanted anymore, what did she want, then? She didn't ask, sensing that Jordan needed to work through this on her own.

Jordan raised her gaze to Emma's, her dark eyes full of emotion. Slowly, she reached out and took Emma's hand into her own. Her palm was damp with sweat, but Emma immediately entwined their fingers anyway. "On Saturday, when I took that woman home with me... I couldn't go through with it. She was attractive, but I didn't want to sleep with her. All I could think about was you. I think..." Her grip on Emma's hand tightened. "... what I want is you."

Emma wanted to sink into Jordan's arms, but she needed to be sure; she needed Jordan to be sure. "You *think*?"

"I want you," Jordan said, now sounding surer of herself, "and not just for one night."

A noise close to a whimper escaped Emma. For a moment, she thought she would burst into tears of happiness, but she held herself in check. "If we do this, I want the real thing, Jordan. I want more than whatever you have with Simone."

"I can't promise you that I'll be any good at being a girlfriend." Jordan's hand shook in hers. "In fact, I'm pretty sure I'll fail and disappoint you a few times while I'm trying to figure it out."

"That's okay," Emma said and softly squeezed her fingers. "As long as it's not the way Chloe did."

"Never." It burst out of Jordan like a passionate vow. "Like I said, I would never be unfaithful to you."

"Good." Emma put her other hand on top of Jordan's too. "Besides, I'm thirty-two, divorced, and a mom. I don't want a girlfriend anyway."

Jordan's eyes widened. "Um, what do you want, then?"

"Eventually, I want a partner," Emma said as firmly as her shaking voice allowed. "Can you do that?"

"I have no idea. But for the first time in my life, I want to find out. It's scary as hell, but I figure we may as well be scared together."

Could it really be that easy? Emma considered it for a moment. Well, it might be—if she was willing to take this leap of faith. "Okay," she whispered.

"Okay?" Jordan whispered back.

"Okay," Emma confirmed.

Their smiles started timidly but then quickly grew into out-of-control grins.

Emma's heart felt as if it might beat out of her chest, half from joy and half from terror. *Oh God.* It was probably crazy, but... They were doing this!

And since they were, she could finally give in to that desire that she had harbored for weeks now and that hadn't been fulfilled last night. "Kiss me."

Jordan's gaze immediately dipped down to her mouth. "I'd argue about who's boss and gets to order the other one around in this relationship..." She shook her head, looking dazed, as if she could hardly believe that she was really in a relationship, but then she continued, "But actually..." She leaned closer. "...I don't..." And closer. "...care as long as I get to..." Her warm breath bathed Emma's mouth, making her forget to breathe. "...kiss you."

Then their lips met in a kiss that was much more tender than the one they had shared in the garage. Jordan's lips caressed hers, making Emma melt against her. She was glad that she was sitting, not sure if her legs still had the ability to hold her up. Her entire body was just focused on one thing—the feel of Jordan's silky, warm lips on hers.

She slid her hands up Jordan's back and wound her fingers through her hair, pulling her closer.

Jordan tilted her head, fitting their mouths together even more perfectly. The pressure of her lips became firmer. She nipped at Emma's bottom lip with her teeth and teased at the corner of her mouth with her tongue.

Emma's lips parted on a moan. Her body seemed to overheat as their tongues slid along each other. An urgent need pulsed through her, and she tried to press closer so she could feel more of Jordan. *Slow, slow,* she cautioned herself. *This is new to both of us.*

But her body needed a full minute to get the message.

They pulled back at the same time and rested their foreheads against each other, both breathing hard.

"God," Emma got out when she remembered how to speak, "that was…"

"If you say *okayish*, I'll have to keep kissing you until you come up with a better description," Jordan said, her voice husky. "And you know how competitive I am. You might end up late to pick up Molly." Her voice dropped another register. "Very late."

Her tone sent shivers down Emma's body. "Is that a threat…or a promise?"

Jordan's heated gaze met hers. "Both."

Emma leaned forward and initiated a second kiss, which was definitely much more than *okayish*. God, she could kiss this woman for hours…for years…forever.

Slow, remember? She nibbled on Jordan's full lips one last time and then pulled back.

Liquid lava seemed to be running through her veins. She felt wonderful, more alive than she had in years. Then she realized something else. Her head wasn't pounding anymore, just her heart and a certain spot between her legs. She started to laugh. "I think we found that hangover cure, Dr. Williams."

Jordan flashed the confident grin that Emma found so irresistible. "Well, what can I say? We surgeons don't just have great hands. Looks like we have great lips too."

"This surgeon," Emma whispered against said lips and then kissed them once more. "Just *this* surgeon. And don't you get any ideas about making this hangover cure available to the masses."

"Never," Jordan whispered back and then found a better way than talking to occupy their mouths.

Jordan leaned in the doorway of the bedroom and watched as Emma changed out of her sweatpants and into a pair of jeans. Her lips quirked into a smile at the irony of it. Normally, she would have the woman she was with undressed and in bed by now, but with Emma, everything was different.

She still couldn't believe *how* different it was. She, Jordan Williams, was in a bona fide relationship! If someone had told her that a few weeks ago, she would have laughed until her sides hurt.

But now it didn't seem like a laughing matter at all—quite the opposite. Every time she thought about it more closely, a tinge of panic skittered down her spine, and even Emma's kisses couldn't completely chase it away.

That was all they had done this morning—have coffee and then lunch and exchange kisses, some tender, some increasingly passionate. They hadn't gone any further. Pacing herself and not letting her hands wander too far had been the hardest and, at the same time, the easiest thing she had ever done. While her entire body burned with the need to touch Emma, it wasn't the same urge that normally drove her.

This wasn't a challenge that would present itself just once, for one night only. Emma wasn't a woman to conquer and seduce; what Jordan wanted to do instead was worship her the way she deserved.

Man. She shook her head at herself. This was only day one of being in a relationship, and she already sounded sappy as hell!

Emma put her shoes on and then turned to face her. Her lips were slightly swollen from all the kisses they had exchanged. The sight immediately made Jordan want to kiss her again. Would anyone notice the freshly kissed look and ask about it? If they did, what would Emma say?

Admittedly, Jordan didn't have a clue how this would work.

Emma stopped two steps from her. "I have a few more minutes until I have to pick up Molly. Can we talk?"

Uh-oh. Already she was hearing the most dreaded words in a relationship. Had she done something wrong? God, since when was she so insecure? "Um, sure."

They went back to the couch, which was now Jordan's favorite piece of furniture in the house.

"So…" Emma pulled one leg up and wrapped her arms around it as if she needed a shield between them. "Are we…um, officially together now? Do we tell people?"

"Of course," Jordan said without even having to think about it. "I thought that's what you wanted." Wasn't it? She had always thought she understood women and what they wanted, but now…

Emma's leg slid back to the floor. "Yes." She pitched to the side in relief, her shoulder coming to rest against Jordan's. "That's exactly what I want. I just wasn't sure if it's what you want. I thought maybe you needed a bit more time to get used to the thought."

Jordan flashed a grin. "I was always the type to get it over with and rip a Band-Aid off quickly."

"Rip a Band-Aid off?" Emma repeated, her brows arched. But her tone was teasing, and the copper sparks in her eyes danced with mischief. "Is that the best comparison that comes to mind to you for us?"

"Well, I'm sure I could come up with something much more flattering and romantic, but the problem is, every time you're near, my brain short-circuits and all I can think of is…"

Then they were kissing again, and her brain was short-circuited, and she stopped thinking anything but *more* and *so soft* and *God, yes*.

When they finally separated, she could hardly remember what they had been talking about.

"Um, you were saying?" Emma leaned against the back of the couch and looked as if she was having trouble focusing her eyes.

Jordan couldn't help the proud smirk. "I was saying…" Oh yeah, now she remembered. "…that telling people about us is fine with me. Part of me wants to shout it from the rooftops." She chuckled about herself.

"Oh, no," Emma said immediately. "No climbing on trees or rooftops or anything else." She cradled Jordan's casted arm in both hands. "I have a vested interest in making sure you don't hurt your hand again."

Her tone and the desire in her eyes made heat erupt deep inside of Jordan. She let out a growl. "How much time did you say we have before you have to leave?"

"Not enough time for *that*," Emma said with a throaty laugh. "If…when it happens, I want to have all night to kiss and touch every inch of you."

Jordan squeezed her eyes shut, fighting for control, then opened them again. "Oh God, I want that too."

They stared into each other's eyes until Emma tore herself away. "And if it's okay with you, I'd like to wait until we told Molly. I don't want her to find out by walking in on us or something like that."

"Sure," Jordan said, even though waiting wasn't normally her modus operandi. Emma was worth waiting for.

"Thank you," Emma murmured against her lips and then kissed her one last time before getting up. "I have to pick up Molly."

Jordan followed her to the door on legs that felt a little weak. "Are you sure you're okay to drive? I could pick her up."

Emma shook her head. "I'm fine after that miracle cure of yours." She winked at Jordan. "Besides, the teachers won't let her go with you. I need to put you on the list of people authorized to pick her up first."

Wow. Jordan's head started spinning. Would that be the first step toward becoming a stepmom? Was she ready for that?

"How about you? Are you all right?" Emma reached up and caressed Jordan's cheek. "You look a little…"

"I'm fine," Jordan said. At least she hoped she would be. She snuggled her cheek into the touch. "So, do you want me to come over tonight so we can tell Molly about us?"

Emma hesitated and let her hand drop away. "I'd love for you to come over and have dinner with us, but maybe we should wait a little before we tell her. Moving…leaving behind her other mom…getting used to a new school and new friends… It's a lot for a six-year-old to take in. I don't want to overwhelm her with too much, too soon."

Emma was the expert when it came to the well-being of her daughter, so Jordan nodded. "Just let me know when you think it's time to tell her so I can prepare for that talk."

"You," Emma tapped her nose and then leaned up to kiss her lightly, "are just too cute."

Instead of an answer, Jordan deepened the kiss.

Chapter 21

On Friday afternoon, Jordan went over to Barbara's house.

Barb's cane leaned against the wooden bench in front of her home while she was sprinkling used coffee grounds mixed with wood ash around her rose bushes, the way she did every few weeks. When she saw Jordan coming, she straightened with a groan and wiped her hands on her gardener's apron. "Hi there, stranger. I haven't seen you in ages."

"Ages? Hello, I picked you up from bingo on Monday."

Barb tsked. "As I said, ages. Is everything okay?"

Heat rose up Jordan's neck. "Everything's fine. More than fine, actually." She had spent most of the week with Emma and Molly, sharing meals and babysitting duties. God, it was so domestic. It still amazed her how much she enjoyed it. Two months ago, she would have been bored out of her mind. Or maybe that wasn't true. Maybe she had just always assumed she would be.

She took the long-handled garden claw from Barb and urged her to sit on the bench and rest while she worked the ash/coffee grounds mixture into the soil. It was a bit of a struggle with just one good hand, but at least it distracted her from her nervousness. "I…um, spent a lot of time with Emma this week."

"Oh?" Barbara studied her closely.

"Yeah." Jordan threw her full body weight into the twisting motion. "She and I… We've grown close." *Man.* She could have slapped her own forehead. That sounded like her awkward coming-out to her sisters when she had been fifteen.

"Close?" Barb repeated, arching her silver eyebrows. "You mean close like you and Simone?"

"No. Close like..." Jordan paused to wipe her damp forehead. She swallowed against the lump in her throat and searched for a comparison Barb would understand. "Like you and Monty."

Barb's eyes widened. Then she bounded up from the bench with a speed and energy that belied her seventy-four years. The garden claw toppled to the ground as she engulfed Jordan in a hug. "I'm so, so happy for you. For both of you."

Jordan had a feeling they were both beaming like maniacs. "Thank you." She cleared her throat. "We're taking it slow, so we haven't..."

"Oh. That's fine, dear." Barb affectionately patted her cheek. "Back in my day, people didn't jump into bed at the drop of a hat either, and it didn't hurt them any."

For the second time within minutes, Jordan felt her cheeks heat. "No. No, that's not what I meant, although...we're waiting for that too. I meant to say that we haven't told Molly yet."

Barb lifted her hand to her mouth and giggled like a young girl. "Don't worry. She won't find out from me. But you are planning on telling her, right?"

"Of course. I want to do this right," Jordan said, staring at the ground. "That's why I thought maybe I would ask Emma out on a date. I mean... Because of Molly, she doesn't go out much, and the last time she was at a nice restaurant, she had to leave early because Molly got sick, so... Do you think she would like that?"

Barb squeezed her good hand. "I'm sure she'll love it."

"Could you...? Would you be willing to watch Molly while we're out?"

"Of course," Barb said immediately. "When?"

"Would tomorrow be too soon?" She couldn't wait to take Emma out.

Barb smiled. "Tomorrow is fine, dear. I'll stock up on cookies and picture books."

Jordan bent and kissed her wrinkled cheek. "Thank you."

Emma hummed contentedly and snuggled her cheek against Jordan's shoulder. A hammock for two was heaven on earth, even if getting into it without toppling Jordan to the ground had been a challenge.

But some things were worth the risk—and that wasn't just true for their nightly cuddle session in the hammock.

The peaceful mood was interrupted when Jordan started to fidget. The hammock began to sway more wildly.

Grunting, Emma opened her eyes and lifted her head off Jordan's shoulder. "What are you doing?"

Jordan froze. She had picked up a twig and was using it to scratch inside her cast.

"Jordan!" Emma snatched the twig away from her, broke it in two, and threw the pieces into the bushes. "You're a doctor. You should know better than that! What if you hurt yourself?"

"But it itches like crazy," Jordan grumbled and now used the pinkie of her good hand to scratch.

Emma took hold of her hand to stop her. "Your scratching-every-itch days are over, darling."

Jordan stopped her attempts to scratch and lifted her head. Her face was just inches from Emma's. "Oh yeah?"

"Oh yeah. Unless I'm the one doing the—"

Jordan's lips were on hers before she could finish the sentence.

Emma moaned into Jordan's mouth as their tongues met. She felt her T-shirt being tugged out of her jeans, and a warm hand slid up her side. Moaning again, she pressed closer, ran her own hand up Jordan's body, and cupped one soft breast through Jordan's shirt.

Mmm. So good.

Her world tilted on its axis, and it took her a moment to realize that it wasn't their passion that had caused it; it was the hammock.

Gasping, they pulled back and balanced out the hammock before they ended up on the ground.

"You," she kissed Jordan's warm shoulder through her T-shirt, "are dangerous."

"Me?" Jordan drawled. "You were the one who grabbed my boob."

"Are you complaining?"

"No. Definitely not."

Emma felt Jordan's lips form a grin against her skin before Jordan planted a kiss on her forehead.

They settled back down, but soon, Jordan started to fidget again.

"Stop scratching!"

"I'm not scratching. This time, it's just…"

At the tension in Jordan's voice, Emma peeked up and put a hand on Jordan's upper chest. "What is it?"

"Um, I was wondering… Well, tomorrow's Saturday, and Barb said she'd love to watch Molly…"

The nervous stammering made Emma smile. She loved this self-conscious version of Jordan because she knew no other woman had ever seen this side of her. All they had gotten was the suave seducer.

"So…" Jordan cleared her throat. "Would you like to go out with me tomorrow night? I thought we could drive to Pasadena and have dinner and—"

Emma stopped the babbling with a kiss. "Yes," she breathed against Jordan's lips.

"Yes?"

"Yes," Emma said. "Was there ever any doubt as to what my answer would be?"

Jordan cocked her head to the side. "Well, the last time I asked you out, you shot me down in two seconds flat."

Emma chuckled as she remembered the day she had moved in. Hard to believe that it had been just seven weeks ago. The woman who lay in the hammock with her seemed so different from the swaggering charmer who had fed her lines and asked her out for coffee.

"So," she asked, "where are you taking me?"

Jordan shook her head. "Not saying. It'll be a surprise."

"Oh, come on. How am I supposed to dress for our date if I don't know where we are going?"

"Just dress casually," Jordan said. With a wink, she added, "But sexy. I'll pick you up at seven, if that's okay."

Emma nodded. "Seven sounds great." She'd put it in her planner—this time using red ink—as soon as she got back inside. But first she had to find out where they were going. Maybe kisses would work as a bribe. Determined, she set out to try.

Emma was very relaxed about the idea of going out on a date, at least until around six o'clock on Saturday evening. This was Jordan, after all. They'd had dinner together many times during the previous six weeks.

But when it was time to get dressed, she could no longer fool herself. This was a real date, not having macaroni and cheese with Molly right next to them. She wouldn't be dining with Jordan, her friend; she would be going out with Jordan, the woman who left her breathless.

Emma pulled one outfit after another from her closet and then discarded them all. Nothing gave off that sexy yet casual I-just-threw-this-on vibe that she was going for. Soon, the entire contents of her closet were dumped on her bed in one big heap, and she was about to collapse on top of it in full wardrobe panic.

She hadn't had a date in over ten years. If you didn't count the interrupted dinner with Wendy, the last date she'd gone on had been with Chloe, which didn't exactly boost her confidence, considering how their relationship had ended.

Desperate, she reached for the phone. Whom to call?

During the past weeks, Jordan had become the person she called when she needed advice, but that was out of the question.

Lori. Her down-to-earth friend had always given her sound advice.

She tapped the contact and put the phone to her ear while pacing the length of the bedroom. As soon as Lori picked up, she blurted, "I've got a date."

For a few moments, only silence filtered through the line. "Um, hello to you too. I'm fine, and it's raining in Portland. Thanks for asking." Then Lori paused. A screech made Emma pull the phone away from her ear. "Did you just say...? You've got a date! Emma, that's great! See? Didn't I tell you? Baby steps and you'll be fine."

Emma exhaled sharply. "Yeah, well, we're not exactly taking baby steps. It feels more like leaping off a cliff headfirst when it's pitch-dark outside."

Springs creaked, probably as Lori dropped down onto her couch. "Don't tell me you already slept with her!" She laughed. "Go, tiger! It's that yummy neighbor of yours, isn't it?"

"No! Yes. I mean..." Emma would have flopped down onto the bed too, but she didn't want to wrinkle the pile of clothes. "Yes, it's Jordan, but it's not what you think. It's different. *She's* different."

"Different than what?"

"Different than I thought she would be if I let myself get involved with her. She's sweet and funny and charming as hell, and now she's asked me out on a date, and she said to dress casual, but Lori, it's not casual." She lowered her voice to a whisper, even though Molly was in her room, listening to the soundtrack of *Frozen* for the thousandth time. "I think this might be serious. Get-my-heart-broken-into-a-million-little-pieces serious."

Lori said nothing for several seconds.

"Lori? You still there?"

"Still here and breathing...I think. Wow. I sure didn't see that coming. I thought you'd not want to get involved ever again—and certainly not within a few months of moving to California! What happened?"

"Jordan happened," Emma said, and then she did drop down onto the bed, wrinkles be damned. She curled up on her side and buried her face in her favorite sweater at the bottom of the pile.

"But that's great, isn't it? New love, romantic dates, hot sex..." Lori sighed dramatically. "The most exciting thing that happened to me all week was when a guy in the park hit me with his Frisbee. He wasn't even all that good-looking, and he only asked me out for coffee because he was afraid I'd sue him. I'd trade that guilt-trip-coffee-date with Mr. Frisbee for a date with your yummy neighbor any day."

That made Emma smile. She let out a playful growl. "Nope. Sorry. She's all mine."

"Is she?" Lori asked, now completely serious.

Emma slowly breathed in and out. "Yes," she said. "I think she is."

"What's got you in such a panic, then?"

"Hello?" Emma waved her hand, even though Lori couldn't see it. "Asshole ex-wife, messy divorce, year from hell... Need I say more?"

"I know. I'm not trying to belittle what happened. I just hope you won't let it stop you from taking a chance at something real with your yummy neighbor."

"Jordan," Emma said. "Her name is Jordan."

"Oh, I don't know. I kind of like 'yummy neighbor.'"

"Me too," Emma murmured under her breath. "I really like her too."

"Great. Now that we have that sorted, let's get you dressed," Lori said in her efficient-executive-assistant voice. "Do you still have that outfit that made Brendan from HR nearly barbecue his own hand at that office party two years ago?"

Emma stared at the heap next to her. "I think so. Somewhere beneath this avalanche."

"Excuse me?"

"Nothing. I'm looking." She scrambled off the bed and started digging. Only thirty more minutes until Jordan would be here.

Jordan looked at herself in her favorite clubbing outfit—the one that always guaranteed her a second look from women, sometimes even the straight ones. She grinned at her reflection and then twirled to make sure her ass still looked good in these pants.

It did.

See? she told her reflection. *Dating isn't that difficult.*

She imagined Emma running her hands down the bare V of skin the shirt left free at the front, the way some of the women in the club had.

The touch, even if it was just imaginary, sent a bolt of desire down her body. But at the same time, it felt wrong. This outfit was the bait she had used to entice other women. She couldn't wear it on her first date with Emma.

Grumbling, she took it off, not bothering to be gentle so it wouldn't tear.

Then she stood in front of her closet and stared inside. What outfit would signal her intentions and tell Emma she was serious about her?

Oh, for fuck's sake! Since when did she waste so much time thinking about what to wear? *Just pick something and be done with it!*

But despite her admonishment, she wanted to look good for Emma. She wanted Emma to be proud to be seen with her.

Finally, she decided to wear something she'd be comfortable in, knowing Emma would want her to be herself. She had picked the restaurant with the same thing in mind.

When she was dressed, she glanced in the mirror and was once again grateful she kept her hair short so she wouldn't have to deal with that wild mop. She dabbed a bit of CK Be on her pulse points and took the flowers she had gotten earlier out of the water.

Squaring her shoulders, she marched to the door. Time to collect her date. Good thing they lived right next door to each other. She'd taken so much time getting dressed that she would have been late otherwise.

Instead of crossing the patio and knocking on one of the French doors, the way she usually did when she went over to Emma's, she circled around to the front of the house. She wanted to do this right, and that included ringing the doorbell.

God, she felt like a high school boy picking up his date on prom night. At least she knew no overprotective parents would open the door.

She heard the racket of little feet running down the hall.

"No opening the door without me, Molly," Emma shouted.

"But it's Jordan," Molly shouted back.

"You can't know that. Wait for me."

Jordan couldn't help smiling at the familiar exchange.

Then the door opened, and Jordan's smile faded away as her lips formed a breathless "wow."

Like Jordan, Emma was wearing jeans, but unlike Jordan's slightly loose, boot-cut pair, hers seemed to practically be painted onto her curvy body. Knee-high boots showcased her gorgeous legs, and her silk top allowed a glimpse of her sexy cleavage without revealing too much of it.

"Flowers," Jordan said, still staring. She thrust them at Emma.

Emma licked her lips, wrenched her gaze away from Jordan's outfit, and turned her attention to the flowers. "Three bouquets? Not that I don't appreciate it, but isn't that a little much?" she asked with a smile.

"Oh. Um, no. This one," Jordan nodded at a bouquet of apricot-colored roses with pink tips, "is for you. The smaller ones are for Molly and Barb."

"Aww. That's really nice of you." Emma took a step toward her. The intoxicating perfume she wore teased Jordan's nose.

Everything in Jordan screamed at her to lean down and kiss Emma hello, but she wasn't sure that was such a good idea in front of Molly.

Before she could decide how to greet her, Molly asked from behind Emma, "Flowers? For me too?" She squeezed between them so she could see the bouquets. "Look, Mommy! I got flowers too!"

"I know. Aren't they pretty?" Emma caressed her daughter's head. "Have you thanked Jordan?"

Molly wrapped her arms around Jordan's hips. "Thank you for the flowers."

"You're welcome."

Barb's chuckle drifted through the open door. "Thank you from me too. They're beautiful—and you don't look half bad either."

"Yeah, she looks okayish, doesn't she?" Emma added, but her hungry gaze that roamed up and down Jordan's body said something else.

"Let's go before you do serious damage to my ego," Jordan said. As much as she enjoyed spending time with Molly and Barb, she couldn't wait to be alone with Emma.

As they headed toward the garage, Emma tried to stay one step behind Jordan, so she could ogle her a little longer. God, no wonder women couldn't resist her. She looked good enough to eat!

Jordan wore a short-sleeved, light-blue shirt that showed off her athletic arms, the top two buttons teasingly open to reveal a bit of smooth skin. Her dark blue jeans looked almost like a pair of men's pants, just hinting at the female curves beneath. A brown suede jacket was thrown casually over one shoulder. The look was lethally sexy, making Emma wonder how she had managed to resist her for weeks.

As the garage door swung open, she forced her gaze away. "Let me drive."

"Nah. I want to take you out in my sports car."

"I could drive your car," Emma said.

Jordan turned and shot her a look before wordlessly continuing on to the driver's side of the car.

She shouldn't have been surprised. Chloe had never let her drive her car either. It was a control thing that seemed to be typical for surgeons.

Jordan pressed the button that unlocked the car and pulled open the driver's side door. But instead of getting in, she held it open and turned an expectant gaze on Emma. "I thought you wanted to drive?"

"Wow. You're seriously letting me drive your car?"

Jordan shrugged. "You let me babysit your daughter. I figure I should show some trust too."

"Thank you." Emma hurried over before Jordan could change her mind. "I promise not to feed your baby as much sugar as you gave mine."

"Hahaha." Jordan lightly pinched her butt as Emma slid past her and behind the wheel. Then she rounded the car and got in on the passenger side, where she admittedly looked a little out of place.

Emma reached over and squeezed her leg for a moment. "Seriously... thank you. Knowing you trust me means a lot."

Jordan nodded as if she didn't know what to say.

Smiling, Emma took her hand away. She put them both onto the steering wheel and caressed the soft leather. "Nice," she purred.

"Very nice," Jordan said, her voice husky.

Emma looked up.

Their gazes met, and for a moment, Emma fully expected the car to go up in flames.

"You look beautiful," Jordan whispered and leaned across the middle console.

"So do you," Emma managed to get out before their lips met in a heated kiss.

Ten minutes later, they were still kissing, still in the car, which hadn't moved an inch.

Finally, it was Jordan who pulled back first, breathing heavily. "If we don't want to spend our first date in the garage, we should get going."

"Oh, I don't know. That doesn't sound so bad at the moment." Just looking at Jordan made her hungry for something other than food.

They both leaned forward for one last kiss before Emma started the car. When she pulled out onto the street, she realized that she had no idea where they were going. "Um, directions?"

Jordan guided her to Pasadena, the next city over, and to an all but full parking lot, where Emma pulled smoothly into the last empty space.

"Very nice, baby," Jordan said and leaned over the middle console again as if to reward her for her driving skills with a kiss.

But Emma stopped her with a hand to her chest. "Emma," she said firmly. "Not *baby*. I'm an adult, and I want to be treated like one."

Jordan blinked. "It's just an endearment. It doesn't mean that I see you as a child. That couldn't be farther from the truth, believe me."

"Still," Emma said. She knew she was probably overreacting, but this was important to her.

Jordan studied her. "Chloe called you that, didn't she?"

Emma nodded, her lips pressed together so tightly it almost hurt.

"I won't call you that again." It sounded like a vow. Jordan reached over and softly touched her leg. "How about darling?"

"That's fine."

"Sweetheart?"

"Acceptable too."

"Cupcake?" Jordan's eyes twinkled. "Sweetie-poo?"

"You!" Emma reached across and pinched a spot on her hip. When Jordan jumped, she gentled her touch to a caress. She couldn't help laughing. Somehow, Jordan always managed that—making her forget the bitter memories of the past.

Jordan squeezed Emma's hand, which still rested on her hip. "Come on. Let's head inside and enjoy our date." She got out and came around to open the driver's side door for her.

"Thank you." Emma climbed out and looked around. She'd never been in this part of Pasadena before. The side street didn't exactly look like a prime dating spot, and as far as she could see, there weren't any fine Italian or French restaurants in the vicinity.

But Jordan seemed to know where she was going. Guiding Emma with a light touch to the small of her back, she crossed the parking lot.

Emma liked how her hand felt on her back, warm and secure, but also setting off tingles that ran through every inch of her body.

At the other end of the parking lot, a neon sign saying *diner* flashed. Beneath it hung another sign, this one made of metal, announcing the name of the restaurant: Heavenly Burgers.

Emma turned her head toward Jordan. "You're taking me to a burger place for our first date?"

Jordan stopped midstride. Her confidence, which she had exuded like a pheromone a second before, visibly wavered. "If you'd rather go somewhere else, we can—"

"No. This is perfect."

"Yeah?" Jordan searched her face.

Emma smiled. Chloe wouldn't be caught dead in a place like this, which made it even better. She wanted this to be their place, Jordan's and hers, with no memories intruding. "Yeah." She leaned up and kissed Jordan to reassure her. "Let's go in. I hear a burger calling my name."

Jordan breathed an audible sigh of relief and held the door open for Emma.

Emma entered ahead of her and looked around.

Wow. This wasn't the greasy joint she had expected. It was a classic 1950s-style diner. A Formica-topped counter stretched the length of the room, lined with vinyl-cushioned chrome swivel stools. The black-and-white-checkered floor gleamed as if it had just been cleaned. A jukebox in the corner played oldies, and a fan whirred overhead.

The hostess guided them past a glass case displaying pies that made Emma consider skipping dinner and going straight to dessert.

They slid into a red vinyl booth along one wall.

The hostess handed them two laminated menus. "Rosey, your waitress, will be with you in a sec," she said and walked away.

Emma looked up at the mural of a pink Cadillac that decorated the wall next to their table. "Very retro," she said with an appreciative nod. "You almost expect to step outside and discover that Dwight D. Eisenhower is still president. I like it."

Jordan laughed. "Wait until you try their burgers...or their pies." She let out a low moan. "De-li-cious!"

As if on cue, a waitress in a pink dress appeared next to their table and greeted them.

Once she had taken their drink order and walked away, Jordan nodded down at the menu in her hand. "Are you sure this is okay? I don't want you to think I'm being cheap or—"

"I don't think that for a second. This is comfortable, and I think at this point, that's what we need most—to become more comfortable with...with us." Emma pointed back and forth between them.

"Exactly what I thought."

They looked at each other, and a complete understanding passed between them, the type that Emma had thought she might never have again, and certainly not with her womanizing neighbor.

"Is it strange for you?" she blurted out. "Being out on a date and everything?"

Jordan's long fingers played with the saltshaker on the table. "I've been on dates before, you know? I like women, and that doesn't mean just in the bedroom. I like their company."

A bit of insecurity reared its ugly head, but Emma swatted the feeling aside like an annoying fly.

"I like your company most of all," Jordan added, making Emma's jealousy melt like ice cream in the California sun. "But yeah, this is a bit strange. I've never been out with a woman that I know so well already."

"What about Simone?" Emma couldn't help asking.

"Having dinner with her felt different—like enjoying time with a friend, not like being on a date," Jordan said. "And with most of my dates, I could rely on small talk about what each of us is doing for a living, where we're from, and so on. But I know that about you already. I know what kind of pie you'll likely choose for dessert, and I know the way you just brushed a strand of hair out of your face means you're a bit embarrassed but mostly pleased about something I said."

Emma caught herself swiping another strand of hair behind her ear. Heat rushed to her cheeks. She had never known she was doing that. When she looked across the table at Jordan, she realized that she already knew a lot of little details about her too—that she would order a peanut butter burger, if the restaurant served it, that she would run her fingertips over the contours of the giraffe on her cast while she thought something through, and that she would argue over who got to pay for dinner.

The waitress returned to the table with their drinks. "What can I get you to eat, ladies?" She looked from Emma to Jordan.

They hadn't even looked at the menus, too caught up in their conversation.

Emma skimmed the menu. "I'll have the classic cheeseburger. Hold the onions, please."

Jordan grinned, her eyes smoldering before she returned her attention to the menu. "For me, the turkey burger with Camembert and fig jam, please. And no onions for me either." She looked at Emma. "Want to share some sweet potato wedges?"

"Sure."

The waitress scribbled down their order. "Coming right up."

When she walked away, Emma gave Jordan a skeptical look. "Fig jam? On a burger? Is that actually edible?"

"I have no idea, but I'll never find out if I don't try, will I? Sometimes, you just have to take a risk to find a new favorite dish."

Emma felt her skeptical expression soften into a smile. "Do you think it'll always be like this?"

"Like what?"

"Us using food analogies to talk about our relationship."

Jordan returned her smile. "I have no idea. But I'm looking forward to finding out."

Emma slid her hand across the table and entwined their fingers, not caring how the waitress might react once she returned with their food. "Me too."

They had been sitting in the car, kissing, for the last twenty minutes. Several times, one of them had reached out to open the door, but the other had pulled her back for just one more kiss.

Finally, they couldn't avoid it any longer.

"You know," Jordan said as they climbed out of the sports car, "I'm starting to think of our garage as a very erotic place."

Emma chuckled. "Yeah. Me too."

The slightly husky sound of her laughter ratcheted up Jordan's body temperature another notch. She reached for Emma's hand. "I'll walk you home."

"Thank you, kind lady."

Too bad that they were at Emma's front door within seconds.

Without letting go of her hand, Emma turned toward her. "Thanks for a wonderful evening. I think that was the best burger I have ever had in my entire life, and the banana cream pie..." She let out a low moan that made Jordan shiver. "It was to die for."

"And the company?" Jordan asked.

"Oh, that was pretty okayish too."

Jordan could have bet money on her saying exactly that, and the familiar response made her smile.

They stood facing each other in front of the door.

Emma jingled her keys. "Um, I would ask you in, but Barbara is here, and we haven't talked to Molly yet, so..."

"It's okay," Jordan said. That was another first for her. Usually when she went out with a woman, they both knew that the evening would end with them having each other for dessert instead of a huge slice of pie. But she wanted to build something lasting with Emma, so waiting was fine—even if her body didn't share that opinion.

"Thank you for understanding," Emma said. "And thanks again for tonight." She leaned up and kissed Jordan.

Her tongue teased and stroked in a way that made Jordan weak in the knees.

God, if Emma had found out the exact way she liked to be kissed so fast, Jordan could only imagine how mind-blowing it would be when they finally slept together.

When they broke apart, both were breathless and clung to each other for a few more moments.

With a bit of pride, Jordan watched Emma fumble with the keys before finally getting the right one into the lock. It was good to know that she wasn't the only one who was affected. Not that Emma's passionate responses had left any doubt about it.

Emma opened the door a few inches. Sounds of the TV drifted over from the living room. Just inside the house, Emma paused and turned again. "Good night."

Jordan couldn't resist stepping closer to steal one last kiss. "Good night," she said after kissing Emma breathless. "Sleep well."

"I might need some help from my favorite battery-operated device to put myself to sleep tonight," Emma said, her voice hoarse.

Jordan's breath hitched. Then realization dawned. "Oh. You mean your e-reader."

A mischievous smile curved Emma's well-kissed lips. "Maybe," she said before stepping back and closing the door between them.

With a low groan, Jordan put her good hand against the door, either to prolong the contact or to keep herself upright; she wasn't sure. The only thing she was sure of was that she had found her match in Emma.

Chapter 22

A HIGH-PITCHED WHINE FILLED THE treatment room as the cast tech turned on the saw.

Emma swallowed against the lump in her throat and clutched Jordan's good hand more tightly. She wanted to look away but was unable to tear her gaze off the metal saw blade descending upon the cast.

"Don't worry," Jordan shouted over the noise of the cast saw. "The blade doesn't rotate. It only vibrates. It can't hurt me."

Even knowing that, Emma couldn't relax. It looked as if the blade would slice into Jordan's skin as it worked through the green fiberglass. Then a second line was cut on the other side of the cast.

By the time the cast tech turned off the saw, Emma's ears were ringing and her hands were damp with sweat.

Next to her, Jordan was vibrating with impatience. She looked as if she wanted to rip off the rest of the cast. "Don't pinch my skin," she told the cast tech, who was now using some kind of spreader to widen the cracks in the cast.

Hope stuck her head into the treatment room. "Is she giving you any trouble, May?"

The cast tech smiled. "Not more than the average doctor." She used a pair of scissors to cut through the padding, then parted the cast and slid it off Jordan's thumb.

"Finally!" Jordan beamed like a prisoner being freed of her shackles. But when she directed her gaze to her arm, a frown marred her face and she blinked as if no longer recognizing the limb as her own.

Truth be told, it did look a little strange. She had clearly lost some muscle tone, so now it seemed thinner than the other arm. The skin was dry and flaky. Emma would provide TLC and put some lotion on it as soon as they got home.

The orthopedic specialist who had reviewed Jordan's X-rays earlier stepped into the room.

Reluctantly, Emma let go of Jordan's hand to give him some room to work. He had Jordan flex her wrist and carefully moved it this way and that. "Any pain?" he asked.

Jordan shook her head. "It's a little stiff, but otherwise it seems to be fine. I'll be back in the OR before the week is over."

The doctor laughed. "Oh no, you won't. It'll be at least three to four weeks before you can operate again, and even then, you should start with easy, laparoscopic surgeries, and you'll definitely need backup in case you need to open up the patient."

"Three weeks?" Jordan echoed, looking as if he had just told her she had to go to jail.

"Could be four or more," he answered. "No strenuous activities for this arm for a while."

"Come on, Jordan. You knew that," Hope said. "After six weeks in a cast, you don't have the dexterity you need to handle surgical instruments right away."

Jordan scowled at her. "Anything I can do to speed up the recovery process?" She directed a hopeful glance at the orthopedic specialist.

"Make a couple of appointments with a hand therapist," he said. "He or she will help you mobilize your carpals and stretch the ligaments so you'll regain full range of motion. But it will still take three to four weeks."

Jordan looked so crestfallen that Emma reached for her good hand again and rubbed the back of it with her thumb. But as much as she felt for her, she also couldn't help being a little relieved that Jordan wouldn't return to work full-time just yet. Sometimes, she wondered how they would manage to find enough time for each other with Jordan's demanding work schedule, her own job, and Molly. This was like a grace period that would give them a bit more time to grow their relationship before everyday life intruded.

With their work done, the cast tech and the orthopedic surgeon said good-bye and left.

Emma perched onto the edge of the treatment table next to Jordan, wrapped one arm around her, and kissed her cheek. "It won't be that bad."

She leaned even closer and whispered into her ear, enjoying the shiver that she felt go through Jordan. "I promise to keep you busy until you can return to the OR."

A hint of the old, confident grin replaced Jordan's sulky expression. "Oh yeah? How will you do that? The doc said no strenuous activities for this arm."

"Oh, believe me, I'll find a way. Plenty of ways, actually."

Hope cleared her throat and looked back and forth between them. "Um, guys? What's going on? The two of you... Are you...?"

Heat shot into Emma's cheeks as she remembered they weren't alone. She moved away, but only an inch or two, and bit her lip while she waited for what Jordan would say.

Jordan rubbed her newly mended arm, brushing off bits of lint and flakes of dead skin. "Yes, we are."

Hope stared at her. "Uh...what exactly are you?"

"Together. Girlfriends. Partners. A couple. Whatever you want to call it." Jordan raised her chin and looked into her friend's eyes. "Go ahead. Tease me all you want. I deserve it for swearing up and down that I would never get involved with anyone."

Hope's jaw worked.

Emma prepared to jump in and defend Jordan should the teasing get too bad. Despite her bravado, Jordan had a vulnerable side, and she wouldn't allow Hope to lay into her too much.

But all Hope got out was "wow." She shook her head. "When did this happen?"

"We've been dancing around it for a while, but it took us until last week to admit that we want to give this a try," Jordan said.

"You could have talked to me, you know?" Hope said softly.

Jordan studied her discarded cast. "I know. But I could barely admit it to myself, much less anyone else. I always thought me and relationships don't mix."

Finally, Hope smiled and gave Jordan a pat on the shoulder. "Congratulations. I'm really happy for you."

Jordan narrowed her eyes at her. "That's all you're going to say?"

"Well, you didn't tease me when Laleh and I got together, so I figure now it's my turn to hold back. But can I just say...wow." She continued to shake her head. "Just wait until I tell Laleh—and some of the nurses around here. Hearts will be breaking all over the hospital."

That was one of the things about Jordan's return to work that had Emma worried.

But Jordan merely shrugged. "Good thing we have some great cardiologists on staff." She slid off the treatment table and reached for the discarded cast.

Emma wrinkled her nose. "You're not taking that smelly thing home with you, are you?"

"Of course I am. It has your giraffe and Molly's heart on it."

Aww. Jordan could be amazingly sweet. Emma's concerns melted away, at least for the moment. Smiling, she followed her to the door.

Hope walked with them to the elevator. "If she gives you any trouble, call me," she said to Emma.

"Thanks, but I'm sure I can handle her."

The ice-blue eyes crinkled at their edges as Hope smiled. "Yeah. I think you can."

"Hey!" Jordan protested. "I'm standing right here, you know?"

Emma cradled the newly bared hand in both of hers, lifted it to her lips, and tenderly kissed the healing wrist. "Come on. Let's go home."

The next morning, Emma glanced up from the blog post she was proofreading for a client. Of course, the hammock was still empty, and so was her mug since Jordan hadn't been over to bring her a second cup of coffee.

Amazing how much she missed that little ritual—how much she missed Jordan.

Molly seemed to miss her just as much. She had pouted earlier, when Jordan hadn't been there to walk her to the car and buckle her into her booster seat, the way they had done it almost every day for the past two weeks or so.

Jordan fit so smoothly into their lives, but now the structure of their days would change.

Jordan had headed off to work when Emma had barely gotten up. A quick kiss at the French door and she had practically skipped off, a big grin on her face, like a kid going on a field trip. She was happy for Jordan, really, but at the same time, she wished their time together, with both of them being home, would never end.

The thought of Jordan as a kept woman made her laugh. No, that would never happen. Jordan loved the operating room too much to stay away for long.

They both would have to learn to adjust and make it work somehow. Good thing her schedule was flexible. She was able to work whenever she wanted so she would have time off when Jordan was home.

She could only hope that Jordan would be willing to make some adjustments too. In her marriage with Chloe, it had felt as if Emma had been the only one making compromises, and she knew she never wanted that kind of relationship again.

Her phone vibrating on the desk wrenched her from her thoughts.

She slid it closer to herself so she could check the display.

It was a message from Jordan.

Hello to my favorite VA. How's your day going?

Aww. So Jordan hadn't forgotten her completely now that she was back in her element. Emma nibbled her bottom lip. Should she tell Jordan she missed her? No. Then Jordan would feel required to say it back.

I miss my second cup of coffee, she typed instead.

Look in your top drawer, came Jordan's answer. *It's not coffee, but I hear it goes well with it.*

Emma pulled it open. There, on top of her calculator and a tape dispenser, lay a package of white chocolate macadamia cookies that hadn't been in there yesterday.

Yum! Thank you! How did you manage that?

What can I say? I'm magic.

Yes, Emma answered. *Yes, you are.* She gave herself a mental kick and added three more words: *I miss you.*

This time, it took a moment until the answer arrived.

I miss you too.

It felt good to read that response, even if Jordan might just have said it because she knew it was expected of her.

Another text message arrived before she could think of an answer.

Really.

Emma smiled, finally allowing herself to believe it, and typed, *No good-looking nurses around?*

Nurses? What nurses?

Good response.

Jordan answered with a smiley face. *I have to go. They are having me assist with a lap chole. Boring. But at least I'm in the OR. Looking forward to seeing you tonight.*

Me too, Emma answered. She put the phone away and then tore open the package of cookies. Munching contentedly, she opened a new browser tab with her free hand and typed in "lap chole," just to get an idea of how Jordan was spending her day.

Jordan pulled the cap off her head, stripped out of her scrubs, and tossed them into the laundry hamper. The muscles in her right arm screamed at her, but it was a good kind of pain.

After she had spent hours doing rounds, intake interviews, and endless paperwork, they had finally let her into the OR. Granted, it had been only appies and lap choles, and she had been assisting for the most part, but she'd still experienced the rush she felt during every surgery.

Now she couldn't wait to get home and share her triumph with Emma.

Without taking the time to shower first, she slipped into her jeans and shirt and tied her sneakers, grateful that she no longer had to have help doing that.

When she headed toward the staff parking lot, a voice from behind stopped her. "Jordan?"

She turned.

Venita, the X-ray tech, jogged after her. "I thought that was you. Are you back at work?"

"Yes." Grinning, Jordan wiggled the fingers of her right hand. "Almost as good as new."

Venita's dark eyes smoldered. "Good to hear that." She pointed over her shoulder, back to where two nurses were just stepping through the staff exit. "Betty, Susan, and I were going to Friday's for a beer. Want to come?"

Jordan hesitated. She did feel like celebrating, and she'd always had a good time at Friday's. But a glance at her watch revealed that it was already half past six. Their last surgery had run a bit late, so if she wanted to make it home in time to at least say good night to Molly, she needed to be on her way.

"Maybe another time," she said.

Venita leaned closer—close enough so Jordan could feel the heat emanating off her body. "You sure?" she whispered into Jordan's ear. "I could make it worth your while."

Past experience told her it wasn't an empty promise. Jordan had wondered how she would handle invitations like this when they came up. She had imagined that she would decline with a hint of regret or at least mixed feelings. After all, it was a reminder of a part of her life being irrevocably over.

But she found that shaking her head was astonishingly easy. "I'm very sure. Have fun at the bar." She waved at Venita and walked past her. After two steps, she paused. If she left it at that, she would probably have to go through this again. It was better to clear this up once and for all.

She turned around. "Venita?"

A grin broke out on Venita's face. "Changed your mind?"

"No. I just thought you should know why I won't have a beer—or anything else—with you now or in the future. I met someone."

Venita laughed. "You meet many someones."

Jordan shook her head. "Not like that. This is a very special someone, and I'm actually in a relationship with her."

The grin turned into a frown. "I thought you don't do relationships?"

"I didn't—until now. But Emma makes me want to try. So please don't take it personally if I'd rather go home than go to the bar with you."

Venita muttered something under her breath, then sighed and smiled again. "Good luck."

"Thanks." She headed for her car without looking back. Maybe she could make a quick stop on the way home and get a bottle of champagne. From now on, all her celebrations would include Emma.

Chapter 23

JORDAN HELD VERY, VERY STILL. Normally, she hated handing over an instrument once she had started a procedure, but when Emma had asked if she could try, saying no was not an option. So she sat with her bare leg extended between them on the couch, the foam pad strapped to it, and quietly gave instructions.

"Now you wrap the long end of the thread around the needle holder twice, grab the shorter end with the needle holder, and pull it through the loops." Jordan guided Emma's hands as she pulled the thread tight. "Great. Now repeat it twice, but just loop the thread around the needle holder once this time."

The tip of Emma's tongue poked out from between her lips as she focused on completing the suture.

Jordan had to bite back a grin at how much she looked like her daughter right now.

She cut the thread, took the needle holder with the curved suturing needle from her, and looked down at the foam pad she had brought home from the hospital to practice on. "Not bad."

Emma touched the sutures on the fake wound edges with her fingertips.

Was it wrong of her to find the way Emma caressed the foam pad strapped to her leg pretty erotic? She couldn't tear her gaze away.

"Yours look better," Emma said.

Jordan chuckled. "I'd hope so. I do this for a living after all." She had practiced for hours since the cast had been removed three days ago. Her dexterity still wasn't up to par, but her frustration had quickly faded once Emma had joined her on the couch. "You tied your first surgeon's knot. Congratulations."

Jordan leaned forward and gave Emma a congratulatory kiss. She had intended for it to be just a light brush of their lips, but when Emma brought up a hand and slid it around the back of her neck, the kiss deepened.

She nipped at Emma's bottom lip and then slowly sucked her tongue into her mouth.

Emma made a sound of pleasure deep in her throat. Her fingers tangled into Jordan's hair in an attempt to bring her closer. She shifted until she straddled Jordan, molding their bodies together.

God, she felt so good. Jordan wrapped her arms around Emma to hold her in place, enjoying the fact that she was finally able to use both hands to touch her.

Emma seemed to make it her mission to reduce her to a trembling mass of desire. She slipped one hand beneath the hem of Jordan's T-shirt and let it roam over her overheated skin. Her fingers brushed one breast as if by accident, then returned to cup her through the barrier of her bra.

Jordan drew in a long, shivery breath. Need spiraled through her, barely held in check by a thin thread of control. All she wanted was to strip off their clothes and make love to Emma right here and now. She slid one hand down the curve of Emma's hip and into the back of her yoga pants. She loved that Emma wasn't the skinny type. Her body was real and lush and so damn sexy. She splayed her fingers over one butt cheek and squeezed.

Emma surged against her with a loud moan.

The sexy sound made Jordan's head spin. But it also reminded her that this wasn't the time or the place. "We need to…God…stop, or we'll wake Molly."

Since Emma had started to explore her neck, pulling back took a Herculean effort.

Emma stared at her with heavy-lidded eyes before crawling off Jordan's lap and slumping against the back of the couch. Her hand fluttered over her kiss-swollen lips and down her body as if she barely recognized it. "Wow," she muttered. With flushed cheeks, she peeked at Jordan. "Sorry. I didn't mean to—"

"Don't apologize." Jordan reached over, took Emma's hand, and brought it to her lips for a kiss. "Never apologize for wanting me. I just don't want our first time together to be on the couch, where Molly could hear us."

"Yeah. A quickie on the couch was not what I pictured for our first time either."

So she had pictured it. Jordan grinned. Her heartbeat slowly returned to normal. She tucked her T-shirt back into her jeans and unstrapped the foam pad from around her calf. Her hands were too unsteady now to get back to suturing practice. "I think I should say good night now and head home before you make me lose what little bit of self-control I still have."

"Could you stay a little longer?" Emma asked softly.

"Sure." It wasn't a hardship, really. The last thing Jordan wanted was to head home into her cold, lonely bed. God, they really needed to talk to Molly soon. Saying good night and heading into separate beds was getting harder every evening.

"There's something I'd like to talk about," Emma added.

That sounded serious. "What do you want to talk about?"

"Um, sex."

That made Jordan's gaze fly up to Emma's face. An eager grin tugged up the corners of her mouth. "Oh, sure. I'm always happy to talk about my favorite topic."

"I…uh, I'm not talking about the fun part of it."

Jordan smirked and cocked her head. "There's an un-fun part when it comes to sex?"

Emma stared at her lap, making her hair form a curtain that hid her face for a moment.

Sensing that this was serious for Emma, Jordan stopped grinning and softly touched her knee. "Okay, let's talk. What's on your mind?"

Emma sat up straight, swiped her hair behind her ears, and turned her head to look at Jordan. "I'm very grateful that you're being so patient and considerate. I know you don't usually wait so long to—"

Jordan stopped her with a soft touch of her lips to Emma's. "As our wise neighbor once said to me, back in her day, people didn't jump into bed with each other either, and it didn't hurt them any. I enjoyed getting to know you as much as I will enjoy getting to know your body."

"Me too," Emma said with a warm smile. "I don't want you to think that I don't want this to happen…don't want us to happen."

"After the way you just kissed me, there's not a doubt in my mind."

"Good. But…before it happens, I think we should talk about how to stay safe."

"Oh. You mean how to practice safe sex?" Normally, Jordan was the one to broach that subject with women. Her respect for Emma grew.

Emma nodded. "Not a very sexy topic, I know, but…"

Jordan reached for her hand and pressed a kiss to the soft palm. "I find it very sexy for a woman to take charge of her health."

"I didn't need to think about it for the last ten years," Emma said. "At least that's what I thought. But after Chloe…after I found out she wasn't faithful, I got tested immediately."

Jordan's grip on Emma's hand tightened. "And?"

"Clean bill of health, thank God."

Jordan kissed her palm again and tried not to think of other potential outcomes. She would have torn Chloe limb from limb if she had given Emma anything. "I'm clean enough to eat off too—pun intended." She winked to lighten the mood.

"You got tested? When?"

"I get tested regularly, but the last time…two weeks ago."

She could almost see Emma flip through her mental calendar. "That's when we got together," Emma said after a moment.

Jordan nodded. "I always tried to be as safe as I could be, but I'm not taking any chances with you."

Emma leaned forward and kissed her, this time more tenderly than passionately. "Thank you."

"No thanks necessary. That wasn't entirely selfless, you know? In the past, I used dental damns and gloves most of the time, but with you, I'd love to touch you and taste you with nothing between us."

Emma's cheeks flushed. "I want that too."

The huskiness of Emma's voice made Jordan weak in the knees. Good thing she was already sitting. "So now that we've established that, can I go back to ravaging you if I promise to do it quietly?"

Emma stalked across the couch like a tigress and placed one knee between Jordan's thighs. "What makes you think you'll be the one doing the ravaging?"

For a moment, Jordan was too breathless to answer. "Experience," she finally got out and was surprised at how hoarse her voice sounded.

Emma shook her head. "That was in the past. It's time to make some new experiences."

Heat simmered between them. Jordan leaned forward and nipped at Emma's earlobe.

A shiver went through Emma, and she grabbed hold of Jordan's shoulders to keep herself upright.

"Well," Jordan said, "there's one more thing we need to do before there's going to be any ravaging, no matter who's the ravager and who's the ravagee."

"Yeah?" Emma's eyes had gone a little unfocused.

"Mmhm." Jordan nibbled on that tempting earlobe once more and then stopped so she could look into Emma's eyes. "We still haven't told Molly."

Emma stiffened against her and sighed. "I know."

That was not exactly the enthusiastic response Jordan had been hoping for. *Great.* She slid to the side, away from Emma.

She had tried to be patient and let Emma take this important step in her own time, but now she was starting to feel that Emma was stalling for no good reason. What the heck had to happen before she was finally willing to tell her daughter about them?

Before she could decide how to broach that topic without starting a fight, her phone rang.

"It's not the hospital, is it?" Emma asked.

"No," Jordan said before even having looked at the display. "I'm not on call." When she withdrew her phone from her pants pocket, she realized it was Simone calling.

Sorry, Simone. Now's not a good time. Making a mental note to call her back later, she raised her finger to reject the call.

"Go ahead and answer," Emma said.

"Are you sure? We were in the middle of talking about—"

"I'm sure."

It was pretty obvious that Emma was looking for a way to delay talking about when to tell Molly, but Jordan decided to let it go. It had been a long, exhausting day for both of them. Maybe it was better to talk about it over the weekend, when they had more time.

With a shrug, Jordan swiped *accept* and lifted the phone to her ear.

"Hey, you," Simone's affectionate voice came over the line. "How's the hand?"

"Almost back to normal," Jordan said.

"I'm very happy to hear that, and my reasons aren't completely unselfish."

Jordan smiled and turned on the couch so she could look at Emma while she talked. "Why's that?"

"I just found out that I'll be in your neck of the woods in the very near future. So…want to practice your fine-motor skills?"

"Uh…" For the first time in her life, Jordan didn't know what to say to that. She'd never told Simone no, not even once, but now she'd have to. She *wanted* to.

But not on the phone. Simone was much more to her than a one-night stand. Her old friend deserved to be told in person.

Emma gave her a curious look and mouthed an "is everything okay?"

Jordan forced a smile and nodded.

"Jordan?" Simone asked. "Are you okay? Your hand isn't—?"

"It's fine. Really. And I'd love to have you over." *Just not for that.* "When's your flight landing at LAX?"

"My client needs me there on Monday, but I thought I could fly out on Saturday so we can spend some time together. The flight I have my eye on touches down at four thirty on Saturday afternoon."

"Great. I've got Saturday off. I'll pick you up."

"Thanks," Simone said. "I'm looking forward to seeing you."

Jordan hoped that would still be true after she told Simone she'd have to sleep in the guest room. "Um, yeah, me too."

They talked for a minute longer and then ended the call.

When Jordan put the phone away, Emma moved closer on the couch and lightly touched her leg. "Is everything okay?"

"Yeah. I hope so. That was Simone."

"Oh. Is she coming for a visit?" Her voice was carefully neutral, but Jordan picked up the tension behind it.

"Yes. She's got a new client whose headquarters are in LA. That's why she was here when you met her. She's flying in on Saturday."

Emma sighed. "So much for my plans to spend the weekend with you. Instead, you'll spend it with your ex."

Jordan grimaced. "I'm sorry."

"No, forget what I said. I'm being silly. I know she's more than just your ex. She's your friend, right?"

Jordan nodded. "And that's all she ever was." She looked into Emma's eyes, wanting her to see how sincere she was.

"Well, a friend with benefits," Emma said. Wrinkling her nose, she added, "*Great* benefits, from the way it sounded."

Jordan groaned as she remembered that Emma had heard her and Simone having sex the night she had moved in. Amazing how her life had changed since then. "Now they are *your* benefits," she said firmly. "Just yours."

"They'd damn well better be." Emma kissed her passionately, as if putting the seal of possession on her.

The last thought Jordan had before she gave herself over to Emma's kisses was that they apparently had not one but two more things to do before the ravaging could start: They had to tell Molly about them, and she had to let Simone know about the new sleeping arrangements.

It was already ten o'clock. Molly had been asleep for hours, and even Jordan had reluctantly kissed Emma good night and headed over to her side of the house.

But Emma knew sleep wouldn't be an option for her anytime soon. She was wide-awake, pacing the living room. Thoughts of Jordan and Molly and Simone and Chloe bounced through her mind in a jumbled mess.

She and Jordan hadn't exactly fought, but she could tell that Jordan was running out of patience. And she was right. They had to tell Molly. A few stolen kisses here and there or some hot make-out sessions on the couch weren't enough. Jordan deserved more—and so did she.

Heck, she wanted to tell Molly. She wanted them to be a family.

But those damn what-if thoughts just wouldn't stop tormenting her. Every time she had finally worked up the courage to tell Molly, one of her doubts overcame her and made her freeze at the last second.

What if things between her and Jordan didn't go well? What if Jordan one day decided monogamy and family life weren't for her after all? What if she realized she wanted her freedom more than she wanted Emma? What if they ended up separating and Molly lost another person she loved?

Stop it, she finally told herself. Yes, she had been hurt before, and yes, there were no guarantees, but Jordan wasn't Chloe.

If she wanted this relationship to work, she had to trust Jordan. She had to face her demons instead of letting her life be dictated by them.

And that included telling Molly about them.

Well, her and Chloe.

That was another thing she feared. She had a feeling her ex-wife wouldn't be overjoyed to hear she was in a new relationship—not so much because of Emma but because of Molly. While Chloe didn't exactly fall all over herself to make enough time for their daughter, she wouldn't want another woman to take over as a second parent for Molly.

Did she really have to tell Chloe? A part of her stubbornly insisted that her ex didn't deserve to know. Another part was eager to tell her, to show her that she wasn't sitting around, missing her and feeling sorry for herself. She had moved on with her life.

Finally, she shoved all other feelings aside and let reason prevail. Jordan would play a big part in Molly's life, and no matter what had happened between them, Chloe was still Molly's other mother, so it was only fair to tell her.

No time like the present, right? She reached for the phone that lay on the coffee table. At least this was something she could do while she worked up the courage to tell Molly.

Phone in hand, she paused one last time. It was getting pretty late. What if Chloe was already in bed—maybe with her little assistant?

So what? Then Chloe wouldn't pick up, but at least she would have tried.

Not allowing herself to hesitate again, she scrolled through her contact list until she found Chloe's number.

The phone rang and rang. Just when Emma thought the call would go to voice mail, Chloe picked up.

"Hi, Chloe. This is Emma. I hope I didn't wake you."

"No. I just got back from one of my late-night runs."

"Oh. Good. Um, do you have a minute? I've got something to tell you. But if this isn't a good time for you, I can—"

"It's fine. What's up?"

Okay, that sounded promising. Maybe they could have a civilized conversation. "I thought you should know that I...I met someone."

Chloe was silent for several seconds. "I knew it! That was why you wanted to move to South Pasadena, wasn't it?"

"What? No! I only met her after we moved here." So much for having a civilized conversation.

Chloe let out a sound between a grunt and a snort. "Well, it certainly didn't take you very long to get involved."

The old anger sparked alive inside of Emma, but she reined herself in. Chloe wasn't worth getting upset over. She had a new life and had found a new love. "You don't want to go down that road, Chloe. I wasn't the one who got involved with someone else first. And it's been a year since we separated. That's not exactly fast."

"Whatever. You can do whatever you want, Emma. We're no longer married, so you don't need my permission to hook up with someone."

"I'm not calling to ask for your permission. I just wanted to let you know."

"Yeah, well, thanks, I guess. Just do me a favor and keep her away from Molly. I don't want our daughter to have to get used to a new stepmom every year."

For several moments, Emma couldn't speak. Then she wanted to say so many things at the same time that she didn't know where to start. At the last second, she discarded several options that would have only led to them shouting at each other. Someone had to be the adult here, and obviously, it wasn't going to be Chloe.

"Molly already knows her." She raised her voice and spoke right over Chloe's groan of disapproval. "We haven't yet told her that we're together, but—"

"Good," Chloe said. "You should keep it that way for the time being."

"I don't think I can do that," Emma said. "We were thinking about telling Molly soon."

"Be reasonable, Emma! If it's true that you only met once you moved to California—"

"It is! She's my neighbor."

"Yeah, well, then you've barely even known the woman for two months! You need to be sure this isn't a rebound thing or something temporary before you introduce her to Molly as your new partner."

"A rebound thing?" Emma echoed. "Don't flatter yourself."

"Whatever. It's still not a good idea to bring Molly into this so soon. She's five, for Christ's sake!"

"She's six, not five."

That shut Chloe up, but only for a second. "Do you honestly think that one year would make much of a difference if you had to explain to her why Mommy is crying and why this new person she barely got used to has disappeared from her life?"

Emma squeezed her eyes shut to ban the mental image from her mind. Great. Just what she needed—for her ex to pour salt in her wounds and stir up her doubts. "I...I will think about it, okay? Maybe I'll wait for a while longer. But, Chloe... It won't be very long. I want a relationship that is honest. No hiding or sneaking around. That's what I always wanted, and it's what Jordan wants too."

"So that's her name? Jordan?"

Emma stepped up to the French door and touched the cool glass while she imagined Jordan standing in her bedroom and looking out into the dark backyard too. "Yes," she said, not trying to hide the warmth in her voice, "that's her name. She's a really great person. Decent and understanding and wonderful with Molly."

"Guess I'll meet her on Saturday," Chloe said.

"Saturday?"

"Yeah. If you hadn't called me tonight, I would have told you tomorrow. I finally got the weekend off and can come visit Molly."

Yeah. Right. Molly. Emma had a feeling all Chloe wanted was to sniff out the new woman in their lives. "You haven't managed to visit Molly once since we moved, not even on her birthday, and now that I'm in a new relationship, you suddenly find the time on such short notice?"

"You know I can't always predict my schedule," Chloe said for about the millionth time in the last ten years.

"Yeah, right." Emma closed her eyes for a second and then opened them again. "Okay. You can come—on two conditions."

"Which are?" Chloe asked warily.

"First, if you cancel this visit, I'm going to kill you," Emma said, making her voice as hard and sharp as steel. "I won't allow you to keep disappointing Molly. Once I tell her you're coming, you'd better be here, no matter what. I don't care if one of your patients pops a fake boob or you have to crawl all the way from Portland because the flight was canceled."

"Yeah, yeah. I'll be there. What's the second thing?"

"You have to promise to be civil to Jordan. Do you think you can manage that?"

"Of course," Chloe said. "I'll be on my best behavior."

Emma didn't believe that for a second. She didn't look forward to that meeting. The only good thing was that Chloe wouldn't be able to get her scalpels through airport security. Maybe she should make sure Jordan didn't have any in the house either.

Then she remembered that Simone would be flying in for a visit on Saturday too. *Oh God.* Two exes were about to descend on their home! Even if she wanted to, she wouldn't have the peace and quiet to tell Molly about them this weekend.

Chapter 24

JORDAN WOKE AND BLINKED INTO the darkness. A warm body was cuddled up to her, and another source of warmth had settled on her feet. It took her a moment to figure out that she and Emma had fallen asleep in the hammock, where they had spent the evening kissing and talking. Tuna had rolled herself into a little ball at the bottom of the hammock.

"Emma," she whispered.

A cute noise of protest drifted up from Emma, and she burrowed more closely against Jordan's side.

God, she felt so good. Jordan inhaled her sleepy scent. For a moment, she considered just closing her eyes and going back to sleep. She wasn't eager to spend the night alone. But Emma had to get some work done tomorrow, and their exes would soon arrive for a visit, and they both needed to get a good night's sleep before that.

"Emma." She gently shook her shoulder.

Grunting, Emma opened her eyes and stared at her without comprehension. "Mmm?"

"We fell asleep. Come on. Let's go to bed." She helped her out of the hammock and walked her to her side of the duplex.

Tuna sent them a glare at being woken but hopped down from the hammock and followed them. She trotted through the open French door into Emma's side of the duplex and then turned to see if they were following.

In the last couple of weeks, the cat had extended her territory and now went back and forth between both units, adopting Emma and Molly as her humans too.

When they paused at the door instead of following her inside, Tuna let out a demanding *meow*.

"Hush! Don't wake Molly, cat!" Jordan turned to face Emma and gently reached for her hand. "Are you nervous?"

"Why would I be nervous?" Emma asked.

"Because of tomorrow… Seeing your ex and all that."

Emma sighed and looked down as if suddenly finding her shoes fascinating. "Yeah, a little. It probably sounds stupid, but I feel like I only really grew up in the past year. I've been Chloe's partner and then her wife my entire adult life, but now… I learned to be my own woman—and I like the person I am without her, but I feel like I need more time to really become that person."

Jordan rubbed the back of her hand. "That makes perfect sense." She hoped Emma would never have reason to say something like that about her. "Listen, if it would be easier for you if I stayed out of your way while Chloe is here, I can—"

"No," Emma said immediately. "I don't want you to stay away. This is your home too. Um, I mean, I know we're not living together or anything, but…uh…Molly would miss you if she didn't get to see you for two days."

Emma's stammering made her smile. "Just Molly?"

"No," Emma said. "Tuna would miss you too." Her lips curling into a mischievous smile, she pointed into her living room, where the cat was still waiting for them to head inside.

Jordan let out a playful growl and took a step closer, right into Emma's personal space. "Want to amend that statement?"

"And me," Emma whispered. "I would miss you. But I know it's probably a little awkward for you, so if you would rather not meet Chloe…"

"Don't worry. I can handle Chloe," Jordan said with confidence. At least if she was there, she could keep an eye on Emma's ex and make sure she treated Emma with respect. "Besides, I would miss you too."

Now both serious, they stared into each other's eyes. The emotional pull between them was like a strong current that tugged Jordan closer until their bodies were tightly pressed together.

"Stupid exes," Jordan murmured. "You've got no idea how much I want to be alone with you."

"Oh yeah," Emma answered hoarsely. "I think I've got a pretty good idea."

Now wasn't the time to talk about them, not the night before Emma's ex arrived for her first visit, but Jordan knew she wanted to move forward as soon as possible.

Just as their lips met in a deep kiss, Tuna let out another loud *meow*.

Groaning, Jordan broke the kiss. Fate just wasn't with them this weekend.

The next afternoon, Emma took an hour to get started on her monthly task of sending invoices to her clients. At least it distracted her from looking at the clock every few seconds, wondering whether Chloe would actually show up or call to say that something had come up again.

When the doorbell rang, she didn't know whether to be relieved or dismayed. She wasn't expecting anyone else, so it had to be Chloe.

As she got up from her desk and crossed the hall, she automatically picked up a toy that Molly had left behind and pulled open a drawer to toss in the pile of today's unread mail. Then she paused and shook her head. What the heck was she doing? This was her home, not Chloe's. If her ex-wife didn't like the way it looked, so be it. Emma didn't need her approval anymore. She put the mail back on the chest of drawers and set the toy next to it.

Resisting the urge to smooth possible wrinkles from her shirt, she opened the door.

Chloe stood before her, casually holding a huge wrapped package under one arm. Her carefully layered hair looked as if she were coming straight from an appointment with a hairdresser instead of just getting off a plane. She was dressed in her dark gray three-hundred-dollar slacks and a silver silk shirt that didn't sport a single wrinkle.

Emma remembered complimenting her on that very outfit, but it wasn't exactly what she would have chosen to wear for playing on the floor or romping around in the backyard with a six-year-old.

"Hi, Emma. Aren't you going to let me in?" Chloe asked with a light smirk.

"Um, yes, of course." Emma realized she'd been blocking the doorway and moved aside.

Chloe's gaze swept Emma's body and then the hall, taking in the pile of mail on the chest of drawers, as Emma had predicted. "Nice little house," she finally said as Emma led her to the living room.

Jeez. Only Chloe could manage to make a compliment sound condescending. Had her ex-wife always been like this? Maybe she was just trying to hide her anxiety at seeing her again and meeting the new woman in her life.

"Thanks," she answered. "Molly and I love it here."

It was a message to Chloe, one she apparently understood, because she gave a grudging nod.

"Where is she?" Chloe asked, looking around.

"Outside, in the backyard with Jordan. They are building a birdhouse."

For a moment, something like pain flashed in Chloe's eyes, then her confidence was back and she just nodded.

Emma couldn't help feeling a little sorry for her. She couldn't imagine not seeing her daughter every day or being replaced by someone else in Molly's life.

Chloe put the gift-wrapped package down on the coffee table. "I'll go say hello." She squared her shoulders and strode toward the French door.

"Wait!" Emma hurried after her. "I'll come with you." No way would she let the two of them meet without her. Her guts twisted with worry as she followed Chloe outside.

Molly hopped up and down next to the newly built birdhouse. "Is it dry? Is it dry?"

Carefully, Jordan touched the edge of the red roof and then looked at her finger. "Yep. Looks like it is. Have you picked a spot to hang it?"

Molly ran to the mulberry tree to look for one.

Jordan massaged her right wrist with her left hand while she waited. It was still pretty stiff. Maybe building a birdhouse hadn't been the smartest idea, but she had promised Molly, and she had vowed that she would never be like Chloe, who didn't seem to think much of breaking her promises to her daughter. Who knew if she would show up this time? If she didn't, the birdhouse would be a good distraction.

The French door opened for the third time in the last hour.

Jordan turned, expecting to see Emma, who either wanted to ogle her butt as she bent over the birdhouse or to caution her to be more careful with her wrist.

But instead, a stranger stepped onto the patio, followed by Emma.

Good thing Molly's presence had kept her from calling out "ass or wrist?" before turning around.

"There!" Molly pointed up the tree. "I want it there." Then she turned, and her eyes went wide. "Mama! You really came!" She raced across the backyard and threw herself into the stranger's arms.

"Of course I came," Chloe said. "I promised, didn't I?"

Yeah. This time and about three times before. Jordan bit her lip to keep herself from saying it. She stood up from her kneeling position next to the forgotten birdhouse. For only the second time in her life, a wave of fierce jealousy swept over her. It wasn't just because this woman had once held Emma's heart; she discovered that she also couldn't help envying her status in Molly's life.

Ridiculous. She had never even wanted kids.

But somehow, the six-year-old bundle of energy had conquered her heart as fast as her mother had. She had truly fallen hard, not just for Emma, but apparently for family life too.

She shook her head at herself and then stood stiffly as she watched Chloe talk to Molly.

Emma's ex-wife was a good-looking woman; she had to give her that. Not really Jordan's type, but attractive nonetheless. She had the toned body of a runner and the confident posture of a surgeon. Collar-length hair framed her bold face. The sandy-brown strands held a whisper of gray at the temples, lending her a distinguished air.

Slowly, Chloe put her daughter down and stepped toward Jordan.

They were exactly the same height, Jordan noticed as they stood eyeing each other. Somehow, that irked her too.

"Look, Mama!" Molly joined them. "Jordan and I built a birdhouse."

Chloe didn't even look at their construction. She kept her gaze fixed on Jordan.

Nervousness came off Emma in waves as she circled her ex so she was half-facing both of them. "Chloe, this is Jordan. Jordan, this is my ex-wife, Chloe."

Neither of them reached out to shake the other's hand.

"Chloe," Jordan said as evenly as she could. "I've heard a lot about you." *None of it good.* At the last second, she kept herself from saying that bit out loud, but her tone probably spoke for itself.

"Strangely, I heard nothing about you until two days ago," Chloe answered.

"Chloe, please," Emma said and pointedly nodded down at Molly.

"Hey, rugrat." Chloe ruffled her daughter's hair. "I brought you a gift. Why don't you go inside and open it?"

Molly hesitated. She was probably afraid that her other mother would disappear as soon as she went inside. But Chloe seemed oblivious to it.

"Why don't we all go inside?" Emma said, cautiously looking back and forth between her ex and Jordan.

"Yes!" Molly ran ahead of them. "Come watch me open my gift!"

"She means both of you," Emma said. "Do you think you can come watch her without it turning into a pissing contest?"

"Yeah," Chloe grumbled.

"No problem," Jordan said.

Jordan wrapped one arm around Emma as she followed her into the house. She would be civil to Chloe for Molly's sake, but that didn't mean she was above annoying her with that little possessive gesture.

Jordan glanced at her watch. If she didn't want to make Simone wait at baggage claim again, she had to go. She leaned toward Emma, who sat next to her on the couch, and said quietly, "I hate to leave you alone with her, but I need to go pick up Simone."

"It's okay." Emma sighed and looked over at Chloe, who was on the floor with Molly, assembling the Lego animal clinic she had bought her. "It's like our exes conspired to visit at the same time, just to drive us crazy," she whispered into Jordan's ear.

"Looks like it," Jordan muttered. "But Simone doesn't know yet that she's an ex. I will tell her on the way back."

"She's staying here?" Emma raised her eyebrows. "Not at a hotel?"

Hadn't she mentioned that before? It had seemed obvious to Jordan. But then again, it probably wasn't for Emma. *Her* ex was staying at a hotel, after all. *Damn. Maybe I shouldn't take so much for granted now that I'm in a relationship.* "She always stays with me when she's in town. But this time she'll sleep in the guest room, of course," Jordan added hastily.

Chloe looked up from the Legos with a big, toothy grin. "Trouble in paradise?"

"No," Emma and Jordan answered in unison.

"What does 'trouble in paradise' mean, Mommy?" Molly asked.

Jordan gritted her teeth. As much as she felt bad for Molly that her other mother couldn't visit more often, right now, she wished Chloe would live on the other side of the planet—or galaxy, if possible.

"Nothing, sweetie," Emma answered. "Your mama is just joking around." She sent Chloe a look that warned her not to comment again.

When Chloe's attention returned to Molly and the Legos, Jordan leaned toward Emma again and whispered, "I'm sorry we didn't discuss this sooner. If it's a problem for you, I can ask Simone to—"

"No." The shadows darkening Emma's eyes disappeared, bringing out the copper sparks in her green irises. "No," she repeated quietly and caressed Jordan's leg. "That's not necessary. I should have realized Simone would stay at your place. I'm fine with that."

"Really?"

"Really. I trust you. Go pick up your friend."

Jordan kept eye contact for a few seconds longer. When all she could read in Emma's eyes was quiet assurance, she nodded and leaned toward her to kiss her good-bye. At the last moment, she changed course and gave her a peck on the cheek. No matter how distracted by her Legos Molly seemed, she was always tuned in to what the adults were doing. "Be right back."

"Jordan!" Emma's voice made her turn back before she had reached the door. "Do you want to take my car? It's got a bigger trunk than yours."

Her gaze went to the car keys that Emma held out to her. This was an offer of much more than just the use of her car. Emma was offering her acceptance of Simone and their friendship.

She crossed the living room and took the keys from Emma, letting their fingers brush. "Thank you." She wanted to say so much more, but not with Molly and especially Emma's ex-wife listening to every word.

God, she couldn't wait for this weekend to be over and for them to be alone again.

Chloe got up from the floor. "I need to move my rental car. I'm parked in front of the garage, so I'm blocking your car."

Great. Jordan resisted the urge to roll her eyes.

As soon as they stepped out of the house, Chloe rounded on her. Her charcoal gray eyes glittered dangerously. "You think you can just waltz in here and play house with my family?"

"Your family?" Jordan firmly shook her head. "You gave up your place in that family when you cheated on Emma."

Chloe curled her hands into fists. "Yeah, of course she would tell you about that. But did she also tell you how I tried to fight for our relationship and she didn't?"

Jordan faced her squarely. "If she didn't, I'm sure she had her reasons. But that's between you and her." Frankly, she didn't want to hear any details. She preferred not to even think about Emma with anyone else.

"Damn right, it is. But I'm telling you one thing." Chloe took another step forward and drilled her index finger into Jordan's chest.

The impulse to swat that hand away or shove her back made Jordan's skin itch, but she forced herself to stand still and watch Chloe through narrowed eyes. No way would she start a physical fight and risk re-injuring her wrist, especially not with Molly nearby.

Chloe growled like a dog whose bone had been snatched away. "If you hurt either of them, I'll—"

"Oh, no." Jordan let out a disbelieving laugh. "You're not giving me that speech. Not when you are the one who hurt them. If you wanted out or met someone else, you should have ended the relationship first, not cheated on her. A woman like Emma deserves so much better. *Every* woman deserves better."

Chloe lowered her head, not so much like a person hanging her head in shame; it looked more like a bull that was about to charge. "Yeah, well, she deserves better than you too."

Had Chloe asked around and heard of Jordan's reputation as a player? If Emma had told her ex that they were neighbors, all it would have taken was a Google search to find out her last name and where she worked. In the medical community, it wouldn't be hard to find someone who knew her or at least knew who she was.

"Maybe," Jordan said coolly. "But that's not for you to decide—or even for me. Emma is the only one who can make that decision, and I'll do my damnedest to make sure she'll never regret it."

Automatically, her gaze went to the house.

The front door stood open, even though she had closed it behind them. Emma stood in the doorway, staring at her. Slowly, a smile lit up her face.

Their gazes met, and the warm affection—or even love—in Emma's eyes made Jordan forget that Chloe was lurking somewhere behind her.

Apparently, Emma had heard what she had said—and she liked it. Maybe she wasn't that bad at relationships after all.

"Um, I need the booster seat from my car before you go," Emma said. "Chloe wants to take Molly out for dinner once she's finished playing with her gift."

Jordan nodded. "I'll get it for you." Ignoring Chloe's glare, she marched past her into the garage.

A sense of déjà vu gripped Jordan as she jogged through the automatic doors of the terminal. Once again, she was late picking up Simone. Traffic had been bad all the way to the airport, and with Chloe's little confrontation in the driveway, she had left home too late.

When she reached baggage claim, Simone was perched on her suitcase next to the all but empty conveyor belt. As Jordan hurried over, she stood and shook her head. "Let me guess. Your cat made you late again."

"No," Jordan said with a wry smile. "This time, it *was* a woman. Three women, to be exact."

Simone laughed. "Wow. Now one woman isn't enough for you anymore?"

"One is more than enough, actually," Jordan said, not laughing at all.

Simone didn't seem to notice. When Jordan stepped closer to hug her, she leaned up to kiss her.

Quickly, Jordan turned her head so that Simone's intimate welcome ended up a peck on the cheek.

"What's going on?" Simone squinted at her. "Since when are you shy about kissing in public? I remember a time when you couldn't wait until we made it home, so you pulled over and—"

"Yeah, I remember, thanks. But that was then, and now…" She had wanted to wait until they were in the car, not standing around at baggage claim, watching an unclaimed suitcase circle around and around. But maybe the location didn't matter. The first time she had kissed Emma had been in a garage after all. "Simone, I…I have to tell you something. There have been some big changes in my life, and they affect you too."

Simone pulled out the handle of her suitcase. "Let me guess. You're moving, and I will no longer be able to stay with you when I'm in the LA area."

"Um, no. That's not it. I actually like it where I live."

"You and your family lived in duplexes on army posts when you were a kid, right?" Simone asked. When Jordan nodded, she said, "Maybe that's why your house feels like home."

That might have been a part of it, but Jordan was pretty sure that Emma had been the cure for what Simone called her itchy feet.

"So if that's not what you wanted to tell me, what is it, then?" A wrinkle appeared between Simone's finely arched brows, and she gripped the handle of her suitcase with both hands. "You're not sick, are you?"

"No," Jordan said quickly. "No, that's not it either. Well, there was a time when I might have thought of it as a sickness, but…" She took a deep breath. "A lot has changed since your last visit. I have changed. I… I'm in a relationship now."

The laptop bag started to slip from Simone's shoulder.

Jordan took it from her and slung it over her own shoulder.

They stared at each other.

"Um, could you say something, please?" Jordan finally asked.

Simone cleared her throat. "I have just four words for you: I told you so!" Her voice became louder and less shaky with every word. With the last one, she laughed and slapped Jordan's shoulder. "Didn't I? I told you that a woman would sneak into your life the same way that your cat did!"

"Yeah, I guess you did." Jordan rubbed her neck. "I sure as hell didn't see it coming."

A broad grin blossomed on Simone's face. "It's your cute neighbor, isn't it?"

Now it was Jordan's turn to nearly drop the laptop bag. She gripped the strap and stared at Simone. "How did you know?"

"The last time I visited, you couldn't stop looking at her ass."

"I always look—looked—at women's asses."

Simone shrugged. "Yeah, but you looked at the rest of her too. And you gave me the shortest good-bye kiss in the history of womankind so you could come to her rescue when she had that trouble with her car."

Heat climbed up Jordan's neck. Had she really?

People from the next flight began streaming into baggage claim.

Jordan took Simone's suitcase and guided her toward the car.

Simone stared at the Prius. "Don't tell me you sold your sports car for this!"

"What? Oh, no. This is Emma's. I borrowed it because the coupe's trunk is tiny, and I didn't know how many bags you would have."

"Wow. You're sharing cars already. Are you letting her drive yours?"

"Um, yeah." Jordan's cheeks heated again. She opened the Prius's tailgate and put Simone's suitcase into the trunk, so she could have a moment to collect herself.

Simone let out a low whistle. "This is serious, isn't it?"

"Very," Jordan said. They got into the car, but she didn't start the engine yet. She looked across the middle console at Simone. "Which is why you and I..."

Damn. This was why she had never been in a relationship. Breaking up with someone was hard.

Simone reached over the console and put her hand on Jordan's. Her fingers were warm and reassuring. "Don't worry, I get it. That part of our friendship is over for good, isn't it?"

Jordan nodded, relieved that Simone had said it for her. She forced herself to look up and into her eyes. "Are you okay with that?"

"Why wouldn't I be?" Simone asked.

Was she really that easy to give up? Jordan tried not to let her dismay show. "I don't know. I just thought..."

Simone laughed. "Good to know that your ego is still intact." But then she sobered and patted Jordan's hand before withdrawing. "I'm gonna miss it," she said, now entirely serious. "You know me and my body so well. You just touch me and...God!" She exhaled sharply.

Jordan cleared her throat and looked away. What could she say to that?

"Emma is one lucky woman. I hope she knows that."

A smile inched its way onto Jordan's face. "I'm the lucky one."

Simone shook her head, her wistful expression replaced by an amused grin. "God, you really are smitten, aren't you? Seeing you like this will take some getting used to, but I always knew you had it in you."

"It?" Jordan asked.

"Love."

They hadn't called it that yet, but deep down, Jordan knew that was what it was. "That makes one of us," she murmured. For her, falling for Emma had been as surprising as falling out of the tree.

Simone looked over at her. "Let's get going, oh smitten one. I hear a guest room calling my name!"

Jordan pressed the start button that turned on the engine but then paused, leaned over the middle console, and kissed Simone on the cheek. While she would never sleep with Simone again, she would have hated to lose her as a friend. "Thank you."

"All done!" From her place on the living room floor, Chloe waved a triumphant hand at the Lego clinic she and Molly had just assembled. "Okay, let's go. Pizza!"

Molly jumped up but then hesitated. Her gaze went to the clinic. "Can we wait until Jordan is back? I want to show her my clinic."

Chloe looked as if she smelled something foul, and Emma had to bite back a grin.

"You can show her tomorrow," Chloe said.

"Pleeeease! I want to show her today."

Chloe sighed. "All right." She glanced at her watch. "What's taking her so long to pick up her...friend?" She pronounced the word *friend* the same way she would say *hot lover*.

Emma gritted her teeth and shrugged as casually as possible. "You know traffic around the airport can be crazy."

"Traffic." Chloe grinned knowingly. "Sure."

Molly looked back and forth between them, as if trying to figure out the undertones of the conversation.

It took all of Emma's self-control not to throw the remote control or any other object within reach at her ex. God, Chloe hadn't been such an ass when they had been together, had she?

"Molly," Emma said calmly, "why don't you go pick out a nice sweater you can wear to the restaurant?"

"I'll get the pink one!" Molly rushed from the room.

As soon as her daughter was out of earshot, Emma turned toward Chloe. "Are you here to see Molly or to make life difficult for me?"

"I don't know what—"

"Cut the bullshit, Chloe." Emma snapped her mouth shut. *Wow.* In the past, she had never talked to Chloe this way. She squared her shoulders. *Well, maybe I should have.*

"I don't mean to make life difficult for you. I just worry, okay? Molly has obviously grown pretty attached to Jordan, and I can't help thinking…" Chloe got up from the floor and dropped down onto the other end of the couch. She picked up a piece of Lego from beneath the coffee table and examined it closely. "Look. I…I know I messed up. I made a mistake—a huge mistake—and it affected not just you and me but Molly too. I don't want that to happen again."

Emma stared at her. In the ten years they had been together, Chloe had never, ever admitted to any mistake. She didn't know what to say. "It won't," she finally got out.

"You can't know that," Chloe said quietly.

"No, I can't, but Jordan is—"

A knock on the door interrupted. "We're back," Jordan called.

Familiar steps came down the hall, and despite her nervousness at seeing Simone again, that tingly feeling that always swept over her when Jordan approached gripped Emma.

She made eye contact as soon as Jordan entered.

Jordan smiled reassuringly and then stepped aside to let Simone enter.

God, Emma had forgotten how stunning Jordan's former friend with benefits was. A lot of women would have given a kidney for those beautiful corkscrew curls and the perfect white teeth, which shone against her dark skin as Simone smiled at her.

Seeing her next to Jordan, she couldn't help thinking what a gorgeous couple they made. Knowing they were dynamite in the bedroom didn't help her self-esteem much either.

Simone crossed the living room, gracefully weaving through the obstacle course of Lego animals on the floor. When she reached Emma, she immediately pulled her into a warm embrace. "I hear congratulations are in order."

It took Emma a moment to make her arms work and return the hug. Relief trickled through her. At least one of them had good taste in exes. It was impossible not to like Simone.

Finally, Simone pulled back. "Or knowing my friend Jordan, maybe I should offer condolences."

"Hey!" Jordan protested.

Simone didn't look her way; she kept her gaze on Emma.

Friend, Emma mentally repeated. Simone had put special emphasis on that word, as if to let her know that was all she and Jordan would be from now on—no more benefits. She smiled and nodded at Simone. *Message received.*

Chloe eyed Simone with interest. Finally, she got up from the couch. "Hi. I'm Chloe, Emma's ex-wife."

"Simone."

She didn't offer any other identifier, Emma noticed.

They shook hands.

"Mama?" Molly called from the direction of her room.

"Mom duty is calling." Chloe let go of Simone's hand and crossed the room. When she passed Jordan, she paused. With obvious hesitation, she said, "Molly wants you to see her Lego clinic before we leave, so stay put."

Emma stared at her and then exchanged glances with Jordan, who looked just as stunned. Then Jordan shrugged. "I'm not going anywhere."

She and Chloe held eye contact in a silent standoff for a few seconds longer before Chloe nodded and walked down the hall.

Sliding to the side on the couch, Emma offered Simone a place to sit. "How was your flight?"

Simone grinned. "Not half as exciting as your day, it seems."

Emma returned the smile. "I have a feeling with Jordan, my life will never be boring."

Chapter 25

JORDAN STEPPED OUT OF THE women's locker room and nearly plowed into Dr. Soergel. She hadn't expected the chief of general surgery to be at the hospital on a Sunday, but maybe he'd had to catch up on research or his administrative duties.

"Are you on your way out?" he asked and lifted his bushy eyebrows as he glanced from her street clothes to the large clock on the wall.

It was five o'clock. She'd had brunch with Simone this morning and had only headed to the hospital at ten, but her work was done. She had completed rounds on post-op patients, gone over treatment plans with her residents, and done pre-op visits. At the moment, that was pretty much all she could do, at least on Sundays, when they were running only one OR for emergency cases that she couldn't yet take over.

She was itching to get back into the OR, not just assisting but operating herself. Her hand therapist said she couldn't speed up the healing process, but Jordan had never accepted *impossible* as a word that applied to her. Both Chloe and Simone would be gone by tomorrow, so she could go back to working on her dexterity with the foam pad.

"Yes," she said to her boss. "I'm finished for the day." In the past, she would have hung around a while longer, but now she had Emma and Molly waiting at home.

"Do you have a minute before you leave?" Dr. Soergel asked.

"Sure."

He glanced up and down the corridor as if to make sure no one else was within earshot. "I talked to Peter Kistner, the director of the abdominal transplant surgery fellowship program at Duke. He and I went to med school together."

Why was he telling her that? Jordan shifted her weight and waited.

"I told him about you, and he said he'd love to have you apply to their program. You would still have to interview, of course, but I'd write you a stellar letter of recommendation. You'd be a shoo-in."

"Oh. Wow." A few months ago, that would have meant the world to her. She wouldn't have hesitated for even a second before saying yes. There were very few women—and almost no women of color—in transplant surgery, and she would have jumped at the chance to be one of the few. But now she had more to consider than just herself and her career ambitions.

She couldn't ask Emma to come to North Carolina with her. Wrenching Molly from her home only two months after moving here wouldn't be fair. Even if Emma and Molly were willing to relocate, a fellowship would mean two years of never being home before Molly had to go to bed. Two years of very little time with Emma. And even after that, her life would be unpredictable. When an organ for one of her patients became available, she'd have to rush off in the middle of the night, a romantic dinner, or a birthday party.

Her boss squinted at her. "Oh, wow?" he repeated. "That's all you're going to say? I thought you'd be over the moon."

"It's great, and I'm really grateful for your support, but…" Jordan licked her lips. She hadn't told her boss or any of her fellow surgeons about her new relationship status yet. Surgeons were supposed to live and breathe the OR—and she still did, but she was no longer willing to sacrifice her private life for it. "I don't think I can apply to the program."

"What? But you said you could see yourself going into transplant surgery."

"Yes, and it was true." Jordan massaged the back of her neck with one hand. "But that was six months ago. My circumstances have changed. I have a family now."

A frown settled on his face. "I thought you were…" He waved his hand. "You know…"

"I am. But that doesn't mean I can't have kids." She nearly repeated Emma's line about lesbians having fully functional uteruses too but stopped herself. Her boss might not appreciate her sense of humor.

His gaze flicked to her belly. "You're not…?"

"No. God, no." Jordan vehemently shook her head. "But I'm in a relationship now, and my partner has a little girl."

"Ah. I see. There are people who manage to do both—being a parent and a transplant surgeon, you know?"

People, Jordan mentally repeated. What he really meant was *men.* Fathers who spent most of their time at work while their wives stayed home with the kids. Jordan had grown up in a family like that, and she didn't want Molly to grow up that way too. "I know," she said. "But not me."

His lips compressed into a line of disapproval. "Let me know if you change your mind."

She watched him walk away and automatically took a step to follow him. But then she stopped herself. "Thanks for thinking of me," she called after him before heading toward the elevator. Every step was firmer than the one before. By the time the elevator doors slid apart in front of her, she was smiling. No matter what Dr. Soergel expected of her or what her goals had been in the past, this felt right. She wouldn't change her mind.

The doorbell rang much sooner than expected. Frowning, Emma closed her e-mail program and went to open the door. That couldn't be Chloe with Molly already, could it?

But when she swung the door open, her ex and their daughter stood in front of her.

"What are you doing back so soon?" The plan had been for Chloe to take Molly out to dinner before flying back.

"Um…" Chloe glanced at her watch.

Emma was still very familiar with what that meant. "What's going on?"

"Something came up at work, so I have to go in extra early tomorrow. If I leave now, I can take an earlier flight and make it back by—"

"But you said you'd read me a bedtime story before you leave!" Molly shouted.

"I know, Molly, but that was before—"

Molly kicked out at the chest of drawers in the hall, toppling over a vase on top of it, and ran to her room.

Emma caught the vase just in time before it could shatter on the floor.

"Molly!" Chloe called after her. She sent Emma a helpless look, but made no move to go after their daughter.

For a few seconds, Emma was so stunned and angry that she couldn't speak. She wanted to smash the rescued vase over Chloe's head. "I really don't know why I ever thought you would be a good person to have a child with!"

"That's not fair, Emma. I—"

"Not fair? Not fair?" Emma's voice rose. "I'll tell you what's not fair. Making promises to your six-year-old daughter and then breaking them—that's not fair!"

"Calm down. I—"

"Cheating on your wife in the bed you shared with her—that's not fair. Showing up here and trying to interfere with the lives we built—that's not fair."

A rapid knock sounded, and then the door swung open, nearly hitting Chloe in the back.

"Is everything okay here?" Jordan stood in the doorway, looking back and forth between them. "I heard shouting."

"Everything's fine," Emma said through gritted teeth. "Chloe was just about to leave."

"Emma..."

"No, Chloe. I'm through with your excuses. Say good-bye to Molly and then go."

For a moment, Chloe looked as if she wanted to protest.

Jordan walked over to stand by Emma's side in silent support.

Lips firmly pressed together, Chloe stalked toward Molly's room.

Jordan immediately took Emma into a gentle embrace. "What happened?"

Emma sank against Jordan's body and inhaled her soothing scent. "Chloe had said she'd fly back on the red-eye so she could spend more time with Molly, but now it turns out she switched to an earlier flight. Molly didn't take it so well."

"What an ass," Jordan muttered. "Poor Molly." She stroked Emma's back. "Do you want me to make my famous peanut butter burgers for dinner? That will cheer her up."

For a moment, Emma closed her eyes and enjoyed Jordan's soothing touch. God, how could she have thought for even a second that Jordan might be anything like Chloe? Except for their occupations, they had nothing in common. Jordan would never hurt her or Molly the way Chloe had. The last remainder of doubt about their relationship evaporated, and she decided then and there that she would tell Molly about them as soon as her daughter had recovered from Chloe's visit.

She clutched Jordan to her more tightly, but before she could tell her about her decision, the doorbell rang. Reluctantly, she let go of Jordan and opened the door.

Simone stood in front of her, dressed in tight-fitting jeans and a top that was so short that it revealed glimpses of a navel piercing that glittered against her smooth skin.

What a difference to the proper businesswoman in the blazer and pencil skirt that Emma had seen her in earlier! She couldn't help staring.

"Hi," Simone said. "I saw Jordan come home, but she didn't come in. Is she here?"

"I'm here," Jordan said.

Emma opened the door wider. "Come on in," she said while at the same time keeping an eye and ear on Molly's room. No shouting or crying came from it, so she hoped Molly was okay. She would check on her in a second.

Jordan let out a low whistle as she looked Simone up and down. "You're not dressed like this to have dinner with us, are you?"

"No. Makayla called and asked me to have dinner and then go to the club with them. She told me to ask you to come too. Says she hasn't seen you in ages. So?"

Jordan's gaze flicked to Emma.

"You can come too," Simone said with a warm smile at Emma. "The more, the merrier."

"I don't have a babysitter for Molly. And even if I did, Molly had a rough day, so I wouldn't want to leave her." Emma didn't regret it at all. After what had happened with Chloe, she wasn't in the mood to socialize with strangers. She gently nudged Jordan. "But you can go, if you want. I really don't mind."

"No, that's okay," Jordan said without hesitation. Facing Simone, she added, "Tell Makayla and the others hi for me."

"You sure?" Simone asked.

Jordan gave a firm nod and wrapped one arm around Emma's shoulders, pulling her against her side.

The warmth of her body instantly made Emma relax, and she realized how tense she had been.

"Have fun," Jordan said. "I will see you before you leave tomorrow, right?"

"Sure. I'll come by the hospital before my meeting tomorrow morning. You're buying me coffee."

"Oh, I am?" Jordan drawled.

"Yep. And one of those sinful chocolate croissants too." Simone leaned forward, kissed Jordan's cheek, and lightly touched Emma's arm before waving and closing the door behind her.

Jordan held Emma for a few moments longer and then pulled away. "Let me wash up, and I'll get started on those burgers."

A wave of affection swept over Emma. Okay, who was she kidding? It wasn't just affection. It was love. As much as she had struggled not to fall head over heels and keep some semblance of control so she wouldn't get hurt again, there was no denying it anymore. She was in love. But before she could calm her racing heart enough to tell Jordan, she had disappeared down the hall, passing Chloe on her way to the bathroom and giving her a stiff nod.

When the bathroom door clicked closed behind Jordan, Chloe went over to Emma.

"How is she?" Emma asked.

Chloe shrugged. "She'll be fine."

Fine. Yeah. Emma gritted her teeth so she wouldn't shout at Chloe again.

"Please be careful." Chloe's gray eyes were dark like clouds right before a thunderstorm.

"Careful?" Emma repeated, her gaze still on where Jordan had disappeared.

"Can't you see that there's something going on between her and Simone?"

Emma tore her gaze away from the bathroom door. "Bullshit. They're just friends."

"Yeah, just friends until they'll be more," Chloe muttered.

A ball of anger bunched together in Emma's belly and then seemed to explode outward. "I know I told you that you can visit any time, but from now on, there will be rules."

"Rules?" Chloe drew out the word.

"Rules," Emma repeated firmly. "One, you get a nonrefundable airline ticket, and if you ever break your promises to Molly without a valid reason again, I'm filing for sole custody."

"You can't—"

"Oh, yeah, I can and I will. I've had it with you. Same if you ever try to come between me and Jordan again. Just because you're a cheater doesn't mean that she is."

"That's what you thi—"

Emma sharply lifted her hand. "Stop! The rules are in effect starting right now, so think long and hard before you finish that sentence." She pulled the door open. "Good-bye, Chloe."

Jaw muscles bunching, Chloe stomped past her. When she was outside, she turned back around and opened her mouth, but before she could say anything, Emma closed the door in her face.

She stood there for several moments. Slowly, her anger drained away, and laughter burst from her chest. God, that had felt good. She should have done that a long time ago.

Taking a freeing breath, she marched down the hall. First, she would check on Molly, and then she would slip into the bathroom to tell Jordan that she loved her and wanted to tell Molly and the rest of the world.

Jordan splashed water onto her face. *What a day!* In the past, she wouldn't have hesitated to go to the club with Simone to blow off some steam, but now she didn't have even the slightest desire to party or chat up women. All she wanted was to spend the evening with her family and make sure Molly was okay.

A smile stole onto her lips. It might have been crazy, but she felt as if that was what they were already: a family.

Her smile faded away. Emma didn't seem to share that opinion. She still hesitated to tell Molly about them.

Jordan sighed. She would talk to Emma once both their exes were gone. Maybe they could compromise and at least take a few steps in the right direction. For one thing, she wanted to keep a change of clothes at Emma's so she could shower instead of just washing her face. Not that they lived far apart, but since her return to work, she had rarely gone home except to sleep—and if she had her way, that would change soon too.

It wasn't just about sex. It wasn't even about making love, even though that would be an entirely new experience for her too. Of course, she longed to kiss and touch every inch of Emma and make her come so hard that she'd forget that she'd ever been with anyone else, but she also wanted to hold her while she went to sleep and kiss her awake in the morning.

As if conjured up by thoughts of her, the door opened and Emma slipped into the bathroom.

Their gazes met in the mirror above the sink, and what Jordan read in Emma's eyes made her shut off the water and turn around.

Emma closed the door behind her and took two long steps right into Jordan's space.

Before Jordan could say something, Emma's lips were on hers.

The edge of the sink dug into the back of Jordan's thighs, but she didn't care.

Wow. What had gotten into Emma?

Then she forgot all about it as she wrapped her arms around Emma and pulled her closer.

As the kiss heated up, she slipped her fingers beneath Emma's shirt and slid them up the curve of her back and then down her sides. Her skin was so warm and so soft; Jordan could touch her forever.

Emma surged against her with a moan. "Wet," she gasped against Jordan's lips.

"Oh yeah," Jordan whispered hoarsely. "Me too."

"No, I mean… Your hands are wet."

"Let's see if we can remedy that." Jordan slid her hands over Emma's velvet-soft jeans, drying them, and then cupped her butt with both palms and drew her against her thigh.

Moaning again, Emma threw her head back and bared her neck.

Jordan didn't resist the invitation. She kissed and nibbled the soft skin of her throat, loving the gasps her attention elicited from Emma. Gently, she nipped at one earlobe before whispering, "Where are Chloe and Molly?"

"Chloe left, and Molly is—God, Jordan!—in her room, picking out bedtime stories for later. She wants us both to read her one tonight. I told her that I'd check on you and be right back."

That meant they had only a few more seconds before Molly came knocking on the door. Jordan stopped mid-nip, sighed, and moved her hands to a safer spot on Emma's hips. "How about instead of bedtime stories, we tell her about us? As hot as it is to be making out in the bathroom like a couple of teenagers, I want more. I want to spend the night with you."

Emma's pupils were wide with desire, and her cheeks were flushed. She held on to Jordan as if she otherwise might collapse. "I want that too. God, I want that so much. I want *you*."

"But?" Jordan asked. There always seemed to be a *but* where this topic was concerned. She had tried to be patient, knowing it was a big step for both Molly and Emma. But now she could no longer keep the frustration from her voice. Lately, her entire life seemed to consist of waiting—waiting for her wrist to gain back its full range of motion so she could go back to operating, waiting for their exes to leave, waiting for Emma to make up her mind and move forward with their relationship...

If Jordan hated one thing, it was waiting. She let go of Emma and slid out from between her and the sink.

"No *but*," Emma said. "Chloe actually warned me about you before she left, and I told her—"

Jordan slammed her good hand against the sink. "Fuck Chloe! This is about us, not about her. I'm sick of being tarred with the same brush as your ex, just because we're both surgeons."

Emma stared at her, the color quickly draining from her formerly flushed cheeks.

Jordan's first impulse was to take her into her arms and comfort her, but she didn't allow herself to do that. This anger had been building for a while, and she needed to get it out or she would choke on it. "What the hell are we waiting for? What are *you* waiting for? I told Simone about us. I even rejected my boss's offer to recommend me for a fellowship today, telling him that I'm in a relationship now and don't want to be at work 24/7."

Emma blinked. "You did?"

"Yeah. What else do I need to do to prove that I'm all in?"

"Nothing. I—"

Jordan held up her hand. "Yes, I appreciate women, and I slept with a lot of them. But unlike your ex, I never lied about that. I never cheated on a woman. I never told a woman that I love her. But I love you, dammit, so why can't you—?"

"W-what did you just say?"

"I'm not a cheater," Jordan said. "I told you that before. I would never—"

"No. Not that. I already know that." Emma swayed a little and held on to the sink with one hand. "Did you say that you…?"

Jordan paused and mentally repeated what she had just hurled at Emma. *Damn.* Had she really said that? "Sorry," she said but refused to look away from Emma's wide-eyed gaze. "I didn't mean for it to get out that way. But I'm not taking it back."

Emma's eyes became misty. "I don't want you to. Not if you really meant it."

Jordan hadn't planned to say it; she hadn't even allowed herself to think it, but now that it was out, there was no doubt in her mind. She braced herself against the onslaught of emotion before saying, "I meant it." She tried to flash her confident smile, but it felt a little shaky. Damn it, was she tearing up too? "You are my chocolate cupcake with peanut butter filling, and I want the world to know. Can we please tell Molly?"

"Yes," Emma whispered. She threw herself into Jordan's arms and rained down kisses all over her face. "Yes, yes, yes," she breathed against her skin after each kiss. "That's actually what I came in here to tell you. I want Molly and the rest of the world to know about us."

"Um, you do?" Man, and she had gone on and on without even really listening to Emma's replies.

"Yes. But you were on a roll, and I couldn't get a word in." Emma laughed, a sound full of giddiness and joy. She cradled Jordan's face in both hands while peering into her eyes. "I realized it was stupid to keep hesitating because of something Chloe did. God, Jordan. I never thought I would feel this ever again, and certainly not after such a short time, but I love you too."

The words seemed to wrap around Jordan's heart and soothe away the anger and frustration, leaving behind only peace. *Wow.* She had said it. For the first time in her life, she had told a woman that she loved her— and Emma loved her back! It was overwhelming and scary and wonderful beyond words.

They looked into each other's eyes, their faces slowly moving toward each other. Their lips opened in expectation.

A pounding on the door made them jerk apart a second before their mouths could meet. "Mommy? Jordan?" Molly called through the door. "Are you fighting?"

Oh, shit. Jordan bit her lip. Molly must have heard her shouting at Emma.

"No, honey," Emma called back. "We're just…talking. Everything's fine. I promise."

"Okay," Molly said. "I picked out two books. Can you read them to me after dinner?"

"Of course," Jordan called. "We'll be right out, and then I'll make peanut butter burgers for dinner."

Molly's cheering drifted through the door, making them both smile.

They leaned their foreheads against each other for a moment before pulling apart.

"Want to tell her now?" Emma asked.

Jordan shook her head. "Let's do it tomorrow. She needs to recover from Chloe's visit first, and one emotional confession per day is my limit."

Emma laughed shakily. "Mine too. God, I feel like I'm on drugs."

"Endorphins," Jordan said automatically. She felt the same. This was a bigger rush than successfully completing a complicated surgery in the OR.

"Thanks for that scientific explanation, Doctor Williams." Despite the mild admonishment, her eyes were radiating happiness.

Knowing that she was the one responsible for Emma's happiness made Jordan feel as if she were walking on clouds. One last quick kiss, then they left the bathroom. Jordan knew she wouldn't sleep a wink tonight.

Molly sat at the table, dangling her legs and eating the zucchini noodles with meatballs Jordan had made for dinner.

Emma wished she could be as carefree as her daughter, who seemed to have recovered from the heartache Chloe had caused her yesterday. She had barely managed to finish her own plate of pasta, too nervous and too excited to eat more. Today was the day. They had agreed to tell Molly about them over dinner…and now Molly was all but finished, and neither of them had said a word.

Emma couldn't remember when she had last been so nervous before a conversation, not even when she had told Chloe she was moving to California. After yesterday's drama with Chloe, how would Molly react to their revelation?

Jordan seemed to be just as nervous. She had abandoned her half-full plate and kept rubbing her newly mended arm as if it were a good-luck charm. Leaning over, she whispered into Emma's ear, "I feel really silly. Here I am, sweating bullets because I'm about to ask a six-year-old for permission to court her mother."

The old-fashioned expression made Emma smile. "We don't need her permission. I just want her to be okay with it."

Molly stopped twirling her forkful of noodles and gave them a curious glance. "Why are you whispering?"

Like two criminals who had been caught red-handed, Jordan and Emma looked at each other.

Jordan opened her mouth to answer, but Emma put her hand on her arm. "Let me do this."

"Are you sure?" Jordan asked.

Emma nodded. She had been the one who had put this off for much too long, so now she wanted to be the one who told her daughter. "We've got something to tell you, Molly," she said over the pounding of her heart.

Molly beamed. "Are we getting a kitten?"

"Um, no."

"Better," Jordan interjected.

Molly's eyes got round. "Better than a kitten?"

"Hush." Emma gently slapped Jordan's shoulder before turning back to face Molly. "Do you remember when we moved into the new house and you asked me if I would find a new friend?" When her daughter nodded, Emma continued, "I said I probably would one day. And now I found a very special someone."

"Jordan," Molly said with confidence and grinned over at her. "She's my friend too."

"Yes, she is. But, honey, she's a little more than a friend to me." Beneath the table, Emma reached for Jordan's hand and latched on to it, only gentling her grasp when she realized it was Jordan's barely healed one. "I...I love her the way I used to love Mama."

Molly looked from her to Jordan, who nodded and said, "I love your mommy very much too. And you, of course."

"I love you too," Molly said immediately. She slid off her chair, raced around the table, and threw her arms around Jordan in an exuberant hug.

Emma had wanted to take up the ball from Jordan, but for a moment, the stunned expression on Jordan's face distracted her from what she had been about to say. Jordan Williams, suave seducer of women, looked as if she would melt on the spot. *Big softie.*

It was a moment that Emma had dreaded since she had realized Jordan could become important to her and Molly, if she allowed it. She had feared getting hurt again—and getting Molly hurt—if she let a new woman into their lives.

But now that the moment had come, she realized that the joy of seeing her two favorite females in the world bond like this had replaced her fears.

Once Molly had returned to her chair, Emma cleared her throat. "And because Jordan and I love each other, we might want to have a sleepover every once in a while," she said. "Would that be all right with you?"

A tiny wrinkle formed on Molly's forehead as she seemed to think about it. "But what about Tuna?" She looked at Jordan with wide eyes. "She would be all alone in your house. Wouldn't she be scared?"

Emma nearly slid off her chair as the tension drained from her. She stared at her daughter. All that agonizing over telling her, and Molly was worried about the cat?

"Tuna is over here all the time anyway, so why don't I bring her?" Jordan suggested. "She and you could have a sleepover too."

"Yes!" Molly pumped her small fist, almost hitting her plate. "Can we, Mommy? Please! I love sleepovers!"

"Oh yeah. Me too," Jordan drawled. "So, can we?"

Now both of them looked at Emma with pleading expressions.

"Of course," Emma said. "Let's have a sleepover next weekend."

Jordan and Molly high-fived each other, and then Molly asked, "Can I have another meatball? I want one with peanut butter."

That seemed to be the end of the discussion for her. How easy life was when you were six years old!

"Can I?" Molly repeated when Emma didn't react to her request.

"Peanut butter on meatballs?" Emma wrinkled her nose.

"Yes! It's like peanut butter burgers."

Emma shook her head. "You created a monster," she said to Jordan. Her legs shook as she got up to get the peanut butter for Molly.

As she walked by, Jordan reached for her hand and squeezed softly.

Emma slid back onto her chair, still staring at her daughter, who happily smothered peanut butter on her meatball. Finally, a smile crept onto her face. She should have known that Molly would take it in stride. It had been just her anxieties that had made everything more complicated than it needed to be.

She reached for Jordan's hand beneath the table again, then remembered that she no longer needed to hide their relationship and pulled their entwined fingers onto the table.

Hand in hand, they sat and watched Molly devour her peanut butter meatball.

Chapter 26

LATER THAT EVENING, EMMA DROPPED down onto the couch next to Jordan. God, this had felt like the longest three days of her life.

"Finally alone," they said at the same time and then laughed.

Both of their exes were gone, and Molly was in bed.

They sat without speaking for a while, resting their heads together.

"I should go too. Let you get some sleep," Jordan finally said but made no move to get up.

It might have been the sensible thing to do since they both had to work in the morning. But for once, Emma was tired of doing the sensible thing. Now that she had let Jordan into her heart fully and didn't need to hide her relationship from Molly anymore, she wanted Jordan in her bed too—tonight and every night after that.

"Or," she said quietly, "you could stay."

Jordan turned her head, and their gazes met. Jordan's brown eyes seemed to get even darker as her pupils dilated. She moistened her lips with the tip of her tongue. "Won't we wake Molly?"

"Not if we're quiet. Is that going to be a problem for you?" Emma asked with a hint of challenge, knowing Jordan wouldn't be able to resist.

"No. But it's going to be a problem for *you*." Jordan's voice dropped a register. "Because what I want to do to you is not conducive to staying quiet."

The words sent a bolt of desire straight to her core. "Oh yeah?"

"Oh yeah."

Emma stood, took Jordan's hand, and pulled her up from the couch. Her heartbeat sped up with every step they took toward her bedroom. The door clicked shut behind them.

Somehow, she had halfway expected Jordan to tackle her to the bed and ravish her, but Jordan pulled her to a stop in the middle of the room and looked at her, studying her as if she wanted to memorize every feature, every second of this night. Smoldering passion and tenderness mixed in her eyes.

A tingle of anticipation went through Emma. "Kiss me," she whispered.

Jordan didn't have to be told twice. She pulled her close and pressed her lips to Emma's. The kiss started out slow and gentle, just a caress of soft lips, but then quickly heated up as Jordan stroked her tongue over hers.

Emma moaned and tangled her fingers in Jordan's short hair.

Jordan's lips trailed down the side of her neck, and then her warm breath fanned over Emma's ear, making her shiver all over in the most delicious way.

God, she couldn't wait to feel Jordan on her, in her, everywhere. Just the thought of Jordan's skin against hers made her head reel.

As if sensing her unspoken need, Jordan tugged the shirt from Emma's jeans while sucking at the sensitive spot below her ear.

"Bed," was all Emma could groan out as her knees weakened.

"Let me undress you first."

As Jordan lifted the T-shirt up and over her head, leaving Emma in only her jeans and bra, Emma tensed for a moment. Her last first time with a woman had been more than ten years ago—before she'd had Molly. She fought the urge to reach down and cover the slight stretch marks on her belly and the few extra pounds she hadn't managed to lose. Jordan had been with so many women, most of them probably as attractive as Simone. How could she ever compare to them? Her gaze went to the light switch.

"Oh no," Jordan murmured. "Don't even think about it. I want to see you. Every sexy inch of you." She reached around Emma and tried to open her bra with one hand, then cursed and had to use the other hand too.

It took Emma a moment to realize that her fumbling wasn't because her right hand hadn't yet regained its full dexterity. Jordan's hands were trembling. That little bit of nerves made Emma smile. Jordan might have been with many women, but this was new to her too.

Finally, the bra dropped to the floor.

Bared to Jordan's gaze, Emma tried not to fidget.

Jordan cleared her throat. "Wow." Her gaze flicked up to Emma's eyes, then down again. "You're beautiful."

A flush spread through Emma's body.

Slowly, Jordan reached out and traced the curve of one breast with just her fingertips. "Beautiful," she repeated in a whisper. Then she cupped the other breast and brushed her thumb over the hardening nipple.

Emma swayed and clutched Jordan's shoulders to keep herself upright. "Bed," she said again, this time with more urgency.

Jordan popped open the buttons of her own jeans, shoved them down her long legs, and stripped off her shirt, not bothering to be gentle, and then reached around to open her bra.

"Let me."

Jordan dropped her hands.

She reached around Jordan's back and opened the hooks. As she slid the straps down her arms, she let her fingertips brush Jordan's skin, enjoying its smoothness, before moving back half a step to take her in.

Jordan's torso was long and athletic, well-toned muscles playing beneath her skin as she shifted her weight beneath Emma's gaze. Her waist was slim, almost androgynous, but her hips had a sexy curve, and her breasts were fuller than Emma had remembered.

Emma immediately wanted to touch them, but before she could, Jordan stepped closer and drew her into her arms. Their naked breasts grazed as she kissed Emma—hard, possessive, letting her know how much she wanted her.

Emma lost track of everything but the feel of their tongues sliding against each other and their bodies pressing together. The next thing she knew, the back of her legs hit the bed.

Jordan held her with one arm, preventing her from toppling back. Her other hand slipped between them, and Emma felt Jordan's fingers working her button and zipper open.

Her mind already hazy with desire, Emma tried to figure out which arm was the barely healed one. Before she could, Jordan curled her fingers into the waistband of her jeans and tugged.

As the pants pooled onto the floor, Jordan followed them down and knelt in front of Emma. She laid a kiss on her belly and then nuzzled her panties for a moment.

Oh God. Heat simmered in the pit of Emma's belly. Groaning, she feathered her shaking fingers through Jordan's hair.

"I want you." Jordan peered up at her, the expression on her face fierce yet loving at the same time. "Now." Her voice cracked with raw desire.

Unable to speak, Emma nodded.

They locked gazes as Jordan pulled the panties down Emma's legs, followed by her own, and then eased Emma down onto the bed.

The cool sheets at her back made Emma shiver, but then Jordan slid on top of her and all she felt was heat. She loved the way they fit together. Perfect.

Jordan slipped a thigh between hers, and Emma moaned at the wetness painting her skin.

Their breasts pressed together. The contact made Emma suck in a breath.

Jordan held herself still for a moment, then started stringing a row of licks, nips, and kisses down Emma's throat, leaving goose bumps in her wake. She dipped her tongue into the hollow of Emma's collarbone.

Emma writhed against her and brought up her hands to guide Jordan to her aching nipple.

But Jordan just grinned against her skin. "Patience. We're not in a hurry. I want to worship your body and learn all of its secrets." She licked a trail down Emma's cleavage and then nuzzled against the underside of her breast.

Restless, Emma slid one hand down Jordan's scalp, teasing the tiny hairs on the back of her neck with her fingernails.

Shivering, Jordan surged against her, her hips rocking against Emma.

"Patience," Emma said with a grin—a grin that ended the instant Jordan sucked one nipple into her mouth. She arched up with a gasp and pressed Jordan closer.

Jordan switched breasts, circled the nipple with her tongue before flicking it across the hardening tip. One of her hands came up and caressed the other breast.

Yes! Emma clasped her head with both hands and rocked against Jordan's thigh. Her skin heated everywhere Jordan's mouth and hand touched.

The ragged sound of their breathing filled the room.

Jordan circled Emma's areola with her tongue and then closed her lips over the hard nipple and sucked with just the right amount of pressure.

"Jordan!" Emma gasped out. She was too close, too fast, but when Jordan looked up and she saw the hunger in her eyes, slowing down was not an option. She let go of Jordan's head and clasped her hips instead, drawing her more tightly between her legs.

Jordan pressed her face to Emma's neck and breathed hard as if struggling for control too.

But Emma didn't want her to hold back. "Touch me."

With a low groan of need, Jordan slid a hand between them.

The muscles in Emma's belly tensed in anticipation. At the last moment before she could lose all reason, she remembered and gently caught Jordan's forearm. "Your wrist."

Jordan let out a frustrated growl and tried to free herself. "Fuck my damn wrist."

Emma needed a distraction—fast—before Jordan could hurt herself. She softly shook her head. "No, Jordan. No fucking tonight. We're going to make love."

Jordan stilled against her. Her gaze gentled as she looked into Emma's eyes. Cupping Emma's face in her palm, she kissed her, this time softly, full of emotion. "Yes, we are," she whispered. "I love you."

Emma traced Jordan's lips with her fingertips. "I love you too."

Balancing herself on her good arm, Jordan kissed her jaw, her chin, her throat, then down to her breasts. She kissed, nibbled, and sucked until Emma thought she would come apart, and then she gently raked her teeth over one erect nipple.

"God!" Emma bowed her back, pressing against Jordan. Her breathing sped up as she felt Jordan's mouth move lower, and her belly muscles quivered beneath Jordan's tongue.

Jordan kissed and licked a hot trail down Emma's body.

Every cell seemed to vibrate with pleasure. Even her toes tingled. She twisted her hands into the sheets.

Jordan whispered kisses over the sensitive spot where her thigh met her hip.

Groaning, Emma parted her legs in a silent invitation.

But Jordan kissed a path down the front of her thigh. "Patience," she whispered once more against Emma's skin and swirled her tongue over her knee.

Jesus. How could her knee be such an erogenous zone?

"Mmm," Jordan murmured. "You taste good. I can't wait to taste you everywhere." Her lips caressed Emma's inner thigh, up, up, until her warm breath brushed against sensitive flesh.

It was sweet torture. Emma let out a frustrated groan. "Jordan…" Weakly, she lifted her head.

Jordan's nostrils flared. She lifted Emma's legs over her shoulders and then looked up at her. Her dark eyes glittered with desire.

Emma's pulse leaped. "Please."

Jordan ducked her head and dipped her tongue into Emma's wetness.

A jolt of pleasure made Emma arc up. She let go of the sheets and clasped the back of Jordan's head with both hands, struggling to hold back a sharp cry.

Jordan immediately went back for more. She circled Emma's clit with slow strokes, then flicked her tongue directly over it.

"Oh. Oh God. Jordan." Emma pressed herself more tightly against Jordan, who started a languid swirling and stroking motion.

Emma's breath came in short, ragged gasps, and her legs moved restlessly around Jordan. "Don't stop."

Jordan closed her lips over her clit and let it slide back out before capturing it again.

A slow pulsing started deep inside of Emma. She ground her heels against Jordan's back and gulped in air through her open mouth. Her eyes fell closed. She tried to hold back, tried to prolong the pleasure, but when Jordan drew her clit into her mouth again and started to suck, her mind blanked. Lights burst behind her closed eyelids.

She let go of Jordan's head with one hand, pressed the pillow to her mouth, and muffled the shout that ripped from her throat. The fingers of her other hand dug into Jordan's scalp as waves of sensation pounded through her.

Jordan rested her cheek on Emma's quivering belly for a moment before looking up.

The pillow Emma had used to smother her cries of passion fell from her weakening grasp, revealing her face.

What Jordan saw took her breath away.

Emma was lost in pleasure, her eyes closed, her entire body flushed, her face completely unguarded. *Beautiful.* This was unlike anything she had ever experienced, and she could only watch in awe, already dying to taste her again and see her come apart a second time.

Slowly, Emma's eyes fluttered open, and their gazes connected. The copper sparks in her irises seemed to glow.

Emma let out a weak groan as Jordan pressed one last gentle kiss to her swollen clit before sliding up her glistening body.

Only now did she become aware of her own pounding need.

Emma moaned into her mouth as they kissed.

"Emma," she rasped and pressed herself against Emma's thigh. "Not like this. Let me touch you."

But Jordan was already rocking against her. "I'm almost...almost there."

"Wait." Emma eased out from under her and rolled on top.

Through a haze of need, Jordan stared up at her and then reached for her.

"Careful with that hand." Gently, Emma grasped Jordan's right arm, then the left one, and guided both above her head, pressing them against the mattress with one hand.

Normally, Jordan was the one taking control, but with Emma, she didn't feel the need. She left her arms exactly where Emma had placed them, making no attempt to free herself from the gentle grasp.

When Emma dipped the fingers of her free hand into her wetness, Jordan caught her bottom lip between her teeth, struggling not to come right then and there. Jesus, one touch from Emma, and she was a goner.

"Not yet," Emma whispered against her ear and then nibbled on it. "I want to make love to every inch of you first."

Jordan groaned. She wanted to come, but she also wanted this special night to last forever. Helplessly, she stared up at Emma. She had never been so completely at the mercy of a woman, not just physically, but emotionally too. Emma was the woman who held her heart, and that made every touch, every sensation, every gaze so much more powerful.

Emma dipped her head down and whispered gentle kisses against Jordan's lips. "Keep your hands above your head."

The fierceness and passion in her tone made Jordan moan. Who knew that being ordered around by a woman—by Emma—would be so hot?

Emma caressed a path down Jordan's throat and over the arc of her collarbone with her mouth. Wet kisses on her sternum made Jordan's skin tingle.

Then Emma's tongue circled one aching nipple while her finger mimicked the motion around Jordan's clit.

"Emma," Jordan gasped out like a one-word prayer. Her head—her entire world—was spinning.

Emma looked up and into her eyes.

Jordan had slept with a lot of women, but she had never seen this mix of love and desire in anyone's eyes. It was as intoxicating as Emma's touch.

Balancing on one arm, Emma bent down and drew Jordan's nipple into her mouth. At the same time, she slid one finger directly on her clit.

Jordan's eyes rolled back in her head, and a sound she barely recognized escaped her.

Emma moved up and kissed her, smothering her moans. Her free hand came up to again shackle Jordan's arms to the bed.

The lingering scent of their arousal and the soft sounds of pleasure that Emma made while she touched her sent Jordan's senses into overdrive. She rocked harder against her and lost herself in the rhythm they created together.

"God," Emma murmured, slowly increasing the speed and the pressure. "I love this. I love you."

Jordan wanted to say it back, but she was beyond words. She buried her face in the curve where Emma's shoulder met her neck and surrendered to the wave of pleasure crashing over her.

For several moments, sound and sight ceased to exist. She was only dimly aware of Emma curling against her side and pressing a kiss to her shoulder. Jordan lowered one of her arms and wrapped it around Emma. Dazed, she stared into her eyes. The copper spots in the green irises seemed to draw her in, and she leaned forward to kiss Emma.

"I love you too," she whispered, her voice raspy.

Emma caressed the damp skin along Jordan's side, setting off tiny shudders all over her body. "That was incredible."

"Yeah. It was," Jordan said. "But I usually have a little more control than this."

"I love that you don't have any with me," Emma answered with a smile.

Jordan tasted the salty skin on Emma's neck, feeling her pulse flutter beneath her lips. "Everything's different with you." She rolled them over so she was on top and slid a hand down Emma's body.

Emma immediately arched into the touch, even as she softly grabbed Jordan's wrist. "What are you doing?"

"Don't worry. It's my left hand. And I'm trying to find out whether you can have multiple orgasms."

A groan escaped Emma. Her cheeks flushed. "You could just ask, you know?"

"What would be the fun in that?" Jordan playfully circled her navel with the tip of her index finger, then cocked her head and looked into her eyes. "Or don't you want me to...?"

Emma released her grip on Jordan's arm. "I definitely want you to. I have a research question of my own, you know?"

"Oh yeah?"

"Yes." Emma kissed Jordan's jawline and then whispered into her ear, "Just how good are you with your left hand?"

"Let's find out."

Jordan slowly eased awake and opened her eyes. The first light of dawn fell into a bedroom that wasn't hers, and she could make out the outline of clothes on the floor in front of the bed. The gleaming red numbers of an alarm clock next to her read 5:50 a.m.

She had to get up and head to the hospital, but for the first time in her life, she didn't want to. She wanted to stay right where she was.

A warm arm was wrapped around her from behind, and Emma's cheek was pressed to her back. Their legs tangled beneath the covers, and her butt was cradled by Emma's groin. She marveled at how perfectly they fit against each other.

Emma's lips sleepily nuzzled her skin through the T-shirt she'd made her put back on, and one of her hands stirred against Jordan's lower belly. "Do you have to get up?" she asked, her voice slurred by sleep.

"Yeah. Although this," Jordan covered the hand on her abdomen, "makes me consider calling in sick."

"Can you do that?" Emma asked, sounding much more awake.

Jordan smiled at her eagerness. Then she sighed. "I wish I could. But I'll be back on time tonight. I want to have dinner with you and Molly. And once she's in bed—"

A racket of footsteps from the hall interrupted.

Now Jordan was glad Emma had made her put her T-shirt back on because Molly burst into the room within seconds.

They really would have to teach her to knock.

"Mommy, can I—?" Molly slid to a stop in front of the bed, her eyes widening when she saw Jordan next to her mother.

Jordan stared back at her.

A frown of disapproval carved itself into Molly's forehead.

Jordan clutched Emma's hand beneath the covers. Were they moving too quickly for Molly, not giving her enough time to get used to the thought of a new woman in her mother's life?

Molly stomped her foot. "That's not fair!" Her bottom lip trembled.

A lump formed in Jordan's throat. "Molly, I..." She sent Emma a beseeching look, not knowing what to say.

"What's not fair, sweetie?" Emma asked softly, her hand tightening around Jordan's.

"You had your sleepover, but you didn't bring Tuna!"

Jordan nearly laughed with relief. That was what Molly was upset about? "I'm sorry, Molly. You were already asleep when we decided to have a sleepover, and we didn't want to wake you."

Molly let out a dramatic sigh. Her frown disappeared. She bounced onto the bed next to Jordan, crawled over her to the middle of the bed, and snuggled between them as if she had done so a thousand times before.

Jordan blinked but then relaxed back against the pillow for a few moments and caressed Molly's blonde locks. Emma's foot stroked hers beneath the covers. Mmm, she could get used to this.

"Can we have another sleepover this weekend?" Molly asked.

"Oh yeah, definitely," Jordan and Emma said in unison and then grinned at each other over Molly's head.

A bit of heat sparked in Emma's eyes, and Jordan thought that the weekend seemed too far away for that sleepover.

"But now we have to get up," Emma said. "Who wants pancakes for breakfast?"

"Me!" Molly jumped up from the bed. "I want mine with peanut butter," she declared and raced from the room.

Emma shook her head. "You totally spoiled my daughter. Now she wants peanut butter with everything."

Jordan pressed her lips to the hollow of Emma's throat, enjoying the goose bumps that erupted beneath her touch. "And you? Did I spoil you too?"

"Yes," Emma rasped out. "You did. Now I want everything with you."

Jordan lifted her head and looked into Emma's eyes. "You've got it," she said, her voice husky with emotion.

"Mommy! Jordan!" Molly called from the kitchen, interrupting their moment.

With a sigh, Emma slipped out of bed, and Jordan enjoyed the sight of her lush body, covered in just a thin T-shirt, before she put on a robe. "We're coming."

We, Jordan mentally repeated as she jumped out of bed for a quick shower. She had never thought she would be a part of a *we*—or want to be. Now she couldn't imagine her life without them.

If you enjoyed *Falling Hard*, you might want to check out Jae's *Heart Trouble*, the novel in which Jordan's friends Hope and Laleh meet and fall in love.

About Jae

Jae grew up amidst the vineyards of southern Germany. She spent her childhood with her nose buried in a book, earning her the nickname *professor*. The writing bug bit her at the age of eleven. Since 2006, she has been writing mostly in English.

She used to work as a psychologist but gave up her day job in December 2013 to become a full-time writer and a part-time editor. As far as she's concerned, it's the best job in the world.

When she's not writing, she likes to spend her time reading, indulging her ice cream and office supply addictions, and watching way too many crime shows.

Connect with Jae online

Jae loves hearing from readers!
E-mail her at: jae@jae-fiction.com
Visit her website: www.jae-fiction.com
Visit her blog: www.jae-fiction.com/blog
Like her on Facebook: www.facebook.com/JaeAuthor
Follow her on Twitter: @jaefiction

Other Books from Ylva Publishing

www.ylva-publishing.com

Heart Trouble

Jae

ISBN: 978-3-95533-732-2
Length: 312 pages (109,000 words)

Dr. Hope Finlay learned early in life not to get attached to anyone because it never lasts.

Laleh Samadi, who comes from a big, boisterous family, is the exact opposite.

When Laleh ends up in the ER with heart trouble, Hope saves her life. Afterwards, strange things begin to occur until they can no longer deny the mysterious connection between them.

Are they losing their minds...or their hearts?

All the Little Moments

G Benson

ISBN: 978-3-95533-341-6
Length: 350 pages (139,000 words)

Anna is focused on her career as an anaesthetist. When a tragic accident leaves her responsible for her young niece and nephew, her life changes abruptly. Completely overwhelmed, Anna barely has time to brush her teeth in the morning let alone date a woman. But then she collides with a long-legged stranger...

Blurred Lines

(Cops and Docs – Book #1)

KD Williamson

ISBN: 978-3-95533-493-2

Length: 283 pages (92,000 words)

Wounded in a police shootout, Detective Kelli McCabe spends weeks in the hospital recovering. Her only entertainment is verbal sparring matches with Dr. Nora Whitmore, the talented and reclusive surgeon. Two very different women living in two different worlds. When the lines between them begin to blur, will they run from the possibilities or embrace the changes they bring to each other's lives?

Wounded Souls

(L.A. Metro Series – Book #3)

RJ Nolan

ISBN: 978-3-95533-585-4

Length: 307 pages (87,000 words)

Dr. Ashlee Logan has spent the last two years on the road with only her Great Dane as a companion, trying to escape her past. While serving her country, former Navy doctor Dale Parker had her life shattered in a single moment. LA Metropolitan Hospital brings the two women together. Can they overcome their pasts and find happiness together, or are they forever destined to be…Wounded Souls?

Coming from Ylva Publishing

www.ylva-publishing.com

Break Apart

Meg Harrington

Meg Harrington's first lesbian romance novel is a medical romance exploring the fine line between friendship and crush.

Trauma surgeon Elle Matthews had a great thing going in San Antonio until a new colleague convinces her to get closer to her very straight crush, Doctor Kate Low.

Meanwhile, Kate loves her husband and their three children. It doesn't matter that he's distant. Or that he's brought so much of the war back with him to San Antonio.

But she also notices that her burgeoning friendship with Elle is turning into something decidedly more than friendship. Could it be love? And if she does love Elle, is it enough to break apart her marriage?

Falling Hard
© 2017 by Jae

ISBN: 978-3-95533-829-9

Also available as e-book.

Published by Ylva Publishing, legal entity of Ylva Verlag, e.Kfr.
Ylva Verlag, e.Kfr.
Owner: Astrid Ohletz
Am Kirschgarten 2
65830 Kriftel
Germany

www.ylva-publishing.com

First edition: 2017

Credits
Edited by Michelle Aguilar
Cover Design and Print Layout by Streetlight Graphics

Made in the USA
Lexington, KY
09 May 2017